Luther's
Women

Luther's Women

Hughlett L. Morris

The Sequel to *Luther's War*

To order additional copies of this book, contact:
Xlibris Corporation
1-888-795-4274
www.Xlibris.com
Orders@Xlibris.com
26802

CONTENTS

Dedication

To my late mother, Mary Lucy Morris Loftis, who was a great story teller.

To my late aunt, Lillian Mathis Francis, who was a guiding force in my young life.

To my late grandfather, Martin Luther Morris, who kept talking to me and would not let me rest until I wrote his stories.

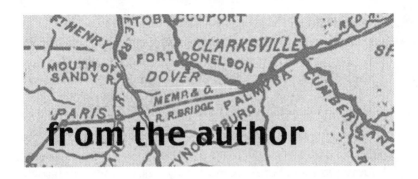

from the author

The Luther stories represent a continuation of my personal and professional interest in people and how they make it through life. The main character is an old man, remembering the events of his life during boyhood and young manhood. The events reflect his physical and emotional development in his coming of age. His approach to sexual maturity is part of that development.

He tells his stories to an unseen listener. They are in the first person narrative: he tells only what he did and observed.

The settings are rural communities in Tennessee and North Carolina. The time is the middle of the 19th century, 1846-1867. The people of the communities are farmers. They are hardworking folks. They live on what they grow in the summer and try to preserve for the winter. There's not much money, less after the War than before. What money there is goes for salt and coffee and boots and oil for the lamps. They are mostly Scotch Irish in heritage and Protestant in religious practice.

Luther tells of two major events during this period of his life. One is the Civil War (*Luther's War*). The other is the journey back home in Stewart County after he leaves the War (*Luther's Women*).

Luther's War is not a historical account of the Civil War, detailing battles won and lost. He is a Confederate soldier, telling experiences in the War as he lived them. His perspective is that of a dog soldier, dealing always with the weather, hunger, loneliness, ignorance, sickness, fear, and death. And above all, he is dealing with the question of what the War is about and what it means to him to be fighting for the South. But he somehow manages to survive.

Luther's Women is about his journey home after he decides to quit the War. The journey is several hundred miles and two years in the making. It takes him from the battlefield at Petersburg, Virginia, to northwest North Carolina, over the Smoky Mountains into Tennessee, and across Tennessee to Stewart County. In both books, he tells of the people that are important to him. Some are men: his Uncle Gray, his cousin Ed, and his fellow soldiers Charlie, Joe Dale, and Billy Jones. But mainly, he tells about the women. Some are mother figures: his mother Harriet, his Aunt Polly, Miz Taylor, Miz Collins, and Miz Tinsley. Others are women his age whom he loves: Nadine, Betty Lou Wood, Maybelle, Josie, Julia, and Narcissa. Some return his passion and his love, but with conditions of their love that he cannot meet. What he learns from all of them about the relationship between a man and a woman leads him on the way to adulthood and manhood.

Martin Luther Morris was my grandfather. My mother was a daughter born to him in later life (age 65). He and I lived several decades apart. There are many connections between his life and mine. I was a boy in the community where he lived and died. Both of us lived in close proximity to Fort Donelson, one of the early major battles of the War. There is oral family history about him. There is also an essay written about him by my older aunt, his stepdaughter, apparently at his dictation. There is also furniture passed down from him to me.

Most important is a formal photograph of him that I have known all my life (it appears on the cover of both books). As an adult, I have often looked at the photograph and wondered about the stories he might have to tell. Finally, I wrote them. They are in part fact and in part what I imagined about that period of his life.

In writing these stories, I have attempted several themes. I wanted to describe what life must have been for the people in the rural mid South at that time. I wanted to describe him as a boy and young man dealing with his sexuality. I wanted to portray the effects of the War on him, his family, and the people he knew. I wanted to touch upon the mysterious and human aspects of the relationships between the "white folks" and the "colored folks" during that time. And I wanted to highlight the lives of women during that time and the limited choices they had in making a life for themselves. It was some of these women that Luther knew, and loved, and told about, that defined his life as a man. I have strong feelings about that message, for I was raised by a family of women, and I have known and loved woman all my life. If I am a man, it is their doing.

These two books are a marked departure from my previous writings of scholarly and technical material about some aspects of speech pathology. They are my first attempts at fiction. I have enjoyed writing them enormously and I hope they bring pleasure to the reader.

Several acknowledgements are in order.

The map of Tennessee is taken from *Civil War Tennessee*, by Thomas L. Connelly, 1979 (p. 22). His citation is: "A contemporary sketch of the war theater in Tennessee. From *Harper's Weekly*."

My thanks to cousin Deanna Nedra Oklepek for her important assistance in matters of Luther's family history. She is a great grand daughter of Luther and Narcissa. Her grandmother was Myrtle Elvira Morris Page, their oldest child.

My thanks also to Evelyn Lee, for her technical advice and for her encouragement, professional and personal.

My daughter Amy Morris has been a primary guiding influence and contributor during the writing, editing, and design of the *Luther* books. I thank her with great gratitude and love.

Lastly, my thanks to my good and faithful iMac computer, Tommyrot, without whom I could never have done this!

Hughlett Lewis Morris
Tucson, Arizona
November 30, 2004

I make good dried apple pies.
You like dried apple pies?

It'd be better if you didn't
kiss me again.

I should have sent you
packin' the day you come.

Naw, he ain't in the wagon. He's
somewheres in the mountains.

Well, that's that.
Can't take any of it back,
can we?

Can you hold off 'til Christmas?

It's about him wantin' to give his
folks a grand baby.

All 'cept you. And you
say you're just passin'
through. Are you?

Do you and that big horse
of yours want to see
the sights of Nashville?

I'll give you my answer
tomorra, after breakfast,
here on the log.

I hope you don't blame me
too much for what I did.

So help me God, you shoot one more time
and you are a dead man!

Photographs are from the author's personal collection

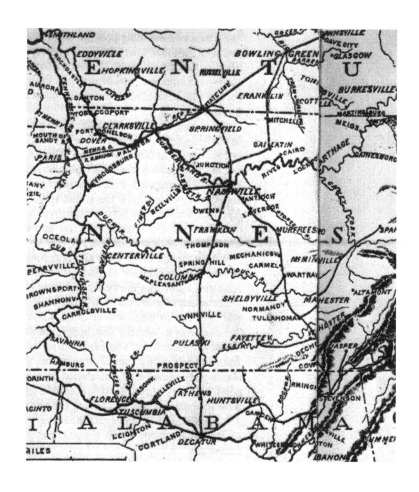

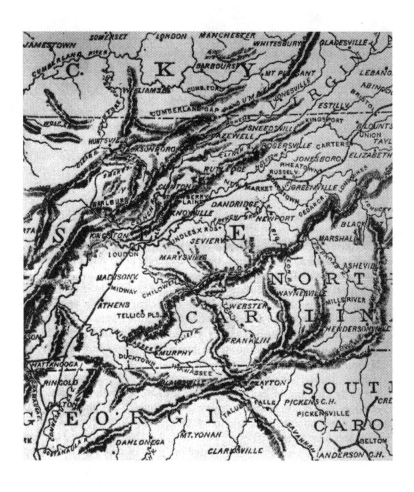

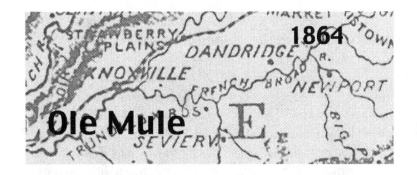

Ole Mule

1864

For about a week, I tried to get along. I went to the sick tent to get some medicine, but they was all out. We was on the move so that I give up tryin' to find much shelter at night. I'd just put my bedroll wherever I could, and as far away from the battle line as I could get, and lay down again. It was early winter by that time. More wet than cold. My bed roll was soaked clean through. No hope in it dryin' out. No hope of gettin' warm.

Sometimes we had a campfire but it would go out on account of the rain. Or it had to be put out if'n there was a advance or retreat. Now I was all the time runnin' hot and cold with a real bad headache most near all the time. I was so weak in the knees I couldn't hardly stand up. At night there was the chills and the sweats and the dreams. The dreams was terrible. I'd dream I was fallin' and couldn't stop. I'd wake up hollerin' and not know where I was.

I quit tryin' to fight. Even if'n I wanted to, the fevers made me shake so I couldn't load my gun and take aim. I was bad sick. Real bad. After about a week, I figured I was goin' to die. I'd seen it happen with the fevers, seen it happen a lot of times. I figured I had to get away if'n I didn't want to die in this hell hole of a War. But I didn't right then have any plan as to how to do it.

One day I was some better, able to get up and I went back agin to the sick tent. *You got any more medicine for my fevers?*

Yep. Not much, but hold your hand. He put some powders in my hand. I swallered 'em with the water he give me. He stood there, lookin' at me. *You in real bad shape, ain't you?*

I reckon so. I ain't getting' any better, that's for certain. We was quiet, standin' there. *The fevers have got me all mixed up. Where do you think we are?* *Don't rightly know for sure. Last I heard we're south of Richmond, aimin' to get there, if'n we can. Some say we're at Petersburg, but I cain't say for sure. They's talk of a big battle in the makin'.* He was quiet, lookin' at me. *You figure you can fight?* I shook my head. *I reckon I can, if'n I have to. Thanks.* I went back to my bedroll and laid down agin and tried to figure out what to do. The time was forenoon. It bein' winter, the sun was low, but I figured it was still in the east more'n in the west. So I figured the way to get out of there was to go to the west of south. Likely goin' back the way we come up from that winter camp.

Right then, I decided to do it. I didn't have any good plan in mind. I just was goin' to take my chances. While I was at the sick tent, I saw that out back there was mules tied up. Maybe 10, 12 of 'em. I guessed they was used to pull the wagons to bring in the wounded. I knowed about that. I'd done it.

It hit me right then what to do. I figured I'd go over that way to see if'n I couldn't just ride off on a mule without anybody stoppin' me. Better do it, while I was feelin' a little better with all them powders. I got my bed roll all rolled up. And I stole a piece of canvas from the bed of another soldier, figurin' I needed it worse than him. I had my old coat on, on top of another'n that I'd took off a dead soldier. Real good boots. Two pairs of britches, one I took off'n of the same pore ole' dead soldier. I felt a little sorry about that, but not much. He was dead and I was alive, and tryin' to keep warm. My old cap didn't look like a Rebel or a Yankee. Just a old cap, that could be pulled down over my ears.

Then I went over to the water wagon and filled my tin. Then to the cook tent, told him I needed some vittles for the road. I had a story ready to tell if'n I needed to, but he didn't even ask. He just give me enough corn pones to fill my kit bag and some halfway cooked bacon and two dried up apples. Thinkin' back to that time, I wonder what he thought, my askin' for some vittles for the road. But he never said a word. Maybe he had somebody tellin' him that all the time.

So I put it all in my kit bag and went over behind the sick tent, circlin' so's I wouldn't have to talk to nobody. I got to the mules. Tried to decide which one was the best, but they all looked the same to me. So I just picked one that was in the back of the lot. It had a bridle of sorts, but didn't have no saddle. I figured I'd have to do without. I couldn't take the chance of tryin' to find a saddle. If'n I tried, somebody would catch me, for sure, and want to know what I was up to.

By that time, the fevers struck again. I was poppin' out sweat and my teeth was chatterin' from the chills. I for sure didn't know if'n I could even get up on that mule. And if'n I could get up, could I stay up there, not havin' a saddle with a saddle horn to hold on to and with some stirrups for my feet. But I did it.

To this day, I don't know how I did it, but I did. It took all my guts, I guess. And I started talkin' to the mule. *Ole Mule, I ain't much for prayin', but I tell you right now that I'm a prayin'. Prayin' that you'll take me away from this God awful mess I got myself in to. Away from all these soldiers killin' each other. Ole Mule, I found out I ain't cut out for fightin' and killin' and I got the runs bad and I got the fevers. I figure I'm goin' to die if'n I don't get myself out of here right now. And I'm sorry to tell you this, but you're goin' to have to get me out, if'n you can. You may not want to, but you're goin' to have to do it. I cain't do it by myself.*

I must of been a sight, this here rag tag soldier, all hunched over, bareback, on this mule, talkin' to hisself. It's a wonder nobody didn't stop me and put me away some wheres. But nobody did. Fact is, there was so much comin' and goin' that nobody paid me any mind. So Ole Mule and me just went right along, like we was supposed to do this. *Ole Mule, what we have to do right now is find out where this camp stops and the country starts. Away from all this fightin'. We don't want to meet up with any Yankees, neither, Ole Mule. Uh oh, that soldier is lookin' at us. Soldier, where you goin'? Down here a piece. Takin' this mule to the old horse lot.* I didn't have no notion if'n what I said made any sense to him. But Ole Mule and me never even stopped, just went on along. In a little while, goin' that direction, I seen there warn't any lean-tos around.

The soldiers was layin' in the open, by the campfires. It was hard by a creek and Ole Mule stopped to drink as he went across. Stooped his head to drink and I near fell off'n him. The soldiers stopped talkin' and looked at Ole Mule and me. *Soldier, where you headed to? Down this way to a sick tent.* My head was swimmin' real bad. Ole Mule was still drinkin, with his head down and I felt myself swayin', tryin' to stay on. *You foller this here creek. Yesstiday there was a sick tent about a half mile that a way. You best get a hurry on. You look danged sick. Gonna fall of 'n that mule.* I hadn't aimed to go along that creek. I had aimed to cross it and get into the timber on the other side, if'n I could. But I figured I better follow his lead else they'd wonder what I was doin'. So Ole Mule and me split the difference. We crossed the creek, but went on up it, like he said. Soon as we got out of sight from them soldiers, we headed into the timber. It was heavy timber, but we could get through it. I was feelin' worse and worse, but I held on as long as I could, tryin' to put as much distance as I could between me and them soldiers.

I must of rode maybe another hour. Couldn't tell much about the sun. It was cloudy and the trees was too tall to see. I recollect wonderin' if'n we was goin' in a circle. I got to the point where there warn't no doubt about it, but what I had to lay down. So I pulled Ole Mule to a stop and slid of'n him. I was skeered to leave 'im loose, for fear he'd run off and leave me afoot. So I tied 'im up halfway to a tree, my hand tremblin' so bad I couldn't hardly do it. And I half laid down and half fell down under that tree, and passed out.

Next thing I knowed I heard a rooster crowin'. Some bare light over ahind me told me that was east. I was feelin' some better. Took my morning piss, ate a piece of corn pone, took a drink of water, and did my duty with the runs. After my guts quit hurtin, I hitched up Ole Mule. *Ole Mule, what do you think we ought to do?* I could see him in the early morning light. *Ole Mule, if'n that's east, we want to go the opposite way, then south.* He just stood there, lookin' at me.

'Bout that time, the rooster crowed again. *Ole Mule, if'n there's a rooster crowin', must be hens about. If'n there's hens about, must be some eggs.* Rooster crowed again. Sun barely comin' up. *Let's me and you go find that danged rooster.* I felt so good, I figured I could walk. *Ole Mule, don't walk so fast. I feel better this mornin', but I ain't fit to trot.* Rooster crowed again. *He's over this a way. We're getting' closer, Ole Mule, must be through the timber this a way.*

Sure enough, standin' at the edge of the timber was what was left of a house. I say what was left, since it was near burned to the ground. The chimley and the chimley wall was still standin'. Spider still hangin' in the fireplace. Pieces of wall here and there but not enough to tell much about what the house had looked like. Rooster and hens was peckin' around. There warn't no other livestock around that I could see. I thought maybe there might be a cow, but didn't seen none. Over on the right was a stable, looked like it was about to fall in. There warn't no fences anywhere to be seen.

Hallo, the house! Anybody at home? Nobody answered. The chickens stopped their peckin', and scattered, but nothin' else. I stood still, listenin' to see if'n I could hear any sounds of battle. Couldn't. It looked like some smoke low in the sky to the north, but that might of been clouds buildin' up. I hadn't come far, but it felt like I'd come a hunnert mile from where I left that camp. Truth to tell, I felt like I was a hunnert mile away from anywhere. *Ole Mule, let's you and me stay here the night and see what we think in the mornin'.*

So we did that. I turned him loose over in the lot. The fence was broke down, but I told him not to go any far. Some winter grass was where it looked like there was water on the ground and he went to grazin'. I petted him some. Never did much pettin' of a mule, but I figured he'd like it as much as the little red mare did. I could always tell she liked it. I walked back to where the house had stood. It had burned down, for a fact. I couldn't see if'n it had been fired by soldiers or if'n it was just a house fire. Didn't matter much to me which, unless it had been fired and the soldiers that done it would come back through here. I poked around some. I stood on what was maybe the doorstep. It was a big flat rock, like the one at our house in Stewart County. A iron bed stead was still standin'. Pieces of the straw tick and the feather bed, scorched brown, in the middle of the bed stead, was layin' on the floor. There warn't many of the floor planks left. It looked like some of 'em had been ripped up. Some more rags was layin'here and there, maybe clothes that had been burned. In what looked like the back room of the house was what was left of a pie safe. No water bucket that I could see. No tin cup or spoon or any kind of dishes layin' around.

But, there, by God, was a meal chest! It was burned on the outside, but still standin'. I opened it up, and it was half full of meal! It was likely to have bugs in it, but I never minded any bugs in my corn meal mush. Back in the front room there was a iron pot and skillet in the ashes by the fireplace. More rags was on the floor, looked like a man's shirt, maybe pants, near burned up. A man's old hat, all bent out of shape was layin' there, by what must of been the doorway, alongside a pair of worn out boots. Not much else that I could see.

I went back out to the stable. *Ole Mule, it looks like the people here got away somehow. Leastwise I don't see any sign of them.* My head started to swim again and I broke out in a sweat. *I better lay down a minute. You tell me if'n anybody comes.* So I laid down by where he was grazin', by the side of the stable, out of the wind. I covered up as best I could. and went to sleep. But I didn't sleep long, I guess. Woke up with a start, thinkin' I heard horses runnin'. I set up. Ole Mule was standin' not far from me, lookin' over at the stand of timber. I didn't hear anything now, but best to be careful, so I led him around to the other side of the stable where maybe we couldn't be seen from anybody passin' by. Sure enough, right then I heard horses passin' by. Maybe not many, but enough to cause us some trouble. They didn't stop, or even slow down, as far as I could tell. Just went on by to where ever they was goin'.

But we stayed out of sight for more than a minute after I heard 'em pass by. I wanted to be sure there was no stragglers, like I was when I got knocked off of the little red mare. The sun was now over to the west. It'd be dark soon. I'd best look in the stable afore it gets too dark to see anything. But there warn't much in there to see. Two stalls, like. A kind of makeshift corncrib, with a fair crop of corn stored. Ole Mule trotted over to the corn and started in to work on it. He acted like he'd never seen corn before. *I don't know, Ole Mule, can you eat corn still on the cob?* He didn't answer but set about doin' what he could with it.

And right then, I found what I was lookin' for, some hen's nests! With eggs in 'em! Corn for him and eggs for me! I hadn't swallered raw eggs since I did it when I was a boy, on a dare. But right then, I broke one and tried to get it to my mouth before it got away. No luck with that one, but got the job done on the next one, and the next one, and the next one. I tried not to think about swallering a raw egg, just got it down as fast as I could.

There warn't much else to tell about that place. Ole Mule and me stayed there that night, and the next. I slept in the stable on the hay. Nested down in the hay, I kept fairly warm. The next night was colder. I wisht Ole Mule would lay down so I could lay down by him. But he didn't. And I wisht the quilts on that bed in the burned down house hadn't been burned up. Truth to tell, I wished a lot of things. But we made do. I got good at swallering the raw eggs. I wanted to save my corn pones from camp for further down the road.

So I built a fire and made meal mush from the meal chest and the eggs and some water. It wanted salt awful bad, but didn't find any anywhere, so I chewed on the end of the bacon I got from camp. That helped. Next thing, I tried to cook some more corn pones to take along. First ones I cooked was too soft. Ate 'em, though. I tried again with more eggs and not as much water. They hung together enough that I could wrap 'em in some green leaves from that wet spot by the stable. I put 'em in my kit bag, figurin' I might not find much to eat where I was headed. It was hard goin'. I was real sweaty and dizzy all that day, but I kept at it. Next morning was still cold, but I figured we'd best get goin'. So I loaded up what I had and stood there wonderin' what had happened here. But not for long. *Ole Mule, we best go.* I took my bearings from sun up, and aimed for the west of south. It bein' winter the sun was low in the sky. Leavin', we went through some right purty country. Good pasture. Good stands of timber. A creek now and then, but nothin' we couldn't get across. We never saw a soul that day or the next. Now I guessed we was a far piece from the battle fields. Never heard any sounds of battle or saw any smoke.

On the second day, it took up a rain about dark time and I shore wisht we had that stable. There warn't nothing in sight for shelter so I crawled under some scrub. It smelled like sassafras. Sassafras is a scrawny bush so it didn't give much shelter and I woke up afore dawn with one of fever chills. I was shakin' like I had the palsy and my teeth was chatterin' something bad. One good thing, it had stopped rainin'. But it had turned a mite colder.

Finally I just had to crawl out from under that bush and move about, to get warm. So I took my mornin' piss and started to run, standin' in the same place. Aunt Polly would say, gets the blood circulatin'. I was holdin' on to Ole Mule's mane, to keep from fallin'. Doin' that helped a mite to get me warmed up and I crawled back under the sassafras 'til it started to get light.

That day, I run into trouble. We was in a stand of timber. I felt good enough to walk, so I was leadin' Ole Mule for a while. But the briars got so thick that I couldn't get through, so I wanted to get back up on him again. It was easier for him with his long legs to get through the briar patch. It was real hard for me to get up on him, since I didn't have no saddle and stirrups to hang on to. So I had to have a log or a rock to step up on. I was lookin' around for somethin' like that to help me up when I heard a man call. *Looky here, what we got.* In front of me, looked like on the other side of the briar patch was two men.

Howdy.
Howdy. The other one nodded. *What air you doin' here?*
I'm real bad sick. Got the fevers. Lieutenant said I could go home. If'n I lived that long. I figured my best bet was to play up the fevers.
You come from the War?
I did. From over around Richmond.
You a Yankee?
No, ain't no Yankee. A Yankee couldn't get home on a old mule. Too far to go.
It was quiet. They was lookin' me over. I was a sorry sight, I knowed, but they wouldn't of won any beauty contest. Long stringy hair. Scraggly beard. Dirty face and dirty clothes. I could smell 'em from where I was. Or maybe I was smellin' me. But they was more filled out than me. Looked better fed, by far. That wouldn't of been hard to do. I hadn't had enough to eat, I guess, since winter camp. And I'd lost some weight from the fevers and the runs, and my clothes was hangin' on me, like I was some kind of scarecrow. *I guess you ain't lyin' about that. Where you come from?*
Stewart County, Tennessee.
Never heard of it.
Over on the mouth of the Cumberland River.
Gol-dang, that's a long ways from here.
I nodded. And started to weave, where I was standin'. All that kept me up was holdin' on to Ole Mule. *I think maybe I'm about to pass out. You boys have a camp near? Where I can set by the fire, maybe lay down, 'til I feel like I can go on?*
They looked at each other. Looked like they was makin' up their mind what to do without talkin' to each other. *We're gonna take a chance on you. If'n you're lyin', it'll be bad for you.* I nodded. It was all I could do to hang on to Ole Mule to keep from fallin'. *Tell you what. I'm gonna help you back up on yore mule.* Nodding to the other feller, *He'll lead the way and I'll foller you. And I'll shoot you if'n you try to get away.* My turn to nod.
They had me. There warn't nothin' else to do but do what he said. I didn't have no idea why they was bein' so hard on me. I

hadn't done a dang thing but come up on 'em. Anyway, he got me back up on Ole Mule. My dizzy spell eased some but I didn't let on that it had. I leaned over on Ole Mule's neck like if'n I didn't, I'd fall off. The lead man went through the briar thicket to the left and we follered. We must a gone near a half mile that way, then he turned to the left again, and come to a little clearing in the shade of two big rocks, right by a creek. And I could see there was a cave, and a fire, and some men settin' around the fire. They was watchin' me as we rode in. I nodded to 'em. *Howdy.* I got some nods back, but nobody spoke.

Then one of 'em settin' over to the left, out from under the hang of the cave, spoke up to the two men who'd got me. *What's this you found?*

He come up on us a mile or two back. Says he's sick with the fevers. Says he's been sent to go home.

He was lookin' now at me. *That so?*

Didn't sound like a question, so I didn't say anything. But I started to sway back and forth, like I was gonna fall off of Ole Mule. I was doin' it on purpose, to show 'em I had the fevers real bad. *Mind if'n I get down and set a spell by yore fire?*

He nodded, and I slid off of Ole Mule, hanging on to his mane. A man by the fire moved over, to make room for me. Tryin' to set, I more or less fell down on my knees, then turned into a squat. Now I started to shiver, and I warn't puttin' that on. *What's yore story?* I pulled my old coat around me as best I could and with my teeth chatterin' told him and the rest of 'em what I'd told the other two. I kept it short, 'cause I was havin' a hard time breathin'. Everybody was quiet, when I got done with my story. *You want a drink of water?*

I thank you for the offer but I better drink out'n my own tin, if'n somebody would reach it for me. Surgeons back at the battlefields don't know what causes the fevers but it might be from drinkin' after somebody with 'em. Some of the doctors had said that. I never believed it but I wanted these men to think it was so. A feller went to Ole Mule and got my tin and handed it to me.

Thankee. I don't want you men to catch the fevers from me. I took a long drink of water. Truth is, I was about to pass out. *You mind if'n I stay here with you boys the night? If'n I stay clear of you, so you won't catch the fevers?* Then I just set there, with my eyes shut, tryin' to keep from keelin' over.

I didn't catch on to all what everybody was sayin' but sounded like some was sayin' it was all right with them, but one was not. *I'm agin it. We don't know hardly anythin' about him or how he come to be here. Mebbe he's a spy. Mebbe he's with the Johnsons. Mebbe this is all play actin', this fever of his. Hit's still day light. Let's put him back up on the danged mule, and send him on his way.*

But the one doin' the talkin', I guess he was the leader of the gang, spoke up. *Yeah, you can stay. Somebody will show you where to put yore bedroll. You want somethin' to eat?*

Mighty nice of you to offer. I got a corn pone and a egg in my kit. But a taste of the meat stew I smell cookin' would set mighty good. He nodded to the man looked like he was tendin' the fire and the stew pot. I handed him my drinkin' cup, holdin' my spoon so they could see I had it to eat with. I took a big spoonful. *By gar, that shore does taste good. I ain't had meat stew since way last summer. Meat was scarce where I come from at the battles.*

I was walkin' a tricky path here. They was eight men to my one. And me so sick I was shakin' so hard I couldn't hardly hold the cup still and get the spoon to my mouth without spillin' it. I warn't goin' to be able to get away, less'n they'd let me. They could take me anytime they wanted to. Only hope I had was to play the sick card, makin' them figure I shore enough had the fevers and that they could catch 'em from me. And that I couldn't do them any wrong. And they'd let me go.

For my part, I couldn't make out anything about them, for sure. There warn't no sign of a uniform that I could see. I could see some rifles standin' over by the cave that looked Yankee to me. But that didn't mean much. They could of been stolen. By that time, I'd been with soldiers from all over the South and the two I'd heard talk sounded like me, like they was from Tennessee or Kentucky. So that didn't tell me much. *You men know much about this part of the country?*

The one doin' all the talkin' shrugged. *Yeah, we know this part of the country. Born and raised around here.* It was quiet. Nobody else was talkin' or doin' anything. They was just lookin' at the fire or at me.

Can I ask a question? He nodded, wonderin' I guess what I was gonna say, maybe, like, what are you men doin' here? Well. I warn't goin' to do that. *Reason I asked is that I'm by myself and I figure I know how to go, but I'd shore be beholden for some help. Maybe you could draw me a map in the dirt about how to get to North Carolina.*

He shook his head. *I ain't much good at that, but Tom here is.* He pointed to one of the men settin' around the fire. *Where do you want to go?*

I think I'm a wantin' to get to the North Carolina line and foller it west to Tennessee.

One of 'em spoke up. *You're gonna have to go cross the mountains to get to Tennessee.*

Yeah, I know. I come up that way with the army.

The man called Tom stirred the fire up, set the meat kettle back, and said so quiet I couldn't hardly hear him. *What army was that?*

No gettin' out of it now. I had to say. *Confederate.* Nobody said a word. I didn't know if'n I'd said the right thing or not. So I just set there, lookin' at the fire, scrappin' the last of the stew out of my cup. Then I stood up, actin' shaky. *All right with you if'n I tend to my mule?* The one doin' the talkin' nodded. I led Ole Mule down to the creek so's he could drink. I filled my water tin, and went back to the fire. I tied up Ole Mule as close as I could get to where I'd been settin'. Then I turned and stood there, lookin' at 'em. *You men want any thing from me? I ain't got much, as you can see. Just what I got on my back, and my kit bag, and Ole Mule.*

One of 'em laughed. *Ole Mule?*

Yeah, I named him that when I stole him from the horse lot back at camp.

Another one spoke. *You dead earnest about gettin' to Stewart County? You bein' sick and all? And ridin' that old broke down mule?* Some of 'em laughed at that.

I set down, afore I fell down. *Yeah, I'm dead earnest. Leastwise about tryin' to. I figure if'n I was gonna die of the fevers I'd a done it already. I've had' em now maybe two months. They ain't any better. Fact of the matter is they's worse, I guess.* It was quiet. *And if'n I die, I'll die on my way back home. Not in some hell hole of this here War.*

The one doin' the talkin' stood up. *Naw, we don't want nothin' of you. If'n we did, looks like you ain't got nothin' to take. You want to go in the mornin'?*

Thought so. If'n you'll let me.

We'll let you. Afore you go, Tom here will draw you a map. One of you show him where to put his bed roll for the night. He motioned to Tom and Tom and him walked down along the creek 'til they was out of sight. The rest of 'em went about their business, doin' this and that. I just set there 'til one of 'em come got me to put my bedroll for the night. The place he showed me to put it was up close to the mouth of the cave. It looked like I could be penned in easy, if'n they wanted to, but there warn't nothin' I could do about that.

By that time, the sun was gettin' low. It'd soon be dark. Ole Mule and me went back down to the creek for another drink of water, and we set there for a while 'til plumb dark. They'd built up the fire and put the stew pot back on. Everybody was quiet, not talkin' to me and not much to each other. It seemed like something was on their mind, but nobody was sayin' what. Somebody give me some more meat stew in my cup. I thanked him, but didn't say anything else. I figured that I better not try to be friendly if'n they didn't want to. And it shore looked like they didn't want to. So I saw to Ole Mule one more time, and went to bed. I lay there, real uneasy, wonderin' if'n they was goin' to let me go. Shorely they would. What else would they do with me?

I woke up in the middle of the night with a start. The fire was low, but I could see or feel a man squattin' by my bedroll. It looked like he was goin' through my kit bag. I set up. *What are you doin' there?* My voice sounded loud in the quiet.

What's it look like? Seein' what you got in here.

Like I told you all, ain't got nothin' in there. Give it back!

When I'm done lookin'.

Elmer, what in the hell are you doin' that for? It was the man that'd done all the talkin'.

I figured I'd better show some spunk. *Give me that kit bag right now!* I sed it in a loud voice that I figured every man there could hear. *Anything you want to know about, ask me. Ain't no need to go rummagin' in my kit bag while I'm asleep, sick and all.*

Go ahead, Elmer, ask him what you want to know. But give him back his kit bag.

Elmer didn't want to do it, but he give me back the kit bag. *What's yore name?*

Luther. Luther Morris.

You a Rebel?

I told you I was.

Can you prove it?

Don't know how. Ain't even got a Rebel cap to show you.

How come you ridin' by yore self?

I told you, I'm desertin'.

Nobody else come with you?

I told you, nobody. I'm ridin' Ole Mule by myself.

Then how come a half hour ago I heard some horses crossin' the creek downstream?

Don't know nothin' about no horses crossin' the creek.

Mebbe they're follering you.

Don't know why they would. I ain't done nothin' but steal a old mule and desert the army. I cain't think they'd care enough to send men out to find me.

When he mentioned horses crossin' the creek, that got everybody's attention and raised up in their bedroll, especially the leader, who was sleeping on the other side of the cave from me. He got up quick. *Bob, you and Tom go down the creek a way, see what you can see or if'n you can hear anything. Might be the*

Taylor gang lookin' for us. I watched them leave. All the men did too. Looked like the Taylor gang was to be watched out for. *Luther, I don't rightly know what to do with you.*

The fire had been built up and I could see him lookin' at me like he was tryin' to figure out what was in my head. *You want me to get my mule and go back the way I come?*

Yeah, that's what I want you to do. Come daylight. You ain't no use to us. And I don't want to have to kill you less'n I have to. You hear what I'm tellin' you?

Yeah, I hear what you're tellin' me.

Elmer was still standin' over me. *Elmer, you leave him alone, less'n I tell you different.*

Elmer went over to stand by the fire. *I don't like it. He just shows up out of nowhere, with this talk about desertin'. All by hisself. Don't make sense.*

It was quiet. I lay back down, wonderin' what I'd got into here. My best guess was that this was a free wheelin' gang, fightin' on their own. I'd heard of sich, when I rode with the cavalry. Question was, who was they fightin'? And question was, was they goin' to let me go?

About that time, the two men come back to the fire. *Don't see nothin', but nothin' to see in the dark. Hafta wait for daylight to look for tracks. Didn't hear nothin' neither, but it's been a while since Elmer said he heard 'em.*

You all heard what I told Luther. Mind you, you leave him be, 'til mornin'. Me and Elmer'll stand watch. Rest of you go back to sleep. Some hours yet afore daylight. But at daylight, we move.

I was overtook with another chill. I lay there shiverin', my teeth chatterin' so loud I figured they'd hear it. Maybe even the Taylor gang could hear it, it sounded to me so loud. Next thing I knowed I was awake, and there was light in the east. Fire was burned low, but I could see the leader and Elmer stretched out by it. Maybe asleep. The chill had passed, but I was as weak as dishwater. I thought about tryin' to sneak off, but sure as shootin' I'd be caught. And they'd figure for sure I was up to somethin'.

So I just lay there. Afore long, I saw the leader stir. He raised up and looked to see if 'n I was still there. I raised my hand to let him know I was, and I was awake. *Can I go piss?* He nodded. I got up from my bedroll, tryin' not to fall over anybody, went over by Ole Mule to piss. I held on to him to steady myself. The time I got back to the fire, the men was all up. The fire was goin' good, and the stew pot was on. One of 'em took my cup, give me some stew and a piece of hardtack.

The men were more talky this mornin' than they was last night. They was talkin' about this and that, about the weather, somebody that snored a lot, joshin' each other. It made me want to be a part of whatever they was. But I told myself that I cain't do that, not if 'n I'm goin' to get to Stewart County afore I die.

Now they started to clean up camp, put out the fire, tend to their horses and saddle 'em up. It looked for sure they was movin' out. The leader come over to me. *Can you ride today?*

I think so, so long as I don't have to ride any fast.

He laughed. It was the first time I'd seen him do anything like he might be a reasonable man. *No need to worry about that, ridin' yore old mule. Tom here will keep an eye on you. Thing is, we're a gonna take you with us until dinner time. Then we'll leave you and go on our way. And you do the same. Don't try to foller us. Be bad if 'n you do. And I got to have yore word of honor that you don't know anythin' about us. No use to lie about seein' us, if 'n it comes to that, but nothin' else. You give me that word?*

Yessir, I shore do. And fact is I don't know anythin' about you all. Just that you let me stay the night with you, and then you went on and I went on. And I'm beholden to you for lettin' me do that. I reckon I was in bad shape last night when I come to your camp. He nodded, and walked away. And we all rode away. It looked to me like we was headed north, then we turned west, at least as best I could tell by the sun. Me and Ole Mule kept up easy enough. They didn't seem to be in a big hurry, wherever they was goin'. Tom rode along not far from me. We stopped at the banks of a good sized river. Everybody took a piss, and watered the horses.

Tom squatted me down on the ground and drawed a map in the dirt. He figured the river was on a line with the North Carolina line. Maybe the line was 50, 75 miles to the south. I'd have to get across the river. He said they was goin' north, so I'd have to go south. I said I would do that, soon as I found a place to ford the river. Then he drawed in the mountains to the west. He called 'em the Smoky Mountains. He said I'd have to get over 'em to get to Tennessee. They was maybe 200 miles away. He showed 'em to run on a slant from east of north to west of south. I recollected comin' over 'em somewheres with the army when we come up from the winter camp. I ast him if'n he'd had some schoolin', to learn about all this. He said he had, and that after the War he was gonna try to get more. I thanked him, and he shook my hand.

The leader rode over. *We're gonna leave you here now. Anybody asks about us, you don't know nothin'.* I nodded, ready to have 'em gone. Then Tom and him rode away at a fast clip to catch up with the others. Both of 'em give a kind of wave back at me afore they rode out of sight.

That was the last I saw of 'em. I never figured out any more about them than I did at the time when they left me there. It looked like they were headed north, but that didn't prove anything. We was always changing directions when I was with the cavalry. I was much obliged that they let me stay with them that night. And obliged that they hadn't done anything to me or to Ole Mule. They could of, and nobody would never find out anything about it.

I set there on that river bank, eatin' what I had in the kit bag, and feelin' mighty alone in the world. It seemed like, for all that, I had liked their company. I never felt that way before, but then I'd not been by myself since I joined up. Always with the other men. So I set there on the river bank, eatin' my last cornpone and dried up apple. I was thankin' my stars that Elmer hadn't thrown them out last night when he was goin' through my kit bag. I'd have to do somethin' about vittles, now that everythin' was gone.

Shorely they could of fed me some of that meat stew afore they left me here!

Well, nothin' to do, but plow on ahead with Ole Mule. At least I had him. And I was not feelin' too God-awful bad. 'Course it was early in the day. Fevers hit me harder as the day wore on. The runs had slacked off some, maybe since I hadn't had much to eat, but I still had that stomach ache, down deep in my gut.

We went, Ole Mule and me, for most of the day along the river. I still hadn't seen any place to ford, so just went on to the west, follering the sun, goin' upstream. I stopped to rest a time or two, take a piss, have a drink of water, let Ole Mule drink, maybe graze a little, while I had a little nap.

But last time I got down from on him, I like to not got up again. I was feelin' real weak, and the fevers was back. My head was swimmin' bad. Finally, maybe middle of the day, I had to just lean over on his neck, and let him go wherever he would. It looked like he was wading his way through a briar patch, but it didn't make no difference to me. It was now so near dark that I knowed we'd have to stop real soon. We was still follering the river.

All at oncet, we come to a clearin', and in the middle of it was a old house. It looked run down but smoke was comin' out of the chimley. I straightened up, and stopped Ole Mule. *Hello the house!* There warn't no answer, but here come a old man out of the door on to the porch that looked out on the river. I staggered down off of Ole Mule and stood by him, holdin' my hands up. The old man stood there on the porch, lookin' at me and Ole Mule.

Who air ye? What'd ye want? I ain't got nothin' fur you to take. You a soldier? Don't look much of a soldier. That shore is a sorry lookin' mule you got. All his words come out so fast I didn't have time to answer him 'til he stopped. When he got to the sorry lookin' mule part, I must of busted out laughin'. He looked at me like he thought I was crazy.

Yessir, he shore is a sorry lookin' mule all right. Can I come over and set on yore porch a spell? I'm feelin' real porely. Could do with a rest.

He held up his hand. *You by yoreself?*

Yessir, I'm by myself. Just me and this here sorry lookin' mule.

All right. You can come set a spell. I'll get you a drink of water in a minute.

I just let Ole Mule stand where he was, and walked over to the porch. I set down, maybe kind of fell down. *You mind if'n I lay down here? My head's swimmin' real bad.* He nodded, and went and got a dipper full of water. I thanked him, and drank it down, and laid down quick afore I could pass out on him. I laid down crosswise the porch, where I could see him pull up a straight chair and set down on it. Looked like he was waitin' on me, I guess, so I started my story. *Name's Luther Morris. Been fightin' the war since I was 15. Got mighty sick with the runs and the fevers in Richmond and I'm aimin' to go home to die.*

You a Rebel?

Yessir. I figured there warn't no need to lie about it, the shape I was in.

You desertin'?

Yessir, I guess you'd say that.

He was quiet, still lookin' at me hard through bushy eyebrows like old men have. *Where you from?*

Stewart County Tennessee.

Where's that?

Feelin' a mite better now, I set up, leaned against a post. *Can I have another drink of that water?* He nodded, and give me another dipper full.

Tennessee's across the mountains, hain't it?

Yessir, it is.

How fur across the mountains is Stewart County? He said Stewart County slow, like he'd never said anything like it before.

Don't rightly know. Maybe two, three hunnert miles.

He looked at me. *You say you got the runs and the fevers?*

Yessir.

You 'spect to make it over them mountains with the runs and the fevers?

I don't rightly know. Only thing I can do is try.

We was just settin' there, talkin', like I said, when all of a sudden, he keeled over and half fell half laid down on the porch. I could see his face to'ard me, and it was all screwed up like he was in terrible pain. I rolled over to where he was layin'. I felt his heartbeat in his neck like I seen the doctors at camp do. It seemed like it was beatin' strong enough. In a minute or two, he opened his eyes and looked at me through them bushy eyebrows. *You still here?*

Yessir, I'm still here. Where do you hurt?

My chest. Hit's in my chest. Guess my heart's goin' bad. My daddy had heart trouble.

You had these spells before? He nodded. *You want me to help you get to bed?* He shook his head. So we just laid there a while. I was stretched out by him but not touchin' him. Nothin' I could do. Mainly I stayed there so's he could see me from where he was layin'.

I can git up now.

Lemme help you.

Don't need no help. But he didn't pull back when I got him by the shoulder, got him on his feet, and back in his chair. I could tell he was sweatin' up a storm. I seen that afore with the soldiers that was wounded and hurtin' real bad.

You want a drink of water? There's still some in the gourd. He shook his head. *I'm alright now. Pain's gone away.* He was quiet, lookin' at me. *You hungry?*

I didn't know what to say. I shore was, but I didn't want to say so outright, him bein' sick. *I could eat somethin', that's for sure. I got some corn pones in my kit bag. Enough for you, too.*

Naw, best save them for when you go on. Then he grinned at me. *You like stewed taters? Maybe some stewed rabbit?*

I figure my eyes near popped right out of my head. *Stewed taters and rabbit! You're puttin' me on. How'd you get that? You making up a story like that jus' to make a man feel bad!*

He laughed at me. *Naw, I ain't. Hit's in the house. All we got to do is build up the fire and heat it up.* He got up from his chair and went in the cabin. I went in after him.

The cabin must of been like the one I seen that got burned up. Only this one was dark inside, so it took me some time to get so I could see. Truth to tell, there warn't much to see. Big fireplace was at one end and a wood pile next to it. I could see a cooking spider with a iron pot hanging over where the fire had burned down.

Best I could see, there was a table with some dishes settin' on it, two straight chairs, pie safe, and a meal chest. On a shelf by the door was a water bucket, with a gourd dipper. His bed roll was spread out on a shelf-like, against the far wall. On the other wall I could see a lot of dried up weeds hanging. It looked like he done some doctorin'. Two old musket guns was leanin' in the corner.

Want me to build up the fire? He nodded, and set down in one of the chairs and put his head down on his arms on the table. *You want me to get you a drink of water?* He nodded. I got him a dipper full. He drank a few swallows, and handed it back to me. The dipper was a cut out gourd, like the one we had at home.

I put some kindlin' on the coals in the fireplace, and it started to flame up right away. I lifted the lid on the pot and, sure enough, there was taters and meat in there. It smelled real good. Right then, my belly started to hurt real bad, and I knowed I had to shit in a hurry. *You got a outhouse?* He nodded to'ard the behind the house. *I gotta go, quick.* He nodded again.

I set there in the outhouse, thinkin' how good it was to have a outhouse instead of having to squat at the trench. It was real good, 'specially with the runs, when you figured your insides was comin' down and out. But the question was, what about this old man? He looked to me like he was bad sick. I figured maybe I better stay with him a few days, if'n he wanted me to. I warn't in no big hurry now, now that I'd got away from the War.

I went back in the house, feelin' some better. With the runs, you always feel better after you shit. He was still settin' at the table. *You surprised to find them good vittles?*

I shore am. You shoot the rabbit?
Naw. Got it with a snare. Plenty of rabbits around here. Only
have to know how to set the snare for 'em. *No need to waste good*
powder and balls to shoot 'em. 'Sides, I cain't no longer see that
good.
What about the taters?
My tater crop from last year. Garden out front gets good sun,
and I had a good tater crop last year. He dished up two bowls, and
handed one to me, and a spoon. *Some corn pone, if 'n you want it.*
Thankee, but this'll do me fine. I took a spoonful. *Well, I*
swear, I never have tasted anything so good in all my born days!
Don't think I had anything so good, since I left home. I caught him
grinnin' at me, me eatin' like I was scared he'd take it away.
You don't have to eat it all. There's enough for suppertime, too.
I pushed my bowl away and laughed. *You must think my*
mama never did learn me any manners. Eatin' like a pig in the slop
trough.
He laughed. *Well, one thing for sure, you was real hungry.*
I set there lookin' at him. It struck me that he looked for all
the world like General Morgan got old. *You feelin' any better?*
I am that. Comes and goes. Now hit's gone. He was quiet. *But*
hit'll be back.
You been havin' these spells long?
Yeah, sometimes.
Sometimes a lot?
What are ye, a doctor? Well, yes, a lot. Big one two days ago.
Thought I was a goner, for sure.
Naw, I ain't a doctor, but I worked around them in the War.
Where's it hurt? I wondered why I ast that. I couldn't do anything
about it, wherever it hurt.
He put his hand on his chest. *Here. And down the arm. I*
guess it's my heart givin' out. I 'member that's what my daddy had
when he died. He was quiet agin. *Maybe my time has come.* He
got up from the table. *I'll get these here bowls washed up, and*
then let's go set a while on the river bank. He did the washin' and
got his stick, and we walked down to a log on the river bank.

The wind was cold and almost by the time we set down, I got a chill. I was all hunched up, trying to keep from shiverin'. But he must of guessed what was happenin'. *You shore ain't feelin' any good yoreself, air you?*

No sir, I'm for sure not.

He was quiet, I guessed thinkin' of what he goin' to say. *Whyn't you stay with me a day or so? Mebbe feel better afore you go on. Mebbe I got some medicine that'd help you.*

I'd shore like to do that, if 'n it's all right with you.

He nodded. *Mebbe we'uns kin catch us some fish. I still got some hog lard to fry 'em in.* We set there, lookin' at the river roll by.

You want to tell me 'bout yore family, where you come from? He moved down to set on the river bank, and leaned agin the log. I moved down too. It put me at eye level with him and the log give some shelter from the wind. And leanin' agin the log eased my back. I was so tired that I wondered if 'n I could talk enough to tell him my story.

But I started out, tellin' him about when I was a boy and goin' off to the War. His eyes was closed and I saw him stiffen up, leanin' into his knees. I could see his hand go to his chest. He was havin' another spell. I went on talkin' like I didn't see what was happenin' to him. I ended up when I left the camp at Richmond. He was quiet the whole time, not movin', eyes closed.

I know what you're doin'. That took me by surprise. I didn't know what to say, so didn't say anything. *You're desertin'.* It warn't said like a question but like he knowed and he was tellin' me what I was doin' when I didn't know it. *No need to try to hide it from me. I know what you're doin'. I can read it in yore face.* I set there, lookin' at the river, not knowin' what to say. *No need to feel bad about tellin' me. I'm a old man, about to die. Cain't do you no harm. Wouldn't, if 'n I could. A man's got to do what he thinks is best for him.* He didn't say no more. Just set there, eyes shut, like he was waitin' for somethin' to happen. Like he was waitin' for me to talk, to tell him how it was.

Well, I warn't goin' to do it. It was none of his business what I was doin'. Or why. Anyhow, I was gonna go off and leave him here and never see him again. Let him set there, by the river. That's what I was tellin' myself.

But then something inside of me wouldn't let it rest. And without my decidin', I started to tell him more. About joinin' up as a boy, not knowin' what I was doin'. Ridin' with the cavalry, the little red mare getting' shot, bein' a foot soldier with all them wounded and dead, killin' that colored soldier, and thinkin' that slavin' was wrong to do. Gettin' sick with the runs and the fevers and makin' up my mind to desert. When I said that word to him, it was the first time I'd said it out loud, to anybody, not even to Ole Mule. I felt real bad that I had to say that about myself. Uncle Gray and Aunt Polly would be 'shamed of me. I was 'shamed of myself.

It must of took me near a hour to tell it, or it felt like it did. He just let me talk 'til I was done. His eyes still closed. One hand on his chest. When I was done talkin' and got quiet, he nodded. More like he'd heard me out than he thought what I'd done was right. It was real quiet. I watched the river water goin' downstream. Lookin' back, I guess it felt good to me then to tell all that story to somebody. Somebody I was gonna leave and never see again.

He raised his head and looked at me. *How long you say you had the fevers?*

Month. Maybe two.

Got the runs too?

Yessir. Had 'em all fall.

Fevers getting' better?

Not so's I can see.

They getting' worse?

I guess so.

You stay with me, mebbe I can cure you. Of the runs for sure.

How you goin' to do that?

I know somethin' about curin' people of sickness. My ma learned me how to do that. Want me to try it on you? Hit'd mean stayin' here a while. Won't take long to cure the runs. Clean out yore insides and give you good water from my spring. But the fevers take more time. You in a hurry to get back on the road?

I guess not. I shook my head. *No, I ain't in no hurry.* Thinkin' to myself, 'specially if'n you can cure me.

Help me up, if'n you can. I got up, not too gol danged steady on my feet myself. But I got him up and we walked back to the cabin. *You go on in and stir up the fire. I'll go see if'n I got a rabbit in my snare.* I did what he told me to and directly he come in without no rabbit. *Nothin' today. Mebbe tomorry. Mebbe tomorry we'll catch us some fish. After we eat a bite, I'm gonna mix up some medicine for you to take.*

While he was putterin' around, makin' somethin' to eat, I looked around the cabin, best I could. Couldn't see much, with the only light comin' in the door. Mostly it was what I seen afore. I could tell now it was a dirt floor. end. I could see some skins on the floor by the bed. There was a lot of something hangin' on the side wall. It looked like weeds and dried flowers. There was maybe pieces of bark and some roots on the floor. Looked like some clothes and a hat was hangin' on some nails in the wall. Supper was meat and tater stew, like dinner. I was real hungry agin. I was right sorry to eat so much. Didn't want to take vittles out of his mouth.

I took another chill right after supper, and he made me go set by the fire, as close as I could get without getting' burnt. He cleaned up the supper things. And he reached under his bed shelf, brung out a jug, and come and set by the fire. I had a drink with him. It was raw stuff and burned all the way down. I hadn't had any whisky since winter camp. *Traded for it last fall. Jug still half full. Maybe hit'll last me 'til spring, they start makin' again. Not much corn in these parts these days.* He took another swig. *You know anythin' about makin' whiskey?* I shook my head, my teeth still chatterin' from the chill. *I use to make some fine likker. Guess I won't do any of that again.*

He offered me the jug again, but I shook my head. He got up, and put the jug back under the bed shelf. *Time to go to bed, put yore roll on the floor on top of these skins. Ain't much pertection from the cold, but hit'll have to do.* He stood in front of the fire, warmin' his back side like I seen Uncle Gray do lots of times. We went out for a piss. It was a real purty night with a half moon. Then we went back in the house. *I'm gonna go to bed. You stay up, if'n you want to. Set by the fire. Tommory, we'll see if'n my medicine will be a cure for you. We'll try to cure the runs first off. Cain't eat anything for two days, maybe three. No water. Jus' drink my tea. Got to clear out yore gut. Get rid of that pisin. You won't like it, but I bet hit'll work.* And he lay down and went to sleep right away.

I set there by the fire for a while, feelin' more easy than I had in a long time. The chill passed on, my teeth stopped chatterin'. My belly didn't feel none too good, but the supper was settlin' all right. So I spread out my bed roll on the skins by the old man, and went to sleep. The middle of the night, I thought that I hadn't done much for Ole Mule, but I guessed he was all right, so I went back to sleep.

Next mornin' I did like he said. Nothin' to eat, nothin' to drink but some tea he made. Tasted so bad I thought I couldn't keep it down. I had to drink it mornin', dinner time, and suppertime. By the second day, I was real hungry, but I stuck it out. Didn't have to shit that second day. Nothing there to pass. Third day, had cornmeal mush and all the water I wanted. Didn't take no more of his tea. And by the fifth day, my bowels looked like they was near normal.

I never had no trouble of that kind again. I asked him what the tea was. He told me, but I never could recollect the name of the weed it was from. When my bowels had settled down, he started me in to chewing a piece of root for the fevers. I kept some in my mouth all the time, and chewed it, and swallered the juice. I did that for as long as I was with him. The fevers never changed. Chills and teeth chatterin' four, five times a day and night. I didn't say anything about it to him. No need to. He could see for hisself. And they got worse after I left that old man's cabin.

I must of been there a week. Maybe more. I kind of lost track of time. I liked to be with him. We went to bed at dark to save what little candles he had, and got up afore daylight. I slept on the floor right by his bed so I knowed when he got up to go take a piss or when he was restless at night. He never complained about hurtin' but I could tell he was. And seemed like day by day he was gettin' more feeble. We didn't do much cookin'.

After a day or two when I went back to eatin' I did most of it. Not much to cook. Made mush with the meal in his meal chest It was about half full when I got there. He had a sack of dried beans that we worked on. I never ast him where he'd got 'em. I kept thinkin' I would, so I could go get more afore I left.

But he didn't want to talk much about such things. I figured if'n he wanted me to do that, he'd say so. I cooked the beans with a little salt pork, cut off of a piece of sow belly, hanging from a hook by the fireplace. It looked good and moldy but that didn't hurt the inside meat none. Flies was swarmin' on the meat, and there'd be more when the weather warmed up. There was some dried up taters on the shelf. They was all shriveled up but cooked up good. There was two or three hard shell squash on the same shelf, but they was rotten on the bottom, so didn't make much of a meal.

We fished every day. I didn't think there'd be any fish, but there was. Mostly little ones, but good enough for a meal. I would cook up some sow belly first to get some grease to fry in the fish in. Every day or two, he'd get a rabbit in his snares. We'd roast them over the fire. He wouldn't let me go with him to his snares, said the rabbits would scare away from my smell. I never heard of such a thing, but I never said anything. Once in a while, he'd bring in some winter greens he'd found on his way to the snares. There warn't many. It was too early for 'em to be out yet. We'd eat 'em raw. They was real bitter to taste, but he said they was good for us. So we got by, even if'n there warn't much to eat. I watched him when we set down at the table. He never et much.

We never talked much. He never ast me anything else about me or where I was from or where I was goin'. And he never said one gol danged thing about hisself. Not if'n he'd lived there all his life, or any family he had, or how he'd got the corn meal or the beans or the sow belly. And in the time I was there with him, I never saw any body else come near the place. I never ast him about any of that. I figured he'd tell me, if 'n he wanted me to know. One evenin', we was settin' by the fire. *You getting' ready to move on?*

I'd been wonderin' when he'd ask that. *No, not 'specially. I ain't in no hurry. It's right peaceful here.*

We was quiet. We was just settin' there, waitin' for it to get dark, so's we could go to bed. *You figure you kin stay on a few more days 'til I get back on my feet?*

I figure I can. Be good to see some signs of spring here by the river. Mebbe take more of yore fevers medicine. I was still havin' the chills real bad. As far as I could tell, his medicine warn't helpin' me much. But I didn't tell him that. On the other hand, I knowed as best as I could see that he warn't likely to get back on his feet, as he put it, any time soon, or ever at all.

I could see by the day that he was in more pain and was getting' weaker. And, as far as spring was, not much sign of spring would be seen for several more weeks. Still some ice here and there in the mornin' when we got up and started to stir. But I figured this was his way of talkin' about hisself and whatever was ailin' him. But 'cept for the fact that the fevers was makin' me sick near all the time, it was as good a place for me to be as any.

Anyway, one night when I laid down to go to sleep, I heard him stirrin' in his sleep, moanin'. And, again, just afore daylight, I was half awake, and I heard him or felt him get out of his bed. Like he allus did, when he got up at night, he edged his way to the door, tryin' not to step on me on the floor. I heard the latch on the door fall when he shut it after he was out. Didn't hear nothin' else.

I laid there, waitin' for him to come back to his bed after he'd had his piss. But then it was too long just for a piss, so I got up, feelin' my way to the door. I started out to'ard the outhouse. Some moon shadow made it light enough for me to see him laid flat on his back, on the path, halfway to the outhouse. I squatted down by him.

I never made it. Pissed my pants. Messed 'em, too.
It don' matter. Can I do somethin'?
He groaned, loud, I knowed he was hurtin' a lot. *Ain't nuthin'*
to do. He groaned again and then was quiet. *Mebbe. Mebbe.*
Mebbe what?
Mebbe set down here. Wait 'til daylight. I set down by him,
crosslegged. Close enough that one of my knees was against his
hip. That way he'd know I was there, even if'n his eyes was shut.
Or if'n he couldn't see me in the dark. We was quiet, a long
time. I could hear him breathin' heavy. *Good thing you come along*
when you did. Ain't right for a man to die alone.

I thought about reachin' for his hand, or goin' to get a drink
of water for him or gettin' some cover for him. But I figured I'd
best to stay put. Then I felt him start to twitch. I knowed what
that was. I'd seen that twitch in soldiers on the battlefield, dyin'.
I didn't say anythin'. Nothin' to say. Just let my knee stay where
it was, so he'd know I was there.

The twitches come regular, then just afore daylight, they quit
comin'. I didn't do anything to be sure he was dead 'til good
daylight. But I didn't have to do much lookin'. I knowed he was
a goner, as we'd say in the army.

Well, I had knowed it was comin'. But I hadn't thought much
about it, if'n I'd still be here or what. I knowed his name was
Zeke, but that was all. I didn't know nothin' about a family
name, or a family, as far as that is. I was obliged to him for takin'
me in, when I was sick and all. But we never talked much. I
knowed he was in bad shape, ever since that first day he got all
bent over with the pain. And I knowed he was makin' hisself
some medicine, along with mine. Only thing he ever said to me
about his bein' sick was when he ast if'n I could stay around 'til
he got back on his feet. I was right glad I stayed around. He was
right. Like he said, it ain't right for a man to die by hisself.

It was somethin', I thought. By then I'd seen maybe a
thousand men die or already dead. Well, maybe not a thousand,
but a lot more than a hunnert. Seein' it hit me hard at first, but I
got used to it. You had to, or go crazy. I didn't know but a handful
afore they got kilt. But they was soldiers in a war.

This old man was different. He took me in, fed me, give me a place to sleep. I'd got used to seein' him around. I liked watchin' him around the place, seein' his shaggy head and chin whiskers. I didn't reckon he'd had a hair cut in a year's time, maybe more. And I thought about his scroungy shirt and pants, and smellin' his feet when he took off his old boots. He'd cured me of the runs, and tried to cure me of the fevers. He even talked some to Ole Mule, when he figured I warn't listenin'.

Well, anyway, here he was, this ragged old man, layin' at my feet. I figured he'd lived his life and it was time to go. Now I had to figure out what to do next. I thought about leavin' him where he was and let the varmints get to him. He'd likely not of minded that. He lived in the woods and shorely knowed about varmints and what they do. But I didn't want to do it that way. They'd get to him for sure anyway but I was goin' to try to give him some kind of a burial, like Joe, back in the army, would want to do. And put up some kind of a marker. Anyway, I could use another day or two in the cabin afore me and Ole Mule set off again, to see if'n I could get back a little strength. As Zeke would of said, to get back on my feet.

But buryin' him was goin' to be hard for me to do. The ground was near friz on top but I figured it'd be thawed when you dug some. Right there it was real rocky, so the diggin' would be hard to do. It looked better for diggin' by the outhouse or in the garden, but somehow that didn't seem right.

So I decided to drag him to the edge of the woods, under a real pretty hick'ry tree. Let the hickor nuts fall on him. He'd like that. I had a little time, I figured. It was a cool, drizzly day. It'd be worse if'n the sun got to him quick. Heat makes a dead body start to rot faster. I never will forget that stink on a hot day after a battle had left a lot of dead.

Anyway, just standin' there, lookin' down at 'im, I was startin' to shake with a bad chill. So I went back to the house, had some water and some more of his medicine for the fevers. And I et the rest of the cone mush and beans from yestiday.

Then I went and got the spade, and went back out to him. The flies had started to come, but no buzzards overhead yet.

Foxes and wild dogs, if'n there is any, won't come 'til they see the buzzards. He was stiff, like a dead body gets. It'd soon be limber again, but it's easier to drag when it's stiff. So I got 'im by the feet and dragged him over to where I wanted him, under that hick'ry tree. It was real tough diggin'. I was weak as dish water and my head was swimmin' something bad.

Like I said, the ground was real rocky. I soon come across one I couldn't move, for the life of me, so I had to try to dig around it. I ended up just scrappin' a shallow grave out for him. It was the best I could do. I dragged him in it and covered him up with what dirt I had and as many rocks as I could get a hold off. It warn't much cover for him, but it'd keep the varmints off for a while. They'd likely stay away 'til I was gone, anyway. Well, maybe the buzzards wouldn't. I hate them things. They'd hardly wait 'til the smoke cleared on a battlefield and there they'd be, flopping around. You couldn't scare 'em off for keeps. They'd keep comin' back.

I rolled the biggest rock I could find and could move to the head of the grave to be a marker. Movin' it, I broke out in a cold sweat and couldn't hardly keep from fallin'. When it was in place, I stood there a minute, leanin' against that hick'ry tree. I just stood there. I never was anything to pray. And there warn't much I could say over him. *So long, old man.*

It took me longer to bury him than I had figured. By the time I did my chores for him, it was near dark. So I chopped some wood, took it in, and built up the fire. And I put some fresh corn meal mush in the pot on the spider. There warn't no need to start any beans cookin' tonight. I warn't even sure there was any. While I was doin' that, it come to me that I didn't know much about where he kept anything. I guessed that warn't no need for me to 'til now. Maybe I best look around in the morning. I might not find anything.

But I shore couldn't do much now, since it was so dark inside the cabin. I pulled the pot back off the fire and went down to set by the river where me and him allus set afore it got plumb dark.

Ole Mule come down, to see what I was doin', I guessed. I set there, feelin' like I was the only man in the world. Truth to tell, I hadn't figured he'd die right so soon.

It hit me between the eyes, settin' down there, by the river. I shore didn't know much of anything about him. Maybe I should of asked more. Maybe a neighbor might want to know he'd died. But I hadn't asked and he hadn't said. I guessed he'd lived on his own. It seemed like a lonesome way to live, but I guessed he wanted it that way. Elsewise he'd of done something different. But he didn't die alone. There was that to say. He had me.

It got dark, and I went inside, and et my mush by the light of the fire. I wondered agin how he got along without no salt. I thought to myself, if'n I ever live to get where there's salt, I'm goin' to salt every thing I eat! Twicet!

So I banked the fire, like I did when he was still here and went to bed in my bed roll on the floor. Somehow, it didn't seem right to sleep on his bed shelf. Afore I turned in, I went out for my piss. The new moon didn't give much light. I thought about going around to his grave, but I was starting to feel bad and decided not to. I'd see him in the morning afore I leave.

That night, I had a bad chill, the worst I guess I'd ever had. I couldn't get warm. I tried to build up the fire agin and looked at his bed, and decided he wouldn't care, so I rolled into his. It shore was warmer than sleepin' on the ground, and he had more covers than I had. But I had to keep tendin' the fire to keep it going. You cain't build up a big fire in a fireplace like that less'n you can watch it. It might spark and start the house afire. I finally settled down and got to sleep. But it was a bad night, what with the bad chills, the cold, and missin' him.

Next morning it was cloudy and cold, with a wind from the west. I had my mornin' piss, and it was cold enough that the piss steamed in the cold air. As I stood there, Ole Mule came up. *Ole Mule, what do you think? Is it a good day to travel?* He shook his head. *I guess it is. Let me get some things together, and we'll go.*

There warn't much to get together. The old man didn't have much, and what he had I couldn't load up on Ole Mule. It was mostly what I could eat. I put what little corn meal he had left in a tow sack. I tied it at the neck, divided it up in two parts, one on each side of Ole Mule, like saddlebags. There was a handful of beans but not worth the takin'. I cut up the sow belly in pieces, wrapped them in leaves, and put 'em in my kit bag. No need to worry much about water, but I filled my tin agin. The clothes I had on was better'n his. At that, they wouldn't fit me. He was too small for me. No need to think about a cook pot. I couldn't hang it on Ole Mule. I looked at his old gun, but didn't think it'd be any use to me. It might get me in trouble carryin' it.

So I stood there, lookin' around, to see if'n I'd missed anything of any use. I shore wisht I knowed more about his medicine, but he never told me anything but chew this or take a drink of that. Maybe I'd take the blankets, the ones I slept under last night when I was havin' the chills. When I reached over to fold 'em up, to put on Ole Mule, there at the foot of his shelf bed, under the blankets, was a leather bag with a raw hide draw string.

There warn't no need not to open it, so I did. There in the bag was a gold ring, looked like weddin' band that a woman would wear. And a gold watch and chain, like the one I'd seen Mr. Cherry have. And a gold piece. It looked for all the world like the ones I had sewed in my old coat, but I couldn't tell for sure since it had been a long time since I'd seen 'em. *Old man, you want me to leave these here things with you? Or you want me to take 'em with me? Ain't gonna do you any good to have 'em, and they might come in use to me sometime. So if'n you don't mind, I'll take 'em.* So I put 'em back in the pouch and rolled it up in one of the blankets on Ole Mule.

Then I shut the door to the cabin, put it on the latch. I went up to the grave one last time to pay my respects, before I left. Varmints hadn't gotten to it yet, but the turkey buzzards was flyin' over head. They knowed he was there, waitin'. I got on Ole Mule and rode away.

It looked like the thing to do was to stay by the river. It looked like it was flowin' up from the south. And I reckoned that North Carolina was to the south. At least, goin' by the river,

Ole Mule would have water that way, and there was some new grass on the river bank for him to graze. I figured I had enough vittles to get by on for a few days, maybe more. Truth to tell, I guess I warn't even thinkin' much about anything, just feelin' real bad. A cold wind blowed hard. I started havin' more chills. And I was lonesome, Lord, was I lonesome. It felt like I was all alone in this old world.

That day and the next and the next and the next turned into a kind of a dream for me. We'd stop some times for me and him to rest or eat a bite or have a drink of water or me to piss. I'd look for some kind of wind break for the night. Maybe I'd find a rock or a log to stop at, so's I could get back up on his back. I was getting' weaker, and and loosin' track of time. I didn't have no notion how long we'd been ridin' after we left the old man's cabin. I had water, but run clean out of vittles. Now I was havin' chills all the time. Always hot, then cold, then hot.

I recollect I had only one thing in mind, getting to North Carolina. I recollect joggin' along on Ole Mule, sayin' to myself, keepin' time as he jogged along, *North C'lina, North C'lina, North C'lina.* It seemed like that was the only thing that kept me goin'. It was that I'd be soon in North Carolina, and that much closer to Stewart County. Finally, it got too much for me to set up, and I just leaned over on Ole Mule's neck, hangin' on to his mane, and lettin' him go where he would. That's the last I knowed.

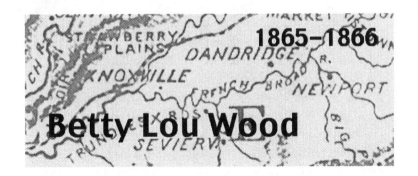

Betty Lou Wood

*Y*ou *got any name?* It sounded like a girl talkin'. I opened my eyes to see a man and two girls lookin' down at me. It looked like we was on the inside of a barn. *You got any name?*

Name's Luther. Luther Morris. I sounded funny, when I said that, like I hadn't talked for a week. *You got any water? I'm powerful thirsty.* The little girl give me a gourd full of water. I raised up so's I could drink, but still spilled half of it. It tasted awful good, like I'd never had a drink of water afore, in my whole life. I had a piss hard. *I gotta take a piss.*

You girls go outside while Luther here and me take care of this.

They went, and he helped me up from my bed roll and held me enough to get to the corner of wherever we was, holdin' me by the arm while I pissed. *Where am I?*

North Carolina. Just over the state line from Virginia. I could see that I had on a long tailed shirt and nothin' else. I thought I'd better ask about my clothes and my old coat but my knees turned to water and all I could think about was getting' back to my bed. But at the same time, I could tell that the fevers was gone. I knowed how it felt to have 'em, and I knew right then that I didn't.

I was shorely weak in the knees, but I felt the best I felt since I took sick back at Richmond. *You got a lot of piss in you. No wonder, we was makin' you drink all the water you could hold. Best thing for the fevers. This is the first time you got up to piss. Me and the girls have been takin' care of you. And you ain't over the fevers yet.*

So, I thought, the girls have seen me nekkid, I guess. But right then I didn't care who'd seen me nekkid. There warn't much to see, anyway. It looked like I was all shriveled up, and I felt that way, too. He helped me lay down again, and I closed my eyes. *Can you hear me?* I nodded, or tried to. *You been real sick and still ain't so good. Here, drink some more water and go back to sleep.* I heard the last part of what he was sayin' like he was far away. I was halfway asleep. *Much obliged.* I said that, or thought I said that, and must of gone back to sleep. After that I don't remember much of anything. Sometimes I'd have the shakes, my teeth chatterin'. Then I'd be hot and throw back the covers. The man would come and get me up to go piss and drink more water. He'd talk to me but I didn't know what he was sayin'.

Sometimes I'd wake up to the little girl settin' there with her dogs. She didn't talk, just set there lookin' at me. Sometimes there was a woman settin' there, sometimes feeding me corn mush. I recollect that I dreamed a lot. I dreamed I was in Bumpus Mills with Uncle Gray and Aunt Polly. I dreamed of the War all the time. I was watchin' the Yankees come at me and I couldn't get away. I thought I was on the little red mare, follerin' Charlie through a swamp. I saw the little red mare get shot by the cannon ball, layin' there, more times than I can count. Every time, I'd try to stop her getting' kilt but I couldn't.

Time after time, I seen the colored soldier's face, the one I shot, lookin' up at me. And many a night I would wake up in the dark and not know where I was or how I got there. Somebody put my water tin next to my head and I took to reachin' out for it to tell me where I was. At the time, I didn't know the passage of time. When I was better, Preacher told me it was near a month that I was laid low, most of it out of my head.

But come one mornin', I woke up to the rooster crowin'. It made me think of the burned up house. I had to piss real bad. I crawled over to the corner where he'd took me afore. Was that yestiday? I couldn't tell. I wondered what they'd done if'n I'd had to shit. The man must of taken care of that some how. I shore did owe him and the girls a lot. I crawled back to the bed roll.

The long tailed shirt kept getting' in the way of crawlin'. It got in the way of pissin', too. There was a big wet spot in front where I hadn't got it out of the way.

I laid there, thinkin'. Last thing I recollected for sure was feelin' so bad. Hot, cold, chills, headache, a real bad headache. I was so weak I couldn't hardly stay on Ole Mule. I recollected that I just laid over on his neck, hangin' on the best I could, to keep from fallin' off, and lettin' him go where he would. That was the last thing I recollected, so I must of blacked out. When was that? I set up, of a sudden. Shit fire, where was Ole Mule? I owed him a lot and I didn't want to lose him. He had to take me to Stewart County.

I was layin' there thinkin' about everything and wondering about everything, and in come this man. He set down by me. *You feel up to hearin' a little talkin'?* I nodded, or thought I did. *I thought maybe I'd tell you a thing or two about how you got here. Then I'll let you go back to sleep if'n you want to. My name's A. J. Wood. Most folks call me Preacher, 'cause I do a little preachin'. My little girl, Thelma, found you in a ditch about a mile, mebbe more, to the north of here. Her and the dogs was out, looking for wild flowers, she said. Dogs got ahead of her, started to bark like holy cane.*

She went to see what was causin' the fuss, and there you was, layin' in the ditch. A mule standin' there by you. Said she didn't stop to look much at you. Jus' called the dogs off and come home to tell me. I was busy at the barn. I thought about leavin' you be, but on second thought decided it was my Christian duty to see what I could do. So I hitched up the wagon and them and me brung you here and put you in this stall.

I laid there thinkin' of what he was tellin' me. *Seems likely you saved my life. I'm much obliged, more'n I can say.*

You don't have to say anythin' right now. You've been real sick and still ain't well. But you're getting' better. There'll be time to talk then. I got to get to work. I'll see you later on today. Looks like you got a little company to set a spell with you. And he got up and left.

About that time, here come two dogs follered by two girls. The little'un first. Well, not so little, but littler than the other one. She was tryin' to quieten down the dogs that was barkin' like fury at me. Then come the big girl, with a bowl and a spoon. *Can you set up to eat?* I scooted up as best I could, to lean against the wall behind me. I tried to pull my shirt tail down and my blanket up to cover my crotch since I didn't have no drawers on. I took the bowl from her. *I 'm much obliged to you. I am a mite hungry.* It was corn mush, and tasted better than I ever ate in all my life. I scraped the last bit of mush out of the bowl with my finger.

She laughed. *Don't have to lick the bowl. There's more where that come from.* She reached over to get the bowl and my hand touched hers, just for a minute. But it was a good minute, and I thought Oh Lord, can we do that again? It'd been so long since I was close to a woman. I'd forgot how it felt. *Thelma, you go get him a drink of water.* Thelma took the dogs and went.

Her and me just set there, lookin' at each other. Mebbe I was tryin' to think of somethin' to say. Maybe she was. I know I looked a mess. Long dirty hair hangin' down in my eyes. Scraggly chin whiskers and sideburns. My hands was god awful dirty, pro'bly my face, too. At least the long tailed shirt I had on was clean, except where I'd pissed on it.

She shore was not a mess, She had brown hair, kind of wavy, hangin' down her back and on her shoulders. And she had the purtiest face I swear I ever saw in all my life. No, not any purtier than Nadine, just different. Her blue eyes was lookin' at me like I was somebody she'd seen afore. It turned out that I looked a lot like one of her brothers, but I didn't know that then.

She had a halfway smile, like she knew a funny that she warn't gonna tell anybody, much less me. And she had on some kind of a dress with little flowers on it. It fit like it was too big for her but I could see the shape of her bosums where her shawl had come open. I just set there, lookin' at her, likely with my mouth hangin' open, like I never saw a purty woman afore in all my life. *You got any name?* I tried to answer. *Luther. Luther Morris.*

Mine's Betty Lou. Betty Lou Wood. The other girl and the two dogs come in. *This here is Thelma Wood. She's my sister.* She got up. *Thelma, you give him the drink of water. I got to get back to the house.* She looked at me. *You want to set up a while and talk to Thelma?*

I'd be proud to do that, if'n she can stay a while. She took the bowl and spoon and the drinkin' gourd from me and went out the door. I turned to Thelma. *Them's right good lookin' dogs you got there.* She nodded, lookin' at 'em, like she was studyin' 'em for the first time. *They got names?*

She shook her head. *Just call 'em Dogs.* She changed her mind. *That one I call Skunk. He's allus smellin' like a skunk. Other one I just call Dog. They're good for watch dogs. Dog is. He'd bark at anything. Skunk, he just stands there and looks.* She fell quiet, still lookin' at the dogs. *It was Dog that found you. He was barkin' like he'd treed somethin', and I went to find out what it was. Thought maybe it was a snake. There you was, layin' in the mud in the ditch, side of the road. A mule was standin' there by you. The mule didn't even have a saddle on. A kit bag tied, kind of, to the reins.*

That's my mule. I call him Ole Mule. He brung me from Virginia. Did you lead him here when you brought me? Is he here?

She nodded. *He's out back in the lot. Daddy was right proud to find 'em. Said he needed another mule. We had two, but the soldiers took one of 'em when they come through.*

I figured I'd better settle that right away. *I'd be proud to have yore Daddy use him while I'm here with you all. But I need him to go on home.* Maybe Thelma would tell that to her Daddy, if'n the subject come up. I wanted to let him know for sure that I didn't mean to give Ole Mule to him. *I guess I want to sleep a little if'n that's all right with you.* I settled down in my bed roll. *Afore I do, I sure do want to thank you for findin' me and getting' yore Daddy to save me. I might of died if'n you hadn't done that. I'm much obliged to you.*

She gave a little smile, first I'd seen on her face. *T'warn't nothin'. It was Dog that found you.* She got up, took the dogs and went out the door.

I needed to piss again, but this time I figured I could walk some. I got to the corner without havin' to crawl. And I stood there thinkin' that it shore was queer that after so long with the fevers they was gone. Or leastwise I felt like they was gone.

I turned around, leanin' against the wall, and looked around some. It looked like just a barn, like many a ones I seen in Stewart County. The cracks between the logs let in some light so I could see what was there. It looked like I was in a stall, but there warn't any manure on the floor so I guessed not any stock was kept there. Some tools and bridles was hangin' on the walls. Some tow sacks was in the corner, looked like they was empty.

My bedroll was a pile of hay, up against the wall. Past my bedroll was what I was lookin' for, my clothes. There they was, piled up, with my old coat on top. I staggered back to my bed and reached over to feel the hem of my old coat. I could feel both of the gold pieces me and that fellar had sewed in, when I went to Clarksvul, as he would say, with him. Wonder what happened to them? Maybe I can find them when I get back. And I went to sleep wonderin' if 'n I'd ever get back.

When I woke up, I was feelin' mighty thirsty. There was Thelma and her dogs settin' by my bed, and a bucket of water with the drinkin' gourd. *Want a drink of water?*

I shore do. I think I must of drunk enough water to float a john boat since I woke up. I took a long drink, bein' careful to keep my shirt tail down to cover me up. *I thankee. You folks have got good water. You got a spring near here?*

She nodded. *The spring's in the spring house, on the other side of where the house is.*

My Uncle Gray's house, we'd keep milk and butter and stuff in the spring to keep it cool. Do you folks do that too?

She nodded. *Ain't got any milk yet. Cows ain't fresh. You hungry?*

I could eat somethin' if 'n you can spare it.

Dinnertime in a little while. She reached ahind her, brought out some pants. *Betty Lou says maybe they'd fit you.*

You turn yore back, and I'll see if 'n they do. She did, and I finally got 'em on, by leanin' against the wall. They was a little big, but not much. I'd find a piece of rope to hold 'em up, if'n I had to. I set down again, and put on my boots. First time I had 'em on since I come here. I felt real good, weak, but good, with no fevers.

Can I turn around now?

Yep, you shore can. But I got to set down again, afore I fall. The sun was comin' in a crack in the wall right on her. We was settin' across from each other. I guess we was studyin' each other. She was a right purty girl. Her yellow hair was done in two braids down the back, and one on top feedin' one of the ones in back. Her eyes was kind of gray. And she had a real nice face, looked like she'd washed it good that morning. There was freckles on her nose. Leastwise, that's what Aunt Polly had called 'em. She had some too. I hadn't seen this girl Thelma smile, but oncet. Maybe she didn't smile much. The dogs was layin' by her. *Is it a far piece to the house? I don't know if 'n I can make it.*

It ain't far. Daddy brung you over a walkin' stick. An' you can lean on me.

Afore we go, can you tell me something? She nodded. *How long have I been here?*

Near four weeks by my count.

I been sick all that time? She nodded. *You and yore family been takin' care of me all that time?* She nodded. *That's mighty good of you. I'm much obliged, more'n I can say.*

Daddy said it was our Christian duty.

Well, maybe that and then some.

She was quiet, frownin' at me. *You got a mama and a daddy?*

My daddy died, I was a boy. Mama married again, moved away. I live with my Uncle Gray. Me and my brother Sam. He's a mite older than you, I guess.

You and him got any dogs?

I nodded. *Got some dogs around the barn. Ain't as well trained as yore's are. They mind Sam better'n me.*

She was quiet agin, studyin' the dogs. Then she looked up at me. *Where'd you come from?*

Tennessee.

That over the mountains?

I nodded. *You know the sun comes up in the east and goes down in the west?*

She giggled. *Anybody knows that.*

Well, look here. I made a map in the dirt floor of the barn. *Here's North Carolina, where you live. Here's where the mountains are, I guess. And here to the west is Tennessee. And I live right about here.* I made a spot where I figured Stewart County was.

Where's our farm? She was leanin' over my map in the dirt, lookin' at it.

I don't rightly know. Maybe yore daddy can help us there. Ain't much of a map. I ain't had much schoolin'. You been to school?

She shrugged. *Went to school afore the War started. Teacher left to go to the War. Betty Lou can read and write. Better'n me.*

Maybe after the War is over, you and me can go to school.

Maybe. She was gigglin' again. *Won't you be too old to go to school?*

Maybe. But I'd like to. Here I am, been to the War, and I don't know much of anything.

Eddie used to talk like that.

These here pants you brung me, they Eddie's?

Nope, they're Charlie's. She got up and left with the dogs, without another word.

Betty Lou was at the door, with a bowl and a spoon. *You'll have to drink water. Ain't had no coffee in a long time. Cows ain't in fresh yet, so we ain't got sweet milk yet. Maybe soon.* She set down where Thelma had been. The sun was shinin' on her like it had on Thelma.

I took the bowl and spoon from her. *I thankee for this. I hate to be such a bother to you, bein' sick and all. Maybe I could walk to the house and set up at the table. It'd save you some trouble.*

Daddy says not yet. He says for you to walk around some in the barn afore you try anythin' else.

The beans was real good, tasted better than anything I'd had in a long time. They could of used some salt, but, like I said, I knowed salt was not easy to find in those times. *Mighty fine beans. You are a real good cook.*

She shook her head. *Ain't nothing to cookin' beans. Beans and water, put it on the stove all mornin'. Them has a little side meat in 'em. Side meat is about gone. I told Daddy about that yestiday. He said he'd try to get some somewhere.* She fell quiet, lookin' at me. *You're feelin' better, ain't you?*

A lot better. I still got some chills and headache and some nightmares at night, but for sure I'm gettin' better. I grinned at her, tryin' to get her to smile again. *Maybe I ain't goin' to die on yore hands, at least not yet. Mighty good of you folks to take me in.* I fell to eatin' the beans. *Can I ask you, you know why yore daddy did it? What with the War and all. Must of been a lot of soldiers in the ditch these days.*

She laughed and it tickled my soul to hear her laugh. She was shore one purty woman without laughin' and when she laughed, all hell broke loose, as a soldier I knowed oncet would say. *Well, that's for sure. Prob'ly there's lots of soldiers in the ditch nowadays.* She frowned, thinkin'. *I don't rightly know why Daddy decided to try to save you. He's real soured on the War, worse than ever now with all that's happened.* She didn't finish. Then she cocked her head, eyin' me. *Maybe it's 'cause you favor my brother Eddie.*

You want to tell me anything about Eddie?

No. I got to go. I handed her the empty bowl and spoon. Then she changed her mind. *We all miss Eddie a lot.* She was frownin' again. *Not that we don't miss Charlie. We do. But Eddie was different. He was real good to Thelma and me. Always laughin' and singin' and carryin' on. Real quiet with him gone. Wisht we knew what happened to him. I'm talkin' too much.* And she got up. *I'll send Thelma in, after you rest a while. Maybe you and her can go for a little walk. Need to get yore strength back.*

I laid there thinkin' about what she'd said. Maybe it wouldn't be best if'n I stayed around. Maybe it'd be too much for them to stand. I must of gone to sleep, thinkin' about that. But I got awake, hearin' Thelma and the dogs come in. *You want to sleep?*

Not right now. It'd be good to set here with you. I ain't done anything like that for a long time. I'm real weak in the knees. We was quiet, me lookin' at her, her lookin' at the dogs, rubbin' their ears. *Can I ask you a question?* She nodded. *How long did you say I been here?*

Maybe four weeks, by my count.

You and Betty Lou and yore Daddy took care of me the whole time?

Warn't much to do. You was asleep most of the time, 'cept when you was out of yore head. She fell quiet. *Daddy told us he thought you was gonna die. He let me and the dogs set with you some. Wouldn't let Betty Lou, on account of her havin' to take care of the house and all.*

You got a mama?

She died when I was born. She was quiet, lookin' at me. *You remember what yore mama looks like?*

I do, but it's been a time since I seen her.

I never saw my mama.

Must be hard to take. We was quiet. *Betty Lou said we could take a walk. You want to do that?* She nodded. *You got a stick somewhere here I can use? Keep me from fallin' in a ditch again.* She giggled and went and got a walkin' stick, I guess the one her daddy had brung for me. She watched me get up, slow, but I made it. We went out the door of the barn, but never got far. My legs give out. I had to set on a big rock and then we went back. I near fell in my bed roll. The fevers had left me that weak. Thelma and the dogs left me there and I went to sleep again.

I was dreamin'. I was at the War and the Yankees was comin' at me. I was tryin' to get away, but I was tied down. So I was hollerin' for help. A man's voice woke me up. It was Preacher Wood. He was squattin' down by me. I could feel his hand on my shoulder. *Luther? Luther? You awake?* I looked up at him, knowin' it was him and where I was. *You was dreamin'. You done that a lot since you been here. It's all right. Get it out of your mind. Now that you're awake, you feel like some supper?*

Yessir, if'n you can spare it.

We can spare it. Ain't nothin' but beans and corn pone, but there's enough for you. He grinned. *So long as you don't eat like a horse.*

I raised myself up and looked at him, maybe for the first time. He was maybe 55, 60. Stocky. Red face. Hair not too long, not as long as mine was, mostly brown with some gray in it. Chin whiskers trimmed. *You need to piss, afore you eat?* I nodded. *Let's see if'n you can make it to the outhouse. Ain't no need to smell up the barn worse'n it already is.* He was still grinnin'. Didn't offer to help me up, but after I was up handed me the stick.

We went out of the barn, him talkin'. *I ain't got many chores to do this time of year. Too early to plow. Ground's still too wet. The cows ain't fresh so don't milk. Girls take care of the chickens. I slop the hogs. There's a sow, two shoats, and several pigs from her. The old boar is somewhere around here. Don't do much for him. But you watch out for him, if'n you're out and about. He's big enough to push you over with one shove. He ain't mean, just troublesome.*

What do you do for a bull?

Take the cows to a neighbor's bull. He's done us good past few years.

By that time, we'd gotten to the outhouse. I stood there, leanin' against it. *It looks like you got a right nice place here.*

He shrugged. *I reckon it is. We get by on it.*

Soldiers never bothered you?

Just oncet. You need some help getting' in and down?

No, I think I can make it. I went in, got through, and come out. *You must of had a good corn crop. Good shucks in there to wipe with. Ain't seen that since I left home.*

He laughed. *That's so.* Then he turned serious. *I made the last crop on my own with the girls and neighbors. All of us around here helped one another. All the boys had gone to the War.* He kind of guided me back to the barn and to my bed roll and I fell in it like it was the best bed I ever saw.

My dreamin' bother anybody?

He shook his head. *Don't know as the girls ever knowed about it. Hit's nothin' to worry about, yore dreamin'. You seen and done some terrible things. Best get it out'n yore mind some way, elsewise they'll stick with you.*

Well, him and me must of done that walk enough times, I got so I could do it all by myself. I don't recollect how many days that was. Then one day, Thelma come down with dinner. *Daddy says ask you if 'n you feel up to comin' to the house for supper. I'd shore like that. You think I can walk that far?* She grinned. *Mebbe. The dogs and me and yore stick will help you along.* So sure enough we made it. It felt real good. I washed up and set at the fire 'til supper time called in the kitchen. It looked like the kitchen at Uncle Gray's. There was the cook stove in the corner, all fired up, and the heat felt real good. Betty Lou was workin' at the stove and the table. She showed me where to set. It warn't quite dark out yet, so's there was enough light through the window and from the stove to see how to eat. I watched her in the half light. She shore was a purty woman.

The next week or two follered the same pattern. Early mornin' mush by my self, dinner and supper with the family. I was up more, walkin' more. I walked to the out house, down to the pond, over to the lot where Ole Mule was. I had got stronger by the day. I was still comin' to grips that I was gettin' over the fevers. Maybe the old man's medicine had done the job. They just took some time to take effect. I still had the dreams about the War, but I paid heed to what Preacher had said about them and I tried not to let it worry me. I had them dreams for years to come. I figure every soldier that's been in battle has 'em.

One day he come to the barn afore dinner. I'd just got back from a walk down to the pond, over to the lot, and back, and I was settin' on a log, whittlin', passin' time, thinkin' maybe I better move on. *Good mornin'.*

Good mornin'. Looks like a fine day.

It does. I folded up my pocket knife and put it away. *I want to thank you again for gettin' me out of the ditch. I 'spect you saved my life.*

My Christian duty. He was quiet, lookin' at me. *You look like you're getting' yore strength back.*

I am, thanks to you and the girls, and all them good beans.

Well, mebbe it was the beans that did it. Then he looked at me straight. *I got a offer to put to you.*

Yessir, I'm listenin'. I was thinkin', wonder what this is goin' to be.

Got two offers. First one is, this is a Satiday, and I'm preachin' tomorrow. If'n I'm able, I try to be clean and decent when I go to preach. Looks like today is a fine day, and after dinner I'm gonna go down to the pond to wash up. Figured you might like to do the same. We got a place on the pond where the spring feedin' it comes in. Water stays clean. It's past the pasture and the cows cain't get to it to keep it stirred up. Good place to wash up. 'Cept in winter, of course, when it's too cold. Men folk go on Satiday. Women folk go middle of the week. So I figured I'd go down today. You want to come?

Yessir, I really do. That'd feel mighty good. I ain't had a bath in a coon's age. Get rid of some of these army lice, pesterin' me.

Better warn you that the water'll be cold.

I don't mind that. You ain't by any chance got any soap? I'm real dirty.

He laughed. *I reckon you are, at that. We got good strong lye soup. Take off yore hide, along with the dirt, if'n you ain't careful. That's settled. We'll go after dinner.* He was still standin' square in front of me, his arms folded. *Another thing.* I thought uh-oh, here it comes. *You been here for some time and we don't know anythin' about you. I figure it's time to find out, and I figure you are up to the talkin'.*

I'm up to the talkin', all right. And I ain't got nothin' to hide. Well, nothin' I cain't talk to you and the girls about. You want to ask me some questions right here and now?

No, I thought about doin' it that way. But best if'n the girls hear what you've got to say too. So this evenin', after supper, you'll have yore chance to tell us all at the same time.

Sounds like a fair deal, and I'll be ready.

He turned to go. *Dinner'll be called directly.*

I walked back in the barn. Yestiday I seen that Ole Mule looked real scruffy. I'd seen a curry comb in there, and so maybe this was a good time to clean him up some. So I got the comb,

and went out to find Ole Mule at the feed trough. There warn't
nothing in it. Maybe he was just bein' hopeful. So I cleaned him
up, him standin' right there. *Ole Mule, you stand still. Watch out
and don't step on my foot. What I don't need right now is a broke
foot. That'd fix us all right. You shore do look scruffy. Stickers and
cuckleburrs in yore tail and yore mane. And dusty all over. It looks
like you don't belong to nobody. Well, you do. You b'long to me and
I b'long to you. And don't nobody forget it.*
I was quiet, workin' him over. *You ain't seen much of me
lately. But I guess you knowed I been sick. Real sick. Got worse, ever
since we left that old man's cabin.* All of a sudden, I recollected
that leather pouch I took from his bed. It must still be in my kit
bag, 'less'n these folks took it. It didn't seem likely they were that
kind. But if'n I learned anything in the army, it was that you
never know about folks and what they'll do. I'd better look in
the kit bag for that pouch.
I kept on cleanin' him up. *You know what, Ole Mule. Maybe
you saved this old boy's life. I don't recollect much about them days
and nights after we left the old man's cabin. Don't even recollect
if'n I got down of yore back at night to sleep. And, if'n I got down,
how'd I get back up, not havin' any strength in my arms and no
saddle stirrups to climb up on? Must of found a rock or a log. Cain't
picture you kneelin' down for me, like I oncet saw a trick horse do.
But howsomever you done it or I done it, weun's done it. All I can
recollect is feelin' so sick I could die. Don't know what I held on to.
I guess I just laid down on yore neck, hangin' on to you and yore
mane as best I could, and lettin' you go.*
I got done with the curry comb. *Ole Mule, you look right
good. As good, I guess, as you'll ever look. Now don't take any offence
at that. I know that I wouldn't win any beauty contest at a pie
supper myself. We're just two of a kind. Les' go down to the pond for
a drink of water.* We went down, Ole Mule at his usual walk. I
remembered feelin' that walk, and thinkin' North C'lina, North
C'lina, North C'lina, in time with his walk. We got to the bank
and he took a long drink. Standin' there, I looked around, maybe
for the first time.

It was a real purty farm place. For sure, it looked like good farmin' land. Some of it was hilly. The house was set down in kind of a valley with the barn and the horse lot and the pond. I could see what I figured to be the spring house and a little gully leadin' from the spring house to the pond. That was what was feedin' the pond. There was a kind of a marsh on the other side that dreened off the pond when it got too full. Uncle Gray didn't have anything like that on his farm, but I'd seen it on farms where I had hired out. It was a good way to do it, if'n everythin', the spring and the pond and the runoff, was in some kind of a line up.

New grass was showin' through, in the pasture up on the hill behind the barn. Maybe six or eight cows was up there, grazin'. They looked like a Jersey mix, if'n I knowed right. A mule was up there, too, grazin'. Seein' the pasture greenin' up hit me that it was might nigh spring time. I'd been on the road two months since Richmond. Maybe longer. I'd ask about the time of year tonight when we was doin' the talkin'.

We done what he said we'd do. We had our bowl of beans and corn pone for dinner. When we got through, Betty Lou brung out some clean clothes, and a piece of soap. They smelled real good from hangin' in the sunshine. Him and me walked down to the pond, around the edge maybe twenty five feet, to where the spring water come in, and it was clear. We shed our clothes and waded out. Like he said, it shore was cold, real cold. It took yore breath away, getting' in. I was gonna take the clothes I had on in to wash 'em, but he said to leave 'em, that Betty Lou would wash 'em. He said it would do 'em good to be in biling hot water. I hated to make more work for her, but I done what he said.

Nekkid, I could tell he'd been a hard worker all his life. He looked like he had strong legs and arms. The hair on his chest and at his crotch was kind of gray, like his head and chin whiskers. He warn't a tall man, maybe no taller than me, but big around the chest. I'd hate to get in a rasslin' match with him. He looked like he'd th'ow me first off. Lord, lord, I hadn't thought about those rasslin' matches with Billy, back at the winter camp, in a long time. It were only a year ago, but seemed like longer than that.

We had our baths. You got used to the cold water after you was in it for a while. Took our turns with the soap. I watched the lice float up around me. I hoped to hell they'd get off me and drown. I soaped up my head and chin whiskers and under my arms and my crotch real good. That's where the lice was likely to be. We didn't talk much.

It felt real good to be clean, mighty good. I'd been dirty for long time. It seemed like forever. Aunt Polly made us take a bath every week. In winter, it was ahind the cook stove. Recollectin' that seemed like it was a whole lifetime ago. I guess it was, considerin' what all I'd been through since then.

We got out of the water and dried off as best we could. He handed me some of the clothes he'd brought down. They was a long shirt, and pants, and even drawers. *I tell you sir, I ain't felt this good in many a day. I cain't think how to thank you folks enough for all you've done, takin' me in and all.*

He nodded. *I know what you mean.* He stood and looked at me. *Charley's clothes look right enough on you.* He shook his head, like he was tryin' to clear his mind. He nodded at me agin, and said somethin' I didn't catch. Then he turned and walked back to the house, leavin' me standin' there.

I fooled around at the barn 'til supper was called. Mostly I was lookin' to see what was there. It looked like any barn in Stewart County I ever saw. One good saddle, another that could use some elbow grease. Enough gear for several horses or mules, if'n mules it were. No sign of any hay to amount to anything. I guessed he was plumb out or it was in a stack somewheres else.

There was still a fair amount of corn in the corn crib. He must of had a good year last year. There warn't much manure in the stalls. Pro'bly it was just from winter now that the live stock was out in the pasture. It didn't look to me like enough to spread over much land but I guessed it would have to do. I walked back down to the pond for somethin' to do, and took Ole Mule along for a drink. *Well, Ole Mule, looks like I'll find out the lay of the land after supper. If'n I read the signs right, me and you will be asked to stick around a while.*

Supper was called and we set down to our beans and corn pone. He said grace, same grace he'd said dinner and supper since I been eatin' with them. I wondered if'n I was a preacher I'd try something different sometimes. But it didn't matter to me, so long as he didn't pray too long. There was a man in Bumpus Mills that I hired out for that would pray so long everything got cold. His wife would finally stop him, afore he got done.

Thinking about that made me recollect what she'd put on the table. Allus she had beans, but a lot of other stuff too, like fried ham and red eyed gravy and fried taters and biscuits and gravy and fried apples. And tomatoes, when the garden was in. I loved them tomatoes with a little salt on 'em. And roastin' ears. I tried to quit thinkin' about all that and pay attention to the beans on my plate.

We got done, and Betty Lou and Thelma cleared the table, and we all went in the other room. He built up the fire, and set down. *Some coffee would shore taste good right now, but we ain't got any.* Lookin' at the fire. *God knows we ain't got much of anything.* He turned to me. *But we have to be thankful for what little we got. Now, Luther, now's the time to hear yore story.*

I'm right willin' to tell it to you, but afore I start, I want to know if'n you'uns want the long story or the short one.

He leaned back in his chair and did a big belly laugh. *Well, I guess you better make it a short one, if'n we didn't want to be here all night. Anybody has questions, they can ask.*

So I started out, with my mamma and daddy, and Sam, and Uncle Gray and Aunt Polly, and Stewart County. As I talked I could see their faces and the room in the firelight. Him and Thelma was watchin' me as I talked. Betty Lou was lookin' mostly at the fire.

The room looked like the front room at Uncle Gray's. There was a big fireplace with a spider hangin' to the side. Wood was stacked up to the side. A dresser with a mirra was over by the door to the kitchen. Candlesticks on it, but they warn't lit. The only light was from the fire. Clothes chest on the other side. One rocker, where he set, and several straight chairs, where we set. There was two beds, one in each corner, by the door 'tween them, that led to another room. I felt just like I'd been here afore, maybe all my life.

Betty Lou stopped me. *Where's Stewart County from here?*

I don't know for sure. Best I can say is yore farm is in North Carolina right next to Virginia, and maybe in the middle along that state line. I don't know about that. Best I know North Carolina and Tennessee is end to end, with Tennessee to the west. North of Tennessee is Kentucky. Stewart County is next to Kentucky like yore place is next to Virginia. I turned to him. *Do you think that's right?*

I'd say that's about right. Not that I know. I never have been over the mountains, but I hear tell Tennessee is over them. Go on with yore story.

So I went on, with joinin' up with the Rebels when I was 15. I was uneasy about talkin' about that, since I didn't know what side he was on. But he didn't say anything, so I figured I was safe. I talked about bein' at Fort Donelson and joinin' up with the cavalry. I told 'em about my little red mare but didn't say much else about her. Then on to Chattanooga and Knoxville and the winter camp and then Richmond. Just named 'em, nothing more than that.

When I got to what happened at Richmond, I was on real uneasy ground. It looked like their two boys went to the War and never come back. Here I was, I was goin' to tell 'em I went to the War and couldn't take it and run away. But I figured there warn't no use in lyin' about it, so I went ahead.

To tell the truth, I never was much of a soldier. A feller told me oncet I couldn't hit the side of a barn with a cannon. But the main thing was I couldn't take all the killin'. Even if 'n I done the killin', and I did. I kilt a lot of Yankees. But I got so I couldn't take it any more. After I come to see that, I started in helpin' take care of them that was wounded and tryin' to put away them that was dead. So that's what I did mostly after I left the cavalry. I ain't ashamed of it. That was needed and I could do it. Maybe doin' it saved my life. I don't know. Yore two men maybe warn't so lucky. I'm real sorry about that.

They was just lookin' at the fire. *Them battles is what you're dreamin' about, ain't they?*

I nodded. *Yessir. I want to put it aside in my mind, but the dreams won't let me do it.*

Well, no need to dwell on it now. Hit's over and done with. Hit'll be better with the passin' of time. We take it for granted them was some real hard times for you. Go on with yore story.

Then I caught a bad case of the runs and then I caught the fevers. I've seen men die of them and I figured that was goin' to happen to me. So I decided to try to get back home afore I died. That warn't the whole story, of course. I left out how I figured the South was gonna lose the War and what I thought about slavin' and that I didn't know why I joined up, in the first place. I figured they didn't need to hear all that. Maybe they had slavin' in their family. And maybe they didn't want to hear this boy sayin' that the North was gonna win. 'Specially since they'd lost their two boys to the War already.

He saw that I was done. He cleared his throat. *That's a right good story. It ain't easy for a man to talk about, especially that last part.* I knowed what part he was meanin'. *You been through a lot. I sure as hell wish we could hear Eddie and Charlie tell their stories.*

How long they been gone?

Charlie, nigh on to two years. We got word he'd been killed at Shiloh.

Yessir. That was a bad battle there. Eddie?

Eddie just shy a year. I tried my best to get him to stay home but he wanted to go awful bad. We got in the garden and some corn. Then he went north to join up. Said he'd go fight and then come home, settle down. Ain't heard from him since. Don't know if'n he's alive or dead.

Yessir. That's mighty hard to take.

Cain't be helped. He wanted to go real bad. Would of been wrong to hold him back, even if'n I could of. The girls didn't say anything. He got up and poked at the fire, stirrin' it up some. Turned around, warmin' his back side. I couldn't see his face. It was in the shadow. He cleared his throat again. *Well, now. I told you there was somethin' I wanted to talk to you about.* He set back down, lookin' at me. *First off, you know that weun's are the Wood family. Names A.J. The A. stands for Adam but most folks call me A.J. I do some farmin' and a little preachin' on the side.* Laughin' to hisself. *Some folks say it ought to be the other way around. But I got to make a livin' and preachin' don't pay much. I'm the only preacher hereabouts. Mostly the folks here are Freewill Baptist, but I ain't particular. I take my turn with the Methodists and the Church of Christ, if'n they want me. There's a Methodist preacher in the next county. Him and me trade off some. Weddin's, buryin's. Revivals in the summer time. You been baptised?*

Yessir, when I was a boy.

He nodded. *I love to preach. Been doin' it since I was called to preach when I was a young man. Just got married to Betty Lou's mama.* He looked back at me, grinnin'. *Folks say I'm good at it.*

I bet that's the truth. I was wonderin' what that had to do with anything. Maybe he just wanted to talk about something else than his boys.

Me and the boys done some right good farmin'. Now they're gone and it's just me. He fell quiet. I could see now where this was goin' to lead to. *You don't owe us anythin' for getting' you out of that ditch. Our Christian duty to do that. But I was wonderin', are you in such a all fired hurry to get back on the road to'ard Stewart County. I mean, now that you plainly ain't gonna die, leastwise any time soon.* He laughed when he said that last part.

I laughed along with him. *I guess I ain't, at that. You want me to stay around here a while, help you do some farmin'?*

He clapped his hands, and got up again, his back side to the fire. It looked like he couldn't set still. *Yessir, that's what I was wonderin'. I don't want to sound pore mouth, but I figure we got some hard times ahead, all of us. War's gonna come to end any day now, I reckon, and the North is gonna win it. Only the Good Lord*

*knows what's gonna happen next. Some of the young men families
are dependin' on to do the farmin' ain't comin' back. Reckon my two
boys won't. Families are gonna have to go on without 'em, best we
can. Weun's are in better shape than most. I'm 55 years old, and I
can still do a good days work. Betty Lou here knows how to do a lot.
Thelma too. But we shore could use some of yore help with the
hard work. You don't have to say right now. Think it over. Let me
know in a day or two.*

*Well, sir, I don't have to think it over, not at all. I'll do it, if 'n
you'll have me.*

He clapped his hands again and set down again. *Sounds mighty
fine to me. Yessir.* He stopped rockin'. *I plumb forgot to ask, do you
know anythin' about farmin'?*

My turn to laugh with him. *I reckon I do, at least Stewart
County farmin'. I'm just a country boy, farmed all my life. I farmed
with my Uncle Gray, and hired out when he didn't need me and
somebody else did. Earned my keep that away. I maybe ain't as
good as yore two sons, but I'm willin' to try.*

He clapped his hands again. *That was what I was hopin' to
hear you say.* He got up. *Well, that's settled then. We can all go to
bed, with that settled.*

Afore we do, can I ask a question?

Ask away.

What time of year is this? I've plumb lost track.

He laughed a good belly laugh, happy I guess that I'd said I
would stay and help him. *I can see how you would. Thelma here
is our time keeper. Thelma, what time of year is this?*

*Daddy, I figure it's near the end of March. A woman at church
helped me make a calendar for this year, goin' by a old one she had,
and the signs of the moon.*

Good girl, We depend on you to keep us on track.

I got one more question, if 'n I can ask it.

Ask away.

What's happenin' with the War?

He shook his head. *We don't hear much regular. Sundays
somebody most of the time has had news. I didn't go preach last
Sunday so we ain't heard anything since two weeks ago. Last we*

heard, the word was that Grant was closin' in on Richmond. It shore don't look too good for the South. I reckon I'll hear more tomorrow. The girls won't go. I'm preachin' at Flat Lick and it's a right far piece to go. I won't ask you to, but you can come if 'n you want to. Maybe we can all go when the roads get better. We'll take the wagon, with my mule and yore's. It's real muddy now to try it.

We all got up from our chairs. It seemed like that warn't anything else to say right then. He walked with me out to the barn. *It shore is dark tonight. I figured you might need some help to keep you out of another ditch. We ain't had oil for the lantern since last year. I guess you can use a candle if 'n you need light bad in the barn.*

I reckon I can get along soon's I learn the lay of the land. Don't want to fall in a ditch or, for that matter, the pond.

You mind sleepin' in the barn?

Don't mind at all. I like the smell of a barn.

Even the cow shit?

I laughed. *Even the cow shit. Tell the truth, the smell of cowshit ain't nothin', compared to the smell of a battle, or after a battle is over. After it's over, and the weather is hot, the dead bodies, well, I won't ever forget that smell.* We stopped short of goin' in the barn. *I'm right sorry I got started on that.*

I reckon you and a lot of others won't forget it for a lifetime. But, Lord be praised you lived to tell it.

Yore sons didn't, though.

Yes, that's so. He cleared his throat. *Well, where was I? Yeah, you sleepin' in the barn. There's a bed in the other room where Charlie and Eddie slept. Betty Lou and Thelma slept in the other bed in the front room 'til after Eddie left. Then they moved in to that bed in the other room. Betty Lou's getting' to be a woman now. Needs some privacy.* Laughs. *Gives me a little privacy too, in case I was to bring a woman home. If 'n you can feel yore way in, I'll say goodnight.* And I heard his footsteps going back to'ard the house.

I figured I needed to talk this whole thing over with Ole Mule, but I couldn't do it right then. It was so dark, I couldn't see my hand in front of my face. I recollected a battle I was in once when it was this dark. It started, and then the retreat was sounded. Never did know on what side, but didn't matter. Everybody fell back. It was too dark to fight. You couldn't tell who you was fightin'.

Anyway, I felt my way on in to the barn and to the stall where my bed roll was. Barked my shins a time or two, but I made it. Walkin' around in the dark made me wonder about snakes. I bet they had 'em in this country. Stewart County did. Spring time, they'd be comin' out soon. Maybe I'd better see if'n I can move my bed roll to the loft. I couldn't recollect right then where the ladder goin' up was. I lay there tryin' to think through what had happened tonight. Maybe I was too quick to say I'd stay. Truth to tell, I didn't hardly know these folks. I'd have to talk about it tomorrow to Ole Mule.

Nothin' much happened for a few days. The spring rains kept on. It warmed up some. The pastures greened up. Creeks filled up. The spring had run over its path to the pond, and made everything down there muddy. Preacher went on his mule in the pourin' rain to Flat Lick to preach. He come home for dinner soaked clean through. After dinner, he kept us at the table to tell us that he'd heard that Richmond was likely to fall. There was more bad news. Word was that the Union Army was marchin' through South Carolina and tearin' up everythin' in its path. They was burnin' houses and store houses. Killin' live stock. Tearin' up railroads. Then movin' on to the next town.

He sed everybody's teeth was on edge, not knowin' if'n they was comin' this way. He sed a man was gonna ride to the south to see if'n he could learn which way the army was headed. But we wouldn't know anythin' for a while, 'til he got back. I thought to myself that I could do that if'n I had the little red mare. But as good as Ole Mule was at some things, he wouldn't be any good at that. *Preacher, I could do that scoutin', if'n I had a good horse.*

That's mighty good of you to offer, but I guess there's no need right now. He left right after church. Best we leave it to him. But I'll tell the people next Sunday that you offered.

The south in South Carolina means it is to the south of us, don't it?

Thelma, I think you got that right. To the south of us. And, if'n I recollect my map right, an if'n they are headed to Richmond, they'd go to the east of us. Preacher, you ever been to the South Carolina line?

No, never have. But I figure it's maybe two, three hunnert miles straight south of here. He sed he'd go some east of south. I think he'd been down that way afore. Had family down there.

We set there, thinkin' about what that meant. I didn't want to scare these folks, but I'd seen what soldiers turned loose can do to the countryside. *Preacher, could I say somethin' about all this?* He nodded. *I don't want to scare you all, but didn't you say you had some guns?* He nodded. *Well, maybe tomorrow you better get 'em out and we'll see what we got. Just in case.*

He nodded again. *Yeah, I think so. We'll do that first thing in the mornin'.* So we did that. We set on the porch and he brung out his guns and the shot and powder he had. There was three, two old muzzle loaders and one I'd seen the Yankees have on the battle field. And some shot to go with that one. We talked about how they was loaded and aimed and fired. Didn't practice none, since we wanted to save the powder and the shot in case we needed it.

Betty Lou was right there and took her turn at handlin' the guns. Preacher said she was a right good shot. Afore the war she'd gone squirrel huntin' with her brothers. She didn't say much, but I could tell she had a feel for the guns. So we was ready, or as ready as we'd ever be. I knowed weun's couldn't put up much of a fight if'n the raiders come through. But it made us feel like we was doin' somethin', and not just settin' there. He put the guns in the corner of the front room, behind some clothes hangin' on pegs.

We never needed 'em to fight off the Union soldiers. The man from the church was back the next Sunday and sed the army was goin' east of us by some two hunnert miles on their way north. But he sed word was that seemed like the Union Army was takin' revenge on the people of South Carolina. I heard that was what happened, after I got home again.

I spent more time right then with Thelma than Betty Lou. Thelma and me walked all over the farm. She showed me where the fences was and how they let the cows in to the pond and for milkin'. Her and the dogs and me spent some right good times doin' that. Two of the cows birthed calves. Preacher was busy doin' something else and so her and me saw to 'em. Then we brung the cows and the calves to the barn. So we had sweet milk with our corn pone and beans.

I helped her gather the eggs and we cleaned out the hen house part of the barn, made a place for the settin' hens. In about a week or two, we had baby chicks. I'd plumb forgot about baby chicks. The dogs slept around the barn. They woke me up many a night, with their barkin'. Good thing they did, to scare away the foxes from the chickens. Still and all, we figured we lost some to the foxes. A fox is real sly about that. We took to havin' chicken for dinner from time to time. I knowed how to wring their necks and dress 'em, from watchin' the folks at home. Betty Lou could wring their necks too, but she didn't like to do it. I didn't mind doin' it, if'n it meant chicken on the table for dinner.

I hadn't seen much of Betty Lou. She was allus busy around the house, and kept to her self. But I started to get some time with her by helpin' her with the wash. She did the washin' most every Monday. The wash kettle had to be filled up and a fire built under it, so's the water would be hot. And the tub filled for rinchin' the clothes after they was washed. Then wringin' and hangin'.

First off, she acted like she didn't need any help, but little by little, she let me build the fire and haul the water from the spring house. That took a fair number of buckets. She didn't talk much, mostly answered questions, if'n I didn't ask too many or push her to answer. It turned out that Preacher had married twicet, oncet to her and her brothers' mama and again to Thelma's mama. Her mama had died of sickness and Thelma's mama had died when Thelma was born. Thelma had already told me that. She said Preacher had had several women friends since then. She said he had one now, that I might see sometime, maybe at church.

Truth to tell, while I was helpin' her with the wash, I warn't backward about touchin' her hand when I could do it natural like, like handin' her something. It didn't seem like she was holdin' back, so I kept doin' it. It felt real good. At night, I could picture how it would feel to hold her in my arms. But I figured I better keep my distance.

Nobody had said a word about which side of the War they was on. I figured they was for the South, elsewise when I told 'em I was a Rebel they'd of made me leave or somethin'. But it seemed like they didn't want to talk about the War at all. I guess it was because they'd lost the two boys. It must have been hard on them seein' me wear their boys' clothes. Just one time Thelma said I had on a shirt that Eddie wore a lot. But she just said that and didn't carry on about it. But the next day, I heard her talkin' to the dogs. *They ain't really kilt. They're gonna come back home one day. You wait and see.*

Preacher and me had our Saturday trips to the pond. I tried to cut my scraggly hair and chin whiskers with the barn shears to keep my hair out of my eyes, but it was tough goin'. So I was clean most of the time, but I 'spect I looked like the wrath of God. Anyway, one day I was helpin' Betty Lou with the washin'. *Can I ask a favor of you?*

She stopped hangin' up clothes and looked at me. Her hands was on her hips. She looked like she might and she might not. *Maybe. Yeah, ask away.*

You cut yore daddy's hair? It allus looks real good.

She nodded. *Every oncet in a while, I do. Why? You want me to cut yourn?*

That's the favor.

I've been wonderin' when you'd ask. Looks like you been tryin' to do it yoreself with the barn shears. She giggled. *It must of pulled some to do that. And the back of yore head looks like a rat's nest.*

I bet it does. I cain't see the back of my head.

I'll tell you what. Tomorry, you get the grindstone all set up. It's in one of the stalls in the barn. I'll bring down the kitchen shears and we'll sharpen 'em. They need sharpenin' anyway. And that was that, and she went on, hangin' up her wash.

Well, we did it that way. I got the grindstone all set up and cleaned up some. The wheel turned real good. I turned the wheel and she did the sharpenin'. It looked like it warn't easy to do, holdin' the shear's blade right next to the wheel, so the sharpenin' would be even. But she knowed how to do it. We done the barn shears too. *You come now and set on the stump out there and I'll give you a hair cut 'til Kingdom Come.* We went out there. I was a mite s'prised she was so friendly to me. 'Til then, she'd been more than a little cool to me, sayin' good morning and this and that but not much more.

Take off yore shirt. I'm gonna cut off a lot of yore hair and ain't no need to get it in yore shirt. I did. She watched me do it. It seemed like there was something goin' on, something special about me takin' off my shirt with her standin' so close. Afore I knowed it, I was getting' some hard. I held my hands over my crotch to keep her from seein' what was happenin'.

She cut away, hummin' some kind of song as she worked. She seemed like she was havin' a good time doin' it. I was for certain havin' a good time havin' her do it. She cut away. The hair fell ever'where, all around me, like leaves fallin' in the fall of the year. She cut in the front, in the back, on the sides, on the top, and my chin whiskers. To make matters worse for me, I guess you'd say, she used her fingers to brush away the hair she'd cut. She'd wipe the hair away from my neck and my shoulders and my back and worst of all, my chest. She kind of rubbed the hair off. And oncet in a while, she'd blow the hair away, gettin' right up close to me. When she got to my chin whiskers, she was real close, lookin' at my face, and with her tongue between her teeth, like this was takin' some careful studyin'.

Oh Lord, bein's so close to her was near more'n I could stand. Her face was near the most purty thing I ever saw in all my life. Blue eyes, hair pulled back, tied with a rag. Her skin was fair. Pink lips, so close to me. I wondered how they'd feel to touch. Pro'bly they'd be soft and warm. I hadn't ever kissed a girl since I did Nadine. Dulciemay and me never kissed. And I never kissed that woman back there at the winter camp. I wanted to grab Betty Lou by the arms and bring her face to mine and kiss the daylights out of her. I about died right then and there. I got harder and harder. I thought I'd explode right then and there. But luck was with me. She got done afore that happened. She stood back, lookin' at what she'd done. *You look right decent. It'll be better with a wash. You and Daddy leave some soap down at the pond?* I nodded, 'cause that was all I could do. *Well, go on down and wash. Get the hair off of you. I'll send Thelma down directly with a clean shirt.* And she took the shears and headed back to the house. Well, I might nigh run down to the pond, shucked off my pants as fast as I could and got out in the water deep enough to cover me, kneeled down, and thinkin' about those lips and her smell, it took maybe two licks to let it go.

I set there in the water, still breathin' hard. I was thinkin' I hadn't studied about a woman like that in a long time, not since Dulciemay. Elsewise it was a case of usin' my hand in the middle of the night when I woke up with a hard. Even that quit when we was fightin' a lot on the way to Richmond. Then, when I got sick, I never had that feelin' at all. Not even in my dreams. I missed them dreams. I'd had them since I was a boy. Anyway, here the feelin' was again, and real strong. I wondered if'n Betty Lou had feelin's like that. Back then, I never knowed much about women that way.

Betty Lou sent me with this here clean shirt. I looked up to see Thelma standin' there on the bank. *You want me to th'ow you that piece of soap from over there by the rock?*

Please, if'n you would do that. She went over and got the soap and th'owed it almost in my hand. *You, girl, are a right good th'ower.*

Eddie and me used to play catch with a hedge apple. He was to get me a real ball to play with some time. She was standin' maybe twenty foot away from me, so I figured I could wash my head and chest and still be decent, as Aunt Polly would say. Thelma stood there, watchin' me wash. I looked up to see that she was startin' to cry, her face all scrunched up and rubbin' her eyes.

What's the matter? I laughed. *Am I that ugly?*
She said through the cryin'. *Naw, it ain't that. You ain't all that ugly. It's just that with yore hair cut and all, settin' there in the pond, you look a lot like Eddie. Makes me wish he hadn't gone to the War. Don't see why he had to be kilt.*
You mean, instead of me.

I guess that was what she was thinkin'. All of a sudden, she turned and run up to the house, leavin' me thinkin' what she'd been thinkin'. I set there in the pond, watchin' her go. There warn't nothin' to say. It was sad, but it was so. So I finished up washing and got out of the pond. And I put on the clothes with the clean shirt she had brought down. And I wondered if'n this was Eddie's shirt. And I wondered what he'd looked like. And while I was at it, I wondered what I looked like! I hadn't seen myself in a mirra since that day me and them two boys got leave from Fort Donelson and went over to Dover.

I stood there, wonderin' how many years ago was that? That year I was about to turn 16, so it would be 1862, I reckoned. The next year I was ridin' with the cavalry. The next year was when I was at winter camp, so that would be 1864. So this was 1865, by my figurin', and I'd turned 19 sometime after I left Richmond. If'n I had any luck at all, I'd be in Stewart County when I turned 20.

Preacher said I could move my bedroll to the loft, if'n I wanted to. So I moved it and what little else I had up there. Funny, after sleepin' all this time on the ground, I didn't want to do it anymore. The hay loft was clean, as hay lofts go. I raked up enough scattered hay for my bed. I put it two, three feet from the ladder, and right next to the hay mow, where I could look out to see the stars and the moon, if'n I wanted to. The mow was good sized. You could get a good load of hay through it from the wagon below. The pulley looked rusted. Maybe they'd not had much hay to put up here in the last year, maybe two.

So I moved up my bed roll and my old clothes and the clothes that Betty Lou had give me. I guessed they was Charlie's, but maybe some of Eddie's, too. I felt in the hem of my old coat.

The old coat was dirty and tore in a place or two, but the sewin'
me and that fellar in Clarksville had done had held, and the two
gold pieces was still there.

I looked again in my kit bag and the pouch from the old
man's bed was there, and some pieces of corn pone left, wrapped
in a leaf. The corn pone had come from the old burned down
house. Maybe it was from the fellars I'd met on the way. I couldn't
recollect for sure. All that seemed like a dream to me now.

The gold piece and the gold ring was still in the pouch. I
looked at them for a while, wonderin' where he'd got the gold
piece. And I wondered who the gold ring was for. I guessed some
woman he'd loved when he was a young man. Like me, now.
And I wondered what had come of her. But I'd never know. It'd
make a good story, if'n I could write it.

It seemed fittin' that I was there when he died. I liked him,
what little I'd knowed about him. I was real glad I'd been there
when he died. I did what I could do for him. I couldn't recollect
for sure how long ago that was. The varmints had prob'ly got to
him by now. But he wouldn't of cared. He'd of laughed, kind of,
and said what I'd heard afore, ashes to ashes and dust to dust. I
think that means everything goes back to the dirt we walk on. It
didn't seem like the pouch in my kit bag was a safe place for
them, but it was the best I could do. So I put them back.

Well, anyway, I studied where I was and where I'd put things
and where the ladder was, and such. I reckoned I'd be goin' up
and down the ladder in the dark every day. I couldn't take a candle
up, even if'n there was one to take. There was too much danger
of a fire. So I'd have to feel my way around. I slept in the loft
near all the time I was at the Wood place. It was hot up there in
the summer but I got by.

There's more to my favorin' Eddie. One day we was at the
dinner table. *Daddy, where's that picture of all of us took that time
before Charlie left for the War? I want to show it to Luther.* She
turned to me. *We all went to Mount Airy and there was a man
there takin' a picture for a dollar.*

It's in the top drawer of the bureau, in that box with some of yore mother's things. And Thelma's mother's things.

I'll go get it. He nodded, and Betty Lou went and come back with the picture. She held it up for me to see. *That's Charlie, there, and that's Eddie.*

I'd heard about the picture takin' men comin' around. One come to Bumpus Mills, but we never went to see him. I wish now we had. I shore would like to have a picture of Aunt Polly.

Anyway, the picture showed 'em all, standin' in front of their wagon. Preacher Wood looked the same. Betty Lou looked younger and just as purty. Thelma was a little girl. It looked like Charlie had yellow hair, like Thelma's. He had on a hat, so's you couldn't see much of his face. Eddie had dark hair, like his daddy and Betty Lou, and it was shorter than Charlie's. I guess it was like mine, now that Betty Lou had cut it. It looked like he had more chin whiskers than Charlie, but it could of been the light. I looked hard at Eddie, to see if'n I could see how him and me favored. *Can you say how him and me favor?*

Betty Lou looked at me and at the picture I was holdin'. *Well, it's the eyes, I reckon, and a kind of half grin you both carry. And he wore his hair short, like I cut yore's. Charlie wore his'n longer.* She was quiet, lookin' back and forth between the picture and me.

Maybe. Problem is, I reckon, I don't know what I look like.

She laughed at me. *You ain't seen yoreself?*

I shook my head. *No, I reckon not. I've not seen my face in a mirra since I was in Dover when I was at Fort. Donelson.*

Well, we can fix that! You come with me to the mirra above the bureau. So she took the picture and her and me and Thelma went to the other room. She made me stand square in front of the mirra, her and Thelma to the side. Lookin' in the mirra, I saw a man's face. It looked like a hunnert other men I'd seen. Near black hair and chin whiskers, cut short, some hair hangin' over my for'ead but not in my eyes. Sun burned face and neck, like Preacher's, but not as dark. Blue eyes. Aunt Polly said I had the clear blue eyes like my Daddy had. I didn't recollect what color eyes my Mother had. I think maybe Sam's was brown, maybe they was like hers.

Betty Lou held the picture up against the mirra, and looked at it and me. *I don't know. Doin' it this way, I cain't see much how you favor Eddie. But seein' you elsewise, you do.* She took down the picture and we turned away.

Preacher come into the room. *I can see how they favor. That half grin you said, and the way they hold theirselves. But it must be like we're lookin' for it.* That was it. Betty Lou put everything away. We all went about our way.

But several times ahead, when we was with folks that had knowed Eddie, they would remark about it. The next time it come up was at church where we went along with Preacher, when he was preachin'. We was at the dinner table the next day. *Daddy, where are you preachin' on Sunday?*

Salt Springs. Why, you want to go?

I thought maybe. I thought we'd all go. Hitch up the wagon.

He nodded. *We can do that, if'n the good weather holds.*

Luther, you want to hear Daddy preach? He's real good.

I bet he is. I'd be real glad to go.

It'd do us all good. I ain't been off of this place in two months, I guess.

You gonna wear yore fancy dress?

I might. And I'll work on one for you. Last year's is too short. You're growin' like a weed. Let's leave the dishes and you and me go see what we can find in the chest. We need something with a big hem we can let down. And off they went.

Preacher and me stacked the dishes for them to do and he filled up the teakettle and set it on the stove for hot water, later. And we went out back. *I ain't asked you but I need to know now, can I use yore Ole Mule?*

Yessir, you shore can. I don't have any idea how he will be behind a plow but we can see what he can do.

I reckon you've seen my mule Jake. I'm down to him. The soldiers took the other two I had. I hated to have them do that, but I was thankful to the Lord they didn't do worse.

You want to tell me about that sometime?

Yeah, I will. When we got time, and I want to talk about it. I nodded. *Anyway, pullin' the wagon to church, like Betty Lou said, will take two mules. I can make it with one, but it's a lot easier with two.*

Yessir, I can see that.

Well, we went to church all right. The girls got all gussied up. Betty Lou worked on a real purty dress for Thelma and she looked all grown up. Even had her hair down on her shoulders. I'd cleaned up all the boots best I could. Betty Lou looked like something special. Thelma's dress was blue and green. Her's was kind of pink and red. Her hair was down on her shoulders too, and pinned back over her ears.

You two girls look like you never did a lick of work in all yore born days. They giggled. I meant it. The words sounded silly to my ears, but I couldn't think of any better ones. I'd killed a chicken and Betty Lou fried it up and put it and a pot of beans and some cornpone in a basket. I reckoned there'd be dinner on the ground after church, like they called it in Bumpus Mills.

We started out good season in the morning. It was a real pretty spring day, all green and sunshine. Some of the flowerin' trees was out. Preacher and me hitched up the mules. Ole Mule acted like he knowed what that was all about, and he never caused a speck of trouble. Matter of fact, he never caused any trouble at all, workin' with Jake. You never can tell about a pair of mules. Sometimes they don't get along at all. But Jake and Ole Mule did.

Preacher and Betty Lou rode up front on the springboard and me and Thelma in the wagon bed. It 'minded me of that time I went down that hill with them wounded soldiers in the wagon bed. A lot had happened to me since I did that. *You know how to sing?*

I guess I can get by. Uncle Gray allus sed I had my Daddy's ear for singin'. You like to sing?

She nodded. *If 'n I know the song. Daddy's real good at leadin'
the singin'. He sed oncet my mama was a good singer. He met her
at a church meetin'. He sed he could hear her singin', one out of the
crowd.*
It was too noisy to do much more talkin'. Thelma and me
jus' looked at the signs of spring. We must of gone another five
miles down the track and then we come upon the church. It
looked for all the world like any church I ever saw in Stewart
County. It looked like it had been white washed some time ago,
but that had faded to a kind of gray.
There must of been some twenty five people gathered around
the outside, talkin'. The wagons and buggies was tied up to trees
all around. Some ridin' horses, too. Everybody looked all cleaned
up like we was. When we got down, the girls went off to where
the other girls was standin' and talkin'. Preacher made my
acquaintance with everybody. *This here is Luther Morris. He's stayin'
with us a while, to help me put in the crops. He's from Tennessee.*
The men shook my hand, some of the women, too.
He yore cousin?
Preacher laughed. *No, not as far as I can tell.*
I figured he might be. He favors Eddie a lot, don't he?
Preacher just smiled. *He does, don't he? We've remarked about
that.*
I said the church house looked like one I knew from Bumpus
Mills on the outside. It was the same for the inside. A platform
and a pulpit was in the front with a high winder behind. It made
light shine down on Preacher like it was light from Heaven. A
heatin' stove was in the back, and maybe ten, twlve rows of pews
between the stove and the pulpit. They was no where near full
on that day. Thelma and me was in the middle on one side, in
back of people setting on that side.
From what I could see the people looked for all the world
like Bumpus Mills. There was women and younguns' of all ages.
Thelma nudged me. *See that woman across over there in the gray
dress? That's Miz Henderson.* I saw who she meant, but I didn't
know who Miz Henderson was. I nodded. Lookin' at the men, I

could see that save for two big size boys, they was all as old as Preacher and a lot older. It hit me what that meant. The young men my age and a mite older had all gone to the War. None had come back, at least, was here today. I was real uneasy about that, wonderin' what them people would make of my bein' there.

We got to the end of the singin'. *Good mornin' to you all.* I heard a lot of good mornin's back to him. *This is shore a bee-au-tiful day, ain't it.* Again, there was some answers back to him.

Afore I begin to preach the sermon, let's see what we got for news. First off, I've got some. Over there in the back of the crowd is a friend of my family. Name of Luther Morris. He's been fightin' in the War since he was fifteen and come down bad sick with the fevers in Richmond. He was let go to go home to Tennessee. Not far from our place he got real sick and fell off his mule in a ditch. Praise the Lord. We found him and was able to nuss him back to health. He'll be stayin' with us for a while to get back on his feet. Luther, stand up, so's people can see who you are. I did like he said and near everybody turned around in their seat to look at me. I wondered what was goin' on in their mind. I set down. *Anybody else got any news?*

At first, the news was about everyday things. Who was sick and needed some help, what roads a wagon couldn't get through, some cows that had got loose, and things like that. Then a old woman and a man stood up and told 'em they'd heard their son had been killed in the War. It was quiet after that. Then a young woman holdin' a baby said she hadn't had word from her husband since Christmas. She thanked them that had helped her and said if'n she didn't hear any word soon she'd try to go down to Asheville where her family was.

Then a man asked Preacher if'n there was any word about Eddie. He said no. Then the same man turned around to me. *Can you tell us anything about the fightin' at Richmond?*

I stood up and looked at 'em. I was scared to death to talk. What's in God's name was I gonna say? *Well, I can tell you what I saw and heard afore I got sick enough to die.* The church house was real quiet.

I was a foot soldier all the way from Chattanooga to Richmond. We walked all the way. The fightin' got worse and worse. The Rebel army is in bad straits, real bad straits. We ain't got much to eat. The water's bad. Guns we have to fight with are old. When it rained, we all was wet and cold. A lot of soldiers got sick with the loose bowels and the fevers. My job was to help with the sick and the wounded and bury the dead, if'n we could. I done that 'til I couldn't carry on for the fevers. Soldiers for the South are brave men and I've seen 'em fight hard and good. But the army for the North is too big and too strong to be overpowered. I quit talkin' but for some reason didn't sit down.

You figure General Lee will surrender?

Oh Lord, I thought, what am I goin' to say to that? *I'm just a country boy just turned 19 years of age and I never heard a general say anything.* Now I was near startin' to cry. I coughed and cleared my throat. *But you ast me and I'm goin' to tell you what's in my heart. This here War just cain't go on. Too many good men killed already and more to come if'n it don't stop.* I looked at the man that asked the question. *Yessir, I hope it is the Lord's will for General Lee to surrender and put a end to the War.* And I set down, lookin' at my hands in my lap and at my feet. Nobody said anything else.

I'm gonna preach today about trust in the Lord in times of trouble. So Preacher started, and I guess he preached a good sermon. I never heard much of it since I was still shakin' in my boots about what I had done. I raised my head, all right enough, and looked at him while he was preachin' but I never heard a word of what he was sayin'.

But a funny thing happened. Thelma's hand was next to mine on the bench and we held hands while he preached. To this day, I can't say if'n I reached for hers or she reached for mine. But it felt real good to me to have her little hand in mine, and I'll never forget it.

Preacher got done. He didn't do no invitational but said we'd sing that song about Beulah Land. I was feelin' better by that time and could sing along with the best of 'em. He said the last prayer, prayin' 'specially for loved ones that couldn't be with us. Didn't mention soldiers, just loved ones. But I'm for certain everybody knowed who he was talkin' about.

After we broke up, the men folk stood around while the women folk set out dinner in some of the wagon beds. I stood by Preacher, mainly since he was the only one I knowed. They talked about this and that, mostly farmin' talk. Nobody said anything to me 'til after we got our plates and went over to squat under some trees. Preacher got called away from where him and me was squattin', but I stayed put. Up come a man, squatted down by me with his plate. *Name's Luke. Luke Jones.*

Name's Luther Morris. Howdy. I set down my plate to shake his hand. *Jones is a good name. I had a real good friend in the army named Billy Jones.*

He went on eatin'. *What happened to him?*

I went on eatin'. *I don't know. He got sent one way, I got sent t'other. That happened a lot in the army.* I looked at him out of the corner of my eye. He warn't much to look at. Just a farmer. Red faced like everybody else from the sun. Looked like he had on a clean shirt. Reddish brown hair was showin' on his chest, and around his hat. His chin whiskers was thin and scraggly. Looked like he was some older than me but younger than Preacher.

Lucky for you Preacher found you.

Thelma come up. *Me and the dogs found him. In a ditch.*

That so?

I'm much beholden to her and her dogs. If'n they hadn't of found me I'd of for sure died in that ditch. She grinned at me and went over to where Betty Lou and the girls was settin' on the ground eatin'.

She shore is pretty to look at, ain't she?

You mean Thelma? That she is.

He kind of laughed and shook his head. *No, I don't mean Thelma. I mean the Preacher's other daughter.*

Betty Lou?

Betty Lou. He got up and got his water tin, and come back. *You favor a drink?*

Thankee, but we brung our own water. It's in Preacher's wagon.
He grinned at me. *This ain't water.*
I shook my head. *Thankee anyway. I guess not.*
What's the matter? You 'fraid Preacher won't like it if 'n you do?
I don't reckon he'd care. I just don't want any.
You soldiers have moonshine at camp?
Sometimes.
You ever drink it there?
Yeah, I had some there. I laughed. *Sometimes too much.* I
stood up, to go put my plate in the wagon.
He stood up real close to me, not real steady on his feet.
*What's the matter, you too proud to drink with me, you bein' a
soldier and all?* I didn't like the way he said that and I wanted to
get away from him. He must of knowed that, and he took hold
of my arm, makin' me near droppin' my plate. *I gotta take a piss.
Le's go over yonder and take a piss. They's somethin' I want to ask of
you.* He had hold of my arm real hard and I figured I better go
along if 'n I didn't want to start somethin'. And I shore didn't.
I nodded. *I could use a piss. Let's walk over by our wagon and
leave my plate and we'll go on yonder.* We did that, him holdin'
my arm like he thought I was goin' to get away. I would of done
that for sure if 'n I could of without raisin' him to a ruckus. He
put his plate by where I put mine and we walked over into the
trees ahind the church house. We had our piss, standin' there, not
talkin'.
He handed me his water tin again from under his arm. I
thought, all right, do it. So I did. *Betty Lou shore is purty, ain't
she?*
*She shore is. Preacher and his family's been real good to me,
takin' me in.*
You reckon you gonna stay around long?
I guess long enough to help him do some farmin'.
Long enough to do some courtin'?
Well, I don't know about that. Hadn't thought about it much.
I started to walk back toward the church, and he took hold of
my arm again, this time with a iron grip. We stopped walkin',

and he made to turn me to'ard him. *I mean to come courtin' to her.*

I nodded, not knowin' what to say. *She know that?*

I ain't told her.

You told Preacher?

Not yet. I mean to. He let go of my arm. *I ain't got a wife. Meant to marry up with one and her and her family moved on when a wagon train came through, headin' west. She sed I could come along if'n I wanted to, but I didn't want to go.* He was quiet, lookin' over to where Betty Lou and the women folk was settin'. *I've been taken by her since she was a girl.*

You want me to lay off, is that it?

He turned his head to look at me. *Yeah, that's it.*

Right then, Preacher broke away and come over to where we was standin'. *What in the cat hair are you two jawin' about?*

We was talkin' about spring plowin'.

Well, Luke, it's time to think about that. Luther, the women folk say it's time to head home.

I reached out to Luke to shake his hand. *I'm glad to meet you.* We shook hands, and Preacher kind of led me back to the rest, and everybody got ready to go.

We got back to the house and unhitched and Thelma and me and dogs took the mules to the pond to drink.

I seen you talkin' to that Luke Jones. I don't like him much.

Why don't you like him?

She shrugged, studyin' the mules. *I don't hardly know. He's allus lookin' at Betty Lou, funny like.*

Does Betty Lou know that?

She shrugged. *I guess so. Daddy says he is a good man. But he drinks too much moonshine. Do you drink moonshine?*

I've had some, in the army.

You like it?

It ain't bad. Not if'n you don't get carried away.

She laughed at me. *You ever get carried away?*

Oncet or twicet I have. We was quiet. *You figure yore Daddy knows how he looks at her?*

She shrugged. *I guess so.*
Well, it turned out he did. A day or so later we was workin'
in the barn after a day's work in the fields. *Mind if'n I ask you
what Luke and you was talkin' about at the church house?* I busied
myself with hangin' up the harness. *Maybe it ain't any of my
business.*
I didn't rightly know what to say, but seemed like I owed it
to him to tell him. *He said he was stuck on Betty Lou.*
He nodded. *Yeah, yeah, I figured that.*
Looks like he's wants to come courtin' to her.
Yeah, I figured that, too. We set down on the log outside the
barn. *He ain't a bad man but he ain't a good man, if'n you know
what I mean.* I nodded, not knowin' what to say. *He's too old not
to have a wife. I reckon he's had bad luck with women. None of 'em
he liked have taken to him. I reckon it's his own fault, but that ain't
here or there. Last woman he liked went west with her family on a
wagon train. I figured he'd go too but he didn't. Mebbe her brothers
scared him off.* He fell quiet, lookin' down to the pond. *I've seen
the way he looks at Betty Lou, like he wants her bad.*
You think she'd take him?
He got up. *I don't rightly know. And I don't rightly know if'n
I want her to. Maybe if'n you stay long enough, she'll take to you.*
And he walked back in the barn.

Nothin' more was said. We started in farmin' hot and heavy.
One week we had heavy rain and couldn't get to the fields. But
there was a lot else to do. There was five more new calves and
there was them to take care of. None of the cows had any trouble
but one. She went off to the other side of the farm to have hers.
Preacher missed her and it took us a livelong day to find her and
the calf. The calf was down in a gully and couldn't get out. The
old cow was standin' there in the gully by him, lettin' him suck.
We had to lead them all the way down to the end of the
gully to get him out. Preacher said he ought to name him Luther,
since he was found in a ditch! We all had a good laugh about
that. And Luther was his name, from then on.

Anyway, that meant we had a lot of sweet milk. More than we could drink or churn, so ended up we put it in the slop fur the hogs. Two of the sows had pigs so we had to separate them from the rest. I knowed about doin' that. If'n you have the little ones in with the sows, they can get mashed. The old boar come around oncet. He must of smelled the birthin'. Preacher drove him away and built up the fence. A boar will kill little pigs.

Like I said afore, we had a lot of chickens. The settin' hens was doin' their job real good. There warn't no chicken feed, save for table scraps we didn't give to the hogs. But they got along with just scratchin' in the chicken yard. One or two nights the foxes got away with some. I don't know what the dogs were doin' at the time. Preacher said never mind, we could give some to the foxes, if'n they didn't make a habit of it.

It turned out that the two mules worked together real good. Preacher had good harness and a doubletree And we'd hook 'em up to the wagon and the plow and a way they'd go. Like they'd been doin' it together all their life. Preacher was real glad to have Ole Mule. Spring plowin' with one mule is hard to do. The mule cain't give you enough power to dig in the plow like it ought to. We plowed the rise first, leavin' the bottom land to last, to dry out. It warn't real creek bottom land like at Uncle Gray's but it was low layin' and it took some time dryin' out afore you wouldn't be mired in the mud. We plowed the risin' land around the direction of the rise so it wouldn't wash. I never had seen that done afore.

He had near enough seed corn and got the rest he needed from a neighbor. The neighbor brought his team so's that made the job go a lot quicker. We had it done but for some of the bottom land in three days. He wanted to wait on that 'til he had beans to plant in the hills. I never had seen it done that way, but it made good sense. You let the bean vines grow up the corn stalks. We did that plantin' by hand after he'd got the seed beans. I knowed the seed taters was in the loft, by the smell. Betty Lou and me spent a mornin' cuttin' them up so each piece had a eye. And we planted 'em the next day. He had a real big tater patch, as big as any I ever saw. The rest of the garden would have to wait 'til we got the right seeds. He meant to do that on a trip to Mount Airy with Miz Henderson.

Thelma had pointed me to Miz Henderson that day when we all went to Salt Creek to church. And Preacher had said somethin' to me about wantin' some privacy in case he brought a woman home. Well, it turned out the woman was Miz Henderson. The next week after Salt Creek he went to church by hisself and when he come home, he brung her. Better I say, she come with him but in her buggy. The girls and me was settin' outside under the oak tree cuttin' the taters for plantin'. I got up to take the lead reins of her horse. *Howdy.* The girls said howdy too.

Howdy to you all.

This shore is a right purty horse you got.

I'm right fond of her. I brought her with me when I came over here from the Piedmont.

Can I help you down? Preacher just set on his mule, smilin' at us.

If you please. She got down, holdin' my hand. *But I can do it by myself.* She turned to me, down, smilin' a real purty smile. *I've had a lot of practice.*

Preacher got down off'n his mule. *Luther would you take these two horses off'n our hands.*

I laughed. *I see that old mule of your'n turned into a horse at church.*

He laughed a belly laugh with me. *The power of prayer, my boy.*

I did that. Guessin' that Miz Henderson was stayin' a while, I unhitched her horse, give her and the mule a rubdown. Then I took 'em down to the pond for a drink and turned 'em loose in the lot. Thelma and Preacher had took two more chairs to the shade of the oak for Preacher and Miz Henderson. I watched Thelma give her my cuttin' knife and pan and she went in cuttin' the seed taters. I figured this was time to give them by theirselves, so I busied myself over at the woodpile, kind of watchin' 'em as I worked.

Miz Henderson was a right good lookin' woman. She was build on the comfort side, as Uncle Gray would put, not fat but

not thin. Her hair was a red brown and put on top of her head,
what hadn't come loose and hangin' down here and there. I could
hear her laugh, clear over to the woodpile. It looked like her and
Betty Lou was talkin' as they cut. Thelma was just settin', a dog
on each one of her two sides, a hand on each of 'em, and they
was enjoyin' that hand, old Dog, especially. Preacher, he was just
settin there, with what somebody in the army called a shit eatin'
grin on his face.

She stayed the night. And next mornin', Preacher went home
with her on his mule he wished was a horse and he stayed there
that night. At least he didn't come in 'til mid mornin', still with
that grin on his face. I had Ole Mule hitched to the wagon, ready
to go spread some manure. I made up my mind to tease him
some. *What in the cat hair are you doin' comin' in this hour of the
mornin', out tom cattin' around.*

He laughed, lookin' happy that I was teasin' him man to
man. He hitched up his mule to the wagon. *Why, you don't know
nuthin! I done done a days worth of work afore I come here.* He
was talkin' like a colored man.

Yeh, I guess so, depends on what kind of work you talkin' about.
I was talkin' that way too. We both laughed. *Ain't none of my
business but you jes as well tell me afore you bust wide open!*

*You're right. It ain't none of your business but, if'n you'll stand
still and listen I'll tell you afore I bust wide open. Miz Henderson
last night said she'd marry up with me.*

I looked at 'im, cockin' my head to one side. *That afore or
after she went to bed with you?*

He purtin' nearly howled. *Why you bastard, what d'you think?
I can't do it anymore?* We was both laughin'.

But I stopped laughin' and offered my hand to him. *All teasin'
aside, I'm real glad for you. She seems like a real good woman.* He
shook my hand. I couldn't resist a partin' shot. *And she's a good
looker, too!*

He pulled me to him, and give me a bear hug. Then he
pushed me away. *I'm much obliged for what you said. And I'll tell
her. All 'cept that last part. If'n she thinks you figure she's good
lookin', she may drop this old man for somethin' younger!*

Naw, no danger in that. I bet you already told her how good she looks. Maybe a hunnert times. When you gonna tie the knot? Not for a while. They's too many things to settle, on both sides. I ain't told the girls yet but I bet they know somethin's afoot. Belle ain't never had no children. She's a mite uneasy about Thelma. She says she'd come here if'n that looks like the right thing to do. I don't know if'n it is. That'd mean another woman in Betty Lou's kitchen. Might not go down too good. So maybe we'd live over at her house. Don't know.

I nodded. *Yeah, I hear tell a woman likes her own kitchen.*

Another thing I meant to tell you. Luke Jones is comin' to court Betty Lou this Sunday, after church. I nodded. *That all you got to say about that?*

Yessir. I guess so. He looked at me like he thought I had somethin' else to say about that, but I didn't. So he went one way and I went the other. But what he said and how I felt about Betty Lou set me to thinkin'. And I studied about that for some time. I was for sure certain that he wanted me to court his daughter, with the idea of settlin' down here to make a life on his farm. I could see how that could work out for him, and maybe me too.

And I shore was taken by Betty Lou, what little I knowed about her. A man could fall hard for a purty woman like that. And it looked like she was a good worker. But didn't I want to go back to Stewart County? And didn't I want Nadine? And hadn't Nadine's daddy told me afore I left for the War that him and Miz Cherry would favor me coming back there to farm with him? It seemed like I was in a real muddle, but the times I thought about it, Stewart County and Nadine won out.

Sure enough, come Friday here come Luke Jones. He rode up a little while after dinner time. Preacher must of knowed he was comin' since he stayed around the house and sent me back to the field. We was movin' the cows to a different pasture. Thelma and her dogs and me was doin' it, when she looked back at the house. *Here comes Luke Jones. Is he comin' to see Betty Lou?*

It looks like it. You figure she likes him?

She shrugged. *Guess so. Elsewise she'd told him not to come.*

From where we was, I could see Betty Lou and Luke and Preacher settin' on the porch. Then, after a little while, they stood up and Preacher went to the barn and Betty Lou and Luke walked over to the spring house, out of sight. It sounds like, tellin' it, that I was just standin' there gawkin'. The cows and us was movin', but I reckon maybe I was gawkin! I was thinkin' to myself, well, is this a good thing, or not?

It must of been a good thing for Betty Lou and Luke, since he kept comin' back. Sometimes he'd come on a Friday, and sometimes on a Sunday. On the second or third time, I was at the gate of the lot when he rode up. I reached out for his reins and he give 'em to me. *That's a right good lookin' horse you got there.*

Thankee. I favor her a lot. I swapped for her last year. She's right good under the saddle.

Want me to take her to the pond and brush her up some for you?

He got down. *That's mighty nice of you to offer. I'll walk along with you to the pond.* Standin' there, we watched the mare drink. *I come off right strong to you last time we met. Meant no offense.*

No offense taken.

But I'm still wonderin' about you.

Ain't no need to wonder. I'm just passin' through.

He nodded. *Yeah, I know that's what Preacher said. But a fellar can change his mind.*

I turned to him, and looked him square in the eye. *I tell you what. If'n I change my mind and decide to court Betty Lou, I'll tell you right off, man to man.*

He nodded. *I don't know if'n I can believe you, but sounds fair.*

One thing.

What's that?

I hear tell there's a play party comin' up. Place called Sugar Creek?

Yeh, school house. Sugar Creek.

You takin' Betty Lou?

She said she'd go with me.

Will you cause any trouble with me if 'n I dance with her some?

I'll try not to, lessin' you hog her all the time and try to get close to her, dancin'. You like to dance?

I shore do. Do you?

Aw, I ain't much of a dancer. But I like to try. With that, we parted company. He went to the house to see Betty Lou and I went to do chores at the lot.

Next day at the dinner table, I asked about the play party. *We ain't had one since the War started. The women folk think it'd be a good idea now. Betty Lou says she'll go with Luke. I reckon he'll come for her in the buggy. I figured Thelma and you and me would take the wagon. Maybe take along some beddin'. Sleep in the wagon bed there. Won't be much moon to see by to come home. I still got some oil for a lantern but seems foolish to use it for that.*

How far is it to Sugar Creek?

Maybe five mile, the other way from Salt Lick. Hit's south of here. Right good track if 'n it don't rain. We'll leave after dinner, take somethin' along to eat for supper there. He grinned. *You're gonna be in the favor of a lot of women. You saw at church, ain't hardly any young men in these parts. All of 'em went to the War. You'll have to spread yourself around. Dance with all the women.*

I bet you old men can hold your own.

Yeah, I bet so. But it's hard for a old man to get ahead of a young fellar like you at a play party.

Stewart County they have a caller at a play party. Do they do that here?

Thelma giggled. *You're talkin' to him?*

I might of knowed. I reckon you'll do the callin' and the dancin' too. He laughed his belly laugh. *I've been known to try.*

I was watchin' for a chance to talk to Betty Lou when she was by herself. It seemed like she maybe knowed I wanted to and every time I thought I could she went off to do somethin'. Finally the middle of that week, I come in from the barn just as she was goin' to the spring house for water. *You need help with them buckets?*

She shrugged. *I can do it. Been doin' it since I was Thelma's age. But you can come along if'n you want.*

I took that to be a yes, so I took one of the buckets from her and we went to the spring house. It didn't take but a minute to dip the buckets in the spring to fill em up. But I wanted her to talk to me. *Can we sit here a while? There's somethin' on my mind I want to talk about.* She shrugged again, but she set down by ne on the log there. *It ain't none of my business but do you like to have Luke Jones come courtin'?*

She frowned. *You're right. It ain't none of your business. And I don't know why you're askin'. But I guess I'll tell you anyway. He asked me if'n he could come and I said he could.* She made a face at me, still frownin'. *I bet I know what you're about to say. Same as what Daddy said. He's too old for me.*

Well, I wouldn't of said it to you but now that you have, I could say he's near the age of your Daddy.

She frowned agin, like she was peeved. *You and Daddy didn't have to tell me that. I got eyes in my head! I know that. But he's real good to me. Says real nice things to me, like I'm the purtiest girl he ever saw. And he's got a good farm and he's a good farmer.* She turned to me. *Besides, they ain't no more men around here. My age, they all went to the War and never come back.* She fell quiet, lookin' down at her hands. *All 'cept you. and you say you're just passin' through. Are you?*

I nodded. *That's what I planned on.*

Then what I want to know is, what is it to you, what I do?

Well, that was the question. She'd ast the question of me and I had to come up with a answer. *You all have been mighty good to me and I feel like I'm part of the family.* I stopped, lookin' for the words to say. *Like maybe I'm standin' in for yore brothers.*

She give a kind of laugh. *Let me ask a question for you. Ask it.*

When you look at me like I've seen you do, are you lookin' at me like a brother would?
Boy howdy, she had me nailed to the barn wall. I didn't know what in tarnation to say. She just set there, lookin' at me, with that frown cloudin' up her purty face. I figured I'd better fess up, right then and there. *Betty Lou, you got me. You got me right 'tween the eyes. I shore ain't lookin' at you like a brother would. I'm lookin' at you like a man looks at a real purty woman. The real purty woman that you are. I cain't seem to help it.*
She reached up to tuck a piece of hair back under her head rag. I had a terrible need for her to touch my face agin, like she did at the hair cuttin'. Then she give me a hard look. *But you ain't gonna do anythin' about it, are you?*
I shrugged, layin' my hands to the side. The hand on her side was near touchin' hers. *I cain't. I like it here a lot and I like yore family a lot and I shore like to be with you. But I've got to get back to Stewart County and my family.*
And some girl you got back there. And she moved her hand away from mine.
And some girl I got back there. She sed she'd wait for me. I hired out for her daddy and he said . . .
She cut me off. *I don't want to hear any about that. You're gonna do what you're gonna do. And that's that. Just don't look at me that way any more.* She stood up and looked back at the house. *Now let me tell you how it is with me. I better get out of this house if'n I can. Daddy's gonna marry Miz Henderson for sure. Bring her to live at our house.*
She stopped talkin' and dipped a gourd of water and handed it to me. I took it, with a nod, and took a drink. I rinsed it out, and took a gourd full for her. She held it, lookin' down at it like she never seen it afore. *Daddy needs a woman in the house, in his bed. And Thelma needs a mama, more'n a sister. So, I guess Luke is the way out for me.*
So you'll marry up with him.
If'n he asks me.
He will.

I guess so. She looked at me. *That's what you wanted to talk about?* I nodded. *Well then, let's take this here water back to the house.*

Now I seen her in a different light. I'd been lookin' at her and thinkin' about her as a real purty young girl who knowed her way around the house and maybe the farm. For sure, all that was so, but here was something different. She'd looked at what was comin' down the pike, as people say, and she'd done some figurin' about her life, and what she was gonna do about it. It looked like she had it all planned out. I thought well of her for doin' that.

The trouble was, she'd got under my skin. Now I watched her move around the house and outside and I seen that she moved around like Dulciemay had. Like she was dancin'. And I couldn't get out of my mind the way her fingers on me had felt that day when she brushed away the hair she had cut off my head and my face. And the feelin's I had when she did that. I wondered how it would feel or how she'd feel with my arms around her, holdin' her so close you couldn't tell what was her and what was me. At night, thinkin' about that, I'd get hard and harder and harder and harder and I'd have to use my hand to get it over with.

But that was my feelin's or maybe my guts. My mind was on a different tack. If'n I looked at it cold heartened, I didn't want to stay around here in North Carolina. Stewart County was where I belonged and Stewart County was where I was goin'. Just a question of when and how. That bein' said, no need not to enjoy myself while I was here. If'n I could.

Next thing happened was the play party at Sugar Creek. Luke come in the buggy for Betty Lou. She looked real purty, in a dress that was kind of red and she had her hair tied back with a red ribbon. I'd never seen her look better. *Luke, you goin' to have yore hands full at the play party.* He knew what I was talkin' about but he didn't let on.

He grinned. *How's that?*

Why, keepin' track of that purty woman you're takin' to the party! Every man for miles around are goin' to want to dance with her.

He was still grinnin'. *Ain't it the tuth. Mebbe I better take a stick along to beat 'em away.*

Betty Lou heard us talkin' and she grinned. *You two men beat it all carryin' on like that. Makes me think you never saw a girl dressed up for a play party.*

He reached for her hand. *I never did afore now.* And right in front of me and Thelma she kissed him on the cheek. He was taken aback, I guess, and just kept on smilin' at her as she went back in the house.

You gonna keep your word to me?

What word is that?

I grinned. *You said I could dance with her at the play party and you wouldn't get riled at me and pick a fight.*

He was still lookin' after her. *Well, I cain't keep her from dancin' with anybody she wants to, I guess.* Then he turned to me. *But afore I say I won't pick a fight with you, I want to know if'n you're gonna keep your word.*

What word is that?

That you're just passin' through.

I nodded. *Yeah. I'm goin' to keep my word on that. I'm just passin' through. But, I better tell you, I shore like to dance!*

So we all went to the play party like Preacher had said, with vittles and bed rolls. It took us over a hour to get there. Thelma rode up front with Preacher and I set back in the wagon bed on some of the bedroll to make the ridin' a little easier. Preacher and Thelma was a purty sight. She set real close to him and he had his arm around her, the other holdin' the reins. Lookin' at them I wondered how it felt to be a man with a daughter. It must feel good, I thought.

The wagon track led through some purty country but no different from what I'd seen comin' down from Richmond, a little hilly with some good pastures comin' in good and green. Mostly cows. A few horses. A farm here and there.

We could hear the party afore we got there, the singin' and the stompin' as the dancers went through the call. It sounded real good. I couldn't keep from smilin', as we pulled up, and settled the team and the wagon for the night. And we got in that school house as quick as we could.

The dance right away was Skip to My Lou, and I asked Thelma if'n she'd be my partner. She nodded and we went with the others through the call. Skip, skip, skip to M'Lou! Skip, skip, skip to M'Lou! Skip, skip, skip to M'Lou! Skip to M'Lou my darlin'! I'll get another'n as purty as you, I'll get another'n as purty as you, I'll get another'n as purty as you, skip to M'Lou my darlin'. Flies in the buttermilk, shoo shoo shoo. So many verses I can't recollect 'em all.

And there was so many play party songs I can't recollect 'em all. But I knowed most of 'em back then. And I could sing 'em as we danced, stompin' our feet in time with the music. Like a lot of them parties back then, there warn't no need for a fiddle. We'd do both the singin' and the dancin'. At this party I'm talkin' about a old man with a fiddle come in about half way through. He could fiddle all right enough but you couldn't hardly hear him for the singin' and the stompin'. We listened to him between sets, when everybody needed to cool off. The school benches had been pushed against the wall, over by the heatin' stove, to clear the floor for dancin'. Them bein' short of men, some of the pairs was both women. I'd knowed that to happen in Stewart County. Some men just didn't love to dance, like I did.

Preacher called out Ole Dan Tucker! And I went and got Betty Lou from where she was standin' with some other women. I can see it and hear it now. Ole Dan Tucker was a fine ole' man. He washed his face in the fryin' pan. Combed his hair with a wagon wheel. Died with a toothache in his heel. Git out the way Ole Dan Tucker. You're too late to get yore supper. Supper's done and breakfast cookin', left Ole Daniel standin' lookin'.

Oh Lord, I recollect that dance! Betty Lou was a real good dancer and she fit in my arms like we was made to do it. And around and around we went. Finally the set was done, with my right arm around her waist, her hand on mine, and her left hand holdin' my left hand, out in front. *Walkin' that way, I took her over to Luke where he was standin' watchin' the dancin'.* *Here she is. She's a real good dancer.* She laughed and moved away from me to him, and put her arm through his. And they moved to the next dance. I stood there watchin' them.

They make a good lookin' couple, don't they? I turned around to see a right purty woman standin' by me. *You the man named Luther?* I nodded. *Name's Maybelle. You want to dance?* So we did. She was as good at dancin' as Betty Lou, maybe better. After the dance, we went over to the water can, and had a drink. We stood there, watchin' the dancers. *You stuck on her?*

I laughed. *Maybe. She's a right good lookin' girl.*

Yeah, she shore is.

I turned to her. *But she ain't the only right good lookin' girl here.*

She laughed, a good hearty laugh, straight from the belly. *So you noticed.*

Afore I could answer, the next dance started. It was Ole Dan Tucker again. Me and Maybelle really got into it, stompin' our way through it. I let the others do the singin' and paid my attention to Maybelle. She was more a armful than Betty Lou and looked like she liked to be close.

So when the call come for it, I held her real close and we went around the floor like we was the only ones out there. Holdin' her that close, my arm went all around and my hand was on the edge of her bosom. And she didn't mind one bit. Just like that I was getting' hard. Not terrible hard, just so's I could feel it. And I thought what the hell, I twirled her around to face me, her dancin' back'ards. We were close enough that I knowed she felt me. But she didn't mind. We pulled apart and finished the dance. Supper's done and breakfast cookin! Left Ole' Daniel standin' lookin'! *You want a drink of water?*

She laughed her belly laugh. *You got anythin' stronger?*

I laughed with her. Here was a woman that knowed her way around. *Not right here I don't.* She laughed agin. Now it was plumb dark and some candles had been lit, and one coal oil lantern. We went and had our drink for the drinkin' gourd. I looked at her, standin' there, for maybe the first time. She was a real good lookin' woman. More a woman than Betty Lou. She must of been my age, maybe a year older. Her brownish hair was pulled to the top of her head, comin' loose from the dancin'. Looked like she had brown eyes but I couldn't see for sure in the half light. A big mouth, looked like it was easy for it to grin, and give that belly laugh. Like I said, she was a armful of woman. She looked like she'd be as soft to squeeze as a feather pillow.

You here for long?

Don't know for sure. Maybe not. I'm passin' through. On my way back home to Tennessee.

You been in the War long?

Yeah. Since I was 15.

You heard the War is over?

I stood like I was froze. *No, I hadn't heard that. Is it true? How'd you hear it?*

Feller came by the farm this mornin'. Stopped by to see if'n I could feed him. I did. Didn't have much but I give him what I had. He come down from Virginny, said Lee had surrenderd.

Preacher must not of heard it. I better find out what he's heard. I looked at her. *That can wait. Here I got a good lookin' woman that wants to dance with me.* She grinned, and tucked some hair up on top that had fell down on her face. She had trouble with one cow's tail, as Aunt Polly would of called it, and I reached up to do it for her. She reached up and helped my hand do it. I thought to myself, Oh Lord! *Let's dance!*

We did. I danced with some more women, spreadin' myself around, like Preacher had said. Thelma and me went around on some calls. She was a good dancer for her age. But I never danced agin with Betty Lou. Mostly I danced with Maybelle. She was real good, better'n most of the women there. And we was a good pair. What I had forgot, she knowed, and led me through.

Preacher caught my eye and grinned his big shit-eatin' grin at me. Sure as hell, he knowed what was going on.

It was the last call. Everybody was give out. When it quit, I held on to her. *Name's Luther. Luther Morris. I'd be right proud to see you agin.* She stayed there in my arms, and grinned. *Maybelle. Maybelle Atkins. My place is over by Salt Lick church. Mebbe you'll come to see me afore you go. I make good dried apple pies. You like dried apple pies?*

I give her my best smile. *I shore do. Maybe I'll do that. Preacher know how to tell me how to get to yore place?*

She laughed. *He knows how. That man knows how to get to all the places where there's a woman.* And she moved away, left me wonderin' why she'd said that that way.

The party died down about midnight. I don't recollect when we had our supper or if'n we had it. My mind was on the War endin' and my guts was on Maybelle. I figured she meant business about them fried apple pies and I was goin' to do some foller up, as we called it in the cavalry. And when I could, I'd have to find out what Preacher had heard about the War endin'. Anyway, afore I quit about that night, I ought to remark about two things. One was that I was the only young man there. Luke was I guessed the next youngest. Then Preacher and his friends.

So the young men had gone to the War and not come back yet or wouldn't ever come back. I felt real out of place about that. Nobody said anything about it but I figured I knowed what they was thinkin'. The other thing was that there warn't no babies. Some reason, I guess. All the men havin' a family was gone.

Anyway, everybody bedded down as best they could. Preacher and Thelma slept in the wagon bed. I put my bed roll over under a tree where the mules was tied. I never did see Betty Lou after the party died down so don't know where she slept. Pro'bly with some women friends. Or maybe Luke.

Next morning was Sunday but there warn't any church I guess. All I know is that Preacher and Thelma and me went home in the wagon. But afore everybody left, they all went around and said to everybody what a good time they'd had. They said that to me, too. The women especially. I guess I'd danced with every last one of 'em afore the night was done. All I know was that next mornin' my feet was shore sore and I couldn't hardly get my boots back on.

I hunted up Maybelle afore she left and told her I'd had a real good time dancin' with her. In the daylight she wanrn't as good lookin' as she was at the night afore, but she was still better lookin' than most of the women there. She was harnessin' up a real purty horse to a buggy. *You need some help doin' that?*

I guess not. I been doin' it since I was a girl, age of Thelma.

That shore is a purty horse.

She is, ain't she? I've had her since she was foaled. She'd druther me ride her than be hitched to a buggy. She turned to me. *Maybe I'll let you ride her when you come to see me.*

You figure there'd be dried apple pies maybe Wednesday?

I can see to it that there is. About dinner time. And she got up in the buggy and rode away, leavin' me standin' there, wonderin' what I'd got myself into.

Anyway, there was a lot of talk about if'n the War was over. By the time we all left that mornin' to go home, the word had spread. It looked like it was all from that man Maybelle had talked to so I figured there was more to be found out. But Preacher and me and some more men figured it was so. Truth to tell, folks was real quiet, when they talked about it. I guessed they'd knowed it was comin' and here it was.

Going home, Preacher and Thelma was in the wagon, swingin' their feet off'n the back. I could hear 'em singin' play party songs. I set up front, drivin' the team, lookin' at the purty countryside, wonderin' where Betty Lou had got, and thinkin' about Wednesday and Maybelle. We got home to find Betty Lou and Luke settin' on the porch, lookin' like old married folk. *I got to get home but I wanted to wait for you all to get here to hear the news. Old Mr. McMinnville come by a hour ago, said the word from Mount Airy was the war was over. General Lee surrendered, up in Virginny.*

We stood there a minute lookin' at Luke, thinkin' about what he said. Nobody said we'd heard about it at the play party. 'Twarn't no need to. Luke's news was for certain. Preacher spoke up. *Well, that's real good news, Luke, ain't it? What we been prayin' about. We don't rightly know what it means, for the North to win, but weun's have to hope for the best.*

Thelma was thinkin' about it. *You think maybe Eddie will come home now?*

Betty Lou took her hand. *Maybe. But I got this feelin' that he won't. I got this feelin' in my heart that he's gone for good. So don't you go getting' yore hopes up.* Thelma nodded. Looked like they both was about to start cryin', but they didn't, they just hugged each other.

Preacher, I want to have a word with you, if'n you will. Can we walk over to the pond. Preacher nodded, and him and Luke went that away. I unloaded the wagon and Betty Lou and Thelma carried everything in the house. Then I drove the wagon down where it set by the lot, unhitched the mules, and turned 'em loose. It warn't the right time to water 'em. Preacher and Luke was still at the pond. Betty Lou and Thelma had come out to set on the porch. When I saw Preacher and Luke start back, I did too, guessin' that somethin' was up. So the three of us was there when they come up.

Preacher was the first to start. *Thelma, Luke here has asked me if'n it was all right with me if'n him and Betty Lou got married? I told him it was. But we wanted you to know that, first off.*

Betty Lou took hold of Thelma's hand. *We want you to come and live with us, if'n you want to.*

We'd be real proud if'n you did that.

But you can stay with me, if'n you want to.

Thelma looked at us all. *Do I have to say right now?*

No, you shore don't. Fact of the matter is, you could live with me for a while and them for a while. Whatever you want to do.

Well, that was that. It looked like Betty Lou had it all worked out, just like she said that day at the spring house. She walked Luke out to his buggy, and kissed him, and he drove away. We went in to eat a bite of supper. Nothin' more about that was said. I couldn't for the life of me see if'n Betty Lou was happy about marryin' Luke. She looked the same as she always looked. Just went about her business and after supper her and Thelma went into the other room where they slept.

Me and Preacher set by the fire place for a while, talkin' mainly about farmin' and what needed to be done tomorrow and next week. I could hear Betty Lou and Thelma talkin' in the other room but couldn't get anything about they was sayin'.

Then him and me went outside, around back for a piss. We stood there, lookin' at the sun goin' down. *You feel good about this?*

I reckon I do. Looks like it's what Betty Lou wants to do. She's a strong woman, like her mama. If'n she wants it to work, I guess it'll work. He was quiet. *Luke is a good man. He gets a little hot under the collar sometimes. And he likes his likker more'n I'd like. But he favors her a lot. Has since she was a girl. And he's a good farmer so she'll have a good life.*

I never did water the mules. I'll go do that afore I turn in. It was near dark but I figure they wouldn't give me any trouble.

I'll come with you.

Down there at the pond, we waited for them to drink. *You know maybe you could of had her, if'n you wanted.*

Maybe.

But I guess you didn't.

Well, I did and I didn't. I'm still bound to get back to Stewart County and her home is here. I don't want to stay and she wouldn't want to go.

Did you ask her, if'n it's any of my business.

I laughed. *Well, it's shore your business to worry about your girls. No I didn't.* It was quiet agin. *You reckon you and me are about done farmin'?*

I reckon so. Another week or so will do it. Get all the plantin' done.

I'll stay till we've done.

I'd be obliged if'n you did.

We turned the mules into the lot. It seemed like there was still some talkin' to be done. He set down on the log and I set there beside him. *What do you figure it means, the War bein' over.*

He shook his head. *Oh Lordy, I don't know. I guess things'll be unsettled for the next year, maybe more. Maybe it won't touch us much, We're out of the way from much goin' on.* Weun's will have to go ahead with our farmin', have to feed our families. He fell quiet. *Maybe some of the young men will be back to help with that.* He fell quiet agin. *I don't know if'n the Yankees will bother us much. Like I said, we're out of the way here. But, then again, maybe they'll come through, causin' trouble. Like they did in South C'lina. I just don't know.*

If'n I can do it, I'll leave you Ole Mule.

That's mighty nice of you to offer. Let's see how things go.

I looked up at the sky. The stars was startin' to shine through. *Can I ask you another question?*

He laughed his old belly laugh. *If'n I know the answer.*

You got plans with Miz Henderson right soon?

He really let loose with his belly laugh. *You are just full of questions tonight!*

You don't have to tell me. I was just wonderin', what with Betty Lou marryin' up with Luke, and all.

You don't have to be sorry for askin'. We're talkin' here man to man. Yeah, her and me have got plans. She said she'd marry up with me, whenever it seemed right. But like I said to you afore, they's matters to be settled. She's got a little farm too and her house is better'n mine so I don't rightly know how it'll be settled. Her and Thelma get along good, if'n Thelma wants to live with us. She never had any younguns, and she's taken with the notion of a daughter. He laughed again. *You got any more questions?*

Yessir, I do. Can you spare me and Ole Mule on Wednesday?

Well, now, I reckon I can. You plannin' on goin' somewhere? No, let me guess. A old man like me ought to be able to make a good guess where you want to go on Wednesday. He did a kind of laugh agin. *Does it have anythin' to do with dried apple pies?*

You been readin' my mind!

No, I ain't been readin' your mind, just your crotch. I seen you dancin' with Maybelle Atkins at the play party. She's a good lookin' woman. Makes danged good dried apple pies. And for sure she makes a good armful for a man to hold on to.

I figured that, dancin' with her. I let it be quiet. *Am I goin' to make trouble goin' over there?*

Naw, you ain't gonna make trouble goin' over there. Not for her. She likes men and takes 'em when she can. Pickin's purty lean these days. Right when the War started she was spoke for by a man some miles away. But he went away to the War without a fare thee well and I guess she ain't heard from him since. I never knowed if 'n she was broke up about it or not.

He fell quiet. *She ain't had a easy life. Lives with her daddy. He acts like he's deaf as a post, but I ain't so sure. I never seen much of her mama. Word was she died some years back. Frank is well off. Never seemed to like for much. They had a real good herd of horses that her and her Daddy raised and sold. Them soldiers comin' through I told you about took most of 'em. Word was that she stood up to 'em and turned out she kept her stud and some brood mares. Don't have to worry about Maybelle Atkins. She'll get along. Like I said, she likes her men. You go and enjoy yourself. A young man like you needs to do that. But no, you won't be makin' trouble by goin'.*

I warn't too sure about that but I kept thinkin' about how Maybelle felt in my arms at the play party. I shore wanted to see her agin. So, on Tuesday evening, I went to look for Betty Lou. She was out back. *You think I could have a clean shirt tomorrow?*

She stopped what she was doin' and stood lookin' at me, her hands on her hips. *I reckon. There's one hangin' on the line over there from yestiday's washin'. What are you gonna do, go callin' on Maybelle Atkins?* She warn't grinnin' when she said that. Matter of fact, sounded like she was on the edge of gettin' mad. *I saw you dancin' with her. You and ever' other man. Sniffin' at her like she was in heat.* She looked down at the ash pan she was workin' at. Then up at me. *Well, are you?*

Yeah. That's where I'm goin'. Don't you want me to?

She shrugged. *Lordy, it ain't up to me to want you to. You want to, go? Go.* And she turned her back on me. Well, I figured

I knowed what that was about. But I warn't goin' to talk anymore about it. So I went to the clothes line and got the clean shirt and went on about my business. She never said anything more about it and I didn't either.

Preacher had told me how to get to the Atkins place. I got there on Ole Mule without any trouble. It looked like it was a real nice place. There was a good lookin' house, and a big barn, bigger'n I ever saw in all my travels. It must of housed a lot of stock in the winter. Some cows was over to the side in a pasture that looked real green. That'd make good grazin'. I didn't see no horses anywhere around. I halloed the house, but twarn't no need.

Maybelle and her daddy come out on the porch. It was a big porch, looked like it stretched all the front of the house and around one side. *I see you found yore way here! Luther, this here's my Daddy, Frank. Daddy, this here's Luther. Luther Morris.* I saw that she was talkin' some loud to him. Preacher had told me he was a little deef.

I walked over and shook his hand. *I'm glad to meet you, Mr. Atkins.*

Call me Frank. You here to see our horses?

Yessir, I'd be proud to see 'em.

Well, you go ahead. I'll stay here and wait for you to come in. Maybelle took my arm. *You want to see my prize mare?* I nodded, not knowin' what else to say. I follered her over to the barn and down the hall to a stall where there was one of the purtiest pieces of horse flesh I ever saw. *Ain't she a beaut?*

She shorely is. You take good care of her. She shore does look good. I walked around the mare, pattin' and rubbin' her like I used to do my litle red mare. But this one was bigger and dark chestnut colored with black tail and mane. I kept walkin' around her, rubbin' her and talkin' to her.

You look like you know your way around a horse.

I try. And I told her a little about my little red mare and how she'd got shot.

That must have been real hard to take. She was quiet, watchin' me and her mare. *Tell you what. You ride bareback behind me? We'll go see Black and the mares out with him.*

I can do that. I been ridin' Ole Mule since I left Richmond, bare back. I kind of laughed. *And nobody like you to hold on to.*

She let out one of her belly laughs and pointed to where the saddle and gear was. *I'll get ready.* And she went into another stall, and come out in pants, I guessed maybe a pair of her daddy's. Her shirt was tucked in, but tucked in tight so I could see where her bosums was. Her hair was pulled back and tied with some kind of ribbon. Yella hair and brown eyes, that crinkled up when she grinned. And she grinned a lot. I stood there, holding the bridle, lookin' at her.

She grinned. *What? You ain't ever seen a woman in pants before?* Well, I hadn't, but I warn't goin' to tell her that. *Pants make ridin' a lot easier than a danged skirt.*

I never in all my born days seen any pants and shirt that looked any better. You are one good lookin' woman. I laughed and shook my head. *I bet you been told that afore.* And I handed the reins to her and our hands touched each other, and I didn't let go but stood there grinnin' at her, holdin' on to her hand. By that time, I figured I knowed what this was all about, and it was more than all right by me.

Them brown eyes was sparklin'. *Maybe. You want to stand here, holdin' my hand or you want to go see my horses?*

Maybe I can do both. You s'pose? One thing, afore I let go yore hand, when do I get a dried apple pie?

She let out another one of her belly laughs. *Man, you want it all, don't you?*

I laughed along with her. *I wouldn't say no to that.*

She let go my hand and led the mare out and got up in the saddle. I got up ahind her and not even askin' if'n I could, I put both arms around her middle. It shore did feel good to do that and I got as close to her as I could, as close as the back end of the saddle would let me. We rode maybe a mile through timber. The path was cleared enough for us to get through but it was close from time to time. It made me think of when I got knocked off the little red mare and Dulciemay found me.

But I didn't think about that much 'cause her mare went into a good gallop and Maybelle and me was rockin' away together. My hands moved with the motion and first thing I knowed, they was at the bottom edge of her bosums. She didn't move 'em so they stayed there. It felt real soft and I wanted more. And I had to move back a hair 'cause I was so hard I was hitting the saddle.

Right about then, we come to a big clearing and scattered around the clearin' was a herd of horses. I could tell the stallion apart from the others easy, even from a distance. He was big, maybe 15, 16 hands, and looked like he was as black as the ace of spades. I slid off the mare, lookin' to see if'n they was gonna come up to us, but none of 'em did.

I reached up to help her down and she half slid into my arms and into a hug and then we was kissin' like it never was goin' to end. Somethin' come over me, and I led her over under a tree or maybe she led me, I don't know which. *This here gonna count as a dried apple pie?*

I tried to say it did, but her mouth was in the way with the kissin'. We went at each other without sayin' a word, but knowin' or feelin' what we was doin'. That first time with her was somethin' real special.

And I can picture it now as I tell it to you. I set her down, and got off her boots, then mine, watchin' her all the time. Her purty yella hair was all mussed from ridin' in the wind and hangin' in her eyes. Her overhalls was easy but when I got to her shirt I had to be careful not to bust a button, it was so tight. I tore off my shirt and got down my pants and drawers over my hard. Just her undershirt and drawers was left. She took 'em off, watchin' me all the time. The sight of her nekkid filled my eyes. I wanted to keep on lookin' and I wanted to go ahead. So I raised up and she raised up and we come together, first slow, then fast, then it was over, like a thunderstorm has passed.

We laid there in the new grass with our hands still on each other. I was still laughin' out loud with a bellow that had started when the lightnin' had struck me. She started to giggle. *Are you always so noisy?*

I stopped laughin', long enough to talk. *I never done that afore.*

What? Laughed out loud?

That, too.

Well, there ain't much more to say about that. Maybelle wanted to be with me as much as I wanted to be with her. I ain't never seen a woman that liked to be with a man so much. Not that I've seen so many women in that way. But she shore was a pleasure and she learned me a lot about bein' with a woman. I never had no notion there was so many ways for a woman and a man to come together. And she loved 'em all and I loved 'em all. I took to goin' to her daddy's place ever' chance I got.

Sometimes we'd go ridin' out to where we could be by ourselves. Sometimes she'd say he was out in the fields and we'd stay in the barn. But we never went in the house and I never slept in the bed with her. Sometimes I'd see him, sometimes not. When I did, he was allus real friendly to me. I figured he must of figured out what we was doin', but he never said nothin' to me about it. A time or two, he'd ride out with us to see the horses. We'd talk about the horses and the foals, and their strong points. Him and Maybelle knowed a lot about horses. I learned a lot from hearin' them talk.

Truth to tell, Maybelle and me never did much deep talkin', leastwise at first. But little by little we got so we warn't in so much a hurry that we could spend some time talkin'. I recollect a day, we was layin' in the grass, lookin' at the clouds. Me on my back, her gathered to my side, playin' with the hairs on my chest. *You ain't told me much about yoreself. I don't even know where you come from.* So I told her what I called the short story of how I come to be here, leavin' out a lot of it. It must have been enough. She ast a question or two, but not any to amount to anythin'.

What about you? Yore mother died? When'd she do that?

That ain't so. It's a story my daddy made up to cover up what happened. I was 15, she left my daddy here and went back to Charlotte. She took me with her. There warn't any more childern from the marriage. She told me she didn't want to live up here in the country any more. And Daddy didn't want to go to Charlotte. So she went and he stayed. I guess there ain't many hard feelin's between them. They're right civil to one another when he takes me down. But she ain't never been back up here. She rolled over on her back agin. *I'm twenty year old and I better get married afore I'm a old maid.* She giggled. *Maybe I'm a old maid now!* She put her hand over on me. *You figure I'm a old maid now?*

I put my hand on hers. *Naw, you're a far cry from bein' a old maid. But I know what you mean.*

She moved her hand away, and set up and looked at me. *Well, are you goin' to marry me?*

I couldn't tell if'n she meant it or she was just foolin'. I decided to act like she was foolin'. *Now what kind of a husband would I be to a purty woman like you? I ain't got nothin' to offer you, 'ceptin' this.* And I leaned over and kissed her hard. *And that ain't goin' to put any vittles on yore table for you and yore youngun's.*

She pushed me away and set up. *Naw, I've knowed from the start what you and me was all about. There ain't no tomorras.* And she got on top of me, and away we went agin.

This 'tween me and her went on for near all spring and into the summer. It seemed like I couldn't get enough of just lookin' at her. She had a body that was all pink and white, that looked like it was made to be kissed all over and loved by a man. And I kissed her all over, every part of her. I couldn't get enough of her and most of the times she was ready. There warn't no more talk about any tomorras. Just havin' the pleasures of today.

Then one day, when I got there, her daddy come out and sed Maybelle was gone. She was gone to Charlotte. He sed her granny on her mama's side was real sick, and Maybelle had to go tend to her. He sed she left yestiday morning early and told him to tell me goodbye and that it had been good knowin' me. I thanked him for tellin' me. He said to come back to see him any time. I said I would. And I rode away, tryin' to figure it out.

Truth to tell, I guess it was a good thing to have happen. There warn't no more tomorras for Maybelle and me than there was for Betty Lou and me. Maybe not as much. She knowed it and I knowed it. So, sooner or later, we had to quit bein' with each other like that. At the time, I wondered if'n it was her that decided to leave for Charlotte. I wisht she 'd of said goodbye, but maybe it was better this way.

But, Lordy, she was some woman for a man to be with. I'll not forget them feelin's if'n I live to be a hunnert. And I spent many a night after she was gone, thinkin' about her and how she felt, outside and in. Like I said, I learned a lot from Maybelle Atkins about how it could be 'tween a woman and a man. I guess the main thing it did was to turn me on to all that and to make me want more. The soldiers at winter camp would of said what she did to me was to make me horney. I never figured out where the word had come from, but I knowed well and good what it stood for.

So I quit goin' to the Atkins place. First Wednesday come along and I didn't go. That evenin' Preacher and me was out, tendin' to the stock. *Word is, Maybelle Atkins is gone.*

Yessir. Her daddy said she went down to Charlotte, to help with her grandmama that's ailin'.

I take it you didn't know she was goin'. No, you don't have to answer that. Ain't none of my business.

I don't mind you askin'. No sir, I didn't know anything about it. It feels quare that she didn't say goodbye to me.

I can see as how that would be. He was quiet. *You gonna miss her? Her and her dried apple pies?* He was grinnin' when he said that.

Yessir, I'm goin' to miss her real bad. Her and me had some real good times with each other.

He looked at me sideways. *You know you ain't the first.*

Yessir, I figured as much. But that didn't pay me no never mind. I liked her a lot. She shore is a pleasure for a man to be with.

Don't hold it agin her. Seems like she growed up to be mighty needy for somebody to love her. Some women are like that. Some men too. Betty Lou's mama was like that. Thelma's mama warn't. He shrugged. *But we didn't have much time with each other to find out.* That was all we said about that. But I got to learn later on in my life what he was talkin' about.

It was not real hot that year and the rain was just about right for the corn to grow. We got it laid by in good season. I say we did, mostly it was me and the mules. I didn't mind. Preacher had done a lot for me and I didn't mind doin' all I could to help him farm.

It looked like it would be a good year. There was maybe six, seven calves all together, so more than a plenty milk. We even give some in the hog slop. The varmints were kept from getting many of the chickens, so we had eggs and chicken to eat. The garden come in real good, with plenty of pole beans and creepers like squash and punkins. We dug the taters earlier and they were dryin' in the loft by the cookin' stove chimley.

I figure I ought to say right here that it felt like to me then that I had put the War ahind me. I warn't dreamin' no more dreams from the War. I never any more had to say how or why I'd left the fightin'. To be sure, I was all right enough regretful that so many of the young men from around had gone to the War and not come back. But there warn't any thing I could do about that. My time in the War seemed like a long time back, and I let it stay there.

It looked like now it was a good time to leave for Stewart County. We was settin' on that log by the barn, whittlin'. *You think weun's are about caught up farmin'?*

Looks like it. He quit whittlin'. *I reckon I know what you're gonna say.*

I laughed. *You figure you readin' my mind agin?*

I figure I am. He turned to me. *You done your share of farmin' with me. I reckon I can get along without you.*

I don't know how to thank you enough.

You don't have to try. Past year, you more than earned yore keep. He fell quiet. *You reckon I cain't talk you into courtin' Betty Lou and settlin' down here in North C'lina?*

I reckon not. I'm partial to here a lot but I yearn for Stewart County.

I can see that.

We let it go at that. Two or three days after that Preacher had gone over to the Henderson place. I was done with my chores and so I went over to help Betty Lou hang up the wash. *Daddy told me this mornin' afore he left that you was fixin' to leave.*

I reckon it's about time. I been livin' offn' your family for near a year, I guess. I stood there, watchin' her. *I'll be right sorry to leave you all. You all have been real good to me.*

She stopped hangin' and looked at me, grinnin', hands on her hips, like she did sometimes. *Well, you know you don't have to leave. You could stay here and marry me. Or maybe Thelma in a year or two.* Turning her back on me, she went back to hangin' up the wash. *Or maybe marry up with that Maybelle Atkins.* I couldn't think of what to say so I guess I just stood there, holdin' the shirt I was gonna give her next thing. She turned back around, hands on her hips again. *You don't have to say anything.* Like she could read my mind. *I know all about you goin' to the Atkins place to break horses. You may be breakin' horses but that ain't all you been breakin'.*

Takin' that shirt out of my hand. *Only thing that gets me is how come you went all the way over to the Atkins place and Maybelle when I was right here in yore reach! How come you didn't see me? Ain't I purty enough for you? Or mebbe you think I wouldn't lie down with you? Or mebbe you was afraid I'd make you forget that girl Nadine or whatever her name is. Well, let me tell you, mebbe I could of, if'n you'd give me the chance.* She just stood there, lookin' right through me, half mad and half cryin'.

The words come to me. *Most all of what you said is so.*

Well, I guess that's good for me to know about. She held out her hand. *Give me somethin' to hang.* I did. She hung it up and turned back to me, halfway mad again. *But it's too late now even if'n you wanted to. I'm goin' to marry Luke.*

You sure you want to do that?

She nodded. *I'm sure. He's rough around the edges but he's a good man inside. All he needs is a good woman like me. I can do it and I'm gonna do it. You tell me, what else can I do? Eddie and Charlie gone. Daddy courtin' Miz Henderson, you leavin'. I cain't do this farm by myself, all the young men around here kilt in the war!* She looked like she was gonna start to cry. I started to go to her. She backed up against the wet clothers hangin' on the line. *No. don't you touch me! You cain't touch me now! And don't start talkin'! Just hand me them clothes and let's get done and get away from here.*

I did and she got done, and picked up the basket and walked away fast enough to let me know that she was done talking to me and didn't want to be follered. At the time, it seemed like she did the right thing. She'd said it all, and there warn't anything else to say on my part. And I guess not hers. I had went to Maybelle 'cause we both knowed there warn't no strings along with it. It looked like if'n I went to Betty Lou there'd be strings that I didn't want no part of. I made up my mind when I left Richmond to go back to Stewart County. And I guess back to Nadine.

Truth to tell, time had passed and I'd done so many things that I couldn't hardly remember what Nadine looked like. But Stewart County was on my mind and I warn't goin' to let no woman get in the way. Not even Betty Lou, who was on my mind a lot, or maybe not my mind, if'n you know what I mean. She shore was some woman. But so was Maybelle Atkins.

So it looked like it'd be best for near everybody if'n I got out of there as soon as I could figure out how. The main thing was what to do about Ole Mule. I didn't rightly see how Preacher could do the farmin' with just one mule. I owed Preacher a lot. He saved my life. But if'n I didn't have Ole Mule, the only way I had to go was to walk. I just couldn't figure out what to do about that.

Maybe the next week, a neighbor come by on his way back from Mount Airy. Preacher and me was pitchin' hay up in the loft. He pulled up to the barn and got down off'n his horse. *Howdy.*

Preacher quit pitchin' and got down off 'n the wagon. *Howdy. You care to come n for a drink of water?*

Much obliged, but I best be on my way. I just stopped by to give you a piece of mail.

Where it come to?

Mail in Mount Airy. I been there to see a man I do some business with. Word was out there was a letter to a Preacher A. J. Wood and I said I was comin' this way and they asked me to bring it to you. All the time he was talkin' he was fishin' around in his saddle bag. Right then he come up with a folded piece of paper and handed it to Preacher.

I'm much obliged for gettin' this. You shore you won't set a while?

Naw, I got to get on. I guess I'll see you at church next time you come to Flat Lick. And he put his horse in a trot and went on down the road.

Preacher stood there lookin' at the piece of paper. He hadn't talked about it to me but I figured he couldn't read much 'cept for some of the Bible and I figured he read that by heart. The paper warn't my business but if'n it had been, I couldn't of read the writin' either. *Let's go find Betty Lou.* He headed to the house. I didn't know if'n I ought to, but I follered. *Betty Lou!*

What's the matter, Daddy? She come out on the porch, Thelma, too.

He handed her the piece of paper. She unfolded it and looked at it. I saw her wipe her mouth, nervous like. *It looks like it's from somebody named Comer Hicks. If'n I can read his writin' right. Looks like he wrote the 25th day of March of the year 1865. Let me have a minute lookin' at it afore I try to read it to you.* She set down in a chair there on the porch and I could see her mouth some words as she read the writin' on the paper. She looked like she was goin' to cry, but she give a sniff or two and looked up at Preacher. *Some words I cain't make out, but here's the best I can do.*

And she started out to read. *To Preacher A. J. Wood, Flat Lick Church, Mount Airy, North Carolina. I write to you.* She stopped and said she couldn't make it out. She started up again. *Yore son Eddie Wood.* She stopped agin and started up agin. *Him and me at Richmond.* She stopped agin, then started up agin. *I saw him shot and fell.* She looked up and kind of waved her hand. *The call to fall back. He was a good man and a good soldier.* She stopped and wiped her cheek with her hand. *Told me about you and Betty Lou and Thelma. I am right sorry to tell you this. Comer Hicks, Ashville, North Carolina.*

She kept on lookin' at the paper like she thought she'd read it wrong. Then she held out her hand to Thelma and Thelma took it and went over to her and hid her face in Betty Lou's dress. I started to go off of the porch, maybe to the barn, thinkin' this warn't no place for a stranger to be, but Preacher motioned for me to stay put. So I did.

He cleared his throat a time or two. *Well, that was mighty good of Mr. Hicks to do. Yes, that was mighty good. We are much obliged to him for doin' it.* He cleared his throat again. *Let's all set down here a minute and recollect about Eddie and what a fine young man he was.* Thelma had stopped her cryin'. Them three set in the porch chairs and I set down on the porch. *I reckon we all knowed that Eddie had been kilt in the War but this here word from Mr. Hicks brung it back to us agin.* Betty Lou was lookin' straight ahead, not cryin', not givin' any sign of what she'd read from that paper.

Daddy, what are we gonna do for a marker for Eddie?

Preacher looked over to Thelma, clearin' his throat again. *You know, my big girl, that's a right good thing to think about. Let's think about that some, like where we're gonna put it and what it'll look like. Betty Lou, what do you think about that?* For a minute, I thought she hadn't heard him, but I saw she had when she turned her head to him. I could see now where the tears had run down her face. She still didn't say anything. Just shook her head just a little. Preacher stood up. *Well, no need to make up our minds about that now. Luther and me have to go do our chores.* And we walked on over to the barn, leavin' them settin' there on the porch.

I felt real uneasy about bein' there, now worse than ever. The letter from Comer Hicks had brung back to this family that their two boys had stayed in the War and had fought and been killed. And I had run away and come here and was still alive. But there warn't any use in talkin' about it any more. We all knowed how it was and why. Best thing I could do was to finish up with Preacher the best I could, and get out of their sight.

I never knowed much about what they did about a marker for Eddie. The next day or so I saw Preacher workin' on a kind of cross but he give it up when Thelma said she'd druther have a big rock for a marker. Sometime that week after breakfast, Preacher said him and the girls was goin' to walk up the hill where the cow pasture was and would I watch the place while they did. I knowed what he was tellin' me, so I stayed around while they did whatever they did. I was obliged to him for settin' it straight that there was no need for me to go along. Nothing more was said about Eddie or the paper that was sent by Comer Hicks or where they'd put a marker. I never saw it, to know what I was lookin' at.

Thelma was still keeping track of the time and she told us that it was the first of September. I kept putting off making my mind up about leavin'. It looked like the best I could do was to use one of my pieces of gold to buy a horse from Frank Atkins and leave Ole Mule for Preacher. But a piece of gold was worth more'n a horse, even one of Frank's good ones. And I hated to leave Ole Mule behind.

Then one morning while I was still tryin' to make up my mind, Preacher and me was pitchin' hay up in the hay loft. Thelma was around somewheres with her dogs. Luke had come by in his buggy and him and Betty Lou had went somewhere. I was in the wagon, pitchin' up, and Preacher was in the loft stackin' it to make room for more. Sudden like, I heard somethin' break and Preacher yelled somethin'. Right off, I figured he'd fallen through where he'd told me to be on the lookout for. I jumped down from the wagon bed fast as I could and got in the barn to find him layin' there.

First off, I figured he was dead. But I felt his throat and his blood was thumpin' so I knowed he was still alive. He was all twisted together where he'd fell and his head was all bloody. I figured I needed to get help from somewhere, so I run out of the barn and hollered for Thelma to come. I figured next to make him as easy as I could without movin' him. But when I tried to straighten his legs out he hollered like crazy and I knowed somethin' was broke. About that time here come Thelma and the dogs. She looked at him and started to cry. *Is Daddy dead?*

Naw, he ain't dead. But I 'spect he's bad hurt. You and me have got to do somethin'. We ought to get Frank Atkins here. He's the closest thing we got to a doctor. And we ought to get Miz Henderson here. She'll know what to do too. What you and me have got to decide is do you stay here with your Daddy, and I go get 'em, or do I stay here and you go.

I was real proud of Thelma. She quit cryin' as quick as she'd started and studied her Daddy for a minute. *You think I can do it?*

Yep. I know you can. I can saddle up Ole Mule and him and you can do it. Do you want to do it that way? She nodded. *You know the way to the Atkins place?*

What if'n I go tell Miz Henderson first off and she can tell me for sure how to get to the Atkins place?

Yep, that's the way to do it. All the time I was unhitchin' Ole Mule from the wagon and saddlin' him up and shortenin' the stirrups and talkin' to him like I allus did. *Ole Mule, we need you one more time. You're goin' to have to carry Thelma to get help for Preacher. You go fast but watch out for branches to knock her off, you hear?* By that time, Thelma was ready. She hitched up her skirt and I helped her up in the saddle. The dogs were all hot to go too but she told 'em they better stay here. I didn't think they'd do it, but they did. Anyway, with a wave of the hand, her and Ole Mule was off and runnin'.

It was a long day settin' there by Preacher, waitin' for somebody to come. I tried to recollect what I'd seen the doctors in the War do about legs that was broke. I guess maybe they tried to fit the pieces together, if'n they could find the ends of the pieces. Then they'd tie the leg up to hold it in place. I figured if'n worst come to worst I could do that. But Frank Atkins could do it better, I figured. He had horses that must need doctorin' all the time.

I finally went and got some water and tried to wash the blood offn' Preacher's head. It looked to me like the cut warn't too deep. I'd seen enough cuts on the face and head to know there was a lot of blood. The blood made you think the cut was worse than it was.

What worried me was that he was still knocked out. It looked like more trouble was inside his head than outside. I kept puttin' a wet rag on his head and talkin' to him but he warn't doin' anything. Just layin' there, his eyes closed, not movin', like he was dead. I knowed he warn't though, since I kept feelin' the thumpin' in his neck. Nothin' to do but wait.

I guess it warn't long, but it seemed like it was, that Miz Henderson pulled up in her buggy. I was shore glad to see her and told her so. She set down by Preacher and looked him over, mashing here and there with her hands, and opening his eye to look in. I told her what I thought about the leg and that his head was hurt more inside than outside.

I think you are right about that. When Frank Atkins comes, we'll let him fix up the leg. I know about people with jarred brains. It happens sometimes when you fall or get hit on the head. Trouble is, ain't anything to do to cure it. We just have to wait 'til he comes out of it. Make him rest as easy as we can. She fell quiet, lookin' at 'im. *The next days will tell the tale.* All the time she was holdin' his hand and rubbin' his hand and arm and around his face. I could see she was real troubled.

Right soon after that, Frank Atkins and Thelma rode in. Frank had his horse doctorin' bag and he went through the same motions that Miz Henderson had and he come up with the same story. He sed he'd best set the broken leg while Preacher was out, so it wouldn't hurt him. So he did that. I watched him and for sure it looked like he knowed what he was doin'.

Thelma took Miz Henderson in the house to get some rags to tie up the leg tight. I knowed about that from the War. That

was a good thing to do, to give Thelma something to do. She
was real worried if'n her Daddy was goin' to die. Tell the truth,
so was all of us. It shore didn't look too good, him layin' there,
just barely breathin'!

Right about then here come Betty Lou and Luke Jones in
the buggy. When she seen what had happened, Betty Lou near
come apart, thinkin' like Thelma that her Daddy was dyin'. Tell
the truth, I was real struck by how good Luke Jones was with
her, holdin' her hand, and such like. When she calmed down, he
looked Preacher over and sed he guessed we was right in what we
thought. We'd all just have to wait and see.

Then come three more buggys with folks from around.
Everybody looked Preacher over. Nobody had anything different
to say, but one woman said a good sign was that he had a good
color. Miz Henderson said that was so and that she hadn't noticed
it. I hadn't, neither. All this time, Preacher was still layin' where
he fell. They was talk about if'n he ought to be moved to the
house, but they figured now to wait 'til near dark. And maybe
not then.

Then the wait set in. The women folk went in the house and
rustled up some dinner. Frank Atkins and some men set with
Preacher while Luke Jones and me finished putting up the hay. I
worked in the loft and right away I seen what had happened.
There was one place to the left of the open place of the hay loft
that the timber had rotted away. Preacher had showed it to me
when I first started to sleep up there and I stayed away from
walkin' on it. I guess he didn't pay enough mind to it when he
was forking the hay. There it was, where he had fell through. I
guessed that he went feet first. That was why he broke his leg.
But I couldn't see any place from up there that he could of hit his
head. But anyway he did, and that was that.

So Luke Jones and me wound up the job of puttin' the hay
in the loft. He ast me if'n there was any more in the field. I said
there was, maybe one or two wagons. He said he'd get some
neighbors and them and him would help me get it in while it
was dry. He did just that and we got in the hay in the days to

come, afore it rained. I was much obliged to him for the offer. I couldn't of done it while it was still dry.

That started me thinkin' that Betty Lou was right. Luke Jones was a good man. That and the way he was so gentle with her. I figured that, unless there was trouble of some kind, he'd be a good husband to her and daddy to her youngun's. The picture of her with youngun's by him give me a jolt, but I knowed that was the way it was meant to be.

Well, things settled down that day. Luke Jones and me unloaded the hay. The women fixed some dinner. Somebody set with Preacher but he stayed the same. Thelma set with him most of that day after dinner. We all talked about it and decided what to do.

Betty Lou wanted to send for the doctor but that was hard to figure out. One come to Mount Airy now and then but the nearest one for sure was at a place called Winstum Salum. I never had heard of it. Frank Atkins said he'd see what he could do. He had to get back to his place to do chores but he'd come back tomorrow. Luke had to do the same. Betty Lou walked him out to his buggy and give him a good long good bye hug and kiss. Miz Henderson would stay a while. She'd be back tomorrow. A neighbor man and woman said they'd stay if'n we needed them. Betty Lou said much obliged but she guessed not. But she'd send Thelma if'n we did. They all left, sayin' they'd be back to help.

They talked more about if'n we ought to move 'im to the house, but figured it was best to let him lay there in the barn, covered up. Miz Henderson put some rags at his crotch, to catch the piss. She said not to worry about that, or if'n he messed his pants. The thing right now was not to move him.

We made a hay bed roll for me right by him and I'd sleep there of a night. She sed for me to hold his hand where him and me lay and to keep squeezin' it. She said that was so his brain would wake up from the squeezin' and when it woke up, he'd squeeze back. Well, I never heard of such a thing but it made sense to me and so I sed I'd do it. Thelma said she wanted to sleep by her Daddy and we sed she could, on his other side.

We did it that way for three days and nights. Miz Henderson would come the daytime and help Betty Lou and set by Preacher while I did what farm work there was to do, and split wood for the cookin' stove. Preacher and me had hauled in a lot of wood on our off days and the woodpile was good sized. But winter was comin' and I'd need to tend to that afore I left. That thought brought me up short 'cause I started to see that maybe I'd better not plan on goin' anywheres anytime soon. We'd have to see what happened next to Preacher.

We all tried to get him to take a drink of water from time to time. Sometimes it looked like he did and sometimes it just run down his face. Miz Henderson went on trying to feed him, too, with a little chicken soup and thin corn mush, but I couldn't see that he was takin' it. Keepin' him clean warn't no problem since he warn't puttin' anythin' in his body.

Frank Atkins come every day to see to his leg and put on clean rags. And on the third day after he fell, he moaned when Frank was tendin' to his leg. Miz Henderson was standin' by and started in cryin'. That was the first sign, she said, that Preacher's brain was wakin' up. Then there was another sign of that. That night, in the middle of the night, when I squeezed his hand, he squeezed back.

Well I tell you, it was all I could do from wakin' up Betty Lou and Thelma to tell them. But I reckoned it'd keep 'til mornin'. By mornin', he was squeezin' back about half the time. When I told the girls, they both started cryin' and Miz Henderson too when she drove up in her buggy.

I don't think they budged from his side all day and kept squeezin' his hand and rubbin' his face and his arms like, as Miz Henderson said, they was wakin' up his brain. And they said they talked to him and sang to him the whole day. I believe it, but I was out doin' chores. There warn't no more change that day 'cept that Miz Henderson was for sure that he swallered some water and corn mush. And the next day was the same but for more women folk neighbors come with vittles and help in the house and to set with him.

Then on the night after that, I'd dropped off to sleep when he woke me up, squeezing my hand. *Where in tarnation am I?*

I just nearly whooped when I heard him say that. *Why Preacher Wood you are layin' on a bed of hay in yore barn!*

Luther, is that you?

Preacher, it's me all right.

My leg hurts awful bad.

It's got a right to. You fell and broke it.

He laughed. *What'd I do that for?*

I laughed, from more of a feelin' than anythin' funny. *Bein' pure onry, I guess. You want to talk more or go back to sleep, it bein' the middle of the night and all.*

One more question. Why am I holdin' hands with you?

I laughed. *'Cause I'm here and Miz Henderson ain't. You want a drink of water afore you go back to sleep?*

I don't know. I do and I don't. If'n I move to get to the dipper, it'll hurt my leg.

How about I wet a rag good and wet and let you suck on that?

That's what we did and he went back to sleep, holdin' my hand. I tell you, I was right uneasy he'd not wake up again, but he did. I woke up about daylight, still holdin' his hand. I squeezed and he squeezed back. *You awake?*

I reckon so. He was quiet. *How long'v I been out?*

Three days, mebbe four. You fell through the hay loft. You recollect doin' that?

Maybe. You was pitchin' hay up and I was stackin'. Ain't that right? I recollect thinkin' the rotten place in the floor was about here some place.

Then you must of stepped on it and fell through.

He was quiet agin. *I got a broken leg?*

Yep. Frank Atkins set it while you was out like a light.

He give the first belly laugh of his'n I'd heard. *Hells bells, he cain't fix a man. He fixes a horse.*

Well, that may be so but he did it. He'll be here afore dinner to check you out.

Miz Henderson been here?

All the time. Looks like she's stuck on you.
Yes. Well. Can you get these rags out of my crotch so's I can piss?
I did that and we rolled him on his side so he could piss away
from his bed roll. *This is how I did you when you have the fevers.*
'Cept you didn't have a broken leg that's hurtin' awful bad. We got
him turned back and as easy as he could be.

By that time the rooster was crowin' and it was turnin'
daylight. And here come Thelma and her dogs. And he called her
name and her and the dogs was all over him. They was prob'ly
mashing on his leg but he didn't say anything. Then here come
Betty Lou and it was all over again. Then here come Miz
Henderson and she was beside herself when she saw how good
he was. I told the girls could I have something to eat and they
caught on and we left him with her.

Frank Atkins come about dinner time. He was for sure real
pleased to see Preacher woke up. Him and Miz Henderson looked
at Preacher's leg again and sed it looked all right to them. They
said it would be the thing to do to get him moved to the house.
So me on one side and Frank on the other we got him to hobble
over there and set him on the porch, with his leg stickin' out
straight. The break was below the knee but Frank had put the
sticks to hold it straight from his ankle to up around the hip.

By that time Thelma had told her daddy all about what had
happened and how she rode Ole Mule to get help and all that.
Preacher told her how proud he was of her and that it didn't
surprise him one bit that she could do such a thing.

Everybody left well afore sundown so's to get home in good
season. Afore they all left, they made a plan. Preacher would
sleep in his bed with me beside his bed on the floor 'til he was up
to a buggy ride. Then he'd go to the Henderson place and she'd
take care of him. Frank Atkins could see to his leg there bettern'
here, since the Henderson place was closer to him.

The next day, after I'd helped him piss, Preacher and me had
a little talk. *You think you want to go to the Henderson place?*
Yeees (he sed it long drawn out) *I do.*
You figure you know what that'll lead to?

I reckon I do. She's said she'd marry up with me anyway. This'll be on the road to that, I reckon.

Looks like Betty Lou has set her cap for Luke Jones.

It does, don't it? He looked at me. *You ain't gonna do anything about that, are you?*

I reckon not. Her and me have talked some about all that. I figure this is best and I reckon she does too.

Lemme say this. It won't do her no good to leave her by herself with you. I started to say something. *Lemme finish. You're a young man and you've been stuck on her all along. I know it. I seen it in yore eyes as you watch her. Maybe she's halfway stuck on you. But it won't come out right that way. So you and her can stay here after I go to the Henderson place so long as Thelma is here. But Miz Henderson says there's talk of a school startin' up at Flat Lick and Thelma ought to go. So when she comes to the Henderson place, Betty Lou'll have to go or I'll have to come back, makes no matter. You got anything to say about all that?*

I knowed well and good what he was talkin' about. We'd have to do what he said. *No, I guess not.*

All right. Next thing to say. This farm needs farmin'. I cain't do it now. Will you stay to do it, maybe 'til spring?

I figured that was gonna come up. *Lemme have a day to think about it.*

Fair enough.

Well, he was layin' it on the line, all right enough. And I figured he was right about me and Betty Lou. Left alone in this house, one of us was bound to start somethin' we'd be right sorry for. And that somebody was bound to be me. Hells bells, I was already dreamin' about her and how her bosums would feel in my hands and 'gainst my chest. And how it'd feel if'n she'd spread her legs and let me in. It was enough to drive a man crazy. So I knowed he was right.

All day long and into the night I thought about what he said about stayin' on for the winter. On the side of goin' was that all of 'em had a place to go but me. Frank never said yet when Maybelle was comin' back from Charlotte. Maybe she warn't comin' back. But even if'n she did, it wouldn't amount to much more'n a roll in Preacher's bed with me oncet a week. Last time we did it she seemed like she half way didn't want to. And I shore didn't want to marry up with her! That'd be real trouble all around. So I wondered what there was for me in stayin'.

On the side of stayin', it come down to waitin' some longer afore I could get on the road to Stewart County. I guessed I warn't in all that of a gol danged hurry. I'd have a place to live with nobody botherin' me. Like as not, Preacher would see to it that I had enough vittles to eat. I warn't much of a cook but I shore could get by. And like as not Miz Henderson would have me to dinner from time to time. Mebbe Betty Lou would. There shore was work on the farm to keep me busy and maybe out of trouble, and I liked to farm.

Truth of it all was that I was still hung up on how I was goin' to leave when I went. Ole Mule looked to me like he was real happy here and I didn't know if'n he could make it over the mountains, much less to Stewart County. If'n I didn't take him along I was goin' to have to walk. And right then I didn't want to start out walkin'. That by itself was on the side of stayin'. If'n I stayed for a while longer, maybe I could figure somethin' out.

The next mornin' I went and found Ole Mule. *Ole Mule, do you like it here on this place? I hope you do, 'cause it looks like we'll be stayin' on a while more. We would leave right now but that'd be winter on the road and I don't think we want to do that. And Preacher bein' hurt and all, he cain't do the chores here and he asked me if'n I would. So I just thought I'd tell you what was in the air to be settled. I'm goin' to go in the house now, and tell him.*

So I did. He was real glad to hear that I'd stay on, like he said, 'til he got on his feet again. And he said he'd put me up with vittles and we'd go havers on the new calves been born since I started in helpin' him farm. It'd be up to me to get 'em sold, round about in this part of the country or takin' 'em to Mount Airy. It'd be up to me to get the cows to the bull at the right time. I said that sounded like a fair and square deal to me, and we shook on it. After he had something to eat he went back to sleep. He said his head hurt awful bad.

Midmorning here come Miz Henderson and Luke Jones. I went about my morning chores, Thelma and the dogs comin' along. Betty Lou and Luke was down by the pond. It looked like they were talkin' up a storm. Miz Henderson was fixin' dinner and watchin' over Preacher. After we et, we all set around Preacher's bed. He laughed. *It looks like you are all settin' up with a dead man. Well, I ain't dead yet, by a long shot. And to show it, I'm mighty proud to tell you all that Miz Henderson says she'll think about marryin' up with me.*

He'd already told us that but I guessed he liked to say it. All the time she was holdin' his hand and smilin' at him like he was the only man in the county. *But she says she wants to be sure what she's gettin' into, so she wants me to come to her house 'til I get back on my feet.* He looked up at her, with that shit eatin' grin of his. *Ain't that the case?* She nodded, smilin' at him. *So I'll go over there as soon as you all figure I can travel.*

Then Betty Lou reached over and took Luke's hand. *Well, Daddy, you stole our thunder but Luke and me have somethin' to say, too. We want to get married as soon as you can do the job.* And she smiled at both Luke and her Daddy at the same time. I guess both Luke and her Daddy had already talked about it. *Is that alright with you, Daddy?*

It's mighty alright with me. I'll be proud to do the job, as you put it, just as soon as I can get my leg and my head straight at the same time. Everybody laughed but I saw Thelma lookin' like she was goin' to cry. So I took her hand. *Well, Thelma and me are right glad for you all. Thelma here will have three home places, one with Miz Henderson, one with Betty Lou and one here with me.* I didn't rightly know what I was talkin' about, but somethin' had to be said to make Thelma feel like she warn't bein' left out.

Luke smiled a real good smile at Thelma. *You purty girl are always welcome at our house. I never had a big girl like you in my life, and I'd shore like to do that.*

So it was settled and that's the way it went. First off, in a day or two, Luke and Betty Lou and me made a kind of stretcher like I used in the War. We got Preacher in it, and carried him to the wagon and laid him down in the wagon bed propped up on two feather beds and all the quilts they had to keep him from joltin'. Luke drove the team and did a real good job of tryin' to keep away from the rough places in the tack. Going slow, it took us up to two hours to get to the Henderson house. He moaned and groaned a lot on the way but he made it.

Miz Henderson was at the door and showed us where to put him on the bed in the front room. I could see that the house was a lot like Preacher's 'cept maybe the rooms was bigger. And she had closed up the fireplace and put in another cook stove in the front room. It's a wonder more people didn't do that. Everybody knows a lot of the heat from a fireplace goes up the chimley. That was one of the first things we did when Narcissa and me set up housekeeping on the Cherry place. As soon as we had the money to buy the stove.

It looked to me like that Miz Henderson had money. I never heard anybody say anything about a Mr. Henderson or if'n she had a family or where she'd come from or anything like that. But she was shore stuck on Preacher and she was always kindly to the rest of us, and that was all that mattered. She took to Thelma all along and it looked to me like Thelma was gonna have a good mama at last.

Like I say there was always a good spread at her house for dinner and I recollect for one thing her blackeyed peas and side pork. I never tasted anything so good in my life. Preacher lived up to his word about giving me vittles and I had all I needed of dried beans and side pork and the like as long as I was living on his place. Him and her would show up with a buggy full. Later on, she told me she was goin' to open a store on her place. I took it to mean that was tied in with what she had on her table.

Anyway, once we got Preacher moved, Luke took over some with helpin' with Preacher. I was much obliged for that. Luke's place was closer to Miz Henderson's and he could come and go

easy like. Miz Henderson said he'd better get on his feet as soon
as he could. When Frank Atkins thought he could, Luke got
him a crutch from somewhere so Preacher could hobble around.
I'd seen many of them crutches in the war. Preacher got real good
with it after a while.

Next thing I knowed, Betty Lou and Luke Jones got married
up. Preacher did it, settin' down, and Miz Henderson and me
was the witness. Thelma said Luke wanted to buy Betty Lou a
new dress for the weddin', but Betty Lou wouldn't have it. She
looked purty enough to me in that dress with the flowers she
wore that first time we went to Flat Lick church. I tell you I felt
mighty sorry for my self when I watched her drive away with
him. But I'd made my bed and now I had to lay in it.

With Betty Lou married and off, Thelma went to stay at
Miz Henderson's with her and Preacher most of the time. Money
was found for the schoolteacher for her. Maybe Miz Henderson
paid it. I don't know. But Thelma was real glad to be able to get
some schoolin'. I was real proud for her and wisht it was me. I
don't mean by that, it was me instead of her. I mean I wisht I
could do it too.

One thing I did when Thelma left was to ask if'n she'd leave
her dog Skunk with me on the farm. I was startin' to see how it
was goin' to be on that farm with nobody else around. A dog
would be a lot of company, if'n that's the right word. She said I
could and by jakes when she left with Miz Henderson in the
buggy she told Dog to come along and she told Skunk to stay
and he did. She had a real way with animals. She allus liked Ole
Mule and I told her she could ride him some. Maybe she could
ride 'im to school, when I got so I didn't need him for farmin'!

I have to tell you that first night and the day after everybody
had gone but the dog Skunk, I warn't ready for what I was feelin'.
Lookin' back, it was the first time in my life that I was by myself,
not still at home or travelin' somewheres. All them days on Ole
Mule I was sick and mostly out of my head and didn't care if'n I

made it or not. This here was somethin' else. It was like I had a place of my own and I had to make some kind of sense of what I was goin' to have to do.

A hour afore sundown me and Skunk went over to the lot to talk to Ole Mule. *Ole Mule this here is something I don't know anything about. I never lived in a house on a place with just you and Skunk to talk to. I'm goin' to have to study this to see what I can do. You and Skunk'll have to help me. I figure I can do it, if'n you and Skunk give me some help.* Ole Mule never let on if'n he heard me or not but Skunk set there listenin' to me talk and he wagged his tail a time or two. I figured that was as much as I'd get. So Skunk and me went back to the house. I shut up the chickens and didn't go milk. I figured one night without milkin' wouldn't hurt.

So I stirred up the fire and et my beans and corn pone in the front room. Skunk laid by the fireplace. Preacher wouldn't let the dogs sleep in the house but Preacher was gone and I was in the house and I meant to let Skunk stay in if'n he wanted to. It turned out he didn't, and when I went out to piss afore I went to bed, he went too and stayed out. It felt real quare to go to bed in Preacher's bed but I got over that feelin', and went to sleep right away.

The next morning, I set on the porch with Skunk and went over in my mind what I had to do. One good thing, the hay was in. I was much obliged to them that had helped me. Truth to tell, I hadn't never paid much mind to the neighbors. Some of 'em I guess I'd seen at church and at the play parties but that was all. It looked like I'd have to do better than that if'n I was goin' to be able to work with 'em more. And it looked like I'd have to do that.

For one thing, I hadn't paid any mind to any of the cows that was bullin', and getting' them to the bull in time. I went last time with Preacher and I knowed that neighbor was named Hopkins. And I knowed Preacher and him had said every third calf was his'n, as payment for the bull. I had to study that more. Maybe I'd ride Ole Mule over to the Hopkins place in a day or two to talk to him some.

I figured I could do the fall plowin' all right enough, if'n I knowed what else Preacher wanted plowed sides the garden. Prob'ly that'd be the big corn field on the far side. First off, I'd have to wait 'til a hard frost or two afore I could gather in the corn. And that, I had to say, was the biggest job I faced, doin' it alone. Likely I could use some help to do that.

I looked at the wood pile. It warn't low but it shore wouldn't see me through the winter. So I'd best talk to Preacher about where in the wood lot he wanted me to go. Sawin' a big log is a two man job. So there was that.

I've got to tell you that right that morning it looked like more than I could do. My time farmin' was back in Stewart County, more as a boy than a man, and what little I'd done here with Preacher. He'd called the shots and I'd follered through as best I could. Now it was goin' to be up to me to call the shots and to do the foller through too. And on top of that, do enough house keepin' to get me by. I would shore miss havin' a woman to help out that way.

The next day or so, me and Ole Mule and Skunk took stock around the place. We rode the fences and fixed them that had fallen down. We rode around the cow pasture and looked over the cows and calves. The bull calves would have to be cut if'n I was goin' to keep 'em or else keep one for a bull.

I figured Preacher would say to cull the herd to eight and keep two of the heifer calves and get rid of the rest. Swap with the neighbors or take 'em to Mount Airy to sell. I couldn't tell right then if'n any of the cows was carryin' a calf. One day I left Ole Mule and rode Jake. It turned out he was a good one to ride. I could make do with him if'n I wanted to let Thelma have Ole Mule sometimes. It turned out that Jake was real good at snakin' firewood.

In the house I looked around the kitchen and found what I needed to cook my dried beans, taters and cornbread. I figured I'd cook twicet a week and warm it up 'tween times. Weather was goin' to be cool enough that the beans and taters would keep. One thing, I was low on side meat and I wanted side meat for my beans. It was a real good thing there was plenty of salt and black pepper and pepper sauce. All that and sweet milk or buttermilk would do me, as long as a cow stayed fresh, I'd have to be sure to milk every day to keep one fresh. And I'd have to get some butter from somewhere. I didn't know beans about makin' butter.

Well, I went to see Preacher and him and me talked about what I made of things. He was feelin' fair to middlin' but he still had the bad pain in his head sometimes and he had dizzy spells. Miz Henderson said that was to be expected and 'twarn't nothin' to worry about. I didn't know if'n she knowed what she was talkin' about or was just puttin' on a good front. However it was, she wouldn't let him walk by hisself even when he got so he could on the crutch, for fear he'd fall again.

Anyway, he said I was thinkin' all right and that he'd rustle up some help for me if'n I needed it. She had cooked up a passel of vittles for me to take home, and I et more than my fill while I was there. She said for me to come back for dinner any time I could, that the table was always ready for me.

Thelma was goin' to start school in a week or so and she was tickled pink about that. Miz Henderson had made her a new dress to wear the first day. She said she'd take Thelma the first day or so in the buggy. Maybe Preacher could when he was feelin' better. Thelma said she didn't mind walkin'. It warn't but two miles to the school house. I told her agin she could have Ole Mule when I didn't need him. Miz Henderson didn't have much of a farm, but she had a horse lot and a stable. And a few cows for milkin' and a good chicken yard. There was two old geese about the place that she said was her watch dogs. Them geese shore made a lot of racket if'n anybody got close. Now, Dog was there, too.

It all turned out the way I had figured, mostly. I worked in the wood lot, Jake and me, and hauled in enough wood for two winters, I figured. Most of it was dead or near dead, so it'd burn fast. But it not bein' green I didn't need any help on a two man saw. Preacher come through with the corn pickin'.

It turned out that a bunch of neighbors had done it that way anyway so's I just took his place. Not long after he fell we started havin' frosts and in a week or so, a hard frost made it time to pick the corn. So all the men would go from place to place to pick the corn. All but one had a team left from the soldiers. Him that didn't, we used another neighbor's team and wagon. It was a good crop, mostly. By the time we was done, the corn cribs was full to runnin' over. The fellar at the grist mill would be glad to know that, since he took his turn of corn or meal, whichever he wanted, for every turn he ground. I allus thought that would be a good way to make a livin'.

When we was done gatherin' corn, I did my own shockin' and turned the cows into the corn field to take what was left. In the middle of that, a old cow birthed a calf. Skunk found it one mornin' we was out. It was a real puny little calf. I don't think it would of made it if'n Skunk hadn't found it and if'n the old mother cow didn't know what she was about. She was one I had marked to cull. I hated to do it but you have to cull out the old to make room for the young to keep your herd good. Uncle Gray learned me that. And Preacher went by that too. Afore she was culled, she give us a lot of sweet milk. There for a while I had so much sweet milk that I give it to the hogs.

Well, after the frosts had set in Mr. Hopkins come by one day to say there'd be a hog killin' over by him and I was welcome to come help and bring a hog for the killin'. He told me the day it was to be and how to get there. Come to his place and foller the path by the crick was the short cut. Bring my best butcher knife, two, ifn' I had 'em. We walked over to the hog pen but couldn't see but two. The rest of 'em was up in the oak trees. He pointed out a good lookin' shoat, said he'd be a good one if'n I could catch him and get a rope around his leg. And he left. I went over to get Thelma the next day. Seemed like she was awful good with critters, pigs too. I rode Jake and put Ole Mule on the lead so she'd have a way back home. She was livin' then over at Miz Henderson's.

We got back to the place and she got several ears of corn in a basket and started in to call the hogs. *Soooey! Sooey!* I was struck by her call. It sounded more like a woman than a girl. Here they come running, all but the boar. There was two sows, and two shoats and two pigs born in the summer. She got in the pig pen and talked to 'em like I talked to Ole Mule. I looked around in the barn and couldn't find anything that would do to lead a hog to the killin', it bein' the better part of three mile, I figured. Her and me stood there thinkin' about how to do it. *Only thing I can think of is for me to walk with 'em, givin' 'em some corn as I go. You come on ahind on Jake, if 'n one of 'em starts to get away.*

You thinkin' about takin' the two of 'em?

I guess so. They'd come better if 'n there was the two of 'em.

You figure they'd follow you?

If 'n I had the corn, they would.

Thelma, girl, you are gettin' mighty smart on me! She grinned but like her callin' the hogs the grin was more of a woman than a girl. She'd growed up a lot since I come to the Wood place last spring.

Well, that's what we did. They was gonna kill on a Monday so I went and got her Saturday afore and she stayed at my house, I mean Preacher's house. And we took them two shoats over to the place on Sunday. It took us the better part of the day. Hogs don't walk fast and seemed like one of 'em was allus wanderin' off even if 'n Thelma had the corn. Once we got there, there was a pen for the hogs to be kilt and Thelma led them two in there nice as you please. I made her ride Jake back to the Preacher's place so's she could go home on Ole Mule, and I walked.

Next day I was up real early to get there to help with the killin'. When I stood there, lookin' at what was happenin' I recollected the time I'd went to a hog killin' with one of the farmers I had hired out to as a boy. What I recollected most was the pigs squealing, the big black scalding pot, and the smell of the innards. What we had here was all that and then some.

It looked like they was set up to kill, dress, and hang maybe ten hogs, so it was a big set-up. I never seen such a big scalding pot with a pulley over it to drop in the dressed pig. There must of been 20 men there, workin' to heat the band. The smell of the pig guts was mighty strong. Truth to tell, it brought to mind a battle in the War, all but these was pigs and not soldiers. I asked where could I work and a man told me to go help with the hoist. I didn't really know what a hoist was but they made room for me to pull on the double rope to lift the pig up after it was gutted and into the scaldin' kettle. Down in the kettle, then up for the scrapin' then down and up 'til the hair was mostly scraped off.

The scrapin' was hard work. I did that for a while, too. I'd forgot to bring my butcher knife but a woman give hers to me and I spent some time cuttin' up the meat. That was hard work too. We stopped for dinner in a hurry then back at it. Well, by sundown we had all ten hogs hung, with two more butchered up partly. Everybody had to get home to do chores so we left 'em hangin' there.

The next day was mainly butcherin' so's to hang the meat to smoke. I was thinkin' about what to do about that when the fellar that owned the place came up. *You ever worked a killin' afore?*

Not since I was a boy. Man I hired out to had one oncet. I don't recollect much about what to do.

Well, sir, you did a good job for a greenhorn about it.

I'm obliged to everybody showin' me how.

Preacher tell you how him and me do this?

No sir, I ain't talked to him about it. Did I do something wrong?

He shook his head and grinned. *No, you ain't done nothing wrong. I'm just talkin' about how him and me make a deal with the hog killin'. It goes like this. He brings two hogs, and you done that. We all do the killin' and the hanging. And I smoke his meat in my smoke house for half the meat. You pro'bly know, he ain't got a smoke house. Never did have one. That sound right to you?*

That sounds right to me. I had been studyin' about what I was gonna do with all that fresh meat.

I got some good smoked side meat you can take home with you today. You come back again tomorry and we'll finish up. If 'n you're short on salt, I'll let you have some of that too.

Well, that's what we did. I figured out the man's name was Atkins, a cousin to Frank. Next time I saw Preacher I told him all about the killin' and what Mr. Atkins had said. He was much obliged I'd gone ahead and worked in his place and that Mr. Atkins was a fair minded man to deal with. Afterward I found out that Mr. Atkins had come by to see Preacher and Miz Henderson and brung some fresh meat.

So it turned out that I had all the hog meat I wanted all that winter. It was mighty good. Miz Atkins and the women made sausage and give me some of that. They ground up the meat and salted it and put in some sage from somebody's garden and it was real good. Made good gravy too. I figured I could live on that and fried eggs. Only thing was, at the time, I couldn't make good biscuits. Miz Henderson could make real good biscuits.

I saw Frank Atkins at the hog killin'. First time I'd seen him for some time since Preacher had gone to the Henderson place. We said howdy and talked about the hog killin'. *What are you doin' with yourself now on Preacher's place by yoreself?*

Well sir, things is real quiet. It's just the mules, the dog Skunk, and me. But we get by.

I been thinkin' about somethin' for you. You want to hear it?

I nodded, laughin'. *I'm real surprized you been thinkin' about me.* I was quiet, not knowin' what to say next. *I figured you was maybe mad at me after what happened with yore purty daughter Maybelle and me.*

Well, I was, for a while. But I know a little about women and I figured it was as much her as you. That's why I sent her to her mama's down to Charlotte.

She gettin' along good down there?

I reckon so. I ain't heard but oncet.

She shore is some woman.

She is that. Takes after her mama, I guess. He looked sharply at me. *Maybelle tell you about her mama?*

I nodded. *She said somethin' about that. But not much.*

Well, anyway, that ain't what I wanted to talk with you about. Let's go set on that log so we can hear ourselves talk. I'm a little deef and I've got trouble with all this here noise. We did that. I couldn't figure out what he was gonna say. Maybe he was goin' to tell me it was time to move on, but that warn't any of his business. So we set there a minute while he thought about what he was gonna say. *Well, you know my business partly is in raisin' horses.* I nodded. *My brood mares and the stud horse is turnin' out some good colts. Problem is right now I got too many yearlin's to green break than I can do by myself. Maybelle did a lot of that for me and she ain't here. And she ain't likely to come back, leastwise any time soon. So, I figured maybe you could help me do that. I'd pay you for yore time. And I figured it might be a pleasure to you to do it.*

Well, I almost clapped my hands like Preacher did when he was satisfied. *Mr. Atkins, I ain't heard such a good idea in a coon's age! I'd be right proud to do that. But it'll take some figurin'. Right off, you'd have to learn me how to do it. After that, we'd have to figure out how to get me to the horses with time to do the breakin'. I got chores to do on Preacher's place, and I got to watch over it, and all that.*

He nodded. *Yeah, I thought about that. Let's take the learnin' first. Main thing about breakin' a horse is how you come up to it and make over it. I've watched you with yore Ole Mule. Any man that talks to a old mule like that, he's crazy in the head or elsewise he knows how to come up to a mule! No doubt in my mind you can do it. You'll get into it as you go along. Now, as to you gettin' to the horses. Let's figure if'n this will work. I figure you can get away from Preacher's place for two days at a time to start with. You come over to my place after chores one day, work with me that day and the next and go back that evenin'. I figure I got one, maybe two that will be easy to halter break. We can lead them to yore place and the other four will follow along. I can do the leadin' and you foller along to do the herdin'.*

He laughed. *Maybe we'll bring along Thelma. If'n she can herd hogs, I bet she can herd horses!* I laughed and allowed as how she could, at that. *Anyway, oncet they are at yore place, you can take yore time at the rest of the job. Go at it slow and easy. Best way to do it with the yearlings, anyway. Well, what do you think about that?*
I think a lot of that, Mr. Atkins. I'd be proud to see if'n I can do it. I figure I can, with some learnin' from you. And, like you said, it'd make it a whole lot easy if'n we can get 'em to my place. If'n you don't change yore mind, let's do it!
Good. I won't change my mind. So it's a deal. And he held out his hand to shake and I shook it. We said I'd come over to his place first chance I got and we'd see how it would work out. Anyway, I went over there three, four times. First off I watched Frank work with 'em, then I started to with him watchin' and learnin' me how. I guess he liked what I did. He said I had a natch'ral born feel for the horses and that I'd do good with 'em. So long as I didn't hurry it, take it a step at a time. He said that was when a lot of men went wrong in workin' with a horse.

I never had much to do with a horse afore then. Everybody said they was smarter'n a mule but I took that with a grain o' salt, as Aunt Polly would say. To my eye, Ole Mule was real smart and a horse would have to get up purty early in the mornin' to beat him. But, when I started in with Frank's horses, I saw some things I never knowed afore. A horse is real smart. They recollect what you've done yestiday. And if'n you do it right, it don't take more'n two or three times and they've got it down pat. Leastwise that was so with Frank's horses. Since then I've knowed some otherwise. But that's another story.

Another thing with a horse is that they are real nervous. One of Frank's horses would git scared to death at a grasshopper. She was a real purty mare and she saddle broke real easy but you never knowed what was gonna set her off. Another thing was they was mighty partic'lar about what they et. I tried to feed 'em some of last year's corn but nosiree bob, they wouldn't touch it.

It had to be this year's corn. So Jake got the old, Ole Mule too when he was there, and them horses got the new.

Anyway, it worked out the way he said. We got one of 'em halter broke real easy. I rode Jake over and him and the halter broke one led the way for the rest of 'em to come along. It was a sight to see, that mule leadin' a herd of six horses. Me and Frank got a good laugh out of that. That must have been a week or two afore Christmas. I had 'em at my place for maybe two months. Bein' it was winter, there warn't much farmin' to do, so I spent time with the horses.

When they was all saddle broke, I told Frank he could come and see how they looked to him. So he showed up one day, and I put 'em through their paces. *Luther, boy, you done real good with them horses. I'm real proud of you. Good a job of breakin' as I ever seen.*

Well, sir, I'm right glad you think so. I had a good teacher. You shore do know a lot about horses. And I'm much obliged to you for bein' able to do it. It brung me a lot of satisfaction. I had learned that word from Miz Henderson.

He reached in his saddle bag and brought out a pouch and handed it to me. *Here's something for yore trouble in workin' with my horses. Hit was a big help to me.*

I thankee but you don't need to do it. I did it for the learnin'. Now that warn't exactly so. I hadn't said anything to him about it, but I was hopin' he'd pay me some. I was tryin' to save my gold pieces 'til I got back to Stewart County and I figured I was goin' to need some money to get there! The pouch had some heft to it so I figured it warn't paper money. Leastwise I hoped not. I figured Confederate money was not worth the paper it was writ on. Everybody was sayin' that about Confederate money. *I'm much obliged to you.*

Come over here to the settin' log. I want to hear what you have to say about my horses.

What do you want to know?

Anythin' you can think of that I can tell somebody wantin' to buy a horse. So I started out, talkin' about every horse, tellin' what I knowed or thought I knowed about it. Two of 'em was well broke and couldn't cause anybody any trouble to ride. I recollect one was a dapple gray mare. I told him I figured she should bring top dollar. He nodded. Another, I recollect, was real feisty but was good under the saddle if'n you knowed what you was about. I told him about the one that was skittish about a grasshopper. He laughed and said he'd not forget that. *You ain't said nothin' about the young stud horse.*

Well sir he's a lot to talk about. He must be the purtiest horse I ever seen, all black with a white stockin'. I call him Thunder. Without any doubt, he ain't the easiest horse to ride. You got to let him know who's boss or he'll get away from you. It's happened to him and me more'n oncet.

I can see how that's the case. He shook his head. *Trouble is, I don't know what to do with him. I already got a good stud horse and he won't take to havin' another one around the place.* He was lookin' at the horse I called Thunder, shakin' his head. *I don't know what to do with him. I figure you'll just have to take him off'n my hands.*

I looked sharp at him. *Mr. Atkins, you don't know what you're sayin'! That's a right fine horse. He'd bring a lot of money in to the right buyer.*

He kept on shakin' his head. *No, Luther, I can't take him. You'll have to do it.*

I started to laugh. *Mr. Atkins, you are touched in the head, givin' that horse away.*

No, Luther, I've made up my mind. He turned and looked at me, with what the soldiers used to call a shit eatin' grin on his face, like the one Preacher had sometimes.

Shitfire, Mr. Atkins, I never thought of doin' that! That warn't so either. I knowed when I started in workin' with Thunder that I wanted him real bad. But I figured there was no way in hell I would get him. *At least let me give you back the money you paid me.*

He shook his head at me. *No, I cain't let you do that. You worked for that money, fair and square. I want you to have that*

*horse you call Thunder aside from that. I never had a boy. If 'n I
had I'd of give him that horse.* He was lookin' at the horse. *And
'sides, that's what Maybelle would want, if'n she was here. She
thought a lot of you. But I guess you knowed that.* Then he turned
to me. *Now you go saddle up Thunder and show me what he can
do and we'll take the rest of 'em back to my place.* And that's how
I come to have the big black I called Thunder.

Well, we drove the other horses back to his place, him on his
mare and me on the big black stud horse that was now mine.
Lookin' back, I figure I was a lucky man in them years. But of all
the luck I had, maybe the bestest was the gift from Frank Atkins
of the horse Thunder. The little red mare took me to the War.
Ole Mule got me away from it. And Thunder carried me back to
Stewart County. That's the short of it. Anyway, I was much
beholden to Frank Atkins for what he'd done, and I told him so
near ever' time I saw him. On about the third time, he laughed
at me and said he didn't want to hear any more about it!

Ridin' back to the house the day he give me Thunder, it hit
me of a sudden that nothin' was holdin' me back from getting'
on the road agin to Stewart County. I was feelin' good, with no
more fevers, and no more dreams. The Wood family was settlin'
down, and I didn't owe them anythin'. I'd done the farmin' for
Preacher and the horse trainin' for Frank. I could go now, any
time. I guessed I'd do that, first good signs of spring.

Thinkin' about what I've said about that year at the Wood
place, it seems like nothin' havin' to do with the War ever happened
there. It did and it didn't. To start with, the Wood place and the
places around it all the way to Mount Airy, was out of the way.
There warn't even a good road that passed along that people used
a lot.

Mount Airy was the closest town and it was a good day's
ride, maybe more if'n you had a wagon load or was leadin' stock.
I never did know how many farmin' places there was around
there. One time I counted maybe forty people at church one

Sunday. That was a day with dinner on the ground. There was
maybe that many at that first play party I went to. And there was
a big crowd of men at the hog killin'. Mostly it seemed like
Preacher's neighbors was three, four, five miles away. From time
to time somebody at church had been to Mount Airy. Oncet I
saw somebody or heard 'em talkin' that they'd been to Asheville
or Ashvul, as they called it. That's how we'd got word that the
War was over or President Lincoln was shot. Somebody been
somewhere, come back to tell it.

We heard tell of gangs goin' around the country, causin' a lot
of trouble. That was the cause of our gettin' out all the guns and
powder and knowin' how to shoot. But we never had any trouble
like that. Only oncet do I recollect Thelma sayin' it looked like
somebody had been campin' over the hill on the other side of the
place.

I recollect some news at church about soldier boys. Two
families said theirs was come home but I never saw'em. Two or
three more said they got word theirs was kilt. Must have been
more than that that said they got no word. After that first time
at church when Preacher told everybody about me comin' to his
place, only one old man ever said any more about it. He wanted
to know more about the cavalry than the fightin' at Richmond.
That was plenty good with me. I didn't want to talk about
Richmond.

When I first got to the Wood place, it seemed like nobody
had much to eat. And there warn't any way to get more less'n
you raised it yoreself. Nobody had any money worth anything
so if'n you had somethin' to sell, there warn't any way for sure to
get yore money's worth.

Many a time that year I thought I better give Preacher one of
my gold pieces but I never had to. He always come up with
something. As time went on, that year, things got better. Him
and me took calves over by Mount Airy and he got paid in Union
money, he called it. And he traded for dried beans and salt. Salt
was real hard to come by. We got by with no sugar. He traded
some chickens for sorghum 'lasses. One thing we never had was

lamp oil. They had candles but everybody went to bed at dark anyway. Only time I ever saw lit lamps was at the play parties at night. I had no notion where that oil come from.

The men folk could trade for pants and shirts. I guess they come from off of dead soldiers in the War. And boots. And drawers, most times. That warn't no worry to me. I was wearin' Eddie's. But the womenfolk had it worse. They wore old dresses down to the rag tag end of it. One time Preacher and Miz Henderson went to Mount Airy and got some flour sacks. Her and the women folks made aprons and skirts that went over a old dress. Boots was a worry for them.

I guess I forgot back there to say that Preacher and Miz Henderson got married. It was a little afore Christmas time and they went to Mount Airy to do it. Thelma stayed with Betty Lou and Luke. Preacher had been gettin' better all the time and had gone back to preachin'. I give him a hard time one time that if'n he could preach he shorely could make Miz Henderson a honest woman. He laughed and said he reckoned he could. He was still walkin' with a stick but it maybe was out of pure habit, more'n a need. I figured he liked to do it. And Miz Henderson claimed he was forgetful. I couldn't tell if'n it was so or if'n she was givin' him a bad time. Maybe it was both.

She was still talkin' about runnin' a store out of the front room at their house. Said she figured she could do it come spring. And she laughed, said it'd give Preacher somethin' to do besides preach. Nobody said anything about what was goin' to be done with his place after I left for Stewart County. I figured maybe he didn't want to farm no more. He never said and I never asked.

Well, when Frank give me the black horse Thunder I couldn't hardly stand it. I rode him over the next day to show Preacher and he was real proud for me. He said he never saw a better horse in all his born days. And for me to pick the best saddle and bridle he had in the barn, that no worn out saddle would be fittin' for that black horse. And Miz Henderson come around the house with the purtiest saddle blanket I ever saw. I was near to tears at that. About that time here come Thelma from school on Ole

Mule. She was tickled over Thunder but more so when I said Ole Mule was hers to keep. I'd already told Ole Mule about him and Thelma but I told him again and said much obliged to him for gettin' me to the Wood place. Bein' so proud of Thunder I meant to ride him that Sunday to church but I never got that far.

I got back from Preacher's that day and there standin' in front of the house was a man with a gun aimed at me. *Don't come any further. What do you want here?*

I could ask you the same. What are you doin' on this place, drawin' a gun on me?

I'm drawin' a gun 'cause this is my Daddy's place and I don't know who you are or what you're doin' here.

You must of got the wrong place. This is the Preacher Wood place and he had two sons and they was both kilt in the war.

I'm askin' you again, who are you and what are you doin' here?

Name's Luther Morris and I live here. I'm the hired man for Preacher. He ain't here.

Where's he gone?

He's over at Miz Henderson's place. They got married and he's livin' there now and I'm doin' the farmin' for him here.

He lowered his gun but still held it high. *Where's Betty Lou and Thelma? And Eddie?*

They got word Eddie and Charlie was kilt in the war. Thelma's with Preacher. Betty Lou married up with Luke Jones. What business is that all to you?

Ain't none of yore business what it is to me.

Then it hit me in the gut. *You're Charlie.*

He looked hard at me. *What's it to you?*

Ain't nothin' to me. I was quiet, lookin' at 'im. *But it'll be to yore family. They think you're dead.*

Might as well be for all I gone through.

You hungry? I got some beans and taters and corn pone. He looked like he was goin' to turn me down. *Come on in.* I started to walk to the house. I could hear him foller me.

Don't seem right eatin' some man's cookin' in my own house.
But he set at the table and I dished up the vittles. He et like he
was starvin'. He had three glasses of sweet milk. I ate a spoonful
of beans and taters but mostly watched him out of the corner of
my eye, wonderin' what he was goin' to do next.

What he did was walk out the back door and around the
house, and back to the barn. I let the table set and follered him
out there. *That black horse over that, that my Daddy's?*

No, he's mine.

How come he's yourn?

*Ain't none of your business. But he's mine. You can ask yore
Daddy when you see him.*

He was still lookin' around. *Anything else here yourn?*

Could be. You goin' to fight me about it? I couldn't tell if'n he
was or warn't. He was taller'n me but I figured I could take him.
And I figured I better let him know I would do it if'n he wanted
to. Somethin' was eatin' him bad. That was plain to see. He
didn't say anything more about the horse. *You want to go see yore
Daddy and Thelma now or wait til mornin'?*

He looked at me like he didn't know what I was talkin' about.
What'd you say?

I said do you want to go see yore Daddy now?

Yeah, I guess so. You know the way?

*Yeah, I know the way. Let's get to it. I'll have to get back well
afore dark to do the chores.*

Chores? He looked like he never heard about that. I didn't say
anything but we went out and got on the horses. Thunder started
actin' up, like he did sometimes. Maybe he was showin' off to
the mare Charlie was ridin'. I jes' let him go and he settled down
to a fast run with Charlie and the mare behind. All the time I was
thinkin' about Charlie and what was eatin' on him. He shore was
actin' funny. Preacher was goin' to have his hands full with this.

We pulled up at the Henderson place and they come out to
meet us. We got off our horses and I showed him where to tie up
the mare. And we walked over to the porch. *Howdy again.*

You back so soon. Did you come about any trouble?

Naw, they ain't trouble. I thought, Lord, that shore is one big lie. *I brung you company to set a while.*
Miz Henderson stayed on the porch. Preacher stepped down into the yard, holdin' his stick to steady hisself. He come over to where we was standin'. He held out his hand to Charlie. *Name's A. J. Wood.* Charlie took it and held on to it and they looked at each other. *Oh my God! Charlie, is that you?*
It's me, Pa. And Preacher took Charlie in his arms and held him for a long time. I just stood there. Nothin' to say. Miz Henderson was standin' on the porch. I could see that she brung her apron up to her face.
Finally, Preacher let go and led Charlie up to the porch. *Charlie, this here is Miz Henderson, my wife.* I didn't know what to make of that. I guess Miz Henderson didn't know Charlie afore he went to war. Or maybe Preacher was just talkin' to fill up the time.
Charlie, I'm glad to meet you. Won't you set down over here by yore Daddy? I'll go get you a drink of water. Luther, you come help me. I went along with her to the back porch to get the water. She stopped me. *You figure that's Charlie?* I nodded. *Where's he been? The war's been over for a year!*
He's ain't said anything about that. He was on the place when I got back from comin' here. Wanted to know who I was and how come I was there. I did the talkin'. I got to tell you, Miz Henderson, he's actin' real quare. I cain't tell what he's goin' to do next. So you be ready. We took the water out and Charlie took some.
Can I get you somethin' to eat?
Thankee, no mam, I already et. He set there, holdin' the water, his old hat on his knee, lookin' around at everythin'.
Charlie's been in prison camp. Up north. He nearly died of the fevers and liked to have starved to death. Then he run into some trouble comin' home. Took him near a year to get here but he's here and he ain't kilt like we thought he was. And Preacher wiped his eyes. Charlie just set there lookin' at him.
Up come Thelma on Ole Mule. I reckoned she'd been at school. She let Ole Mule loose in the lot and come over to the

house. I got up to meet her. *Howdy Thelma. You and Ole Mule gettin' along?*

Ole Mule is one good mule. Where'd you get that big black horse? Who's settin' on the porch with Daddy?

I caught her hand. *I'll tell you about the horse after a while. But I better tell you, him settin' on the porch with yore daddy and Miz Henderson is yore brother Charlie.*

Charlie? That cain't be. He's dead in the War!

No, he ain't. That's Charlie. Come in afore noon over to yore daddy's place. He just told yore daddy he'd been in a prison camp up north. Took him a year to get here. Don't mind it if'n he ain't like he was when he left. He's been through a lot. She stood still while I was talkin'. And then she walked onto the porch.

Charlie, that you? It's me, Thelma. First time I seen any feelin's in him. He stood up, dropped his hat, and holdin' the water, stepped off'n the porch to her, and took her in his arms, him cryin' like a baby. I took the water from him. *You ain't kilt! You come home.* Hard to know what she said. He still had her in his arms.

I ain't kilt. I come home. He was still cryin'. Nothin' for anybody to say or do, just stand there and wait.

After a while he let her go. *You know what? You need a haircut.*

He laughed. First time I'd heard that from him. *Guess I do. Maybe you'll do it.*

I cain't do it as good as Betty Lou but I can try.

That's good enough.

Where you been all this time? War's been over a year.

Well, the Yankees got me and sent me to prison up north. I got out after the War was over but I was real bad sick and I couldn't come home right away. You go to school now?

Yeah, I do. I ride Ole Mule.

Who's Ole Mule?

Used to be Luther's mule. He give him to me.

Charlie turned to look at me. *How long you been here?*

About a year.

Where'd you come from?

Richmond.

Preacher stepped in afore Charlie could ask any more questions. He turned to me. *You fixin' to go back to the place?* *Yeah, I better get back to do chores afore it gets dark.* I looked at Charlie. *You comin'?*

Preacher spoke up agin to Charlie. *You're welcome to stay here tonight.*

He looked mixed up again, like he didn't know what he wanted to do. *I'll go back to the place. I want to see Luther off in the mornin'.*

Thelma looked like she was goin' to cry. Miz Henderson just set there, stock still. Preacher started in to say somethin', but I held up my hand to him to stop him from sayin' it. *Then let's go.* I got up in the saddle and went ahead, not waitin' for him. Then I heard his horse ahind me so I knowed he was there.

In the time it took to get back to the place, I knowed I had to make up my mind what to do. Part of me was madder'n hell at Charlie Wood, tryin' to make me leave if'n I didn't want to. Question was did I want to. I got the money and Thunder and nothin' was holdin' me back. It boiled down to that I hated to leave the folks here. But I knowed I had to do that sometime, if'n I was ever goin' to get back to Stewart County. By the time I rode into the lot at the place, I'd made up my mind.

Charlie follered me around. I took off the saddle and bridle and took Thunder to the pond. Brung him back, give him some corn. Then I went in the stall where my kit bag and old coat was, and brought 'em out, puttin' 'em by the saddle. Charlie had tied up his horse. He looked at what I was doin'. *Them yore's?*

Yep.

Saddle too?

Yep. I went on about the chores, him follerin' me around, me not talkin', him not askin' any more questions. It took me a hour, feedin', milkin', gettin' in the eggs, fillin' the water buckets, takin' in stove wood, getting' the fire goin' in the fireplace. It warn't quite dark yet. I dished up my bowl of beans, and corn pone and onion and poured some sweet milk. And I set there thinkin' about all the good times we'd had there at that table. He'd got his own vittles and set across the table from me, still not talkin'. Not lookin' at me much, neither.

I washed up my dishes and put 'em to dry and went in the front room. I reached under Preacher's bed where I'd been sleepin' since he left and pulled out the floor sack of Eddie's shirts and pants and drawers. I took two of everythin' and pushed the flour sack back under the bed. *Them's Eddie's.*

Yep.

You takin' 'em?

Yep. Preacher give 'em to me to wear. I put 'em by the door. Then I went to the corner where Preacher's guns was leanin', and took the Yankee rifle and the bullets and laid them by the door. I was ready for trouble from Charlie about doin' that.

You aimin' to take that rifle?

Yep.

What if'n I try to stop you?

You shore can try. You want to go out of doors to do it? Shame to fight in the house. I stood there waitin' for him to say. I figured he would but he didn't. What he did was kind of fold up in Preacher's rockin' chair. He reached around his neck to somethin' hangin' there and started to finger it. I seen him do that at Preacher's, afore Thelma got there.

It was near dark but I could see his face in the light of the fire. *Naw, I don't want to fight you. Fact is, I'm gonna ask you to stay on a while. Get me started in farmin' again.* Then he was more talkin' to hisself than to me. *Fact is, I never loved to farm like Eddie did. Fact is, I was real glad to get away when I joined up. Fact is, I don't know nothin' about farmin'.* All the time he was lookin' at the fire and fingerin' what it was around his neck. He was quiet. *You know Maybelle Atkins?*

Yep. Thinkin, what's Maybelle got to do with my stayin'?

She at the Atkins place?
No, she's been in Charlotte since fall. He was quiet agin, lookin'
at the fire and fingerin' whatever it was. I was tryin' to do some
straight thinkin'. First off he wanted to get me gone, now he
wanted me to stay. I figured I better stay with what I made up
my mind to do. *No, Charlie, I ain't goin' to stay. You was right first
off. Best thing for me to do is move on. In the morning. You have to
say if'n you want to farm. Yore Daddy would come over and help
you get started. Give you time to get back on yore feet.* I went over
to the door. *I'm sleepin' in the barn. You can take yore Daddy's bed,
if'n you want. I'll see you in the mornin' afore I leave.* And I went
to the barn to sleep my last night there just like I slept my first
night there.

Next mornin' I was up early, just after sun up. I figured I had
the time so I did the chores. Charlie come out half way done and
looked like he tried to help. It looked like he'd forgot how to
milk. He looked like he wanted me to help him do it, so I took
over the cow he was milkin'. I warn't in no mood to talk so not
much was said.

After I took the fresh milk to the spring house, I had my
morning bowl of beans with yestiday's corn pone. Wrapped up
the rest of the fried meat and corn pone in a rag. Filled my water
tin. And was ready to go. He just stood there lookin' at me. I
held out my hand and he took it. I was tryin' to think of somethin'
to say but I couldn't come up with anythin', so I just got on
Thunder and rode away, not lookin' back.

I stopped at Preacher's first. I got there just as Thelma and
Ole Mule was leavin' for school. Then it was my turn to cry,
leavin' her. But we made it through. I told her I'd get a haircut,
like she told Charlie to, and she kind of laughed, cryin' at the
same time. She told me she'd watch after Ole Mule. I asked her
to say goodbye to Betty Lou and Luke. She said she would, and
she left for school in as near a gallop as Ole Mule could do.

Miz Henderson give me a big hug and a pouch with some
vittles and wiped her eyes with her apron. Preacher and me just
stood there, lookin' at each other. I started to say much obliged

but never got through it. He nodded, like he knowed what I was tryin' to say, and said they'd pray for me to get to Stewart County safe. And I rode away not lookin' back.

Frank Atkins place was the last stop but nobody was home. I guessed that was all right. Him and me had said to each other what there was to say. We'd be just sayin' it over agin. It was right funny, I thought. Preacher saved my life comin' here and Frank saved me by helpin' me leave.

So I left, headed on the road west to'ard Mount Airy.

1866

Beulah Gates

Ridin' along, my mind was still on what I'd left ahind me at the Wood place. Lord knows how they was goin' to figure it out. It looked like Charlie was in a real bad way. Not in his body, that I could see any sign of, but in what Miz Henderson would call his mind. I'd seen soldiers in the War that looked like they'd gone crazy. I guess anybody would, sometimes, what with all the killin' and bein' scared to death you'd be next. Charlie warn't the same as that, as far as I could figure it. You might go crazy in a battle, but you'd get over it. I figured it'd take a long time for Charlie to get over it. Maybe he wouldn't, never. I hated to leave 'em all with Charlie comin' home like he was. But it was time for me to go, anyway. Charlie comin' home like he was just forced my hand.

It was real good to be in the saddle of a horse agin. Ole Mule had saved my life, I guess, but a mule is a mule and a horse is a horse. They ain't the same but that they both got four legs and a tail. Thunder was as good as the little red mare but not any better. He was just bigger and had more fightin' in 'im, bein' a stud. You could give the little red mare her head, knowin' she wouldn't do anything crazy like runnin' off with you. With Thunder, you couldn't never tell. Leastwise I couldn't, first off.

Anyway, Thunder and me went on the track to Mount Airy. It was a real nice day but so cold I had on my old coat with the gold pieces and a hat of Eddie's. Or maybe Preacher's. So, I had to get thinkin', what was next. One thing for sure, I had to get over them mountains they call the Smoky Mountains down into

Tennessee. Maybe there was a good track to foller if'n I was where I could find it, but I best not try it by myself. I didn't have much of a recollection of us doin' it comin' this way when I was a foot soldier.

So I had to find somebody to do it with. After I got across I still was in hot water, I figured. I recollected about Knoxville. That's where we fit the last battle afore winter camp. That led me to thinkin' where winter camp must have been. Anyway, Nashville had to be a good piece past Knoxville. Old Joe Dale, back in the army, told me about his home place. Sounded like it was on the Cumberland River, part way from Knoxville to'ard Nashville. I might shoot for that and foller the river downstream to Nashville.

About that time I come to a creek, seemed like a good place to eat a bite and give Thunder some grazing and a good drink of water. It was in the shade of a near mountain bluff, maybe a half mile to the north, I figured. I was about to saddle up agin when here come a wagon with a kind of top on it, pulled the team to a stop. *Howdy.*

Howdy. He got down. *Is that there bluff Cumberland Knob?*

I cain't tell you. I never been this way afore but oncet and I don't recollect seein' that bluff.

I figure it is, by a map a feller drawed us down in Raleigh. You comin' from away?

You could say that. From Charleston.

That in C'lina?

South C'lina.

The Yankees hard on you folks down that way?

He shook his head. *They was mighty hard. It seemed like they was takin' it out on us that the War started.* He shook his head agin. *In a way, I guess we was where it started. Anyway, weun's are goin' west. All the way to Missoury, if'n we hold out.*

Missoury. I ain't good at places. That on west of Tennessee?

I been told that. They's good land out there for farmin' and it's free for the takin'. Federal gov'ment land. Left over from the War.

Well, I swear, I never heard of such a thing. You the only wagon goin'?

He shook his head. *Naw, there's six wagons in all in the wagon train. We started out with three, picked up more along the way. Well, I got to get goin'. My time to lead. Afore you go, I'm headed to Tennessee and I'm lookin' to go with somebody. You think maybe a wagon could use a hand? Mebbe. You might stand here and ask 'em as they come by. One I know that might is Elmer Gates. Him and his missus is travelin' by theirselves and he might need a hand. I cain't say as how he'd take it. He's right quare, from what I've seen of 'im. He'll be nigh at the end of the line up.* And he got back on the springboard and started his team up. About that time another one come in sight. That one was pulled by a double team too.

The wagons was a sight to see. I never seen such afore. The bed was covered over with somethin' looked like flour sack. Must have been canvas like we had in the War. This one had some fryin' pans hitched on the side that rattled along. Thunder and me stood at the side, lettin' them pass. The man drivin' waved when he passed. There warn't any more in sight so I galloped past them and on into Mount Airy.

Like I said, I'd been to Mount Airy oncet with Preacher to git supplies. But I didn't recollect much about it. No need to worry, it warn't all that big. It looked like what I recollected about Dover. Me and Thunder rode around some, gettin' the lay of the land.

I ought to point out here that was the first time in my life I warn't beholdened to nobody. I didn't have to do no chores. I had this big black horse that acted all the time like he was goin' to run away and all that was keepin' him from doin' it was me. And I had money in my kit bag that I worked for. Didn't steal it and it warn't give to me out of the kindness of nobody's heart. I tell you right now I was full of myself that evening.

It looked like I had to make up my mind about somethin'. Right ahead of me was a house that had some writin' but I couldn't make it out. But I recollected that Preacher had called it that day we was here. He called it a boardin' house. Said anybody on the road could get a bed and some vittles there. So I headed there, tied up Thunder at the hitchin' post, and went up on the porch.

Nobody come out so I went in and there was a woman looked like Miz Henderson. I told her what I wanted and she allowed as how I could have it. If'n I used my bedroll it'd be so much. And that I was to keep my boots off'n the bed. And told me when dinner would be on the table. And to leave my gun with her. She said nobody could keep their guns in her house. Preacher's bed was better, but I had it to myself. It looked like sometimes men had to double up. There was three beds in the room. One man snored so loud another man got up and made him turn over. Her vittles was real good and I et my fill twicet. Even there was biscuits and gravy and fried meat that mornin! She shore set a good table.

Next mornin' I saddled up and rode around lookin' to see any sign of the wagon train. There warn't nothin' to see close to town, but when I rode on west I caught up with one of 'em. The driver stopped the mules when he saw me. I held up my hands to show I didn't mean any harm. *Howdy.*

Howdy. He got down off'n the springboard. *You travelin'?*

I shore am, goin' over the mountains to Tennessee. You headed that way with them other wagons?

Yeah. I guess we're in the middle of the bunch. You travelin' by yourself?

Yep, all by myself. I was wonderin' if'n anybody wanted a driver. I'd work for vittles. Wouldn't need no money. I talked to the fellar in the wagon at the front yestiday and he said mebbe. He named Elmer Gates. You Elmer Gates?

Naw, name's Bill Williamson. Gates is the end wagon. He studied me. *You a good rider? Must be with that purty horse.*

I petted Thunder on the neck. *Yeah, him and me get along. I saddle broke 'im.* I grinned. *Cain't sell 'im, 'cause he won't let anybody but me ride 'im!*

Yeah, he looks like he'd be a handful. Look here, I got a thought about what might work. If'n you'll bear with me, I'll see what I can do.

Sounds good to me. What do you want me to do?

You drive my team so's we can keep up while I'm lookin' in to this. I'm goin' to ride my side mule up ahead to talk to Henry Smith. He's at the head of the train. He kind of runs the thing. You want to do that?

Yessiree. So I tied up Thunder at the back of the wagon, hopin' he'd stand still for it. Mr. Williamson got on his mule bare back and rode on ahead after I started his team up. I never drove a double team of mules afore, but it turned out not so hard. I figured them mules been doing this now for a while and had the hang of it.

We was rattlin' along, me looking back from time to time to see if'n Thunder was causin' trouble. He warn't, at least that I could see. I felt a hand on my shoulder. *Where's my husband gone to?*

I figured it was Miz Williamson. I answered her more or less said over my shoulder, *He's gone ahead to talk to Henry Smith. My name's Luther Morris. I'm goin' to drive yore team 'til he gets back.* She didn't say no more but stayed back where she was. After a while, here come Williamson back. I could see now that he was a mite older'n me, but not much. More Charlie's age, I guess. You'd couldn't tell much how he looked with all his hair and chin whiskers and his hat pulled down. Later on it looked like all the men on the wagon train looked like that. I had trouble tellin' 'em apart. One had some gray chin whiskers so I could tell him.

Anyway, he motioned for me to stop the team. *Henry's goin' to talk with the other men. You go up ahead and drive for him while he does that.*

So I did what he said and went ahead full gallop on Thunder to the wagon at the head. I rode alongside. *Howdy. Name's Luther Morris.*

Howdy. Name's Henry Smith. He stopped the team. *Williamson tell you what he was thinkin' about?*

I shook my head. *No, he didn't say nothin' about it. What's he thinkin' of?*

Well, we could use a scout to ride ahead and see if'n the wagons can get through. And the men could all use somebody to spell 'em now and then. If'n they all say so, you can do that. And we'll take turns feedin' you. What d'you think?

That sounds real good to me. You want to ask 'em now or wait 'til time to camp?

Just as well do it now. We won't be campin' anytime soon. You want to drive the team while I go talk to 'em? So I tied Thunder to the wagon like I done afore and got up in the springboard. He got on his side mule and rode back down the line, and I drove the team on down the track.

While he was gone, I set there thinkin' about it. I loved to do the scoutin' in the army. That was a different story than this one. It looked like the question here was to find a track through the mountains that a wagon could take. The track had to be one that a double team of mules could make, with a loaded down wagon! I figured I'd have to learn a lot more about wagons and mules if'n I was goin' to be able to do that. But if'n I could do it at all, it'd mean a way over the mountains with vittles every day. I didn't have to worry about Thunder. He could get along with grazin' and there'd always be water in the mountains, I figured.

After a while, Henry come back up the line. He said all of 'em said this was a good plan. He took over his team and sed there'd be more talkin' about it when the wagons stopped for the night. To'ards sundown Henry stopped his wagon and one by one the rest of 'em come along and stopped. It looked like a good place to stop. It was a big pasture over to the side of the track, big enough to hold the wagons. I counted five. I thought Henry said six but maybe I misheard. I tied Thunder up to a tree, with a long rein so he could graze and walked over to see what was goin' on.

It looked like any camp bein' set up for the night but these folks had these wagons with covers and they warn't soldiers. And I didn't see no guns. I figured if'n they had 'em they'd be in the wagons. There was a creek over past the pasture and men were leadin' mules over there to drink. Women folk was goin' for water. Some fires was built and spiders hung over 'em for cookin'. Henry come over to where I was standin' with Thunder and told me I was to come have supper with him and his wife.

I was with them folks the better part of two months, judging by the full moons. The days all come together. After some breakfast with that family, me and Thunder lit off up the track to see how the goin' would be that day. I'd come back to meet the head wagon and tell him what I saw. Then I'd take turns spellin' the men at doin' the drivin'. Many a time when they was spelled they'd go off to hunt for somethin' for supper. If'n they got a deer or maybe four or five rabbits and squirrels they'd divide 'em up. The stop a hour after sundown meant somethin' like that could be cooked. Elsewise it was corn pone or corn mush and stewed taters. Beans took too long to cook, except one time we stayed in the same place two nights.

Travelin' like that, I never got know anybody much. Aside from Henry and Bill I never knowed any other of the men's names. And never knowed any of the womenfolk's names. I reckon they all told me but I warn't with any of 'em long enough at a time to get 'em straight. I recollect it that I figured at the time they was all a little older than me. The men was, for sure. One wagon had a girl and another'n had a baby. At suppertime when there was the gatherin' there was so much to do that there warn't much time to talk. Maybe they did in the mornin' after I left on my scout. It warn't that nobody warn't friendly. There just warn't that kind of time on the road.

The scoutin' and the goin' turned out to be real easy at first. These folks had been put on the right track, I guess you'd say, and there warn't much chance of getting' off'n it or gettin' lost. Mostly the track was clear. We had some heavy rainstorms along then, but nothin' like we had later on. Maybe twicet I had to ride back to the lead wagon for a shovel to work on a wash out across the track. We never had to cross any creeks of any size at that time.

Then the climb started in to gettin' steep, and you could see the mountains was ahead. The driver that was in the lead would stop anybody meetin' us to find out what was ahead. I was there one time for the talkin'. They talked about goin' over the pass and that we wanted to do that in the daytime for sure, maybe dinnertime.

I asked Henry what a pass was and he told me it was the highest place where the track went over the top of the mountain down the other side. The men talked about it at night when they made camp. They all said we'd have to take one wagon at a time and maybe have to do two double teams, if'n it was real steep. Henry asked me if'n I could drive two double teams, if'n they needed me, and I said I'd shore give it a go. They all laughed at that. I 'spect they was laughin' to keep from showin' their worry. When it quieted down, one of 'em said what about the Gates wagon. Nobody said anything at first, then Henry spoke up. *We'll send Luther back to tell him what we know and what we're goin' to do.*

You mean we goin' to wait for him to catch up?

Naw, I don't mean that. He's had plenty of time to catch up and he ain't. But he signed up with us and I figure it's right to tell him what's ahead. Nobody said anything else.

So the next mornin', instead of ridin' ahead I rode back down the track. This'd be the first time I'd seen the Gates face to face. They'd been way ahind ever since I joined up with the wagons. Only oncet had I seen a wagon comin' our way, looked like a mile off in the distance. I figured it was them but nobody said so. I must have rode near a half hour at gallop afore I found 'em.

The wagon was standin' still, with the mules hobbled over in the grass, grazin'. Here it was middle of the mornin' and they warn't even on the move yet. I hallooed the wagon, with my hands high away from my rifle so's they'd know I warn't up to no good. Right away a woman come out of the canvas cover right ahind the springboard. *You Miz Gates?* She nodded, tuckin' her hair under the shawl over her head. *Name's Luther Morris. I come from up ahead at the rest of the wagon train. Is Elmer anywhere about?* She shook her head. *He's gone to get some firewood to build a fire.* I couldn't hardly hear her, so I moved Thunder closer to where she stood, holdin' on to the springboard. She looked like she warn't a girl but warn't a old woman either. In between. I could see from where I was settin' on Thunder that she was shaky. It looked like she didn't want to look at me, but kept lookin' away. And her hands wouldn't be still. They'd be tuckin' in her hair or smoothin' her apron. I recall thinkin' to myself that she warn't all that good lookin', but there was somethin' about her that caught my eye. A girl come from out of the canvas cover on the wagon, she stood kind of ahind the woman. *My name's Beulah. Beulah Gates. This here's Dory. She's my daughter.* She smiled at the girl. *Weun's are going to Missoury, ain't we?* The girl nodded. *Say howdy, Dory.* The girl said something I didn't hear. I nodded.

I figured maybe Miz Gates was still scared of me. I backed Thunder off. Guess I better say I turned him around. He never learned how to back. *You know when he'll be back? I need to talk to him.*

About that time here come a rider on a mule, movin fast to'ards us. *There he comes, now.* Elmer Gates pulled up between the wagon and me. I could tell he thought I was up to no good, so I held my hands up. *Elmer, he's come from the wagon train.*

He looked from her to me. *What's yore business?*

My hands was still high. *Name's Luther Morris. I'm workin' with the wagon train. I 'spect you know about that.* I figured shorely Henry had talked to him too but maybe not. *They sent me to tell you what's up ahead and how they was going to go over the mountain pass.*

I'm listenin'. And he started to hitch up his team as I talked. He didn't even have a double team. Maybe that's why he'd fell so far ahind. By the time I was done, he was all hitched up with his ridin' mule ahind, ready to go. She said he'd went for firewood but I didn't see any sign of any firewood or where a fire had been. *You go on back and tell them to go on ahead on their own. Me and my mules can do it without none of their help.*

Elmer, don't do that. We got a mountain pass to go over and you know we cain't do it by ourselves. And, 'sides that, I yearn for some women folk to be with, me and Dory. Whyn't you tell 'em to wait for us?

He turned to her and looked at her and drawed back his hand like he would of hit her, if'n he could of reached her. *Woman, you shet yore mouth. You the one wanted to go to Missoury and now you keep causin' me trouble. Git back in the wagon cover. Dory's shore to need you.* And he started the mules up.

I set there on Thunder, watchin' 'em go. I figured they was in real trouble, one way or other. He looked like a wild man and worse yet he acted like one. I couldn't even take a guess where he'd been when he come ridin' up. No places near by that I knowed about and there hadn't been a town for two days. And if'n I read the signs right, he was real hard on the woman. She looked like she was scared to death of him. I figured she had cause to be, from the looks of things. Well, it warn't none of my business, so I set Thunder at a gallop and we passed 'em up. Didn't even wave. Just rode on by. That evenin' when the wagons stopped to camp I told 'em what Elmer had said. Bill Williamson said there warn't anything to be done and nobody didn't say anything elsewise.

The next four, five days we went up over the pass. I cain't say it was easy goin', 'cause it warn't. Every mornin' like always I'd scout ahead and get back to help with the drivin'. Near every night it'd rain like all tarnation and near every mornin' I'd find gulleys was washed across the track. Some of 'em warn't so deep I couldn't fix 'em myself. But some of 'em I had to have help on. What with all the rain, mornin' found everybody and their camp soppin' wet. They had to take time to dry out some, so it was slow gettin' started. So we didn't make much time any of them days.

Aside from that, the uphill goin' warn't as bad as I figured it would be. By and large there was only two places that was real troublesome. On them, you went steep uphill and sharp around a corner at the same time. We cleared the track as best we could and made it with the double team of mules. It was touch and go. The corner was so short that the lead team of mules had to go over the edge and turn and pull at the same time. We took it slow and easy. Them drivers knowed what they was doin'. And them mules was real good. I never had seen better. And the drivers knowed when to lay on the whip and when not.

Findin' a level place to camp overnight was might nigh not possible the closer we got to the top. We had to space the wagons out in any place we found. Every time we had to scotch the wheels to keep 'em from rollin' back'ards back down the mountain. And all the time I was thinkin' about the Gates and wonderin' how on earth they was goin' to make it alone.

So we got to the top. There was a clearing up there, big enough for the five wagons, some end to end, some side by side. It was a real purty place and you could see down the mountain over to the next one. We got up there after the middle of the day, by the sun. Everybody felt real good about what they'd done. Some of 'em talked like they wanted to stay the night up there but it looked like there was a bad storm brewin' to the west. Henry said we better start down. So we let the mules drink but didn't let 'em graze. Thunder and me started on down to scout the way. The goin' looked easy but doin' it on a horse and doin' it in a wagon with a double team is somethin' else. I went back up to tell 'em the first mile was real steep, but with none of them sharp corners.

So we did it like comin' up, one wagon at a time. We got all the womenfolk and younguns out of the wagon to walk down. Put one man drivin', two men on the brake shoes, and a man at the head of each of the mules, leadin' 'em down, gettin' 'em to hold back as best they could. The brake shoes would get hot and start to howl but they held. We made that first mile without any runaways, and camped wherever there was a place big enough.

The storm come along and it rained and blowed like holy terror, and we was all glad we hadn't stopped at the top. No use in tryin' to have a fire that night, it was so wet So we et cold vittles. I allus slept out, but that night it was real hard to find a dry spot for my bed roll, even under a wagon.

The way down on that side of the mountain warn't as steep and crooked as the other side. We did it the same way as afore, me scoutin' ahead, and then goin' down the steep places one by one. It worked out just fine, with everybody's help, and we got down to a gentle slope in three days, as I recollect. When we gathered for supper on that third day, it looked like the worst was over by far. We built a big fire and everybody got warm, for a change. There was two other wagons there, on the way up, one of 'em with a single team. There was some talkin' back and forth but I guess none of our folks felt called upon to tell the others about how hard the way ahead was. At least I never heard them say anything like that.

At the fire, Henry made a little speech. He said how proud he was of everybody, doin' their part. And he said he was talkin' for them all when he thanked me for my help. I was taken aback by what he said, and couldn't find the right words to say, but I told 'em I was much obliged to be able to come over the mountains with them. And for them to stop in to see me, if'n they was ever in Stewart County. Then they asked one of the other men goin' up what town was next, and he said Johnson City. So it looked like from the talk that they meant to stop in Johnson City long enough maybe to work and buy more supplies afore they went on west.

I was standin' there, listenin' to the talk. And the picture come to my mind of the Gates wagon and Miz Gates standin' there shakin'. I just couldn't help thinkin' they'd have to have help getting' over the mountain. *Henry and you all, I cain't help thinkin' about the Gates. They ain't goin' to make it over the mountain without no help. You all need to get on yore way. But I ain't in no hurry. So if 'n you'll spare me some vittles, me and Thunder will go back to see if 'n we can find 'em.*

It was quiet. *That's real Christian of you to want to do. Don't know as I would do it. Elmer Gates can be real mean to start with and worse yet when he's had his likker. You be careful of him, if 'n you go back. He may not want any of yore help. We was against lettin' 'em join up with us, but Beulah Gates begged my wife to let 'em come.*

Miz Williamson nodded. *I don't know. Maybe I did it wrong. But she wanted so bad to go to Missoury.*

What's done is done. He's lagged ahind the whole way. Of course, not havin' a double team maybe held him back some. Anyway, Luther, you want to do that, go ahead. You got my blessin'. I could see him grinnin' in the firelight. *And some of my corn pone.*

Nobody said anything agin my plan, so next mornin' one of the women give me the vittles in a pouch. I shook hands with everybody, women folk too, Miz Williamson gave me a special word to give to Miz Gates. I told 'em maybe I'd meet up with 'em agin, and Thunder and me headed back up the mountain.

On horseback, the trip up the pass and down the other side, now that I knowed the way for sure, was easy. By dinner time I was on top. Goin' down the t'other side, I could tell where the wagons had been and where the washouts was. The rain had washed 'em out agin, but not so bad that I figured a wagon couldn't get through. Then, part way down the other side of the pass, there was the Gates wagon, pulled over to the side. It was a wonder it hadn't tipped over, it was on such a sideways slope. By that time of day, it was near sundown, and it warn't any use going up to the wagon and talkin' to him. I shore didn't want to talk to Elmer Gates in the dark.

So I turned around up the mountain to a place off the track where I could camp. I recollect that it rained that night and the pine tree where I had my bed roll dripped on me. Twicet Thunder woke me up during that night, with his whinney. I got up and tried to build up the fire, thinkin' maybe he heard a mountain cat. I guess what with bein' wet and Thunder bein' uneasy and me wonderin' what I was doin' there, I didn't get much sleep.

But by mornin', it had cleared off and the sun was good and I reckoned the mountain cat had gone his way. At least Thunder didn't seem nervous. So I had some cornpone and a drink of water and set off down to the Gates wagon. I could see they was in a bad place. It was right down mountain from one of them steep climbs and turn a corner. Not the worst one. It was ahead yet up the mountain. But still and all, it was bad. I stopped Thunder maybe thirty foot away from the wagon. I didn't see nobody stirrin', so I halloed the wagon.

Miz Gates come out from under the canvas cover. She looked real bad. Her hair was all wild and her apron was real dirty and her face looked like it was dirty, too. Then I could see that it warn't dirt on her face but black and blue marks around her eyes and on her chin. Soon as she knowed what I was lookin' at, she held her apron up to her face like she was wipin' off the dirt. And her eyes and her hands was movin' all the time. *I come back to see about you all.*

Weun's are all right. She stood there, noddin' at me. *Much obliged.*

Elmer around?

He's sleepin' in the wagon.

Dory?

She sleepin' in the wagon too.

There was some noise around the back of the wagon, and here come Elmer from around ahind there, holdin' a rifle pointed at me. I held up my hands to show that I warn't up to anything. *Elmer, it's Luther Morris. Put yore gun away.*

Huh. You're back agin. What'd you want?

I set there on Thunder, lookin' at the man. He warn't much to see, all dirty scraggly hair and chin whiskers and dirty shirt and pants. He was about a half of a foot taller'n me. And he was aimin' the gun right at me and Thunder. Miz Gates was still standin' by the springboard. *Elmer, it's Luther Morris. He's come from the wagon train.*

He shook his head, like he was just wakin' up, looking at me. *I seen you afore.*

I nodded. *The wagon train is done over the mountain. I come back to see if'n I can help you folks over.*

He stood there, lookin' a hole through me, wavin' his gun at me, like it was a stick. *I done told you. We don't need no help. We just stopped here to rest the mules. Now you git!*

Miz Gates broke in to what he was sayin'. *Elmer Gates, you know we could use some help. You said so yoreself last evenin'. You let Luther help us, or we'll never make it.* And she started in to cry. The girl Dory come out of the wagon cover to stand by her mama, holding onto her apron.

Shut yore mouth, woman. You don't know anythin' about this. This here is a man's work.

That looked like it made her real mad. I could see her hands shakin' as she wrung her apron up in a ball. *I may not know much. At least you are allus tellin' me I don't. But I know for sure we need some help getting' over this mountain. And I say to let Luther help us.* She spoke like she was scared to death to say all that but said it all the same. I recollect that I was near holdin' my breath to see what he was goin' to do next.

He looked back and forth from her to me. Nobody said anything else. I figured he would or he wouldn't, and nothin' I could say would change his mind. He must of stood there a minute and then he walked over to the wagon and put his gun under the canvas. Then he told her to git down from the wagon with the girl. He got up on the springboard and started up the team up the track, cussin' as loud as he could. Miz Gates and the girl follered along on foot and me and Thunder come along last.

Dad gum, if'n he didn't make it up that place and went on up the track like nothin' was goin' to stop him. But he stopped all right when he got to the worst place goin' up on the mountain. It was where there was a real steep climb with two switchbacks back to back. It was Henry that called 'em switchbacks, and you near met yoreself comin' back, they was so sharp. Elmer stopped the team afore he got there but where he could see what was ahead. He set there a minute, lookin' at that. Then he got down from the springboard and went around the back of the wagon.

Miz Gates was watchin' him. *Elmer Gates, you stay away from that jug! This ain't no time to be drinkin' moonshine.* He shook his head in her direction, and got the jug out of the wagon and took a long swig. I watched him wipe his mouth of his sleeve and he reached in the back of the wagon and took out a bull whip. Then he come around front and climbed up on the springboard and started up the team. They got a good start and made it up the first climb and the first switchback. Then they stalled.

It looked like the climb was too steep for 'em to pull that heavy a wagon, and right after the steep climb was another switchback. Where they stalled the ruts in the track was so deep that the axles on the wagon near hit bottom. I knowed that some of the other wagons had trouble at this very spot when they went up even with a double team, and now the fresh rains had washed out the ruts deeper. So there they set.

Elmer started in cussin' at the team, tellin' 'em to get goin', They didn't even strain a leg. Then he started in with his bull whip, and he whipped them pore mules like he hated 'em more than anything else in the world. The whippin' got 'em movin', but all they did was flounder around, tryin' to get away from the whip.

I set there on Thunder watchin' it as long as I could. When I couldn't take it no longer, I jumped off of Thunder, and up on the springboard and jerked the bull whip out of his hand. That made him so mad I thought he was goin' to explode. More likely he was goin' to try to take the whip from me and whip me with it. What he tried to do was to knock me off of the springboard. He could of, too. He was that big and that strong and that mad.

But afore he could do anythin' else, here comes the woman from around the wagon, yellin' at the top of her voice. Like she'd of whipped him, if'n she'd had the bull whip. *Elmer Gates, you quit whippin' them mules! You're goin' to kill 'em for sure. That ain't goin' to help nothin'. You hear me? You leave that bull whip be, and git down off of that springboard, and let's you and Luther and me see what we can do. Will you for God's sake do that? If 'n you don't, weun's are goin' to die right here!* And her bein' so mad, her mad turned into cryin', and she stood there lookin' at him cryin' like her heart was goin' to break. She was a real pitiful sight to see. The girl Dory was standin' there, holdin' on to her mama's arm.

Well, I tell you, I had to hand it to her. What she said must of turned the tables, 'cause he did what she said do. He looked down at her like he didn't know what she was talkin' about. But then he climbed down to where she was standin'. I got down on the other side, holding the bullwhip. I had to lay it down careful like 'cause Thunder was dancin' around like he was about to run away from this here place as fast as he could. I did what I always did when he got that way. I held his head so his nose was next to my face, and I talked to him. It didn't matter what I said, it was the talkin' that did it. Then, just to be sure he would calm down, I led him over to the mules and let him stand there. Didn't even tie him up. And I walked back to the wagon where Elmer and Miz Gates was standin'.

We stood there, lookin' at the wagon, stuck in the ruts. *I got a notion that might do the trick.*

That was Elmer talkin' and it took me by su'prise. It was the first I'd ever heard him say to me that warn't like he wanted to fight. I nodded. *What are you studyin' about?*

I broke them mules and I figure I can get 'em to back up. The ruts ain't so deep back down slope. If 'n I can get 'em to back up and push the wagon down the mountain, out 'n them ruts, we can fill up the ruts with rocks. Not only was he making sense, but that was a lot for him to say at one time. *If 'n they can do that, and we fill up the ruts, then they can go on up the mountain.* He looked at me to see what I was goin' to say.

You think maybe you can get 'em to back up? I never seen a team that would do that on a mountainside. Why don't you try it and see? If 'n you want me to, I can put Thunder out front of the team. Maybe that'll help out.

Miz Gates was standin' there, still with her apron rolled up in a ball, but she'd quit cryin'. And I saw her reach out to touch

Elmer on the arm. Not sayin' anything, just standin' there, touchin' him.

So we did it that way. I figured that the mules must of forgive Elmer for all that whippin'. When he pulled back on the reins, and said his gee haw, they started to back up, slow like, and first thing I knowed they'd backed the wagon down out of the ruts. It beat anything I ever had seen. First off he was cussin' at 'em and whippin' 'em like he hated their guts. Next thing I knowed, they acted like a team of show horses you might see somewhere. And he was a different man. Kind of like there was two men, wrapped up in one.

You figure you can drive the wagon alongside the ruts? He shook his head and grunted at her. *Wagon might fall over.* He looked at me to see what I thought, I guess. I nodded at what he'd said. I figured he might be able to do it, but I didn't want to cross him and maybe set him off agin.

So you want us to fill up them ruts with rocks? He nodded at her and she went at it, with the girl Dory and me helpin'. I forgot to say her and the girl had on britches. Shirt tail tucked in and I swear a pistol tucked in her pants, just like a man would. It didn't make much sense, her so shaky afore, talkin' to him, and here she was with a pistol tucked in her britches, like a soldier. But that's what I seen. Anyway, we all heaved to and found enough of the right size rocks to near fill up the ruts.

Then, oh Lordy, it was the mules' time to be balky. Hard to say why. Mules get that way, from time to time. But they warn't about to budge. I was fearful that Elmer was goin' to let loose agin with the bull whip. I figured that warn't goin' to do nobody any good. I happened to look over at Thunder standin' by, and I figured if'n talkin' to him sometimes did the trick, maybe it would with the mules. I held up my hand at Elmer and went over to where Miz Gates was standin'. I could tell she was back to bein' scared. *What air we goin' to do now? He cain't whip them mules any more. He'll kill 'em.*

I know. He'll kill 'em for sure. I stood there lookin' at it all. *I got somethin' we can try. I don't know if'n this'll work but let's try it out. You and Dory go to the head of one of the mules and talk it to*

*real soft and like it was a special mule of yours. I'll do the t'other
one. And I'll put Thunder in the lead and see if'n he'll behave
hisself and walk at the pace of the mules, pullin' that wagon. Maybe
they'll figure they're supposed to follow him.*

She nodded, and I looked up at Elmer on the springboard
and told him what we was goin' to do. He shook his head, like
he thought it was crazy. But he didn't try to stop us. So afore he
could do anything else, I put Thunder in his place, the women
started talkin' to their mule, I did the same. We must have been
a sorry sight to see, two women in britches, leading and talkin' to
a mule like it was a baby. Me doin' the same on the other side. It
looked for all the world this big black horse was leadin' the way.
And in the springboard was this mountain of a man holdin' the
reins to the mules, cussin' a blue streak at 'em, as we went.

And we went. It worked. The mules must of got the word
that if'n they ever wanted to see a green pasture ever agin, they
better do this. We got over them rocks and went on up the
mountain. I tell you, it was something to see.

It was gettin' dark. There warn't no place to pull off the track,
so the only thing to do was to just let the wagon set in the middle
of it. We hadn't seen hide nor hair of any body all day, so I figured
anybody come by, they'd just have to stop for the night. Nobody
did. Thunder was long gone long ago, but when we stopped the
wagon and I whistled, here he come gallopin' up. He was some
horse, I tell you. I never had a better one.

I recollect that nothing was said about stoppin', Elmer just
did. He looked at me after he whoaed the mules, and I nodded.
Miz Gates and Dory and me got rocks big enough to scotch the
wheels to keep it from rollin' back'ards. Elmer got down and
unhitched the mules and tied 'em up, not sayin' a word. Miz
Gates said I could have somethin' to eat with them, but I thanked
her, and said I had somethin' in my kit bag. Truth to tell, I did,
but it was mighty little.

But I didn't want to get any more mixed up with Elmer and
them. So Thunder and me went on up the mountain a piece and
made our camp under a big beech tree. There warn't no need for

me to build a fire. I didn't have anything to warm up and didn't need the light. So I tied up Thunder on a loose rein, and went to bed. But I could see from where I was that the Gates had a big enough fire, and I could see 'em pass this way and that around it.

Somebody yellin' woke me up. I didn't have any notion how long I'd been asleep or what time it was in the night. There was enough clouds so I couldn't see the stars, and there warn't no moon. Their fire had burnt low so I couldn't see much, but it looked like Elmer was on his knees. I reckoned it was Miz Gates that was yellin', but I couldn't see anythin' of her. Then it was quiet agin. I decided there warn't anything I could do about it. It warn't any of my business. So when it got quiet, I went back to sleep.

It rained agin that night so I was wet and cold when I come to, about daybreak. It looked like somebody was up and movin' about down at their fire, so I decided to go down to see if'n I could warm up some. It was Miz Gates who was up. No sign of Elmer or Dory, but I could see what must of been Dory, sleepin' under the wagon. I ast if'n I could warm up by her fire. She said I shore could and she got me a cup of warm water to drink. Nobody did any talkin'. She got Dory up and give her some warm water. Now that it was daylight, I could see that her face looked black and blue on her cheeks and her jaw. It might of been dirt, but I didn't think so. I didn't say anything about it.

About that time, Elmer showed up from around back of the wagon and took his cup of water. It was still dead quiet but for some birds singin'. Finally I said I'd go hitch up Thunder, and he went to hitch up the team to the wagon. I figured we still had five, six miles up the mountain to go. And maybe halfway from where we was, there was another real sharp turn on a steep slope.

We got to that place about dinner time. It come as a su'prise to me that we made such good time. I didn't do anything but kind of lead the way. Miz Gates and Dory led the mules like they had the day afore, I guess talkin' to them all the way. Elmer, he never said a word to nobody, but he never used the bull whip on the mules, neither. But the mules balked agin when we got to that real bad switchback. Seemed like they knowed they couldn't make it. Elmer started in hollerin' at 'em and cussin' 'em out. Then he started in cussin' at Miz Gates, for makin' him come anyway. She never give him any back talk, just stood there lookin' at her hands or the mule she was standin' by. But I seen she still had on the britches and the pistol in her belt.

I set there on Thunder, takin' it all in. I couldn't think of a thing to do that would get that wagon up that mountain. But just then, like the Good Lord knowed what a mess we was in, here come a wagon pullin' up ahind us, with a double team. I went back to the man in the springboard quick like, afore Elmer could get there. I figured if'n he did the first talkin', he'd scare the fellar off. But glory be when he come up to us, he didn't say a word, but let me do the talkin'. I really didn't have to do much talkin'. The fellar saw what was happenin' and said right away that he'd help. By that time, I knowed how to hitch up a double team to a wagon, so the fellar and me got the job done pretty quick.

What we did was to unhitch Elmer's team, and hitch up his double team. Right away when they started off, I could tell they'd make it. They did. We was in luck. There was a wide place in the track, so's our wagon could be pulled over to the side and the other one could pass. I told the fellar that I knowed the track ahead and this was the worst place and that we'd make it all right by ourselves. Elmer was still not sayin' a word but he helped with the hitchin' and then afore the other wagon left, he said he was much obliged to him.

We got to the top the next day. Maybe it was the second day, I don't recollect. Elmer was still behavin', I guess you'd say. He warn't talkin' much at all to me. He hollered at Miz Gates from time to time, but she didn't pay him no mind. Maybe that was why he hollered at her. But there warn't any more middle of the night yellin' like that one night, and I never seen her face look dirty agin, if'n that what it was.

It looked to me like he paid no attention at all to Dory, but to look at her out of the corner of his eye, as Aunt Polly would say. It was no su'prise that he did, since any body could see that she had the makin's of a real purty woman with the passage of time. But she warn't like most girls, as far as I could see. Like, she didn't talk much and when she did, I couldn't get what she said. Miz Gates could, and when Dory was talkin' to me, she'd tell me what Dory said. But then she never said all that much to me. But, thinkin' back, I recollected how Elmer looked at her, kind of side wise.

We started down right after daybreak. There warn't no problems at first. The slope was gradual and there was no switchbacks. I recollected that one was comin' up, so I did my scoutin' and saw it ahead. I rode back and told Elmer. He nodded, but still warn't talkin' much to me. For my part, I wanted to get that danged wagon down the mountain all in one piece and get away from the Gates. We got to where he could see what I was talkin' about, and he stopped the team.

I've told you afore about how hard it was to go down a steep slope with a wagon and team. The main thing was to hold back the team so the wagon wouldn't start to push 'em along. It takes a lot of know how to keep the team from runnin' away. If 'n they do, the driver ain't able to keep the wagon goin' right. Elmer got down and he watched me go to the back of the wagon to look at the brake shoes.

You recollect that I told you oncet that the thing was to put a heavy man on each shoe, pullin' back on the stave that run the show, slowin' down the wagon. I could see there was a problem to start with. If 'n Elmer and me worked the brakes, Miz Gates'd have to do the drivin', and I didn't know if 'n she was up to doin' that. The shoe on one side was near to bein' wore through, and didn't look like it wouldn't even touch the wheel. Elmer watched me lookin' at the shoe that was near broke. *So, how are we goin' to get down off of this mountain?*

He shrugged. *Danged if 'n I know. Only thing I can think of is to unload the wagon, take all the weight off we can, and lead the mules down.*

Well, I couldn't think of a better way to go. I nodded. *I guess so.* So that's what we did. Truth to tell, there warn't all that much in the wagon that was heavy. We took out maybe three wood chests, two straight chairs, some bedding, some crocks that looked like they had vittles in 'em, some sacks of corn meal, I figured, and one small sack, maybe salt, and some clothes tied up in a bundle. I wondered how these folks could get along on such a pitiful little. The wagons in the wagon train had a lot more. Elmer hisself took out three good sized jugs. Likker, I guess. Miz Gates and Dory watched us, but didn't say anything.

That done, we went to the mules, him on one side, me on the t'other. It was in my mind to tell him what we had to do, but I figured he knowed as much as I did. So I kept quiet. We started down the steep slope, gradual like. When we got to the switchback, I was on the outside first off. The slope was so steep that I couldn't hardly keep hold of my mule's harness and I had to let go, hopin' his mule would hold back enough. Then, the next time, he was on the outside and I guess he had to let go. The mules did right well. Only once in the whole thing did I figure we'd lose it. But it held and we made it through and on down a piece afore we stopped the mules.

There ain't nothing much else to tell. We loaded up the wagon agin. Elmer loaded his jugs. On down we went to a place to camp. I did the same as afore, laying my roll down slope, away from them, eating a little more of my cornpone. But that night, it was the same as afore, with the woman's hollerin', and Elmer movin' around in the light of the fire. Like the first time, I didn't do anything. Next mornin' her face was all gray marked, like it was dirty. Like it had been the other time.

Only other thing I recollect about the trip down was that Miz Gates ast if'n she could ride Thunder. I said I didn't know if'n he'd let her, but she got up there in the saddle, with her britches astraddle, and he put up with it. I got to say she looked real good, settin' there on Thunder. It hit me agin that there was somethin' about her that caught a man's eye. She asked Dory if'n she wanted to ride, but Dory shook her head. But after her mama got down, Thunder let her lead him around some. It looked like she liked that a lot.

By the fourth day, we was down the mountain. By that time, Miz Gates had me callin' her Beulah and she was feedin' me at

supper time. My cornpone had run out. They was about out of
supplies, too. All 'cept the likker in the jugs, I guess. Elmer was
still not havin' much to do with me, more like he was just puttin'
up with me. Beulah and me would set at the fire and talk about
this and that. The more I saw of her, it looked like there was
more to see. But I was keepin' my distance.

Halfway down the mountain, I told 'em they didn't need
me any more and that I'd go on ahead. Beulah begged me to stay
'til we got all the way down, and I said I would. I kept on makin'
my camp away from them. On another night, I heard her yellin'
at him. I couldn't tell what she was sayin', but sounded like she
was real mad, givin' him or Dory what for. I doubted it was
Dory. Maybe that was why I stayed with them 'til we got down
all the way.

We was about to come into Johnson City, Tennessee. First
time I'd been in Tennessee in over a year. Maybe two. I'd lost
count. Anyway, I'd not of knowed where we was right off, but
Beulah Gates could read and she read it on a sign. Elmer stopped
the team a ways out and Beulah and Dory got out and then's
when I told 'em I'd be leavin' 'em there. I shook hands with
Elmer and he stood there like a knot on a log, but finally he said
a much obliged, or something like that. Tell the truth, I didn't
expect any more'n that.

Beulah come up close to me and acted like she was goin' to
give me a hug, but I moved away from her afore she did it. No
need to take the chance of gettin' Elmer riled up agin. Dory come
up to me and shook my hand and said somethin' I didn't get.
Beulah told her she had the feelin' they'd see me agin. I said maybe.
But I thought, not if'n I can help it. I got up on Thunder, and
her and Dory come over to say goodbye to him. She said
something to Thunder that I didn't hear. Then she turned him
loose and I rode away to'ard town.

I was right glad to get shed of 'em. And I was some regretful
that I'd gone back to help 'em. Truth to tell, I warn't even certain,

lookin' back, that I'd been of any help. I guess if'n they had got stopped, like they did, somebody would of come along to help out, like that man did with the double team. One thing about the trip over the mountain made me to wonder. There warn't many other wagons or even horses on the track when the wagon train come over or the Gates wagon. It looked to me like there'd be a lot more.

Well, it turned out I found out that we warn't on the main way over the mountain. There was two other ones, one to the north and the other a good ways to the south that most of the wagon trains went on. Not that it mattered I guess. Maybe just as well for the wagon train, movin' slow. Anyway, that's what I found out later on, down in Greenville or maybe it was Knoxville.

Johnson City looked like Mount Airy, but maybe half agin as big. It looked like there was two main streets where Mount Airy had one. There was some stores and blacksmithys and stables. I could see there was two or three saloons. I was a mite smarter now and I knowed how to look for a boardin' house. I found one on the side street and the woman said the same thing I'd heard afore. Leave my gun with her, keep my boots off'n the bed, and all that. I had money to spend so I asked her where to go to get a bath and a hair cut. It was right near the boardin' house. I left Thunder at a stables, tellin' them to curry him good and look at his feet. Then I went where she said go. I don't recollect much about it, except that I come out of the place feeling like a new man.

After supper at the boardin' house, I walked down the street to one of the saloons. I thought maybe I'd see some of the men from the wagon train, but I didn't.

But what I saw was Elmer Gates, big as life and twice as drunk. He was tellin' some tale about crossin' the mountain. I saw him just as I was goin' in, so I changed my tracks and got out of there afore he saw me. One way or other, he was apt to be trouble, and I didn't want any part of it. So I went on down the street to another saloon and had my whiskey. But I didn't hang around there long. It looked like a rough crowd to me and I didn't want to tangle with 'em. So I went back to the boardin' house and had a good night's sleep. No old man in the next bed snorin', to keep me awake.

Next mornin' I made up my mind to get out of town afore I got mixed up with the Gates agin. I was askin' at the stables about the way to Knoxville and how long a ride it would be and he happened to mention the town of Greenville, down to the southwest. He said that was where the Rebel Army had a winter camp in the War. Not knowin' what side he had been on, I didn't let on that I'd been at that camp when I was a soldier. I went to see it agin.

It was a two day ride from Johnson City. I camped out one night, in the rain. I got real wet, but it warn't cold, so I didn't mind much. The road was a pore one. It looked like nobody had done much to take care of it. I passed some houses here and there but didn't see nobody out and about. It was real purty country. Hilly up by Johnson City, levelin' off down by Greenville. I rode into what little town there was and found a boardin' house and told the woman I'd stay a night or two. She named her price and I paid for one night, and asked about a stable for Thunder. He didn't need the cover, but he was actin' like he had a limp, and I wanted to see what a stable man thought about it. She told me where to go. *You just passin' through?*

Yes mam, on my way to Knoxville. Mean to look around some. You been to Greenville afore?

Yes mam. I was here in the War. Winter camp with General Longstreet. You live here then?

She nodded. *My family's lived here for near on to fifty years. I was here then. More's the pity.* She was quiet. *You recollect where the camp was?*

I don't know for sure. Can you tell me where?

She nodded. *You ride down this road all the way, past the last houses, and on two or three mile. It was in a kind of valley that'll be to yore right, to the west. Ain't much there to see.* She shook her head. *When youn's left to go in the Virginny, folks in town took everything that was there. Seemed like it was only fair to do.*

I couldn't tell if'n she was a Yankee or a Rebel. I recollected that the officers had told us back then that some folks in these parts was Yankees, and that we had to be careful about them. A soldier I knowed said he got into near a fight with a old man over it. *Maybe the army bein' here that long caused you folks a lot of trouble?*

A peck of trouble. Feedin' all you soldiers made it so's the army was allus short of supplies. Vittles was the main thing. At first the pack trains come in from the south, we heard tell, then that line was cut off. Word was that nothin' could get through from the west, over from Knoxvul. So they had to get it best they could. Forage. Steal. Buy it from over the mountains. Anybody could get anything over the mountain could make a lot of money off'n it. A lot of 'em did. She shook her head. *It was real bad. Weun's was as hungry as youn's was. By the time the army moved on, we didn't have much of anythin'.* She shook her head agin. *Weun's still don't. We get by, but don't look for no fancy vittles on my table.*

No mam, I won't. I ain't used to fancy vittles, anyway.

Where you been since the War?

North C'lina. I was sick a long time.

Fevers?

Yes mam.

She nodded. *Lots of soldiers had fevers bad. Lots of 'em in the winter camp. It got so bad, some of the women folk in town took care of the sick. Did youn's know that?*

No mam, we never heard anything about that.

She shrugged. *Well, it was give and take. Sometimes, a Army wagon pack train got through the mountains, we got some of it. Some folks in this town was sorry to see the army move on.* She grinned. *Some of the women, in partic'lar. Maybe you met up with some of them.*

I nodded. *Yes mam, maybe I did.*

I got chores to do. Where you headed now? You thinkin' of settlin' down here? We can use some young men. Most of ours never come home from the War. She looked away. *My two sons didn't ever come home.*

I'm right sorry to hear that. Right now I want to go home. Stewart County, over past Nashville.

Long way to go.

Yes mam, it is that.

Next mornin' I got over to the stable, and here was Thunder hobblin' around like he was goin' lame. It scared me to death. Sometimes you can do somethin' about a lame mule or horse and sometimes ain't nothin' to be done. The man at the stable looked at him, and he went and got the smithy to come and have a look. Back then, a smithy generally was a good horse doctor, in particular about a horse goin' lame on you. It looked like they was real taken by Thunder and was as worried about the hobble as I was. The two of 'em put on some salve and wrapped up the leg tight and said I better stay off'n him for a day or so. The stable man said he had a mule I could ride, if'n I wanted to.

I stayed in Greenville three or four days, I don't know how many for sure. It cost me more of my money at the boardin' house to do that, than I had meant, but it looked like she could shore use the money. And I had to pay the stable man and the smithy somethin' too. They made it easy for me. The boardin' house woman let me work off some of what I owed her by workin' in her woodpile for a day. And the stableman let me do that too by cleanin' out his stalls. I was much obliged to them.

On one of them days, I rode his mule out to where the winter camp was. The woman was right. There warn't much left to show that the Rebel Army had camped there one winter. It looked like there was maybe three fields where the camp was. I didn't recollect that. Maybe I was in just one field, in one part of it, and never knowed about the other parts.

One thing was that there was stumps all around everywheres, where the trees had been cut for firewood. The stable man had said the people in town was real mad about that, but there warn't anythin' that could be done about it. The camp had to have wood for fires. There was a lot of places where the grass had been worn off by where the lean-tos was and where we did all that marchin'. And where the big campfires had been built there was a place, maybe fifty feet across, where the ground looked scorched. I saw some ditches, where the latrines had been, I guess.

My recollections was all mixed up. It'd been cold and wet and I was hungry some of the time. There warn't anything to do but march and go for wood and tend to the fires. Time fell heavy on our hands, and there was a lot of back talk and fightin'. Some of the officers was pure mean and looked like they went out of their way to give us trouble. But it warn't all bad. I recollected Bill Jones and the good times him and me had, talkin' about this and that. And our ras'lin matches. And, like the woman said, the woman Bill Jones had sent to me in our lean-to when I couldn't pay for her myself. Bill was tickled to death to do that. I'd catch him grinnin' at me for days on end after that. I knowed good and well what he was grinnin' about.

Thinkin' about that woman made me think that I hadn't been with a woman for a long time. If'n I'd had a little more money, I'd be tempted to see if'n there was a woman like that in Greenville! But I didn't, and anyhow I didn't figure she'd let me chop wood for her to work off what I owed her.

It must of been the fourth or fifth day that it looked like that Thunder could ride agin, so I settled up with everybody and took off. The boardin' house woman even made me as parcel of vittles for the road. All them people in Greenville was real good to me.

The road from Greenville warn't all that good. It was real rocky in places where there was a wash across it. I went slow, pickin' the best way through, to keep from doin' any damage to Thunder's leg. So it took us near to three days to get there. The road from Greenville to Knoxville hooked up with the road down from Johnson City afore it got to Knoxville. I stopped at the forks of the road, tryin' to be sure I was goin' the right way. Nothin' looked like I recollected from the battle we fought there, on the north side of town, I thought. But of course, back then, I warn't payin' any attention to how the land laid. And maybe I was wrong. Maybe we didn't even come up this way.

Anyway, I was settin' there on Thunder, lookin' around, tryin' to place where I was, just killin' time. There warn't much traffic that day, goin' or comin'. It was mostly buggies and horseback, with one or two wagons. The wagons looked like they was loaded down, with this and that. None of 'em had a cover, except one, movin slow, at the end of the line. The wagon and the cover looked like what I'd seen afore. The driver had some old hat pulled down over his face. There was two of 'em on the springboard. It hit me, standin' there, lookin' at it, that the wagon and the team looked for all the world like the Gates. It got closer to me, and then right afore it got even with me and Thunder, it pulled over to the side and come to a stop.

The driver handed the reins to the other fellar, and got down, and come over to'ard me. Oh Lord, I thought, it's Elmer Gates. But it cain't be. He ain't big enough. *Howdy.* It sounded like a woman. He took off his hat and his hair fell down, and I could see that it was a woman and it was Beulah Gates.

Well, I'll be damned! Beulah, is that you? Is that Dory on the springboard?

Yes, it's me, all right. And that's Dory.

Where's Elmer? He in the wagon?

No, he ain't here right now.

You been on the road all this time?

Most of it. I was lookin' at her while we was talkin'. She looked real tired, but not much worse than the last time I seen her. She was not a purty woman, but she warn't all that bad lookin'. I figured she'd look good with a clean face and a dress like Betty Lou had. There was somethin' about her, maybe the way she talked, or held her head, that made you pay attention to her. I figured that was the case even when she was dirtier than she was now or when she acted scared to death of Elmer. There was somethin' about her. *You got time to look at my mules? They're movin real slow.*

Yeah, I got time. Elmer not lookin' after 'em?
No, he ain't doin' that, and I don't know how.
You plannin' on stoppin' in Knoxville?
I thought we might stop and stay a while here. Maybe get a job some where. We could use some supplies. I see you still got Thunder. It was quiet. We stood there, lookin' at each other and at the wagon where Dory was holdin' the reins. I didn't know what was goin' on, and I warn't for sure I wanted to know. And where the devil was Elmer? *Tell you what. Let me ride ahead and see if'n I can find a good place to camp and I'll meet you headed that way. I'll stick around for the night and if'n Elmer don't give me no trouble I'll look at the mules in the mornin'. But if'n he gives me any trouble, I'm gone from here. Understand?*

She nodded. *I'd be much obliged if'n you'd do that.*

What about Elmer? He likely to cause trouble if'n I start to look at yore mules?

She looked away and back at me. *Naw, he ain't likely to cause any trouble.* I wanted to ask her more about him but I figured from what she said, or didn't say, this warn't the right time to do it. She was shakin' her head. *One thing. We ain't got much vittles left. We cain't feed you like we use to.*

That ain't a problem. I been workin' a little along the way and I've got a little money. You ride ahead 'til you see a place to camp. I'll go see what I can find in the line of something to eat.

It looked like she was about to cry. Her face was all screwed up. Then she shook her head and wiped her face with her shirt tail. She didn't say any more, just nodded, and went back to the wagon, climbed up, and started the team. We went on down the road a piece, and found a place to the side she could pull over to. It looked like wagons had camped there afore. I waved her to do that and I rode on into Knoxville, thinking what have I got in to agin! Every time I get with the Gates, there's trouble of some kind. But she looked so down and out that I felt so sorry for her, didn't seem like there was anything else to do.

At the next crossroads, I found a place to buy some vittles, all cooked and in army tins. I told the man I'd bring the tins back. As I recollect, he was chargin' a lot of money for what he had, but I paid it anyway. It looked like he done this for a livin' and got what he could from the folks on the road. I even got some sweet milk and tea cakes for Dory.

By the time I got back, they'd unhitched the mules and had a little fire goin' from wood they'd scrounged up from somewhere. There must have been a spring somewhere near. They had fresh water for supper and they had washed their faces and tied their hair in a rag. The light was startin' to fade, but there was enough to eat by. They fell to the vittles like it had been some time since they'd had enough to eat. I was a mite hungry myself and so there warn't much talkin'. Nothin' was said about Elmer, and I didn't ask any more questions. I figured she'd tell me, in her own good time.

By that time, it was near dark. Two or three more wagons had pulled up right close to where we was and made camp. Gen'lly, at a camp like that, folks move around, talkin' to folks at other camps, like where you from and where you headed for. Some folks come by our camp and we acted like we was a family, and told 'em we figured we'd stop in Knoxville to get supplies afore we moved on. I did all the talkin' and they moved on without askin' any more questions. Beulah saw to it that Dory went on to bed in the wagon. I hadn't heard Dory say a single word. She'd smile at this and that, but not a word out of her. It was real quare that a girl her age warn't doin' any talkin'. Or not much. But that warn't any thing new. She'd been like that up on the mountain. Beulah never tried to explain it to me. I thought about old Thelma Wood and how she could be such a chatterbox when she let loose. Dory didn't seem natch'ral.

Beulah come back to the fire. She set down close enough to me to talk without botherin' Dory or anybody else. *You terrible tired?*

No, I guess not.

You good for some listenin'?

I figured this was goin' to be about Elmer. *Yeah, I'm good for some listenin'.*

She stirred up the little fire, and put another stick on. I figured she was decidin' what to say and where to start. *Elmer, he ain't my first husband. And he ain't the daddy of Dory. I married up with her daddy when I was fifteen. Dory was borned the next year. She was a puny baby and I thought I'd lose her for a long time. She ain't ever been right in her head. She can do things all right, but she don't talk much and nobody but me can get what she's sayin'. My mama could, afore she died. I ain't had no more babies since. Lost 'em when I was carryin' 'em, or they was borned dead. Dory is all I got or ever will have, I guess.*

She was lookin' at the fire and it seemed like she was talkin' to herself. *Robert, he were a good man. We got along. Lived on his daddy's place and he farmed. Had a right good livin'. But I never got along much with his mama. She was allus tellin' me what to do, pickin' on me for this and that. I couldn't hardly take it, but I had to stick it out. Well, anyway, Robert died over a year ago. He had the fevers and there warn't nothin' nobody could do to help him. He went fast, afore I knowed what was happenin'.*

After he died, it hit me that I warn't happy with his family and that I didn't have to put up with that any more, and that I better get away if'n I could. First thing I knowed, along come Elmer, and I figured he was my way out. Mine and Dory's. Robert had left me with a wagon and a team of mules and a little money we'd saved up from sellin' some cattle. Elmer come courtin' and Robert's family didn't raise any commotion about it. I figured they'd be glad to be rid of me and Dory, his mama, in partic'lar.

At the first, Elmer was for goin' west. He was tenant farmin', like his daddy was, and he didn't go for that kind of life, he said. I shore didn't, either. When he was talkin' about goin' west, he was talkin' about Californy. I was thinkin' about Missoury, but I figured we could make that out as we got along, if'n we could find a way to go. Then I heard at the store about the wagon trains comin' through North C'lina. The word was they was folks that wanted to start a new life after the War. I figured that was fittin' for Elmer and me.

Tell the truth, I got him to lie down with me. Then I told him I was carryin' his baby and he better marry up with me. And that if'n he did, we'd take my wagon and team and my money and join up with a wagon train goin' west. I better go look at Dory. And she got up and went to the wagon.

I watched her go, wonderin' where this was leadin' to. There warn't no need for her to tell me about her dead husband and all that. I got up and went over to the edge of the woods to take a stretch and a piss. Then I come back to the fire that was burnin' low, and put on more wood, thinkin' she was comin' back. She did. She set back down by the fire. I could see her plain, now, in the light of the fire, settin' crosslegged, tuckin' her shirt tail around her. And she went on with her story.

You'll be wonderin' why I'm tellin' you all this. Fact of the matter is, so am I. I ain't never told any body all of this. But you the only friend I have here in Tennessee and I want to tell it to you. You still willin' to hear me out?

If'n you want to tell me, I'm willin' to hear you out.

You still wonderin' about Elmer, ain't you?

I reckon you could say that. Him and me never hit it off much. If'n he finds me here, talkin' to you like this, I reckon there'll be hell to pay. I can fight for myself all right enough, but he's a big man.

Yeah, he's a big man, and a mean one, at that. But I don't figure you have to worry about that tonight. I'm goin' to go on with my story now. The fire was burnin' right good now and I could see her face in the light of the fire, as she started up agin. *Well, there warn't no baby but he never knowed it. And oncet I lay down with him, I had him hooked, you might say, and he wanted to do it all the time. I wouldn't do it, 'less'n he married up with me. So he did, and I moved in with him on the tenant farm where he was. And I took the wagon and the team and the things that was mine.*

There was trouble right off. He didn't take to Dory and she was scared to death of him. He said back when we started talkin' about goin' west, he'd take Dory, then he said he wouldn't. I told him we'd take her, elsewise I wouldn't go. I figured if'n I didn't go, he couldn't. I was the one with the wagon and team. So when time come to go, we took her. She stopped talkin' agin, got up, stood there, rockin' back and forth, huggin' herself with her arms. I could see her in the light of the fire. I didn't say anything. I figured there warn't anything needed to be said from me. Then she set down agin and started in agin. *I got to say right here that I knowed there was a mean streak in him. When we was courtin', I seen him act real mean to a dog or a team of mules or anything like that. One time he flyed off the handle real bad at me when I told 'im he was wrong about something. I don't recollect what it was about. But his face got red and he hollered at me and I thought he was goin' to hit me. My daddy could be mean like that so one part of me knowed what was happenin'. But the other part of me wanted so bad to get away from that tenant farm that I tried not to think about it.*

She stirred agin, takin' the rag off her head, lookin' at it like she didn't know what it was, and then puttin' it back on agin. *I should of thought about it. We'd no more than got on the road than he started in bein' mean. Mean to the mules, mean to Dory, mean to me, mean to the folks on the wagon train that was tryin' to help us. You recollect how he was that time you come back to help us over the mountain?* She didn't wait for a answer, but went right on ahead. *Well, that was no where near as bad as it got. We warn't on the road hardly a week and he started in on me, layin' the blame on me for anythin' that went wrong. And if'n I talked back, he'd hit me or acted like he was goin' to. I never knowed what to look for. One minute he'd be good to me and Dory and the next minute go crazy about somethin'.*

The fire was burnin' low, but I could see her turn and look at me. *And he was actin' like a boar hog, if'n you know what I mean. He was at me, every night, when we camped. I was 'shamed of it, but I was scared to try not to do it. I warn't sorry he didn't want to hook up with the wagon train. They'd find out how he was and it'd shame me real bad.*

That warn't the worst of it. She was talkin' real quiet now. I couldn't hardly make out what she was sayin'. *He started in on Dory. Sweet talkin' to her. Tellin' her how purty she was. Layin' his hands on her. She didn't like it and would cry. He didn't pay no mind to that, but kept on doin' it. Then he got on me to let him do it to me while she watched. Said she ought to know how to do it, big girl that she was.* She started to cry, a kind of a wail, like a animal in trouble. Then she wiped her face with her shirt tail, and I could see her raise up her head. *So I shot him.* It was real quiet. The folks in the other wagons had turned in, I guess, and the only sound that could be heard was some night birds. *Did you hear what I said?*

Yeah, I heard. You said you shot him.

Yeah, I shot him. She started in cryin' agin. *And I'd do it agin. He was a bad, mean man and shootin' was too good for him.*

Where'd you shoot him? Somewhere in the mountains?

Yeah, somewhere in the mountains.

He ain't in the wagon, like you said?

Naw, he ain't in the wagon. He's somewhere's in the mountains.

You want to tell me about it? I warn't sure if'n I wanted to hear about it. But it seemed like the thing to say, now that she'd gone this far.

She stopped cryin' and wiped her face agin with her shirt tail. *He was bad afore you come back that last time but he got worse after you left. Ever' night when we camped, he'd start on me about somethin' I done wrong. If'n I talked back, he'd hit me or else told me he was goin' to. I started right then to figure out how me and Dory was goin' to get away. But weun's had to get a far piece away, else he'd come and find us, and it'd be worse that it had been.*

Now I couldn't see her hardly at all. The fire had gone down to just some red coals. All I could see was just the shadow of her in the pitch black. *Then one night, he told me he was goin' to have Dory. I begged him to leave her alone, but the more I begged the more he said he was goin' to do it. He said it was time for him to do it. He told me he was goin' to do it on the next night. She was*

settin' there by me. I guess she knowed somethin' of what he was
talkin' about. She started in cryin' and holdin' on to me like she'd
never let go. Then's when I knowed I had to kill him.

She stopped talkin' agin. I figured she was tryin' to decide what
to say next. *I know it ain't right to lay this on you, but seems like I got*
to tell someone. If 'n I don't, I'm goin' to go crazy. And I cain't talk about
it to Dory. She won't even sit still for it. She just covers her ears and gets
that quare look in her eyes. Can you stand it?

I can stand it. When I said that, I was wonderin' what I'd do
if 'n the sheriff finds out about her killin' Elmer and drags me
into it. I guessed it was a little too late to worry about that. She'd
already told me she shot him.

By now it was pitch dark. No moon. Hardly any stars to
amount to anything with what I guessed was cloud cover comin'
in from the west. The fire had burned out and it didn't seem like
the thing to do to stir it up agin. So what she said next was kind
of like a voice comin' out of the dark. But she warn't cryin' no
more and so what she said was quiet but strong, and I got every
word.

The next mornin' I made my plan. I knowed where the pistol
was kept and the shot and I figured I knowed how to load it and
shoot it. You seen me with it oncet when you was with us. The
thing was, I wanted him close to me when I shot him and I wanted
him to know it was me that shot him. I didn't want to shoot him in
the back. That'd be the coward's way out. But not just that, I wanted
him to know I pulled the trigger on him that kilt him! She said
them last words all spaced out like she was feelin' agin how much
she hated him.

So I got the pistol and loaded it and put it in my apron with
the real big pocket. And I got out a quilt from my bed roll and put
it on top where I could get at it. And middle of the day, I told him
I'd lie down with him when we camped that night, rollin' my eyes
and all that, to make him think I wanted to do it. He gave me a
bear hug and said somethin' like we'd stop early. I didn't want to

*stop early since I wanted it to be plumb dark when I did it, but I
was scared to say so.*

*Maybe we stopped early. I don't know. All I know is that it
was near dark by the time we got stopped and he got unhitched.
I sed for him to build up the fire away from the wagon, over in
the edge of the trees. I guess he was thinkin' I wanted to put our
bed roll over that way. And I got somethin' for supper. After we
et, I told Dory to go on to bed and I spread out her bed roll a
ways from the wagon under a real big tree. I stayed with her 'til
she was asleep, talkin' about Missoury. She loves to hear me talk
about Missoury. I told her she might hear somethin' in the night,
and that she warn't to be afraid. And that I'd come sleep by her
when we put out the fire.*

*He was settin' by the fire when I done all that, whittlin'. I
come around the wagon with the quilt and took and laid it down
in the edge of the trees on the other side of the wagon from Dory.
And I put the pistol under one corner of it, so's I could reach it.*

Now she was talkin' so quiet I couldn't hardly make out
what she was sayin'. *I laid down on the quilt with my legs to'ard
him, and pulled up my skirt tail so's he could see I didn't have on
any drawers. I called his name, and I could see him get up and
come to'ard where I was layin' down, undoin' his pants as he come.*
She stopped talkin' agin. *And when he was down on his knees in
front of me, I reached up and got the pistol and pointed it at his
chest and pulled the trigger.*

She stopped talkin' agin, and then started up agin. *He fell
down on top of me and I couldn't hardly move, but I kicked my
way out from under him. I stood up over him and loaded the pistol
agin from the shot in my apron pocket and shot him agin in the
back. And I done it agin, jus' to be shore he was dead. And I had
shot for one more time, so I done it agin.*

*I heard tell that when somebody gets shot, they make a noise.
Well, he didn't. He just fell on top of me. He just went down. Only
thing I'm sorry for is that I couldn't see his face when he knowed
what I was doin'. His back was to the fire, so he could see mine, but
I couldn't see his'n. But I trust to God that if'n he could of seen my*

face when I did it, he'd of knowed what I was doin', and more, why.

She was quiet agin. *I hated it that that dress got all bloody. Best dress I had. I should of thought of that and wore a old one. But I had to do somethin' with the bloody dress, so I took it of, tryin' not to get blood all over, and draped it over him, real nice. Then I turned up the corners of the quilt 'til he was near to bein' covered up, and put some sticks and leaves on top of that. He was a big man and all that didn't hardly cover him up, but I figured it would do the job 'til daylight. Funny, my wantin' to cover him up. We'd pulled off of the road a good piece. There warn't nobody around, and not likely to be. But I wanted him covered up.*

I went to the wagon and laid down beside Dory. And I put my arm around her and I knew right then and there that he'd not ever hurt her like he had me. Worse than me, 'cause I'd been with a man afore and I could take it. Even like it sometimes. But she couldn't, and I fixed it all right enough that he couldn't hurt her ever.

She was quiet. *I guess not many folks kill somebody like that. I know you done it, but that was War. This was a war, kind of, I guess. War with him on one side and me on t'other. He allus thought he had me beat, but he didn't. By God, he didn't. In the end, I had him beat.*

She fell quiet agin. I thought maybe she was done with her story. But she warn't yet. *Thing I cain't figure out is why I married up with him in the first place. By that time, I knowed like I said he acted like a boar hog. Robert liked me that way, but he didn't want to do it ever' night. Seemed like sometimes Elmer couldn't think of anythin' else. Worse than that, I knowed he liked to be rough sometimes. I seen him rough with dogs and cats and mules. But I figured that was a passin' thing. I figured he'd quiet down after we was married and settin' out for a new life. Well, I shore was wrong about that. I come to hate him for what he was, deep down inside 'im, in his guts. The likker made it worse, but it was there in 'im, down inside 'im, in his guts.*

I heard or felt her stand up. *I'm done with the story. I'm much obliged that you let me tell it to you. I don't rightly know what you want to do about knowin' it, but I don't rightly care, I guess. I did what I figured I had to do. And I'd do it agin, if'n I had to.* And I heard her walk away, to the wagon.

I poked the coals of the fire and put on some wood. Over to the south of east a half moon showed up through the clouds flying by. I warn't of a mind to lay down, not just yet. Thinkin' about Beulah's story, I could see why she shot Elmer. It was bad enough to put up with him on her part, if'n what she said was so. But she sure as hell was right in doin' what she could do, to keep him off of Dory. That was for sure.

I set there, playin' in the fire with a poker stick. Then I let myself think what I'd been thinkin' all along, ever since I saw her that first time, half scared to death and half madder'n hell. She was all dirty and all mixed up, but there was something about her I couldn't shed my mind of. Maybe I better say my guts. Maybe I better say my crotch. I hadn't been with a woman since Maybelle, and when I let it, it were drivin' me half crazy. Maybelle showed me how it was 'tween and man and a woman. Usin' my hand didn't wipe away the need I had to hold a woman, us nekkid, me feelin' of her from her face clear down to her feet. Lordy, I needed that right then right bad.

Well, Beulah was right over yonder. But from her side of the story, she'd just kilt off Elmer and it didn't seem likely she'd want to tangle with another man right now. I halfway laughed at myself, thinkin' that. She'd pro'bly kick me in the crotch just for thinkin' about it!

But I have to tell you out right that I wanted her. Dirty and ragged that she was, there was something about her that made me want to find out more. There was something about her that got me all stirred up. I never let it get to me when we was on the mountain, what with all the trouble up there with Elmer and gettin' over the mountain, and all that. But when I seen that wagon and her comin' to'ard me, takin' off that old hat and I knowed it were her, it got me. And I knowed all right enough what it was that got me.

I was pokin' at the fire and thinkin' all that and I looked over at her wagon. She was standin' there, in part moon shadow. The way she was standin' there made me figure she was waitin' for somethin'. Not hardly knowin' what I was doin', I stood up and held out my hand to her. If'n she wanted to come back to the fire, she'd come. Elsewise, she'd take it for a good night and get out of my sight.

Well sir, she didn't get out of my sight. She walked back to the fire. We set down, her right by me, crosslegged. I can see it now, in my mind's eye. Her dress tail covered my britches leg on that side, but she didn't make any motion to move it away. It were like she wanted it there. I knowed it was there, and I started to think about what might be to come. She held out her hand and I give her the pokin' stick and she started in playin' in the fire like I'd been doin'. She was lookin' at what she was doin' with the pokin' stick. *You ain't laid down yet.*

No. It seemed like I warn't ready to.

Me neither.

Dory asleep?

She nodded. *She allus sleeps real sound. Not like me. I wake up at anythin'. Allus have been that way.* She was quiet, still playin' in the fire. *I'm obliged that you let me do the talkin' I did. I feel better for havin' said it all out loud.* In the light of the fire, I saw her turn her head to me. *You're a good one to listen. Anybody ever told you that?*

I shrugged. *Maybe. I don't know. Ed allus said for me to be quiet and listen.*

Who's Ed?

A man I know. Part of my family back in Stewart County.

She handed me back the pokin' stick. *Ain't no wonder why you ain't ready to go to sleep with all of what I told you, on yore mind.*

I put the pokin' stick in the fire and watched it start to burn, and I let it be quiet. Then I turned to her. In the light of the fire flamin' up from the pokin' stick, I saw her watchin' me, with a half smile on her face, that face that had got to me. *Yeah, that's on my mind some. I ain't never been with a woman what's shot her husband.*

She gathered up her dress tail and pulled her shawl up around her neck. *I guess not. Ain't many men that have, that knowed about it.* She give a little laugh at what she'd said. *That scare you off?*

Naw, that don't scare me off. I give a little laugh. *'Sides, you ain't got yore pistol handy.* I let it be quiet agin. *But that ain't all of what's on my mind right now.*

You goin' to tell me what's on yore mind right now? She was lookin' at me straight. There warn't no smile nor no laugh anywheres to be seen or heard.

I don't know as how you want to hear this, but I'm goin' to tell you anyway. What's on my mind right now is to put these here arms around you and hold you and kiss you on the mouth 'til the sun comes up!

Then I seen her smile, in the light of the fire. *Well, whyn't you do it afore you change yore mind?*

So, Lord help us, I did. I bent around and took her in my arms and kissed her. It started out all me, but halfway into it, she pulled away and put her arms and hands around my neck and then it was her doin' as much of the kissin' as me. Then she pulled away, with her hands still on my neck.

She looked at me, and shook her head. *I never looked to be kissed like that by you. I ain't been kissed like that since Robert.* She shook her head. *Elmer warn't in for kissin'.* She pulled back so's she could talk. *When I come over here, I figured you wanted me to lie down with you.* She took her hands away and looked at the fire. *I figured you'd want to do that as payback for what you'd done for me, listenin' to my story.*

I took her hand and held it to my face. *Beulah, there ain't no payback needed. I did it as yore friend and 'cause I wanted to.* I turned her face to me and I let it be quiet. *But I've got to tell you*

198 Hughlett L. Morris

I want more than just kissin'. I couldn' hardly think about sleepin' for my wantin' you. She didn't say anything, so I went on with what I had to say. *I want to lie down with you in this place right now. I want to kiss you more and more. And I want to lie down with you, us nekkid. I want to make you forget about Elmer Gates right now. But I got to tell you. I ain't thinkin' just about makin' you forget about Elmer Gates. I want it for me. I want it a whole lot.*

She stood up and I figured I'd said it all wrong and that she was goin' to leave me, settin' there by the fire, with me mite nigh shakin' like I was havin' a chill. But I was wrong about that. What she did was to hold out her hand and pull me up to her. We kissed agin and I was so hard, I figured she could feel it through all the clothes. I picked up my bed roll and spread it under a big tree out of sight from the other wagons. We went down on our knees and, as Maybelle oncet said, the play party started.

There ain't no use in tellin' you about how it was. I was hungry for a woman. She was wipin' her mind and her guts clean of Elmer Gates. Then, of a sudden, it seemed like my hunger for a woman was for her in partic'lar and she was havin' her feelin's for me. Nothin' like that was said out loud, but the feelin's was there, leastwise on my part.

When the storm passed, she stayed with me for a while, her at my side, layin' on my arm. *I don't know anythin' about you, 'cept how you feel here in the dark.*

There ain't much to tell. I went to the War when I was just a boy, not knowin' what I was doin'. I still don't. I got real sick with the fevers and started home. I've been on the road near two years, I figure. I still have a long ways to go. I'm much obliged to the wagon train for gettin' me over the mountain. Now I'm travelin' by myself. I let it be quiet. *You and Dory goin' to stop in Knoxville?*

That's what I plan to do. Find some place to work. Find some place to live. Start over. She was quiet. *I guess I have to ask. Are you goin' to tell on me, about Elmer?*

Naw. I ain't got nothin' to tell. All I know is a story some woman told me. I was quiet. *Afore you ask, I need to say there ain't no strings from what we done here. I needed you bad and you went along.*

She set up. *Yeah, I went along, like you say. But I got to say I needed you as much as you me. All them times with Elmer, I was wonderin' if'n I could have feelin's for a man like I had for Robert.* She bent down and kissed me. *Now I know I can. I'm obliged to you for doin' that.*

Our mouths was still together. *You want to stay here with me? I can show you agin you can do it.*

She pulled away. *One part of me wants to. But, naw, I'd best not. Dory she sometimes wakes up the middle of the night. 'Sides, you and me is done here. Best we leave it as it is.* She got up and I watched her put on her clothes. She bent down and kissed me one more time. *See you in the mornin'.* And she went to her wagon.

I'm goin' to end this story about Beulah Gates. The next mornin' we et what was left of the vittles from the night afore. And I left 'em hitchin' up to go on into Knoxville. Only thing was, Beulah and me kissed twicet, oncet when her and Dory come over to the campfire place that mornin', and oncet when I was ready to ride away. And she felt of my face and neck like she wanted to recollect how they felt to her hand. Doin' that, she smiled that crooked smile of hers that had got me in trouble.

Well, I cain't say for certain it was any trouble. She was a different kind of a woman than I'd ever knowed and I loved that about her. I said Elmer was like two men. Maybe Beulah was that way too. I'd seen her look mighty pitiful, and then God awful mad, and then soft to my touch. But I guess like Betty Lou Wood she knowed what was what and she warn't takin' life layin' down. That come out wrong, but you know what I mean.

I never told anybody about Beulah's story. And I never stayed around in Knoxville long enough to find out if'n Elmer was found. So I rode into town and stopped at a place to eat. The feller there and me got to talkin'. I told 'im where I was headed next, over to Nashville, I figured. He said the right word was down to Nashvul. He said we was in the Cumberland Mountains and that Nashvul was down in the basin. He told me how to start out. He said the goin' was rough. The settlements was few and far 'tween. The only ones he named was Harriman and Standin' Stone, where he figured I'd find a boardin' house. He reckoned it would be a four, five day ride. Maybe six.

So I bought some supplies for the rode, saddled up Thunder again, and we took off. I left, thinkin' about Beulah Gates and her crooked smile and how it had got me. But I knowed there warn't no need to worry about Beulah Gates. She was goin' to get along.

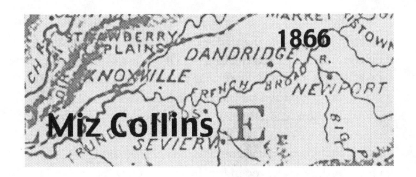

1866

Miz Collins

I don't recollect much about the ride from Knoxville to Harriman, 'ceptin' it was a longer ride than I thought of. That man I talked to in Knoxville said there wouldn't be much on the road, goin' this way. He said there was another way to Nashville, to the south. But he'd heard tell of a lot of robbin' and trouble down that way. Well, he was right about not much goin' the way I went. A wagon and team now and then, haulin' somethin' somewhere. A few buggies, but not many. Men on horseback, mainly, some ridin' by hisself, but more in twos or threes or more'n that.

Truth to tell, I warn't payin' much mind to anything. My mind was on Beulah Gates. My feelin's for her was all mixed up. I couldn't figure out what it was about her that got to me. It warn't anythin' like how it was with Maybelle Atkins. I swear to God it was a good thing I got away from her when I did, else I would want her more and no tellin' where all that would lead me to. More trouble, likely. I knowed it was best for her to go her way and me go mine. But she shore got me all stirred up. Bein' with her left me wantin' a woman more'n ever, and feelin' like I'd never get back to Stewart County and Nadine Cherry.

Anyway, it was a long road. After I got passed a crossroads a man called Oak Ridge, there warn't nothin' hardly at all 'til I reached Harriman. I had et all my travel vittles and had to beg at a house along the way, if'n there was any to beg from, or go without. Thunder had it better'n me, since there was good grazing at night and creeks for waterin' him. And for waterin' me, too.

I will say this, it was real purty country. Some hilly, some valleys. More timber than I'd seen, short of in the mountains we'd come over. I passed two or three crews cuttin' trees. I wanted to ask 'em about the lumber, where it would go, and all that. It seemed like they was a far piece from any town to sell it in. But they was busy, and I didn't stop. There was not more'n a dozen homesteads between Oak Ridge and Harriman that was close enough to the road that I could see 'em. I stopped at two of 'em to see if'n they'd take me in for the night. They fed me and put me in the barn for sleepin'. Fact is, they fed me right good. Game meat and taters and cooked greens and cornpone.

One woman, looked like she was maybe middle age, took to Thunder right away. She said she'd allus wanted a black stallion. I asked her if'n she wanted to try to ride him. She said she'd be tickled to try. And, by gar, she did it. She talked to him first off, and petted him some. Then she tucked up her dress tail and got on, and set there a minute or two, and than away they went. She rode him up and down the road like she'd been ridin' him all his borned days. He showed some spirit, but didn't cause her any real trouble. I was right pleased to watch, she was that good. When I left, I made her the promise of his foal, if'n he ever had one that warn't a filly. Of course we both knowed that was just country talk. I warn't goin' to ever come this way again, foal or no foal.

Harriman was a cross roads, like Oak Ridge was. But it was near the main road, and there was some more to it than Oak Ridge. A fellar at a saloon asked me where I come from and where I was bound for. I told him. He asked if'n I'd met up with any trouble on the road back to'ard Knoxville. I said I hadn't. He said that was lucky, that there was gangs of men, mostly fought in the War for the Yankees, that hadn't never settled down after the War was over. They was ridin' the countryside, lookin' for Rebel soldiers that come home or was passin' through. He said Knoxville and the countryside thereabouts was for the North in the War. He asked me if'n I'd been in the War. I said I had, but didn't say any more than that. Maybe he figured I was a Rebel by what I didn't tell him. Anyway, he said look out for the gangs. I thanked him and left.

I didn't know what to make of what he said. Nobody had give me any trouble since I left the Wood place. But aside from stayin' in a boardin' house and havin' a whiskey at a saloon, I'd kept to myself. Only time I hadn't was in Greenville, and nobody had give me any trouble there. But what he said made me on the lookout.

I figured, from what I'd been told, the next town was Standin' Stone. And it was near a week away by horseback. And I guessed there warn't much in between. I thought maybe I could hook up with somebody goin' that way, but never found no one. I figured maybe it was just as well. Sometimes travelin' alone is better'n with somebody you don't know or don't get along with. Anyway, that's how it turned out.

Since it looked like I was goin' to have to carry a fair amount of vittles with me, I asked around and found a right good set of saddle bags that I could afford. They fit over Thunder's back right good. I'd been using my old coat as a saddle blanket, but I got another one where I got the saddle bags. So I put my old coat on Thunder first, and the saddle bags on top of it. The old coat had got so ragged that I feared my gold pieces would fall out, so I'd put them in the pouch with the other one and the gold ring. Now the pouch went in one of the saddle bags.

When the man where I got the saddle bags found out where I was headed, he said word was that the road warn't too bad if'n it didn't rain. But he said watch out for the places where trees had been felled across the road where there was big mud holes. He was right. A horse could break a leg goin' over one of those places. I was much obliged for him warnin' me about that. I come across them places a lot. It made travelin' slow. I would have to lead Thunder around the edge of the mud hole. In the middle of the way to Standin' Stone, I saw a wagon stuck in a mud hole all the way up to the axles. It looked like the man had unhitched his team and just left the wagon there where it set.

To make matters worse, it come a rain, a heavy rain, almost every day. It seemed like the sky just opened up and let go for all it was worth. It made me think of the times in the War when it rained hard and nobody knowed where we was or even if'n we was still fightin'. Them was real bad times. I didn't want to think about them, but it seemed like I couldn't forget 'em. A time or two I had them dreams about the War. I'd of druthered dreamed about Beulah Gates, but she didn't show.

Anyway, back to the road to Standin' Stone. I was wet clean through a lot of the time but I guess it warn't too bad since it warn't cold. Findin' a place to sleep at night to get out of the rain was the main thing. And travelin' that slow made me get real low of vittles sooner than I expected. I begged some cornmeal at two or three crossroads where there was a grist mill. I saw some houses with younguns around, but they looked half starved to me It looked like they didn't hardly have enough to eat themselves, to say nothing of givin' anything to me.

So I tried to beg at the mills. I better 'fess up that several times I stole what ever I could get a hold of from the gardens. Most likely it was a ear of corn or a squash. I hungered for a tater, but they took time to dig and that was a problem. I tried to get in a hen house to get a egg, but never got one more'n oncet or twicet. They allus had dogs barkin' up a storm. One dog got me by the leg afore I could get away. My leg warn't hurt but my pant leg got tore up. Anyway, I got real hungry on that trip but I never starved. Thunder didn't have any problems with vittles. There was good grazin' ever' where. And a lot of springs runnin' with all that rain. So water for him or me was in good supply.

I guess it warn't a bad trip, for all that. Mostly I felt the need for a body to talk to. I could talk to Thunder, but he didn't give any sign that he knowed I was talkin' to him, like Ole Mule did. Or leastwise I figured he did.

So when I come to a grist mill, I took some pleasure in talkin' to the man there. I guess they felt the same way, 'cause some of 'em was real big talkers. They would chew yore leg off, talkin', if'n you just stood there and let 'em. And I did that. I stood still and let 'em talk. It seemed like little enough to do for them if 'n I was goin' to get a handful of meal in return. Sometimes it was hard to just listen to 'em, since I've allus been a big talker myself.

Some of 'em wanted news from what they called down the road or over to town. They wanted any news I had about what was goin' on, what with the War over, and the President shot, and a new President. One of 'em said the new President was from Tennessee. I didn't know that, but I didn't let on that he was talkin' to a man who didn't know much of anything.

But I reckon most of 'em wanted to do the talkin', so I let 'em How the goldarned rain was bad for the corn. How the land in them parts warn't much good for growin' corn, to begin with. I could see that was true. Most of the land around there was in timber, timber so heavy you could get lost in, if 'n you didn't watch what you was doin'.

Most of them mills was set up so they looked like they would work out. They'd be on a creek that run right smart, with a mill wheel that would turn the grind stones. But one mill made me scratch my head when I rode up to it. It looked to me like it couldn't hardly grind anything. There warn't no creek and no mill wheel. All I could see was two mules walkin' around in a circle, turning what looked like a wagon wheel. The man was a talker and he went on about the weather and this and that, and what I heard in Harriman. When he run down, I spoke up. *Can I ask you a question?*

Ask away.

It don't look to me like yore mill can do much. Turnin' them stones with them mules must be slow goin'.

He grinned. *You can see that, can you?* I nodded. *Well, you know anythin' about makin' whiskey?*

I laughed. *Well, sir, not much. Just that it takes corn and good water and a still.*

You ain't got anythin' to do with the law, have you? You don't have the look of a law man.

I laughed again. *Lordy no. I ain't got nothin' to do with the law. Fact of the matter is they might be after me.*

You a outlaw or somethin'?
Naw. I'm just a tired soldier on his way home from the War.
Well, I'll take yore word for it. It's about dinner time. *Whyn't*
you tie up yore horse and come up to the house with me and have
some dinner.
That's mighty kind of you. Won't yore wife raise no question?
Naw, she'll be glad of the company. *We don't eat fancy, but*
what there is, there's plenty of it for you.
We walked maybe a quarter of a mile away from the road to
a clearing and his house. It was a real purty little place. Chickens
and two or three cows was peckin' and grazing around the house.
I could see a pig pen out back. Something like a old barn was a
piece away from the house. A woman come out, with two half
grown younguns. They told me their names. She said dinner was
ready on the table and we went in and set down. He was right.
There was plenty there. I was hungry as a horse, but I tried not to
show it. I guess I did, though, cause the Missus laughed and said
I was still a growin' boy. I never tasted better stewed taters in all
my life, and I told her so.

They had a lot of questions about where I'd been and where
I was goin', and what I'd seen. The Missus was learnin' the
younguns and she asked if'n I could draw them some maps of
where I'd been. We went out in the yard and I did the best I
could, drawin' the maps in the dirt. When I got 'em as best I
could, she copied 'em on a piece of paper with a ink pen.

After we got done with that, they went off somewhere and
him and me set down in some chairs out front, under a big tree.
It looked like he was in no hurry. *You ast about the mill. Well, let*
me tell you how I work it. I don't make whiskey, but them that do
need corn. So them that farm in these parts bring me their corn. I
keep it in my corn cribs to dry out some. Then them that makes the
whiskey, they come along and give me good money for the corn. I
keep some of it and pass the rest to the farmers that growed it.
He laughed. *I know hit sounds crazy, but it works out. I been*
at it for some years now and I make a good livin' off of it. Revenoorers
come around, I tell 'em all that corn is for my grist mill. They don't

know much about a grist mill, and they go away believin' my story.
He laughed and slapped his knee at the joke on the revenoorers.
*The wife, she don't like it, but she don't try to stop it. So long as I
don't drink their whiskey. And I don't. My daddy, he made whiskey,
and one time there was a bad batch, and he purty nearly died of
drinkin' it. So I stay way from it.*

But that warn't how it was, I guess. We talked a little more
about this and that and I said I had to get back on the road. We
walked back down to the mill. I got Thunder ready to go. I said
much obliged for the dinner and to tell his wife that, too. He
grinned and said I was welcome and did I want a little drink
afore I left. I figured I didn't but I said I would. He went and got
a jug and he took a swig. Then he passed it to me and I took a
swig. It was right good whiskey, maybe the best moonshine I
ever had. And I thought to myself I could drink this all day! I
guess he thought the same. He took another swig, and offered
the jug to me. I took a little one this time, 'cause I didn't
want to fall off of Thunder! And he was at the jug again when I
rode away.

The rest of that day and for some time after I thought about
his set-up. I plainly could see how it worked for the farmers, and
the boot leggers and for him. Truth is, when I was farmin' in
Stewart County I did some of that myself. It warn't the same, of
course. I didn't have no mill for a cover. Narcissa didn't like it
and people got suspicious, and I had to quit. Her daddy thought
it was a good notion.

After I left his place I went past some right good corn patches.
It looked like the crop that season would be good. Then, like
there was a line drawed, I was in heavy timber again. I warn't one
much to be fearful, but this stand of timber was so thick and
spread out so far that a man could be tracked for miles and not
know a thing about it. Ridin' alone, you hear noises that you
know ain't anything, but you get jumpy all the same. And it
turned out that I had a good reason to be jumpy.

I was on that road for maybe three more nights. It had rained off and on all that time, but this night it was clear. I'd gotten in the habit since I was in the timber of turnin' Thunder loose at night. He stayed close to where I was camped anyway and there warn't no use in tyin' him up at night or puttin' him on a hobble. Some people put a hobble on a horse to keep it from roamin'. But I never liked to do that to a horse of mine. On a hobble, it'd be easy to break a leg if'n the horse got scared and tried to get away fast from what was scarin' it.

So this night I'm talkin' about I had turned him loose and set his saddle and my gear by my bed roll and the little camp fire I built. Travelin' alone I allus liked to have a little camp fire. Some men I knowed like to sleep with their head on their saddle, but I never could get the hang of doin' it that way. Seemed like I allus got a crick in my neck. So I just rolled up my old coat for my piller, stirred up the fire a tad, and went to sleep, lookin' up at the stars, thinkin' about Beulah Gates and Maybelle Atkins, feelin' real lonesome.

He's got a horse around here som'ers. I tried to tell where that was comin' from without movin' my head or makin' any noise. Whoever it was, was in back of me. Then I felt somethin' like I knowed was a pistol against my neck. *Where's yore horse?*
He ain't here.
He pushed harder with the pistol on my neck. *I can see that! Where abouts is he?*
He didn't sound like no man, but more of a boy. But his pistol against my neck had me right scared, man or boy. *Whyn't you move yore pistol away from my neck? It's giving me a crick. 'Sides, I ain't goin' no wheres with you standin' there aimin' it at me.* I didn't think he'd do it. If'n I was him, I wouldn't care one whit if'n the other man got a crick in his neck. But he did. He raised up, standin' over me, lookin' down at me. The moon had just come up over the trees. I lay there a minute and then movin' real slow I set up so's I could see what else was around. What I

saw from the light of the low burnin' fire was him holdin' his pistol. There was another fellar, standin' maybe ten, twelve foot away, holdin' the reins of a horse.

You fellars ridin' double?

He answered, smart alec like. *What's it to you?* Then he waved his pistol at me. *Yeah, we ridin' double. That's why I mean to take yore horse. Where is he?*

I figured I better stall for time, if'n I could. They took my horse way out here and I'd be in one hell of a mess. *I don't rightly know. I guess he just wandered off. He does that sometimes of a night. Allus comes back at daylight.*

He laughed, nervous like. *That's one hell of a story.* He waved his pistol at me again. *You don't 'spect me to believe it, do you?*

I shrugged. *It's like it is.*

You mean you cain't whistle fur him? Any man lets his horse go loose knows he can whistle fur him.

I shrugged. *I never learned him to do that. Never had to, him allus comin' back at daylight.* I shifted around, so's I could rest agin my saddle and my kit bag. *You standin' over me like that, wavin' yore pistol at me, makes me nervous. Whyn't you boys set down? It'll be daylight in a hour, he'll show up.* I didn't think he'd do it, but he did, maybe about three foot from me. The one holdin' the horse was still standin', maybe ten, twenty foot away. It was quiet for a minute or two. I was thinkin' what to do. *What'd it take for you fellars to leave me and my horse alone?*

He give a laugh. *You're funnin' me, ain't you? You ain't got nothin' to give. 'Sides, what we want is yore horse.* He was quiet. The other man hadn't said a word. *What've you got to give?*

Well, there's my saddle. It's a real good saddle, bring a good piece of money. It was give to me over in North C'lina by a man who knows a lot about saddles. It's good and broke in. You want to look at it?

He laughed again, nervous like. *We don't need no saddle. What'd we do with a saddle and no horse to put it on.*

I shrugged. *Well, if'n you don't want my saddle, maybe I got something in my kit bag that can buy you off.* I reached slow like over behind my saddle for my kit bag.

What you got in there? Corn pone? He laughed and the other man laughed.

I laughed with 'em. *Maybe some corn pone, maybe some side meat, don't rightly know. I ain't looked for sure since it got dark.* That was pure foolishness, of course. Any man on the road would know what was in his kit bag. *Maybe somethin' else in there could buy you off.* I didn't know what I was goin' to do next. I was just stallin' for time, thinkin' somethin' would come to me. *You ever seen a gold piece?*

I could tell in the half light that got his interest. *You got a gold piece in there? Naw, you ain't. A man like you ain't never seen a gold piece, much less have got one. What're you tryin' to do, trick me? Give me that kit bag. If 'n it's in there, I'll find it. If 'n it ain't, it's too bad fur you.* He kept wavin' his pistol at me.

It come to me what I had to do. I raised up, kind of on my knees. I held the kit bag out to him, but two foot out'n his reach. Then I figured I had him, since he laid his pistol down by where he was settin', and raised up on his knees to reach the kit bag. I let the kit bag fall down on the ground 'tween us. When he leaned for'ard to get it, I went for the pistol, prayin' it was loaded and I knowed how to cock it. I got it afore he knowed what was happenin' and it was loaded and I cocked it. I pointed it dead straight at him and pulled the trigger. He fell over almost on what was left of the fire and on my kit bag.

Right fast as I could, I got up and pointed the pistol at the other fellar standin' by the horse. He looked like he was goin' to piss in his pants. I wouldn't of blamed him if 'n he did. Here was this man, shot his partner, and pointin' the pistol at me. *You get on yore horse and get away from here as fast as you can ride else I'm goin' to shoot you too.* He did,

Well, that was a bluff. I didn't know beans about pistols, ever, and what I knowed in the army, I'd half way forgot. But I figured that you maybe had to reload the thing ever' time you wanted to shoot. And I didn't have no more bullets. So if 'n he'd called my bluff, I'd of been in trouble. But he didn't.

I whistled for Thunder and he come right away to the edge of the trees. The man I shot guessed right. Thunder would of come if'n I had whistled. I thought maybe he'd be scared off by the gunshot, not knowing anything about gunfire like the little red mare did. But he warn't. He waited for me to get my gear and saddle him up. I didn't even take the time to see if'n the man I shot was dead or not. I didn't much care. If'n he was bad hurt, there warn't anything I could do about it, even if'n I wanted to. And right then I didn't. If'n he was dead, that was that. So I didn't even look to see. What I had to do was to drag my kit bag out from under him. When I was tryin' to do it, I wondered what I'd do if'n he started to rouse. I guess knock him in the head and get out of there, kit bag or not. But he didn't, not that I could see in the half light.

So I left him there where he fell, and got out of there as fast as I could, goin' the other way from how his partner had rode. I couldn't ride Thunder out of there. I had to walk him. It was too risky, not bein' able to see where you was goin' in the dark. If'n Thunder had stumbled, he could of broke a leg. Maybe we walked a mile and I figured we was safe enough. So I led him over to the edge of the timber and left him be, and I lay down under what smelled like a cedar tree and waited until daylight.

Truth to tell, I needed to catch my breath. It all went so fast that I didn't know what was happenin' 'til it was all over. Thinkin' it over, it looked like they was two fellars out to see what they could find or steal or rob. They didn't know beans about what they was doin', that was for danged sure. Like, my rifle was layin' right there by my saddle and he never even seen it. Or I guess he didn't. And the other one didn't make a move to help him, he just stood there holding the reins of the horse. And he was so dumb that he didn't figure out that I likely couldn't of shot the pistol two shots in a row. And the first one was real dumb to lay his pistol down to get at my kit bag. It warn't likely that no man trained to be a soldier would of done that. So what ever they was, they was not trained soldiers.

I hadn't killed a man since I left the army. I was real sorry to kill him but at the same time I was mad at him for tryin' to take my horse. I didn't even see his face, it bein' so dark and his hat pulled down. Maybe if'n I had of, and seen that he was a fifteen year old, I'd of let him have the gold piece. But layin' there under that cedar tree, I figured that was wrong thinkin'. A fifteen year old ought to have knowed better anyhow.

It got daylight in the east and I told Thunder what was done was done and we started out again. But I was right sorry I had to shoot him. Wonder what I done with his pistol? I guess I thowed it over in the weeds afore I got away. Good thing I did. I never liked the things anyway. I never had one until years later on the farm place when there was a scare about outlaws. We didn't have any close neighbors at that time, and Narcissa got scared there'd be trouble. She got me to buy one from a man I knowed. But that's another story.

I had another two or three day ride afore I got to Standin' Stone. I told the robber I had some corn pone in my kit bag and I'd told him the truth. But that was all I had in the line of vittles in there and there warn't much of that. So I got real hungry.

On one day, I recollect, I come on a right pitiful farm place. Nobody was around and I went in the hen house and got me two eggs. Then here come a dog, barkin' his head off, runnin' right at me. I thowed some rocks at him. That held him back 'til I could get on Thunder. Reason I remember that was that I dropped one of the eggs in the commotion. But the one I saved tasted mighty good.

Another day, when I got close to Standin' Stone, I stopped at a farm house and begged something to eat. The woman acted like she was scared of me but she went in the house and got me a sausage biscuit and told me to get on my way. I thanked her and got on my way.

I didn't make any more stops to beg 'til I got to Standin' Stone. By then, I was hungry enough to eat a horse. Well, maybe not a horse. Thunder wouldn't of liked to hear me say that. But you get what I mean. I shore was hungry. My stomach was growlin' so loud you could of heard it in the next county. So by the time I hit Standin' Stone I was thinkin' vittles, a real bed, and maybe a drink of whiskey. First off, when I come into town, there was a right big house. I figured it must be a boardin' house, so I tied up Thunder and went right in. There was a man standin' there watchin' me come in.

Howdy. He nodded. *You got a room I can have for a night or two?*

He nodded again. *Maybe. You got any money?*

Lookin' back, I can see why he might of thought I didn't. I'd been on the road for a week, ten days and I reckon I was a sight to scare anybody off. Dirty clothes, dirty face, scraggly hair and chin whiskers. Only thing that might of looked good to him was Thunder and he was tied up out front. *Yessir, I got some money.*

Is it real money or Confederate?

No sir, it ain't Confederate. People still got that?

Some of 'em do. They try to pass it off on me. It's not worth the paper it's printed on, and I won't take it.

How much you want for a room? He named a price, and I stood there lookin' at him like I was lookin' at General Forrest. *Are you puttin' me on?*

He shook his head. *That's the price.*

It was maybe three, four times what I paid in Knoxville. *I've got that much money, but it'd take it all for just one night.*

It's what I get from the folks up from Nashvul. If'n you don't want to pay that, you'd best be lookin' for a boardin' house.

This ain't a boardin' house?

He shook his head. *Cain't you read? This is the 'M-peer-al Hotel.* Later I figured out that's what the sign sed, Imperial Hotel.

Well, I cain't pay that kind of money. Is there a boardin' house hereabouts?

He nodded. *Maybe try Miz Collins. Her place is on down the road, and around the corner at the crossroads. She's got a sign out front, says board.*

I thanked him and got back on Thunder and rode around a little to see what the town was like. I never seen anything like it. There was some real big and fancy houses. It looked like there was some real money in this town. Miz Collins told me later on that Standin' Stone was on a mountain and a far sight cooler in the summer than Nashville. She said the rich folks come up and stayed the whole summer. Some of 'em had a house up there and some stayed at that Imperial Hotel and that was why it cost a lot. She said it was a real nice place, with big rooms and soft beds and a big sleepin' porch around back, for when it was real hot, even for Standin' Stone. She said they set a good table too, but she grinned, not as good as hers!

Well, you can tell by that, that I found Miz Collins place. I can see her still, standin' on the porch, watchin' me ride up on Thunder. She was a big woman. Not heavy set, just big. Taller'n me by a hand. She had a right ugly face and a sour look on it. I don't recollect much about what she had on underneath, but mostly what I saw was a old man's coat. It looked like it had seen its day, for sure. It was some warm while I was there, but I never saw her without that coat on. I told her what I wanted and she named her price and I said I could pay it, and I paid for one night. She told me what I'd heard before, leave my rifle downstairs with her, don't put yore boots on the bed, what time supper and breakfast is on the table, and she didn't set dinner. *You been on the road for a spell?*

Yessum. Maybe a month, maybe more. I come from North C'lina through Knoxvul. I'm headed to Nashvul.

She looked me over. *You are powerful dirty to be sleepin' in one of my beds.*

Yessum, I reckon I am. Is there a place around here I can get a bath?

I reckon you can. She was still lookin' me over, kind of down her nose, since she was taller'n me and standin' on the porch, besides. *Tell you what. There's a horse tank out back. You come around the house and get out of yore clothes down to yore drawers.* She stopped. *You got on drawers, ain't you?*

Yessum, I do. I was real glad I did. She looked like she would whup me if'n I didn't.

I'll cut some on yore hair and chin whiskers while I'm at it. My wash kettle is still warm from today's washin' and I'll put them dirty clothes in it. She grinned, kind of. *Better wash yore drawers, too.* She looked at me right straight. *You wash yoreself real good. I don't let no dirty men in my beds.*

Yessum I will. Only, what'll all this cost me? I ain't a rich man. She let loose a laugh you could hear a mile. She didn't look so ugly when she laughed. *Lord no, I didn't never take you for a rich man, lookin' like you do. You want to do it, we'll do it, and weun's will talk about settlin' up tomorra. Maybe I need some wood cut.* Without waitin' for me to answer, she motioned for me to foller her around back, so I did.

Around back, she pointed to a stump. *Take off yore clothes and set down there and I'll get my shears.*

Now, I been in the army and stripped nekkid more times than I can count. And I did it at the Wood place down at the pond. Didn't bother me none, ever. So I didn't mind getting' down to my drawers in front of her. She looked like she was old enough to be my mother. But I didn't know about it if'n somebody else come along, 'specially a woman. But I did what she said, right down to my drawers, and went like she said and set on the stump.

Then she took the shears to me. I could see all the hair fall around me. She really whacked it off, even my chin whiskers. I started to tell her to leave my whiskers alone. I was gettin' a right good crop of 'em, and I figured they made me look like more a man. But afore I could say anything, she'd gone half way around my chin. I recollect thinkin' I'd not hardly have anything left at all!

You can stand up now. She was lookin' at me. *You don't look half bad with some of that mangy hair gone. Now gimme yore drawers for the wash kettle.* She must of seen the look on my face. *Now, for the Lord's sake.* She put her hands on her hips, like Aunt Polly used to do, *Gimme yore drawers. I'm old enough to be yore mama and not by a long shot are you the first man I ever saw nekkid!* She held out her hand. *T'won't do any good with clean pants if'n you ain't got clean drawers.* She grinned. *And I bet they are sure dirty.* So I shucked 'em off and handed 'em to her. And got in the horse tank.

She was leavin'. *What'll I do for clothes?*

Josie'll bring 'em. And she went over to the wash kettle, holdin' my drawers away from her like they was a dirty rag. I guess they was. *You got any name?*

Luther. Luther Morris. She nodded and I lost sight of her.

The water in the horse tank had been settin' in the sun so it was warm and it was right good to set there and wash up. Truth to tell, the water in the horse tank looked like I warn't the first to be in it, but that didn't bother me none. I caught and snapped some lice that come to the top but nowhere near like what I had when I first got to the Wood place.

I was settin' there, feelin' right good about it all and looked up and there was a real purty girl. For sure, she warn't a youngun girl, like Thelma was, but a woman girl, more near the size of Betty Lou. I was took aback by the sight of her, standin' there lookin' at me. settin' there nekked in the horsetank. She was smilin' at me, holdin' out what looked like part of a blanket. *Miz Collins sent this to you to dry off with. She sent them clothes too* And she dumped 'em on the ground by the horse tank. *They's pants and a shirt. She said put 'em on. Your's is in the wash kettle.* She laughed, coverin' her mouth with her hand. *She said you couldn't have 'em back 'til in the mornin' when they was clean.* She laughed again, behind her hand. *They must have been real dirty for her to say that.*

She just stood there, lookin' at me, settin' there nekkid in the horse tank, her not makin' any move to go away. *What's yore name?*

Josie.

Mine's Luther. I shook my head. *I got to tell you right now, you shore are one purty girl.* She grinned and nodded her head, like this warn't the first time she'd been told that. *You her daughter?*

She shook her head. *She took me in. Me and some more girls to help her do the work.*

What'd you do?

Anythin' there is to do. Help out with the house. Work in the garden. She fell quiet, but she was still grinnin' at me, a real what Aunt Polly would of called, a wicked grin. *You goin' to stay around here a night or two?*

I grinned back. *If'n I can. If'n I got some pants to put on. If'n I can talk to you some. You figure I might?*

Maybe. She was still grinnin' that wicked grin. *It depends on how you look with yore pants on. But I better warn you, afore you start thinkin' elsewise. I don't go upstairs with no man.* Then, like she'd said more'n she ought, she turned away and left.

Well sir, truth to tell, that was what I was thinkin'. She looked like to me she'd be a armful for a man to hold. Her near black hair was cut at her neck and across above her eyes. Them eyes was maybe gray blue, I couldn't tell which. She had a right good size mouth with teeth showin' through when she grinned. And her eyes and her mouth did their part in her grinnin'. It looked like they worked together. She warn't very tall but she had a woman's body that caught yore eye, especially when she was walkin' away from you. Then was when she had that walk, like she was dancin'. Lordy, I was real stuck on her, from that first time I seen her.

Well, from the way she said that about goin' upstairs, I figured right then I knowed what kind of a house Miz Collins kept. It looked like it was more'n just a boardin' house. There was girls here that'd go upstairs with a man. They would, if'n the man could pay. Never no mind to me, I said to myself. It ain't none of my business what they do. Then I thought, maybe it is. I ain't been with a woman for a long time. If'n I could work off a bed and a bath, maybe I could work off that too.

Quick, afore somebody else come, I got out of the horse tank and dried off and got on the clothes Josie left me. Then I went to see if'n I could find my boots, and met Miz Collins comin' my way, holdin' 'em. *You lookin' for yore boots? Or air you plannin' to go barefooted?*

I guess I could. Did when I was a boy, all the time. But maybe I better put 'em on. I set down on the ground and got 'em on.

She stood there over me, her arms folded like Aunt Polly used to do when she was watchin' to see if 'n I was doin' somethin' right. *Yore clothes'll be dry come mornin'.*

I'm much obliged to you for the bath and the haircut and the clean clothes. I guess I owe you some more money. You goin' to let me work some of it off? She shook her head. *We'll settle tomorry. The girls are near puttin' supper on the table. 'Til it's ready, you want to set on the porch or go down to the saloon? Me and Josie have got to go make up yore bed.*

So I went down to the saloon. On the way, I passed the hotel where I stopped. The man there was still settin' on the front porch. It didn't look like much business was comin' his way, if 'n I was to judge. He nodded. *You find Miz Collins all right?*

I did and I'm obliged to you for sendin' me there.

You look a mite better than before. He grinned. *She give you the horse tank and the haircut business?*

I laughed. *She shore did. You know about that.*

Let's just say I've heard about that. He grinned again. *You meet any of the girls?*

Just Josie.

She's a purty one, ain't she? You be careful there. Miz Collins is holdin' out for some rich man to take her away. I doubt she'd think you could cut the mustard.

No, I 'spect not. I'll have to be careful. I thankee for your advice. I guess I'll mosey on. He nodded, and I left him settin' there on the porch of the hotel.

I went in the saloon and had a whiskey. I figured I could afford one on account of I stayed at Miz Collinses instead of the hotel. It was quiet. A couple of men nodded at me and asked where I was from and where I was goin' and all that. I went through my story agin, the short one, as Preacher Wood would call it. Nothin' was said about it. We talked some about the weather and this and that. I paid up, and went back to the Collins house.

Supper was on the table. Josie told me where to set. It didn't look like there was any more boarders that night. And I didn't see anythin' that looked like a Mr. Collins. I never did, while I was there.

Anyway, Josie made my 'quaintance with the other three girls. It looked like they was some older than Josie and not near as purty to my eye. They warn't bad lookin', mind you, but just not as purty as her. I recollect that one of 'em was a red head with freckles. Aunt Polly allus said red head and freckles went together. The other two had some kind of yella hair. Their hair warn't cut like Josie's, but hangin' down on their shoulders. As far as I could see, they had on the same kind of dresses that Miz Collins and Josie had on. Nothing fancy, or anything like that. I don't know what I expected, but maybe somethin' different, if'n like I figured, they took men upstairs. That set me wonderin' if'n upstairs meant where I was to sleep.

Anyway we set down to a good supper and I shore was hungry. I was about to start in but stopped just in time for Miz Collins to say a blessing. What she said sounded for all the world like what Preacher Wood would say. I figured they'd all learned 'em at the same church somewhere. After supper Miz Collins lit a oil lamp in the front room, but we set a spell on the front porch where it was cooler. When the girls got done cleanin' up after supper, they come out too.

They got settled and Miz Collins said whyn't they sing us a song. She started them out on a song I knowed by tune, Barbry Allen. They knowed all the words and it was real purty. One of 'em asked me if'n I could sing. I said I'd been told I could, but I didn't know the words. By her voice, it was Josie that said she'd feed me the words. So she did, or somebody did and I got to sing along with 'em. I recollect that like it was yestiday. It was a real peaceful feelin'. It seemed like I forgot for a while about Beulah Gates and that feller I had shot.

Everybody fell quiet after that. It was a real dark night after night fell but there was a lot of stars. It turned out that Miz

Collins knowed the names of some of the stars and she'd been learnin' the girls about 'em. Her and the girls talked about the stars and what they was called or them stars that looked like they was together. Only thing I knowed about was the Big Dipper. Miz Collins pointed out the North Star and the Little Dipper and how the sailors on the ocean could find their way that way.

Everybody got up and Miz Collins showed me where I was to sleep. She took up the oil lamp and saw me in and then went back down the stairs. I got to tell you I was wonderin' about what Josie had said about men comin' up the stairs with the girls. But I went right to sleep and never heard anything like that that night. If'n they did, they was real quiet about it. To top it off, I didn't even know then that there was two sets of stairs. The next mornin' I figured out that my room was over the kitchen with Miz Collins next to me. It was then that I seen the other set of stairs.

The next mornin' at breakfast, she put to me what she was thinkin' about. It was that she needed some work done around the place and she was willin' to strike a deal with me, me doin' the work and she'd forgive the room money. I said that sounded real good to me.

First off was to chop some wood for her. The logs had been snaked up from her wood lot but had to be worked up into stovewood. I worked at that off and on, for near a week. Some of it was a soft wood like beech but one or two was oak, real hard to work up. I tell you, I earned my keep on them oak logs. I will say this for her, she had a real good ax and a one man cross cut saw.

I done some carpentry work for her too, fixin' a door that wouldn't close right and a piece of the stairs, the back stairs. And I chopped a lot of weeds for her. One day her and me went in to Cookville in her buggy for supplies. She warn't a big talker but when she decided to, I liked to hear her tell about the countryside and people she knowed. She was the one that told me about how rich people from Nashvul, as she called it, come up to Standin' Stone in the summer, 'cause it was cooler up here. She ast me some questions about the War, but nothing that I minded tellin' her. Sometime in there, I told 'em how I'd come across the mountain with a wagon train. One of the girls said her daddy had come that way, too.

On one of them nights, after supper, I walked over to the saloon for some company. Two men come in. From what they said to the bar keep they'd come in from Knoxville that day. There was more to what they said to him than that, but I didn't get it. I was at t'other end of the bar. They had their whiskey and talked to him a while longer and left. Business was slow. The bar keep come over to me, and I had another whiskey. *Did you get what them two was talkin' about?*

Nope, I heard 'em talkin' to you, but I didn't get what they was sayin'.

They come in on the Knoxvul road. Said two days ago this side of Harriman they come across the body of a man. Not come across, I guess. Said he was over to the side, under some trees. Not in the road. Looked like he'd been shot. It looked like he'd been there for a while.

That kind of thing happen around here a lot?

He shrugged. *Not a lot around here, but it does on that Knoxvul road. It seems like outlaw men pick that road since there ain't much out there.* He was moppin' the bar, not lookin' at me. *You come in on that road?*

Yep. I forget when I was on that stretch. Maybe it was near two weeks ago, maybe three. It's a far piece 'tween here and Knoxvul. I said Knoxvul, like he did. That was the way the people in this neck of the woods said it. They did the same thing to Cookeville and Nashville. It was their way of talkin'. *Did they say who the man was?*

Naw. They said they never seen him before. Said the body was startin' to stink.

I nodded. *I was in the War and I know how the dead stink.*

He quit moppin' the bar and raised up to look at me. *So he warn't there when you come along that way?*

Not that I seen. I might not of looked over that way where he was layin' when I passed by. I was ridin' right fast along in there. A man in Knoxvul had told me about outlaws in that stretch and I was tryin' to get here as fast as I ride.

He nodded. Two more men had come in and he went to wait on 'em. Nothin' more was ever said 'tween him and me about the dead man. I never saw the other two men agin, to know who I was lookin' at. I figured maybe Miz Collins might of heard about the dead man and might say something about it to me. But if'n she ever heard of it, she never said anything about it. I wondered then about the law and if'n they was around town. If'n there was such and they was in town, I never seen or heard of 'em. I was right glad they was not. They might have had more questions to put to me than the bar keep had.

Like I said, Josie was the purtiest of the girls at the Collins house. She'd come out and watch me chop wood and rick it up, and we'd talk about this and that. She'd set on a log to the side of me, with her dress tail tucked up around her legs. Some times the dress tail slipped and I could see her legs. If'n she seen me lookin' at 'em, she didn't seem to mind. The top part of her dress looked like it was a mite too smug for her and I could make out her bosums as plain as day. I had to watch out and look where I was choppin' and not at her, else I would end up with a cut off leg!

To make matters worse, it looked like she was goin' out of her way to touch my hand when she was passin' me a dish of beans at the table or handin' me somethin' when she was watchin' me work. I started to look for times I could touch her, and she never drawed back her hand. I hadn't been with a woman since Maybelle and I got to tell you that I thought a lot about how it would be in a bed with Josie. Or in a hayloft. Or anywhere, as far as that was. But I knowed I had to stick to wonderin'. It looked to me like she was maybe 16. Maybe she'd never been with a man, but maybe she had. I shore didn't want to rock the boat with Miz Collins, after all she'd done for me. But I couldn't get Josie out of my mind, better I should say out of my crotch.

I seen what was happenin' at the Collins house one night. We was settin' on the porch, not quite dark. They was singin' and talkin' about the stars. Here come two men down the road with a lantern. They stopped at the hitchin' post. *This the Collins house?* Miz Collins got up and went out to 'em. They talked a little and she called two of the girls to come out. They did and them and the men went around back of the house. She come back to the porch and we set there a while, talkin' about this and that.

Then it was bedtime. She took a oil lamp and her and Josie and me went on upstairs. We got to my room, I could hear 'em talkin' in the other part of the upstairs and for certain her and Josie could of too. But Miz Collins never let on that she heard it. Josie looked at me with a kind of grin, but she never said anythin' about what was happenin'. Miz Collins took the lamp with her when her and Josie went on to their room. I lay there listenin to what was happenin' on the other side of the house.

I was at the Collins house maybe over a week and men come to it maybe four nights out of five. It would go the same way. Miz Collins would go out to the road, they'd talk, and then she'd come back to the house and the girls would go with the men. I'd figured out by then about the back set of stairs goin' upstairs. We'd stopped talkin' when a man come up, but then we went on talkin' about this and that like nothin' had happened. But I knowed what was happenin'. It was what Josie had told me about that first day when I was in the horse tank. Layin' in bed, I would hear the man talkin'. And the girl maybe answerin' and maybe laughin'. Then I'd hear some commotion. Layin' there, hearin' it all, it was real hard to take. I would think about a woman, about Josie, how she looked, and I'd want a woman real bad, and all I could do was use my hand.

I never seen Josie go up with a man. But she got to me. I kept thinkin' about her. And one night, I figured I couldn't stand it anymore, without doin' somethin' about it. So the next evenin' afore supper time, I was at the woodpile, choppin' stove wood for all I was worth. It was real hot that day, and I took off my shirt. It didn't help much, but I got some breeze goin' through. Miz Collins come out with a gourd dipper of water. *You look like you could use a drink of water.*

That's for sure. It's a hot one today, ain't it? I laid down my ax and took the gourd and drank the water. *I want to get this stove wood cut and ricked for you, afore I go.*

You're makin' a good start at it. You made up yore mind when to go?

No mam, I ain't. I give her back the gourd. *You got time to set a while? I'd not say no to a little rest, and there's a question I want to ask of you.*

I got time. We set down on a log there at the woodpile. She tucked her dress tail under her as she set down. Lookin' at her, settin' on that log, I could tell that she was maybe a right good lookin' woman when she was a girl. Nobody else was around, that I could see. *What's your question?*

Now that I was at it, I didn't know how to say it. *You know I've taken to Josie.* I said it like a question, but maybe not.

She nodded. *I can see that. Hit'd take a blind man not to see you moonin' after her.*

She acts like she likes me

I reckon so. She folded her arms. *Where's this here leadin' to?*

Now I had to say it. *I want to take Josie upstairs.*

She took a rag out of her apron pocket and wiped her mouth. *I figured as much. She's a right purty girl, and real easy for a man to talk to.*

She shore is, as purty as a flower. And she's real sweet. Her and me get along, I guess. I was quiet. Miz Collins was still fiddlin' with her rag in her hand. *I want to know what it would cost me to take Josie upstairs.*

She nodded, and wiped her mouth with her rag and stood up. *I got to take the gourd back to the spring house. Leave yore work and walk with me to over there.* We got there and she put the gourd back in its restin' place and turned back to me. *Set here with me.* So we set down on a big log there by the spring house.

She put her rag in her apron pocket and set up straight. *I'm goin'
to tell you no, you cain't have her to take upstairs.*

The way she said it got my back up. *You figure I ain't got the
money? For all you know, I can pay the price. I ain't dirt pore.*

She drawed back, away from me. *Don't rile me, Luther with
yore talk about money. It ain't about money when it comes to Josie.*
She twisted around on the log, to look back at the trees behind
the spring house. *I reckon you can see what kind of a house I run.
Me and the girls have got to earn our keep some way. The girls come
to me, knowin' that.* She looked back at me. *I treat 'em right and
see to it the men do the same. Gen'lly, they don't stay with me long.
Some man comes along and takes 'em off and marries 'em.* She
pointed over to'ard the saloon. *One of 'em lives over there with
her husband. She's real good to me. She comes to see us maybe on a
Sunday. Last time she brung that honey you et at my table.*

She looked away and then back at me. *Josie ain't in to that.
And Lord help me, if'n I can, I'm goin' to keep her out'n it. I'm a
hopin' some good man will come along and marry up with her.* She
was frownin' at me. *You thinkin' about doin' that?*

*I got to tell you the truth. No, I ain't. I'm a long way from home
and I've got a girl there waitin' to marry me. I've knowed her all
my life.* I lied a little. *My family and her family expect me to do
that, and I aim to do that.*

She was still frownin' at me, and she gave a kind of a snort. *I
figured as much. You want to pay to take her upstairs and then get
on yore danged horse and ride away. Is that what you're askin'?*

Well, she had me to rights. That was shore what I was askin',
but after what she'd said, it sounded like it maybe warn't the right
thing to do. Still, I wanted her real bad, so I had to face up to it.
Yessum, that's what I'm askin'. I went on, afore she could say anything.
*But afore I would do it, I'd have to know if'n Josie would want to go
upstairs with me.* I got up and walked around ahind the log where
we was settin'. *I don't want to do it if'n she don't want to.*

She got up and come around to look me in the eye, with her
hands on her hips. *Oh, I can tell you what she'll say. She'll say she*

wants to do it with you. Lord help her, she's as taken with you as you are with her, fool that she is. She's told me as much. But what she don't see is what happens next, after you're gone from here.

You're sayin' if'n I do this, it'll send her down the road with them other girls.

Maybe.

Well, I don't buy that!

You wouldn't. You're a man. You don't hardly know anythin' about this, save what's happenin' in the crotch of yore pants. She walked away from me and then turned back to look at me, square in the eyes, shakin' her head. *I should of sent you packin' the day after you come. I seen you look at her that way and I knowed trouble was comin'. And then I knowed it for sure when I seen the way she was lookin' at you.*

I was cornered and I knowed it. *You feel that way, I better get on my horse and get out of here right now.* Right then, I figured she'd tell me to do just that.

Yeah, you said it right. Maybe I'd better tell you to get on yore horse and get on yore way. She was quiet, lookin' down at her feet and then up at me. *But I won't. There's more to it than that. There's more to it than how I think about it. I got to think about what she's feelin'.* She went back around and set down on the log again, and motioned for me to do the same. I did, wonderin' what she was goin' to say next. She folded her hands in her lap. She warn't exactly smilin'. But she didn't seem so mad at me anymore.

Her ugly face looked almost purty when she started to talk again. *I got no idea what life for Josie will be like. I took her in when she was just a girl. Her daddy was kilt in a gun fight. Her mama tried to carry on, but then she died of sickness. They come from out at Hangin' Limb. Just afore she died, her mama sent for me, and I went, and she ast me if'n I would take Josie and look after her. She said Josie didn't have any place to go. So I did.* She reached in her apron pocket and got her rag, and wiped her eyes and her face. *That'd be five, six years ago. I took her in, and loved her like she was my own. I never had no younguns.*

Now she put the rag back in her apron pocket and straightened her back. *But that ain't what this is about. What this is about is that Josie ain't never been with a man afore.* She looked square at me. *And I want the first time for her to be as good as I can make it. I don't want some man bein' rough to her on her first time, even if'n she's married up with him.* She picked up a corner of her apron, and wiped her face again. *Mr. Collins was good to me that way, even if'n I was as ugly as sin. He said he didn't care about that. And I took him at his word.*

You get what I'm sayin'? Or are you so hell bent to have her that you'll just do it and have it over with? Now she started to cry, her face all scrunched up, what I could see of it with her apron there. Then it slacked off, and she was mad again, lookin' at me like she could hit me over the head. If'n she had anything to do it with. *Damn you! Answer me true! And I don't want no money. Josie ain't for sale.*

And she stood up again, lookin' down at me. *No, Luther Morris, you cain't have Josie, but if'n you do it right, you can take her.* She stood there, lookin' down at me, like she wanted to see in my face what I was thinkin'. Then she turned and walked away, almost as near a run as a woman her age and size could do, like she wanted to get away from me as fast as she could.

Well, I set there. As Billy Jones would of said, she spoke her mind and what was in her heart. But I knowed all right and good enough what she was talkin' about. She wouldn't say I could have Josie, for no amount of money. But she wouldn't stop me if'n I was man enough to get Josie of her own free will and man enough to do it right.

Truth to tell, that was the first time in my life I'd ever thought about bein' with a woman in that way. That may sound cold hearted to you, tellin' it like this, but it's the gospel truth. Like I said, I'd been with just three women in my life then, four if'n you count that woman in winter camp. I guess I had to count her but it was different with her than it was with Dulciemay and Maybelle and Beulah. I didn't have to do anythin' to get her.

Billy Jones paid for her. You recollect that Dulciemay just plain come to me that night. Maybe it was more her takin' me than it was me takin' her. She knowed about men and she knowed what to do and she took the lead. I don't know what to say when it comes to Maybelle. It was plain to me then that she wanted me as bad as I wanted her. I didn't know much, but what I didn't know, she did and we just come together, like it was supposed to be, natch'ral like. Nobody did any talkin' about it. With Maybelle, there warn't no tomorra and I didn't care and I guess she didn't. She didn't even say good bye to me when she left or when Frank sent her away. I never knowed which it was. One day she was there and the next day she was gone. I missed her when she was gone but I never grieved about her. We'd had our good times and they was over.

Then there was Beulah. We'd come together that night. I wanted her real bad and it turned out she wanted me. She said it was to rid her of Elmer. I had to take her word on that. Howsomever it was, we come together that night and next mornin' she went her way and I went mine. But it shore had stirred up my feelin's for a woman.

If'n I went ahead with Josie like it was in my mind to do when I ast Miz Collins, it was goin' to have to be a different story from any of them. I knowed full well what Miz Collins was talkin' about. I'd be the taker and it'd be up to me to worry about what Josie was feelin'. Maybe she wouldn't even know what she was feelin'. I got to tell you that, thinkin' about that, I wanted her even more. I got near hard, just thinkin' about bein' in bed with her.

But what about the tomorras? If'n she wanted to, then we'd do it, and I'd ride off on Thunder, leavin' her here to whatever her life would turn out to be. Maybe I'd leave her with a baby from me. I warn't then and I'm still not the kind of man that goes into prayin', but I tell you that if'n I was I'd of been prayin' about what to do. I wanted her real bad but I didn't want to get into what was right and what was wrong. Settin' there, I knowed nobody could tell me. Only thing to do was to put the question to her.

It happened the same day. I come across her in the kitchen. *Josie, will you walk with me?* She nodded and got done with what she was doin' and we walked out to the log by the spring house. It sounds like there was no place to go at the Collins house but the spring house, and that ain't far from the truth. There was a cow pasture in back, but you had to climb over the fence to get to it. That time of year there was weeds waist high on both sides of the house. The other way led over to the hotel and more houses. So anybody who wanted to talk private like, went to the log at the spring house. We started out and I took hold of her hand like we'd been doin'. She looked at me with that smile that made me turn to jelly.

We set down on the log. She tucked in her dress tail, and looked over at me. I figured this ain't no time to beat around the bush. *I got a question to ask you.* She nodded. *Josie, tonight, will you go upstairs with me?*

She took her hand away, still lookin' at me. *Do you mean what I think you mean?*

I reached for her hand again, but she put it in her lap, out of my reach. *Yes, that's what I mean.*

Afore I give you my answer, I got some questions for you. I nodded. She looked down at her hands in her lap. *You know I ain't never been with a man like that?*

I didn't know it, but now you're tellin' me.

She looked away, across the spring branch. *I'd guess you ain't goin' to stay around here long?*

No, I ain't goin' to stay around here long. I aim to go on to my home in Stewart County. I took her hand again. I thought maybe she'd pull away but she didn't. Her hand was warm and soft, and I raised it to my lips and kissed it. She watched me do it, like she never had seen anybody do that afore. I didn't let go, but kept her hand right there by my lips, talkin' right next to it. *I ain't very good at words. I got to go on my way to Stewart County. But afore I go, what I want most in the world is to be in my bed nekkid with you and to hold you and kiss you with all my might. I want to be so close to you in the bed that there's nothin' else between you and me.* Her eyes was closed, listenin' to what I said. It was quiet. I'd said all I had to say. It was up to her.

She opened her eyes and watched me as I moved our hands down on my knee. *I ain't much taken aback by you askin'. I'm just 16 years old but I know about them feelin's between a man and a woman. And I know sometimes it ain't feelin's but it's money. Like when the girls go upstairs with a man.* She stopped and looked at me with what was most likely her most terrible frown. *Did you pay Miz Collins to go upstairs with me?*

I shook my head. *No.* But I didn't say I'd offered to.

She knows I don't want to be like them girls. Not that they ain't good to me. They are. But I don't want to do it. She shrugged. *Not if'n I can help it. Her and me have talked about it. I told her I didn't want to do it, and she said I didn't have to.* She pulled back her hand and put it in her lap, and looked straight ahead. *I know I cain't get much chance in life, my daddy kilt and my mama dyin'. Miz Collins is all I got.* She stood up and stooped down to pick a clover. *She said I better be on the lookout for a good man to marry up with.* Holdin' the clover, she turned sideways to me. *Air you that man?*

Josie, much as I want you, you know I ain't that man. You know I ain't him that she was talkin' about. I'm just a country boy who's been to the War and now tryin' to get home to Stewart County. I'm not the one to marry up with. I reached for her hand with the clover and she didn't pull away. *But I'm here and now and I want to be with you so much I ache from the wantin' and I swear I'll make it as good for you and me as I can. I'll make it somethin' we can remember all our lives.*

Now she took her hands back. *Yeah, I know about you. You're just passin' through. Like my daddy. Like Mr. Collins. Only they died.* She shook her head. *The only one not passin' through that wants me is Mr. Adams.*

Who's that?

The man over at the hotel. He comes sometimes of a evenin'. He sets with us and wants me to walk with him and he tells me how purty I am.

You like him?

I guess so. I don't hardly know him. She set back down on the log by me. *But I don't hardly know you. Tell me somethin' about you.* They'd already heard what Preacher Wood called my short story so there warn't no use in tellin' her that again. The way she put it, I figured she wanted somethin' different from that but with more in it about me. So I told her about our mother. And about the little red mare. And about how terrible the War was. And how I'd got sick with the fevers and left the War to go home. And how much I liked this part of the country with the mountains and the timber. And how bad I wanted to see Stewart County again.

I looked at her to see her cryin' a little. *I'm obliged for you tellin' me that. I never knowed much about the War, bein' so young.* She wiped her eyes with her apron tail. *You know I like you a lot. Part of me wants to do it with you, wants to do it real bad. But I got to look out for myself and I got to figure out what it means if'n I do it with you and then you're gone to Stewart County.* She stood up and looked at the clover she was holdin' and let it drop. I got hold of that hand and kissed it. She took it away and smoothed her apron like it was all wrinkled. *I got to go. I'll give you my answer tomorra after breakfast, here on the log.* And she ran back to the house.

I set there, watchin' her go, knowin' she was right. If'n she wanted me as much as I wanted her, then we'd pleasure each other in the time we had, the devil take tomorra. But if'n the tomorras took over, she'd not do it. Nothin' more I could say. Only thing I could do was to get on with the day's work. She'd tell me tomorra.

The day dragged on. I worked at the wood pile, choppin' for all I was worth. I was hopin' I'd be so tired at night that I'd go to sleep without thinkin' of her there in the next room with Miz Collins. She was at the dinner table and the supper table but both times she didn't set by me like we'd been doin'. She didn't say anythin' to me but to ask me to pass her this or that. And when time come that night to set on the porch she set over close to Miz Collins with one of the girls 'tween us. Bed time, I could hear her and Miz Collins talkin', but I didn't get the drift of what they was sayin' Like I said, I was dog tired and next thing I knowed it was mornin'. Next mornin' went like it always did. I left the table and did some chores and then went and set on the log.

Here she come and my heart was in my mouth, just watchin' her walk to'ard me. She settled herself next to me, but not touchin'. I wanted to reach out and take her hand but I didn't. It was time to hear what she had to say. *I got a question to ask you.* I nodded. *If'n I do it, will you take me with you when you leave?*

So there it was. If'n I said I'd take her with me when I left Standin' Stone, she'd go upstairs with me. I shook my head. *I ain't goin' to lie to you. I cain't do that.*

She nodded, lookin' down at her hands in her lap. *I figured you'd say that. Then I don't want to go upstairs with you.* She looked at me. *Funny thing is, I'm not for certain I'd of gone with you, even if'n you'd said you'd take me. But I wanted to know.* She shook her head so's that her purty black hair turned this way and that. *Like Miz Collins sed, there's more to this than goin' upstairs. I know in my heart she's right.* Now she reached and got my hand and kissed it. *I'm right glad you come here and stirred up these feelin's in me. I won't forget about you for a long time.* She let go of my hand and she stood up and smoothed her dress tail and not lookin' back went to the house.

I set there on the log for a while after she walked away. Truth to tell, lookin' back, I warn't taken by surprise by how she called it. The minute she asked me if'n I would take her along with me, I knowed what she was leadin' up to. And I guess I knowed in my heart that it was the right thing for her to do. She warn't by no means anything like Maybelle. Goin' upstairs with me and gettin' in the bed with me for Josie warn't nothing to be done just for the pleasure of it. As my Aunt Polly would say, they was strings attached. And I couldn't pick up the strings. Mebbe I should say I wouldn't pick up the strings.

Anyway, what was done was done. It was time to wind up my work for Miz Collins and go on my way. I worked a while on the wood pile. I was near done there. She'd have enough stove wood for the winter to come. Just as I was rickin' the last of it, here she come. We nodded to each other and she stood there with her arms folded watchin' me stack the last of what I had chopped. *I'm about done here.*

Hit looks good. Looks like I got enough wood there to last me through to spring.

Yessum, I think so, 'less'n you folks have a real bad cold spell. I put on the last sticks. *There anything else you want me to do, afore I leave?*

Nothin' more to keep you here, is there?

I guess not. You know what Josie has told me?

She nodded. *She told me this mornin'. You may not like it, but she's got a head on her shoulders.*

It ain't up to me to like it or not. She told me her terms, and I cain't meet 'em. She's got to do what she's got to do, and I got to do what I got to do. We stood there lookin' at each other. Didn't seem like there was any thing else to say. *You got any thing else around the place you want me to do?*

I guess not. Maybe that shelf in the kitchen that's fallin' down. You in a hurry to get goin'?

I shrugged. *Maybe. I was plannin' on headin' out anyway when I got done with the work for you.*

She stood there, arms folded. *You mad at me? You figure that I told her what to do?*

I shrugged. *Maybe. But I got to say that I figure she made up her own mind.* I shook my head. *Naw, I ain't mad at you. You called the shots the way you seen 'em. You owe it to her to do that. You're her mama, so to speak, and it is rightful for you to do that.*

I'm obliged to you for seein' it that way. Now, will you let me tell you what I figure you ought to do?

I'm listenin'.

Ain't no need for you to be in a all fired hurry to leave. If'n you do, that's goin' to tell her that the only reason you were stayin' around was to get her in bed with you. Maybe you feel that way, but there ain't no need to rub her nose in it. So, whyn't you stay around another day or two, show her that there's more to it than that. I got more'n that shelf fallin' down for you to do. 'Sides, it's been real good to have you around the house. I kind of hate to see you go. She smiled, her crooked smile. *Watchin' the way you two look at each other makes me think maybe I'd better be on the look out for a man to smile at me that way.*

I stood there, lookin' at her face that I'd thought was real ugly at first. Now it didn't seem so ugly. As she would of said, there was more to her than was in her face. *Yessum, I'll do that. I can see what you mean. It's the right thing to do, for her and me. I thankee for that. And yessum, you 'd better be on the lookout! Ain't no tellin' what you might turn up under some rock!* We laughed at what I'd said.

So I did. I fixed that shelf and cleaned up her yard and the wood pile and got up on the roof and nailed down some shingles and did that kind of thing. I was with Josie at meal times, and settin' on the front porch and the like. Her and me was friendly to each other but nothin' more than that. I let it be known that I'd be leavin' in a day or two. No men come to the house in them two days. Everybody went about their business as usual. I went to the saloon of a night, and talked to the bar keep about how to get down to the Cumberland River. He said to go down to Gainesbora. Nothin' more was said about the body on the road to Knoxvul. And on the third day, I left.

They all saw me off. I give the girls and Miz Collins a big hug and many thanks for everthin'. Miz Collins got to me by myself afore I went and we settled up. I tried to give her some money, but she wouldn't take it. Josie walked me out to Thunder and kissed me on the cheek. We didn't say much, just that we'd not forget each other for a long time.

It was so, for me. Josie was the first woman I wanted as a man. I can close my eyes to this day and recollect how she looked and laughed and the feelin' I felt for her. But I put it past me. Feelin' for her like I did didn't change me wantin' to go home to Stewart County. And I wanted to do that by myself, not with her, as much as I felt for her. I knowed I had done the right thing, for me. So aside from some recollections', I put it past me.

So I left Standin' Stone with my aim to get to the Cumberland River. Maybe I could hitch a ride on a river boat goin' down to Nashville, maybe even all the way to Stewart County. I recollected that the river went to Nashville, then Clarksville, then Dover. If'n I could get to Dover, I'd be all the way home. The bar keep said maybe that would work.

He even drawed me a map. It showed I could go on this road on past Cookeville and to a settlement named Baxter. There was a crossroads at Baxter, one way to Nashville and one to Gainesbora. He said the river went north from the Nashville road, so goin' to Gainesbora was the thing to do, if'n I wanted to get to the river. Gainesbora was right on the river. I never learned until many years after that Gainesbora was really Gainesboro. Lily told me that. She's a right smart woman. Has to be, since she teaches school. But that's another story. The bar keep warned me that this time of year the river was low, and there might not be any boats runnin' this far upstream.

The road from Standin' Stone down to Cookeville was real purty. It went along the side of a big long bluff. The timber on both sides was heavy. It looked like somebody not knowing where they was goin' could get lost easy. Right afore I got to Cookeville there was a creek and I could hear what must of been a waterfall up stream. There was creeks all around in that country. And I saw some what looked like caves, too. More creeks and caves than was in Stewart County. Anyway, I watered Thunder at the creek. I was standin' there and a feller rode by. To pass the time of day, I ast him if'n the creek had a name. He said it did, Fallin' Water. He ast me how I'd come. When I told him, he laughed and said I'd come down Calfkiller Holler. I don't know why, but I recollect them names.

I made up my mind to ride on past Cookeville and not stop. The road went right through Cookeville. It looked a lot like Standin' Stone but a good size bigger and nowhere near as purty. Like the man at the saloon said, I hit a railroad track when I got to town. The road follered the track and I went on it all the way 'til I come to the crossroads. The sign said Baxter, I figured. My readin' signs was a problem, but I could tell that one from the B. Baxter warn't much. All I seen was the train stop and a few houses and that was it. The feller at the train stop said I was on the right track and that Gainesbora was a long day's ride. I stretched it out to two days. I stopped the next mornin' at a house and bought some vittles from the woman there. I was goin' downhill all the way. That made sense to me since I knowed Gainesbora was down in the Cumberland River valley.

When I got there, I could see that it was a real purty town, like Standin' Stone but on the river. I guess I hadn't paid much attention to where I was afore I got to the Cumberland Mountains. It seemed like I'd of been in some good country when I was ridin' with the cavalry, but I never looked at it that way. I was too busy tryin' to keep up and doin' what I was told. I've heard tell since I was there that Virginny was real purty country but all I recollect there was the War. North C'lina at the Wood place was right flat country. And all I recollected of the Smoky Mountains was that it was hard goin'. Maybe I stopped to look around me sometimes, but not much. Anyway, this was real purty country and I liked the looks of it a lot.

I got to Gainesbora middle of the mornin', and rode straight to the Cumberland River. When I was standin' there on the bank, I almost felt like cryin'. I knowed that all the way downstream was Stewart County. It looked real good to me and it felt real good. I felt like I was at long last gettin' closer to home after bein' so long away. I'd seen a lot of rivers and creeks since I left home, but none of 'em was as purty as this one.

After I got done moonin' over the river, as Bill Jones would of called it, I turned Thunder to the square. I hitched him and went in a store. The sign started with a D, but that was all I could make out. Later on, Mr Tinsley told me it was Draper's Store.

I stood there lookin' around, lettin' my eyes get used to the dark after comin' in out of the sun. And it was dark inside except for the winders in the front and at the back of the store. It was bigger'n any store I'd ever seen, outside of at Clarksville. Bigger'n the one at Dover and Mount Airy. I never went in one at Knoxville so I couldn't tell about that. There was shelves along the side walls. It looked like there was anything there that a man would need or want. And there was a right size crowd in there, men and women and a youngun or two. A man was talkin' to the man behind the counter. *Shorely you know of some man in this here town I could hire!*

No sir, Mr. Tinsley, I shore don't. You know how it is around here. About all the young men went to the War. None but a few come back. Them that did are farmin' on their daddy's place. They ain't nobody else to hire out, that I know of.

The man askin' the question was standin' by the counter, eatin' a piece he'd cut off of a wheel of yellow cheese. It looked like he of a sudden saw me. *You lookin' for work?*

No sir, I ain't, right now. I come down from Baxter to see if'n I can catch a boat to Nashvul.

He cut another piece of cheese and offered it to me at the point of the knife. I took it. It was a real good cheese. *There ain't no boats goin' down to Nashvul this time of year. The river's too low. You just passin' through?*

Yessir, just passin' through. I come from North C'lina on my way back to Stewart County.

That's west Tennessee.

Yessir, up by the Kentucky line.

I been there oncet. The Cumberland and the Tennessee near run together.

Yes sir, they do that.
You want another piece of cheese?
I wouldn't say no. I ain't had much to eat lately.
He cut off another piece, bigger'n the last one and reached it to me. It seemed like he was lookin' me over. *How you goin' to get to Nashvul if'n you ain't got any boat?*
I shrugged. *Ride my horse, I guess.*
You want to show me yore horse?
I nodded. *Thankee for the cheese. Shore, I'll show you my horse.*
We stepped out on the porch and over to where Thunder was hitched. Out in the light, I took a look at Mr. Tinsley. He warn't much to look at. He looked like any other man his age, I guess. Old enough to be my daddy. Old pants and shirt but tolerably clean. Old hat pulled down on his head so's the only thing you could see between his hat and his chin whiskers was his eyes. And I couldn't see much of them. Somebody told me oncet that you could judge a man by his eyes, but I never got the hang of it. He looked to me like any man a farmer his age.
He stopped several steps away from Thunder. He looked at Thunder and Thunder looked at him and me standin' there. *That's a right good lookin' horse you got there.*
Yessir, he is.
You want to sell 'im?
No sir, I guess not. If'n there ain't no boat, I guess I'll have to ride 'im to Stewart County.
He nodded. *You need any money?*
Well, sir, I cain't say that I don't. I was workin' for a man over in North C'lina and I still have a little of that. It ain't much, but I figure it'll do me for a while.
Can I go up to him? He looks like the nervy kind.
I laughed. *He's right nervy all right. I'll walk up with you.* We did, and Mr Tinsley felt him on the neck and the shoulders. *You partial to horses?*
He nodded. *Always have been, since I was a boy. We had 'em around the place when John was a boy. John's my boy. He rode one of 'em off to the War. I sold the others. Needed the money.* I nodded,

couldn't think of anything to say. If'n he wanted to tell me what happened to John, I figured he'd tell me. No need to ask. Thunder stood still to his hand, but kept an eye on me all the while. *What'd you do in North C'lina?*

I'd been fightin' in Virginny and got real sick with the fevers. Started home, got as far as North C'lina and passed out. A farmer and his family saved me. When I got so I could, I farmed with him and broke horses for another farmer. He was where Thunder was from. Then I started to come back to Tennessee.

You come over the mountains. It was more like him tellin' me he knowed what I'd done than askin' me a question.

Yessir, I did, with a wagon train headed for Missoury.

He nodded. *You got quite a story to tell.*

Yessir, I guess I have.

We stood there, lookin' at Thunder, who was takin' it all in. *Tell you what. I got a offer to make to you. Stewart County is a long way away. You ain't even near there yet. You're goin' to have some more money if'n you figure to get there in a year's time. You reckon that's so?*

I didn't want to admit it, but I knowed he was right. I warn't even close to Stewart Country yet. And all I had was a little left of the money from Frank Atkins and the three gold pieces and that gold ring. I shore as hell didn't want to spend the gold pieces now. I figured I'd need 'em when I settled down with Nadine. And I figured I'd give her the gold ring. *Yessir, I reckon that's so.*

I got a month's worth of work I need done on my farm, maybe more. Some of it is hard work but I reckon you can do it. He named his price. I said I reckoned that warn't enough to keep me there, and he doubled it. So I said I'd do it. *Name's Tinsley. Wesley John Tinsley.*

Mine's Morris. Martin Luther Morris.

I'm about ready to go. You got any more business here?

No sir, I'm ready to go with you. One question. Where we goin'?

Tinsley Bottom.

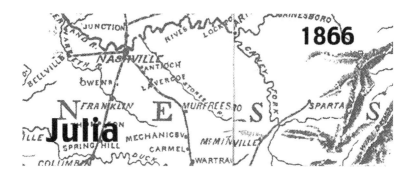

The road led alongside the Cumberland River. It was a real purty river valley and it made me pure homesick to think it went all the way downstream to Dover. Thunder didn't want to go as slow as the wagon, but I got him down to a trot. With that, he'd get ahead and we'd have to wait for the wagon to catch up. He'd stand there, waitin', prancin', like he couldn't see how that wagon could be so slow in comin'. A piece down the road we'd stopped at a creek. Mr. Tinsley and the wagon caught up. He got down to take a piss. *This here is Sugar Creek. School house up Sugar Creek is where they have play parties. You like to go to a play party?* Afore I could answer, he went on. *We turn off up here a piece, to the left. The track goes on up to Tinsley Bottom.*

It named after you?

He nodded. *My daddy's daddy settled it. Called it for hisself. I was born here, lived here all my life. You watch for the turnoff, goin' to the left hand.* And he got back up in the springboard and drove away. We follered him and went past. I let Thunder do his gallop. Half hour later, we come to the turnoff. We'd left the river, but I could see the bluffs of the river valley over to the left, maybe near a mile away. He called it a bottom, so I figured the river made a bend and the bottom was inside the bend. It turned out that was right, but I didn't know it for sure then. I figured we was on the right track, so I didn't wait for him to come. The road up in the bottom was windey, with pasture land on the side of it. It was filled up with scrub, wouldn't be much good for grazin' without some work on it.

We got to a graveyard and I figured that'd be a good place to stop and wait for him to catch up. I let Thunder graze and I looked around some at the tombstones. Shore enough, there was some with the name Tinsley on 'em. The dates on 'em warn't easy to read, but it looked like they went back more'n a few years. About that time, he caught up, and we went on up the bottom to the house.

We got to his place a hour afore sundown. His wife must of heard the wagon comin' and she come out on the side porch. She was a good size woman. Standin' next to her, he come off as a mite puny. I come to learn that she had a sharp tongue. It seemed like she didn't have much of a good word for nobody. I mean nobody. Not him and not her son's wife Julia. She didn't give me much of a hard time. Mainly I tried to stay out of her way. No need to be in her way except at dinnertime and I started right away to take somethin' to the field with me. Or wherever I was workin'. Suppertime mostly, she didn't show up. He said she had bad headaches. Maybe that was why she was so hard to get along with.

He told her who I was and that I'd be hired help for some weeks, maybe more. He said they'd feed me and I'd sleep in the barn. By that time I'd got off Thunder and I figured maybe she'd shake hands. But she just nodded at me. So I was back sleepin' in a pile of hay in a barn agin. Truth to tell, I didn't mind doin' that. It looked like Miz Tinsley warn't all that glad to have me there. I didn't want to get in her way any more'n I had to. I didn't mean to be there that long, anyway. And this way, Thunder was in a stall right across from me. Good for me, good for him.

It turned out I was with them for near two months. Most of what I did was farmin' and what you'd call odd jobs. The first one was to clean out the barn. Some of the stalls needed it bad, knee deep in shit and hay. It stunk to high heaven when it got stirred up. I had to tie a rag over my nose and mouth to stand it. But Mr. Tinsley knowed what he was doin'. I loaded it up in the wagon and scattered it in the garden where the season for growin' was done. I put it heavy on the tater patch. The garden was midsized. I guess they didn't need much.

After that, I did a cuttin' of hay and put it up in the hayloft. Same set up as Preacher had. Then him and me did some work on the house and the outbuildings. And I cleaned out their outhouse. Him and me took some cattle to Gainsbora to market. Took us all day and then some. He drove the wagon and I rode herd on Thunder. I was mindful of how much the little red mare would like to do the herdin'. Thunder did it all right but I could tell he didn't much like it.

While I was at Gainsbora I went back to Draper's Store and asked about river traffic down to Nashville. There still warn't any. The river was still too low this far upstream, the fellar at the store said. He said the boats was gettin' up as far as Carthage. Maybe I could find somethin' down there. I never did. But as it turned out, there was enough to do on the Tinsley farm to keep me busy. And more.

I met Miz Julia on one of them first days. I'd been cleanin' out the stable. And I was standin' in the hallway, with a pitchfork in my hand, gettin' a breath of fresh air from all that manure. Manure was what Mr. Tinsley called it. Up come this buggy. It stopped by the hitchin' post and down got this young woman. She was a sight for sore eyes, brown curly hair blowin' in the wind this way and that from under her bonnet, her skirt caught up in the wind, her holdin' it down with one hand while she started to tie up at the hitchin' post. I come to my manners. *C'n I do that for you?*

She turned to me and smiled a real purty smile. And she answered in a voice so quiet I had to work to hear her. *I'd be obliged.* And she give me the reins. I must of looked like I didn't have no sense, just standin' there, holdin' the reins, lookin' at her. It hit me that she was what Bill Jones used to say bee-you-ti-ful about. Afore he said it, I never had heard the word. She was bee-you-ti-ful all right and enough. Maybe the word fit Betty Lou but there warn't any doubt in my mind that the word fit this woman, standin' there, sort of smilin' at me. *My name's Julia Tinsley.*

Yes mam, I mean, mine's Luther Morris. I couldn't take my eyes off'n her. *I'd shake yore hand but I'm all dirty from in here.* And I pointed in the stable.

She laughed, and it sounded to me like a bell ringin'. *I can tell what you been doin'.*

Yes mam I reckon you can. I finally got around to tying up her horse. When I turned around, she was headed up to the house. I just stood there, watchin' her go. Last woman I'd seen walk that way was Dulcimay. Miz Julia's skirt was longer and there was a lot more skirt than Dulcimay had, but I could tell she walked that way, like she was dancin' to a tune she heard inside her head. Josie had that some of that walk, too. It made me wonder if'n young beautiful women walked that way on account of they was women.

I see you met Julia.

I nearly jumped out of my skin. It was Mr. Tinsley, come up without my seein' him. *Yessir.*

She's some young woman, ain't she?

She shore is.

She's John's wife. They live in the little house on up in the bottom. Now you've met Julia, I'll take you up to meet John. He laughed. *You know you're right smelly, don't you.*

Yessir, I know that. It's hard to clean out a stable and not get smelly. Fact is, I meant to go to river this evenin'. You think Miz Tinsley would loan me a piece of soap?

He nodded. *Yep. I'll go you one better. I ain't been to the river in a week, so I'll get the soap and you and me'll go wash up. Maybe stop to meet John on the way back. Let's do it a hour or so afore sundown. I'll bring along some baked sweet taters for our supper.*

That's what we did. I quit workin' in the stable middle of the afternoon and put the fork and shovels away and here come Mr. Tinsley like he said with a piece of soap and the sweet taters and a water tin. He even brung me a clean shirt. So we rode up in the bottom to'ard what he said was a good place to get in the river and wash up some.

He was in the mood to talk. *The Cumberland starts up near in to Kaintuck. Comes on down south to Celina, then Butler's Landin'.* He pointed to the west. *Right over there it starts to make a big bend, south then east then north. This here piece of land is a good piece of land. Sandy where we're headed. Good dirt where my place is. Parts of it git flooded every year or two, bringin' in some silt.* I nodded. *That's what happens with the Saline Creek on Uncle Gray's place. The floodin' makes for a better crop the next year. So is this whole piece of bottom land yours?*

Naw. The Smith's own up on the hill and out by the road. But my family's been here a long time and everybody calls it Tinsley Bottom. There's a graveyard back to'ard the road where my family's buried. I guess I'll be put there some day.

We got to the river. I'd seen the Cumberland River lots of times afore. There was the time or two when I was a boy and Uncle Gray took me to the river for this and that. But I was a boy and never paid much attention to it. Then I seen it at Dover when I was at Fort Donelson. And agin at Clarksville and Gainsbora and maybe another time or two. But this was different or it struck me as bein' different. It was a wide sweep of a river with bluffs on the other side. It was real quiet and peaceful. Real purty. Maybe I could call it beautiful. Not as beautiful as Miz Julia, of course, but beautiful all the same.

We shucked off our clothes and waded in. *You know how to swim?*

I laughed. *Don't know. Never tried it.*

He laughed. *Ain't nothin' to it. You just wave yore arms and kick. But you have to watch out for this river. It moves its sand bars afore yore very eyes. One minute a sand bar is there, next minute it's moved on by the current.* We washed good. I watched for lice floatin' up to the top but never seen any. I could see what he was talkin' about. Standin' there, I could feel the river current around me, real strong, and feel the sand under my feet, shiftin' away.

I washed my pants and drawers good. And my shirt. I even took my boots in and washed the manure off'n them good. Then I found a shalla place and just set there, feelin' the cool of the river and watchin' it go past me. He come and set by me. *Anybody live over across the river?*

He nodded. *Julia's people live over there. You can see there ain't no bottom land. The bluffs are too high. But they's some real good pasture. Julia's family raise a fair number of cattle.*

Any easy way to get across?

Couple places can be forded when the river's down. Or you can go over with a john boat, if'n you're careful with the current. Elsewise have to go to Gainsbora. Grinnin. *Why you askin'? You figure on goin' over to see if'n Julia has a sister?*

I laughed. *Just askin'.* I shook my head. *Does she?*

Now he did a belly laugh. *I don't rightly know. You'll have to ask her if'n she does. I doubt the sister would want to go to Stewart County with you. They are a real close family. It's a su'prise that Julia married John. And come over here to the Bottom. She misses her family a whole lot.*

He shook his head, lookin' at the river goin' by. *'Specially the way things turned out.* He was quiet. *My wife, she never had a daughter and she don't know how to treat her. Always bossin' about this and that.* He picked up a rock and thowed it in the river, like a boy would of. *And now John's home from the War and he ain't good for much. I feel sorrow for him but I feel as much sorrow for her. Wouldn't blame her if'n she called it quits and went back to her family.* He turned back to me. *Gettin' late, we better go. Eat our taters on the way.*

The house where Julia and John lived was right purty. It had a porch across the front lookin' toward the river bend and the bluffs. It looked like there was a room upstairs. The out buildings was over to the side. Fencing needed some work. There was a pig pen and some chickens here and there. They must of heard us comin' and come out on the porch. There was Julia, and John was standin' next to her, leanin' against a post. He had two crutches and only a half a leg on the right. *John, this here is Luther Morris. Julia, I guess you met Luther.* She smiled at me and nodded. *Howdy, John.* He leaned agin the porch post and offered his hand. *Howdy, Luther. Won't you men set a spell?* She pointed to the chairs. *Tell you what, Julia, I ought to get back. Luther, you want to set a spell? If'n it's all right with you. I'll get back in time for chores.* He nodded and got on his mule and went on up the road to'ard his place.

I'll go get you men a drink of fresh water. And she went in the house.

You gonna be here long? He went to a chair that had arms. He settled in the chair and put the crutches on the floor.

I don't rightly know. I been on the road back to where I come from so long, I guess I ain't in a hurry. I met up with Mr. Tinsley in Gainsbora and he offered me work. I'm right near cleaned out of money so I was glad to take him up on it.

He looked out across the way to the river bluffs. *Yeah. He needs help bad.* Then he looked at me with a halfway grin. His colorin' was fair, not much sun burned. His head of hair was black, and he was near clean shaven. There warn't nothin' else to remark about, about his looks. He looked like many a man I seen in the army. 'Ceptin' he had just one leg. *You want to tell me yore story first off or ought I to go first?*

I guess I'm here on yore territory so I'll go first. That all right with you? He nodded.

Julia come out on the porch with a pitcher of water. Standin' there by John's chair, she near took my breath away with her beauty. Thinkin' back, it warn't any one thing about her, like her hair or her eyes. It was just the whole thing put together. Old John was one lucky man to have her. *You men tradin' war stories?* I couldn't tell if'n she meant it how it sounded or if'n it was just what come to her mind. *I've heard John's here, but if'n you don't mind I'll stay to hear yours.*

I don't mind. It'd save me time tellin' it twice. So she set down, and I told my story agin. Preacher Woods would call it my short story. But I told enough for them to know where I was from and what I did in the War and how I got sick and was found by the Wood family. I told enough about the War so they'd know I knowed somethin' about what happened to John and what he was goin' through.

In the tellin', I tried to do the talkin' to him, but truth to tell I couldn't keep my eyes off'n her. It seemed like she was watchin' me doin' the tellin' like it were a story she'd never heard afore. It was all I could do to keep from bein' flustered, and forgettin' where I was in the story.

After I got through, John nodded and stirred in his chair. I figured he was feelin' pain in his leg that was cut off. I'd heard tell they do, for a long time after. *Ain't much to my story. I fought at Chickamauga and my leg was hit by a cannon ball and they cut it off. It got infected, that's what the doctor's said, and I was laid up for so long I forgot how long. Got back here to the Bottom, near three months ago. Feller got me these here crutches. Told me how to walk with 'em, for all it was worth. I get by. But I ain't much good for farmin'. Like I said, I reckon my daddy can use yore help.*

He fell quiet and I figured that was all he had to say. I stood up to go. *I better get back to help with chores. I'm right glad to meet y'all. I thankee Miz Julia for the water. You folks have got good water here in the bottom. I'll say good evenin' now.* Julia stood up and John got up in right good fashion with the aid of his crutches. *I reckon I'll see you all agin.*

You been to the river? He hobbled over to the porch post.

Yeah, that's where we come from. I been cleanin' out his stable and I reckon I smelled like a polecat. He said maybe I better go get wet, wash off some of the smell. So him and me went, afore we come by here.

He was standin' now, leanin' against the post. *Can I ask a favor of you?*

I nodded. *Name it.*
Go with me to the river.
I can do it. Name yore day.
Tomorra, afore suppertime?
I'll be here.

All day the next day I wondered how he was goin' to get to the river. It was maybe a half a mile from their house to where Mr. Tinsley took me at the river. Maybe he could get on and off a horse, but I didn't think so. Well, I told Mr. Tinsley that mornin' when we was doin' chores what John had asked. *Is it alright with you, if'n I go? We better go a while afore supper time?* He nodded. *Yes, it shore is. It shore is. I'd be much obliged to you if'n you'd do it. Take the time you need. I been waitin' for John to show some life, and maybe this is it. If'n he wants to, and if'n you don't mind, go with him anytime he says. I'd be much obliged to you for doin' it.* So come the time, I saddled up Thunder and went. It was maybe a little over a mile to their house and I could of walked but Thunder needed to have something to do. When we got to the house, I found the buggy hitched up to a fair lookin' mule. I guessed Julia had done the hitchin'. John come out on the porch. We said our howdys.

He got down off the porch and made headway slow to the buggy. Holdin' on to the buggy wheel he turned to me. I stood there, lookin' at him, not knowin' what to say. Then I knowed what to say. *John.* He looked at me. *I hate to put this on you, but I better.*

He didn't let me finish. *You want to know what to do. When I have to have your help.*

I nodded. *I'm willin' to help but I don't know you enough to figure it out without you tellin' me.*

I can still see him standin' there, one pant leg pinned up, holdin' on to the buggy wheel. He nodded. *I know what you're sayin! We're in trouble here. I got to have some help but I don't want to ask nobody for it. Least of all a man who shows up on my daddy's farm what went to the War and lived to tell about it. I don't want yore help but I have to take it.*

He stopped talkin', lookin' up at the chair on the porch. *I set over there in that chair dyin' a little every day, not knowin' what else to do. You show up and I've made up my mind you was sent by God, and by God, I'm gonna use you. You're my daddy's hired hand and I'm gonna use you. Now, I'm tellin' you, I'll tell you when I need yore help. If'n I don't tell you, you leave me be.* And he moved over to the step up on the buggy.

Now them old buggies was made with a wide floor board. I guess it was to put supplies at the driver's feet. Maybe not, I don't rightly know. But John's buggy had a wide floor board. He turned around and lifted hisself up on the step, then up on the floor board, then up in the seat. I could tell it was real hard work for 'im to do that. He must of been real strong in the arms to do that with what little help his good leg could give. When he got set good, he looked at me and nodded, like he was tellin' me somethin'. Truth to tell, he was. And he drove off to'ards the river.

I was left standin' there, holdin' Thunder's reins. First off, I was pissed at him. There warn't no cause, I thought, for him to give me down the road. Then I thought better of it. I figured I'd of felt the same and said the same thing if'n I was him. Maybe worse. I got to say I figured he'd need my help gettin' up in the buggy seat, but by God, he made it on his own. If'n he could keep that up, maybe we could be buddies, like we was in the army together. Maybe we could, if'n he didn't turn sour agin me.

He knowed where to go. I follered him all the way, figurin' it was best to let him take the lead. He stopped the buggy on the river bank maybe 10 foot from the water. By the time I got there, got down and tied Thunder to some willows, he had slid down from the buggy seat and was standin' there holdin' on to the buggy wheel, lookin' at the river. Not knowin' what else to do, I shucked my boots, then my clothes, as quick as I could and stood there waitin' to see what to do next.

He took off his shirt and dropped it. *You'll have to help me take off my pants and my boots.* He said it so quiet I wouldn't of understood if'n I hadn't knowed what to expect. It was easy to do. I knew what to do from the War. I went to him, knelt down on one leg, makin' a place for him to set on my knee that was up, and drawed him down backward to set there. He fought me at first but then caught on to what I was doin', givin' him a place to set to take down his pants and his drawers and his boot. Then I helped him stand on his one leg and I stood up and me walkin' and him hobblin' we got out into the water.

I thought he'd want to get in the water soon as he could, so he could get down in it. But he kept holdin' on to me and we kept walkin' and hobblin' to the deep 'til we was in over our middle.

Then, of a sudden, he let go of me and dived in head first. I tell you, I was scared to death for him. We was now near in the full of the current of the river and I figured he was a goner for sure. Truth to tell, the current was runnin' so strong that I was that much worried about me, and I worked my way back to'ard the bank as soon as I could. Soon as I got good footing I turned to look for him and here he come, swimmin' like a gol danged fish with what Bill Jones would call a shit eatin' grin on his face. He pulled up beside me and set down and I set down by him. *Scared you, didn't I?*

You scared the shit out of me! I thought you was a goner in the current.

He looked out at the river. *I been swimmin' in this here river since I was a kid. Used to swim here with Julia's brothers. They'd come over in a John boat and we'd have water fights and fool around. My daddy didn't like it. He didn't like it one bit. He's scared of the water. Never learned how to swim. Or leastwise that's what he says. Anyhow that's how I come to know Julia. She'd come over with 'em sometimes. Started back when she was just a girl.* He was quiet, playin' in the water with his hand, makin' waves agin the current. *I found out somethin' here today. I come here today to test it. You know what it is?*

*No, guess not. One thing for sure. You ain't afraid of the river,
like me.*

No I ain't never been afraid of the river. Now quiet, almost
talkin' to hisself. *No, what I found out was that I don't need two
legs in the river. One'll do just fine.*

There's not much more to tell about that day. He went back
out in the deep and went up and down like a crazy man. I set
there, watchin' him, thinkin' maybe this would be a real good
thing for him. Maybe it'd give him some hope for something
good in his life.

Well, I guess it did. We went to the river every day I could
get free. Mr. Tinsley told me to do it, if'n I didn't mind, and I
was real glad I was there to do it. Not knowin' how he'd feel about
John's swimmin' in the deep water, I never told him. Anyway he
didn't tell me not to go with John. I figured it was all right so long as
I got my work done. Truth to tell, with all that goin' to the river, I
was as clean as I ever been in my life. Maybe since.

One day of them days, him and me was settin' on the river
bank dryin' off. I turned to him. *I got a question for you.*

He shook his head. *I hope it ain't about the War. I don't want
to talk about that.*

It ain't about the War.

All right.

You want to see if'n you can get up on a horse by yourself?

He shook his head agin. *What kind of a question is that?
What're you doin', trying to push me?*

I nodded. *I reckon I am. I figure you and me are goin' to have
to be buddies like in the army. If'n we was in a battle, we'd have to
lean on each other. Well, I want to know here and now if'n you
figure you can lean on me.*

He shook his head agin and almost snorted. *Shit! I'm already
leanin' on you. You want me to do it more?* He was quiet and I
didn't say anything. I just set there watchin' the river. I figured
this was somethin' he was goin' to have to make up his mind
about. He still warn't talkin'. I got up and helped him get on his
drawers and his pants and his boot. And I got back on my clothes.

He got hold of his crutches and went over and got his shirt and set on a rock there and put it on. *Ain't you gonna try to tell me why I should try it?* *Nope. You know why as well as I do.* He stood up and tucked in his pants. He was shakin' his head. *All right, dammit. Tell me what you're thinkin'.* *I ain't got no clear idea how you can do it. I guess you'll have to study it some.* I shrugged. *We better get goin'. We can talk about it tomorra, if 'n you want to.* He went over to the buggy and got up into the buggy seat like he did. I got on Thunder and went closer to the buggy. *But I figure if 'n you can get up on that gol danged buggy seat, you can shore as hell get on and off of a horse.* And I led the way back to his house and I went on to the Tinsley place.

The next morning it was rainin'. I was in the barn, workin' on gear. First thing I knowed here come John, and he pulled the buggy in the hallway out of the rain. We said our howdys and talked about the rain. *My daddy around?* *I guess he's still in the house. I ain't seen him since breakfast.* He nodded and went over to the house, bein' careful not to slip in the places slick from the rain. He was in there a while and then here he come back with his daddy. I wondered to myself what was goin' on. Maybe it'd really got to him with my question about gettin' up on a horse.

Pap, Luther here has raised the question, if 'n I can figure out how to get on and off a horse with one leg.

Mr. Tinsley nodded, lookin' at me and John and back at me. *What you got in mind?*

I didn't have no notion of what Mr. Tinsley would think about this. Fact is, I was taken aback that John had got him into it. *I ain't got much in mind. But yestiday I saw John settin' on a big rock, puttin' on his shirt. It put me in mind to when I was sick with the fevers and ridin' a mule bareback over in Virginny. I was ridin' by myself. I didn't have no stirrups and I was so weak I couldn't use my arms much. So I had to make do with a big rock or somethin' like that to get me high enough up to get on the mule. Then I had to find one to let me down off'n it. Elsewise, slide off'n it.*

They looked at me, I guess thinkin' about what I'd said. His daddy looked at John. *It might work. You got strong arms.*

It might.

It'd take some doin'!

I reckon it would. I saw him lookin' out in the rain at a big rock by the gate to the cow pasture. He half laughed to hisself. *I'd likely fall and break the t'other leg.*

I guess you might. I recollect when you was learnin' to ride as a boy you started out bareback and you fell off a lot. We all kind of laughed at the picture of the boy fallin' off of the mule. *You want to try it agin as a man?*

Shit. He shook his head, lookin' out at the rain. *A man with one leg! Shit.* He shrugged and looked at us, standin' there. *Might as well try it. Looks like it's startin' to slack.* Mr. Tinsley and me nodded. He looked at his daddy and then me. *You fellers mind gettin' a mite bit wet?* We said no. *Then, Luther, get me that little mule and let's try it.*

Well, it didn't much work that day. I more or less stood by and let his daddy do what he could do to help. But everything was wet and slick from the rain, and John didn't have the hang of it. He'd get his good leg in the stirrup but couldn't sling his part leg over, and he'd kind of slide down. Mr. Tinsley tried to hold him up there but couldn't. The mule got restless and kept movin' away from the rock.

It started to rain hard and they decided they'd had enough for the day. John was downhearted about it and wouldn't say much afore he got up in the buggy and rode away. I can see it still, his daddy standin' there soakin' wet, feelin' sorry for his son and for hisself. I wondered if'n I'd done anybody any good by bringin' it up.

But it turned out I had. Next day John and me tried agin and we got him up in the saddle but he near fell off when he tried to get down. But it looked like his spirit was better and we said we'd try agin. And we did. We kept tryin' to work it out.

Finally, one day right afore supper, his daddy and me was on hand, and still at the big rock, and John made it up and down by hisself. And he didn't fall. I don't know who was the most tickled, John or his daddy or me. Bein' able to ride the mule by hisself made a heap of difference to John. Now he could get about the Bottom by hisself. As far as I knowed he didn't go to the river to swim by hisself but he went everywheres else. I'd see the mule at the Tinsley house sometimes. He'd carry his crutches on the saddle horn to walk with when he got to where he wanted to go. He took to ridin' out to the field where I was workin'. Sometimes him and Julia would bring me dinner out there.

One Sunday not long after, I went to their house afore noon. Julia said she packed up a dinner for us all and we'd go to the river. And she said us two men needed our hair and whiskers cut. Nothin' for me to do but go along but I had two worries about it. In the times John and me had been to the river we'd been buck naked. It didn't seem likely we'd go to the river and not get wet. But I put that aside, figurin' him and me would keep on our drawers. What got me all up in the air was if'n Julia was gonna get wet and what she'd have on. Truth to tell, I wanted her to do it and I wanted to see it real bad.

Like I said, she was a real looker of a woman and I watched her out of the corner of my eye every time I seen her. But I knowed I had to be real careful, things bein' what they were for John. But, truth to tell, I figured she could tell I was stuck on her and she liked it. Then there was the hair cut. Every time a purty woman give me a haircut, I got in trouble. And she warn't only purty, she was bee-you-ti-ful. Maybe she'd do it with my shirt off but my pants on. Or maybe it'd be with just my drawers on!

Well, it all turned out for the good or for the bad, whichever way you want to see it. We went in the river first off. John and me stripped down to our drawers. Julia went over to the side and got out of her dress and waded out in her drawers and whatever you call that kind of shirt women wear under their dress. She didn't swim around but she dipped down in the river and set there, playin' in the water. After a while of doin' that, she'd stand up, then dip down agin.

Her wet clothes was stickin' to her, and you could see her body a man could die for as plain as day. She had right smart of a bosum and I could see her nipples through the wet shirt. Lord help me, I tried not to look but there was no gettin' around it. John was swimmin' back and forth but I knowed he knowed what I was lookin' at. We all played around in the water some, and she said it was time for the haircuts.

She got out of the water, and walked to the bank like she knowed that all the men in the wide world was watchin' her. They warn't, but I shorely was. Like I said, her wet clothes was stickin' to her and I could see her bosums and what Billy Jones would call her beautiful ass. And it were that. She put back on her dress but that warn't much different since the dress got wet and stuck to her all the same.

She said John was first and I helped him get out and on the log. She cut his hair and his chin whiskers, kind of humming to herself like Betty Lou did back at the Wood place. Fact is, she did it like Betty Lou, knockin' the hair away with her hand as she cut, kind of smoothin' away the cut hair with her hand. It looked like she liked to feel of him that way. He didn't show any signs that she was doin' that, not even sayin' anythin' to her, like that feels good, or do that some more, or anythin' like that. It seemed like he should of, his woman bein' so close to him, him settin' there in his drawers and her hoverin' over him in wet clothes and all.

But I knowed I was in trouble for sure when it come my turn. There ain't no need to spell it out. It'd been a fair time since I was with a woman and I shore was taken by her. It warn't just the way she looked. But it was the way she held herself and she walked. I was real stuck on her. But I figured for sure she was out of my reach.

Anyway, just watchin' her come out off the river and workin' on John got to me. I was half hard when I got out of the river, and whatever there was to go went when she worked on me. I tried to wiggle around so it would stay in my drawers and so nobody would see it. I don't know if'n John did but I couldn't see how he could help it, my drawers stickin' out in front so. And worst of all, I could see that she saw what was happenin'. When she was trimmin' my chin whiskers, I saw her look down, hummin' and sort of smilin'. I thought I was gonna shoot right then and there but I tried hard to keep thinkin' how he must feel and I got through it. As soon as she said she was done, I near jumped over to the river as fast as I could, to wash off and get calmed down. Then I got on my pants and she helped him on with his. We had our dinner there on the river bank, talkin' about this and that. If'n he was upset about it all, he didn't let on. He joined in to what we was talkin' about. And we picked up after ourselves and they left in the buggy. I got back in the river agin and used my hand, thinkin' about how she looked all wet.

The next day, I was workin' in a corn field, choppin' out the weeds. Here come the buggy around dinner time and I watched her get out of the buggy, by herself. *John ain't feelin' too good today so he sent me with your dinner.*
He sick to his stomach?
No, his leg is hurtin' him real bad. I had to help him out of the bed. He stayed there 'til middle of the mornin'.
Lord help me, I didn't know what was goin' on but I carried on the best I could, tryin' not to look at her straight, if'n I could help it. *He been havin' trouble?*
She nodded. *His leg's been seepin', I guess you'd call it.*
Is he bleedin'?
No, just sort of yellow seepin' comin' out at the end, where they cut it off.
I nodded. *I seen signs of that when we was at the river. It been doin' that for long?*
Worse the past day or two. I nodded. So we carried on, her handin' me the baked sweet tater and cornpone and she'd brought

fresh water for me to drink. I started out tryin' to keep from touchin' her, but it looked like she wanted to touch my hands and I let her without pullin' away. And I got hard agin, just bein' close to her and havin' her touch my hand.

She settled down in the grass, lookin' so purty I couldn't believe she was there with me. It looked like she had on the same dress as the first day I seen her. It had a long skirt and she kept playin' with it, smoothin' it here and there. I was tryin' to keep my eyes to myself. *Are you gettin' along all right here in Tinsley Bottom?*

Yes mam, I guess so.

Mr. Tinsley makin' you work hard? She could see that my shirt was wet clean through with sweat.

Yes mam, I guess so. But he needs the help real bad. If'n I can get this corn chopped, he'll have a right good crop.

You ever see John's mama?

Not much. Sometimes at breakfast. She don't come very much to the supper table.

She shrugged. *I didn't figure you would.*

She's a different kind of woman than I ever knowed.

She nodded. *She is that. She don't like me much. Didn't want John to marry up with me, him just goin' to the War.* She was quiet, lookin' away, to'ards the timber line. *The Tinsley's are better off than my family. Did you know I come from across the river?*

Yes mam. I think John told me that.

She smiled. *Luther, you don't have to call me mam. We all are the same age.* She was quiet agin. *She figures John married beneath him.* She was quiet agin.

How'd you meet John?

I'd knowed him since I was a girl. But we met at a play party at Harrican school. My brothers and me came. John was a good dancer. He saw that I loved to dance and made up to me. I thought he was about the nicest man I ever met. But I hadn't met many men afore him.

She was quiet, pickin' at the grass. *He come courtin'. Then he ast me to marry up with him. We did it right afore he went off to the War. Like I said, his mama was against it I guess. My daddy warned me that the Tinsley's would think I warn't good enough for him.* She was quiet, suckin' at a piece of grass. *After he went to the War, I tried to get along her the best I could, but I went back home when I could. With him gone I didn't like it here. I still don't.* She got up. *I have to get goin'! I'm much obliged for you listenin' to me.*

I'm much obliged to you for the dinner. I'm partial to baked sweet taters. She smiled and nodded and I handed her up in to her buggy. Maybe in the handin' up, I held on to her hand longer than needed. But she didn't make me let go any sooner. I watched her go.

Then by happenstance I looked in the other direction. There was John settin' on his mule up a rise, a distance away. He set there a minute when she left, and turned and rode away. It looked like for all the world that he was watchin' us.

I was all mixed up from what was happenin'. It looked like John had sent her with my dinner. And it looked like he come to watch us. I had feelin's for the both of them. I had feelin's for him, for what he was goin' through. And I had feelin's for her, wantin' to be with her and wantin' her to touch me and wantin' to touch her. I figured maybe the best thing for everybody was for me to get away afore somethin' come to pass.

It was some days after, him and me went to the river agin. I shucked my clothes. He'd got the hang of it by then, settin' on a log to get off his pants. He called for me to come over to him. *I want you to look at this here stump of a leg.* I went over and looked. I saw what she was talkin' about. The end of the stump looked red and angry lookin'. It looked like it was sendin' out what I heard the doctors would of called discharge. I could see why she called it seepage. *What d'you think is happenin'?*

Well, I didn't know and I did know. What I didn't know was what a doctor would say. What I did know was that it didn't look good. *Does it hurt a lot?* He nodded. *More'n usual?*

He nodded. *Sometimes it's so bad I cain't hardly stand it.* He looked at me. *Funny thing about it is, what hurts so bad is my leg that ain't there.*

I nodded. *I heard of such a thing when I was in the army. Maybe we better get a doctor to look at it. There one in Gainesbora?*

He shrugged. *I guess so. Don't know for sure.*

You want to go see? I'll go with you. We can take the buggy.

He kind of grinned. *You don't think my mule can make the trip?*

I kind of laughed. *Maybe.*

Maybe you ride the mule and I ride Thunder. Maybe he'd buck and thow me in the river and it'd be all over. He went on, afore I could say anything. *You don't have to tell me what you figure the doctor would say. It ain't gettin' any better. It's gettin' worse.* He was quiet, lookin' at the stump of his leg. *He's gonna say take more of my leg off.*

It warn't a question to me but I figured I owed it to him to tell him what I thought. *I guess maybe you're right about that.* It looked to me like it might be blood pisinin' and maybe gangrene might of set in, but I didn't want to say that.

He set there, lookin' out at the river. *Can I ask you a question, personal?*

I nodded. *Ask it.*

Then he was quiet, like he warn't sure of the question. Then he turned to look at me. *You ever have any trouble bein' with a woman?*

I knowed what he meant. There warn't no use in lyin' to him. *No, I never had no trouble that way. But I ain't been with all that many women.*

He was lookin' back at the river. *I ain't ever been able to do it. Not afore you got shot?*

He shook his head. *Not afore I got shot.*

I wanted to ask him, not even with Julia when you married up with her? But I didn't. I figured he'd already told me that. *Maybe bein' shot has made it worse?*

Maybe, but I don't guess so. He set there, quiet, lookin' at the river. *I guess it's just me and bein' with a woman.*

Bein' we're talkin' personal, does it work when you use your hand?

It used to. Not much that way since I got shot. Seems like I just don't care or I can't care or somethin' like that. He was back lookin' at the river. What he said next was so quiet, I couldn't hardly hear it. *You ever try it with a man?*

That took me by su'prise. I shrugged. *Oncet, when I was a boy.* When I said that I was rememberin' that night with Ed.

What'd you make of it?

Truth to tell, I don't recollect much about it. It was a man I knowed since I was a boy. It was a time of high feelin's. He was leavin'. I knowed by then I was goin' to the War. He come and got in the bed with me. I felt a lot of love for him. He was always real good to my family. But I got to say, there was somethin' sad about it, like he was tryin' to tell me somethin'. I turned to look at him. *You had them feelin's?*

Yeah, I've had them feelin's. He started to try to get up. *Let's go set in the river. I got somethin' to ask you.* So I helped him hobble over to the water and we set down in it. We set there for a while, me wonderin' what was gonna be next. Then he come out with it. *You ever brought a baby to a woman?*

I didn't know what to say. I shore hadn't been 'spectin' a question like that, by a long shot. Only women I could of done that for was Dulciemay and Maybelle. I guess maybe that woman at Winter Camp. I shook my head. *I don't know. Not that I know about.* I kind of laughed. *I never stayed around to find out.*

He turned to look at me. *I want you to give Julia a baby for me. You figure you could do that?*

I knowed he was lookin' at me and I turned to look at him square in the eye. We set there for a minute lookin' at each other. *John, you know what you are sayin'?*

He looked out at the river and nodded. *I know what I'm sayin'. I've given it a lot of thought ever since I come home and seen how it was for me and Julia.* He shook his head. *But afore you come, but I didn't see how to do it. When you come, I knowed this was the way. Then I seen you with Julia and I seen you had feelin's for her. I seen what come over you at the time here at the river when she did the hair cuttin'. And I knowed I was goin' to ask you to do it.*

He looked out at the river. *Afore you give me yore answer, let me say some more. My daddy and mama had only one baby, me. From the time I was a boy, he told me he wanted a heir to leave this farm to. After him and me was gone. This place means a whole lot to him. He don't want nobody else outside the family to get it. That's a fact. I bet he's told me that a hunnert times.*

Down inside me, I allus wondered if'n I could do it. But I met Julia and liked her a lot and I figured I could make it. Then I found out I couldn't. She figured it were her fault, but I knowed it warn't. I went to the War to get away from it. I got shot and come home a cripple, not worth much of anythin'. Then, for sure, I knowed I couldn't do it. Then here you come.

He fell quiet and I hadn't figured out what to say. *Here you come and you and me are enough alike to be brothers. Julia has remarked about that, and I figure it's the truth.* He turned around to me and I met his eyes. *I been watchin' you and Julia together. You're stuck on her and she's stuck on you. A blind man could see that. A man with one leg can see that. She takes to you like you are a man. Maybe a man she thought she had but now ain't got. She'd do it for me. More'n that, maybe she'd do it for herself.*

He was looking at the river agin. *If'n she had my baby, they'd keep her here and treat her right.*

I was near struck dumb. I didn't know what to say to him. Then I found the best words I had. *You thought about this a lot? You thought about how you're goin' to feel, knowin' what was goin' on? You thought about if'n there was a baby to come from it? You thought about how you're goin' to feel about that baby, knowin' where it come from? Are you dead sure you want to do this?*

I'm sure. Will you do it?

You want to know right now?

It'd be best, if'n I do.

Give me a little time to think about it. You go swim. I'll be there directly. He did his usual crawl to the water and swum away.

So there I was, settin' buck nekkid on a river bank thinkin' about tryin' to start a baby for a man who told me he couldn't do it and wanted me to do it. He was right about one thing. I was real stuck on Julia, head over heels, as they say. Just thinkin' about her and how she looked and how it felt when she touched me give me them feelin's and made me half hard. Truth to tell, ever since I first seen her, I'd been thinkin' about her layin' down with me somewhere where we was alone and could do what we wanted to. That's the picture I saw when I used my hand at night. I'd pro'bly spilled enough seed, as the Bible put it, doin' that since I first seen her, to make a hunnert babies! But doin' it when John knowed about it and wanted us to do it was a different story. I didn't even know for sure she'd want to do it, but I guessed he must of knowed she would, elsewise he wouldn't of asked me about it.

There was another side to it. I figured him and me was good buddies. I liked him a lot and put a lot of store in the way he was handlin' his life and his problem with the leg. I didn't mean to stick around long but I wanted to have him feelin' good about me while I was here and when I left.

There was still another side to the story that I'd never thought about much, with Dulciemay and Maybelle and Beulah Gates. What if'n I'd give them a baby? And I left, never seein' a baby I'd brought about. If'n it worked here, there'd be this baby of mine I'd never see. He'd have a daddy, of course. That'd be John. Dulciemay and me had talked about that, I recollected, and she said she'd take the chance. I was no more'n a boy and I warn't thinkin' about it then the way I was now. Maybelle and me never talked about it. We just went at it, like there warn't any likelihood of a baby. I didn't know what the story was with Beulah.

Of a sudden, I knowed what I had to do. I stood up and waded out in the river. He come up to me, and set. *Afore I say if'n I'll do it, I want to hear a vow from you.* He nodded. *Raise*

*yore right hand and swear to me as yore brother that if'n I do it
you'll try as best you can not to hold it against me.*

He held up his hand. *I swear to that.*

Then I'll do it.

He looked like he was goin' to cry. His face was all scrunched
up and he kept wipin' his eyes. Then he got to where he could
talk. *I'm much beholdened to you and will be 'til the day I die.
And I vow that I won't hold it against you.* I was real moved by
what he wanted and what he'd said. But I couldn't think of
anythin' to say that had been said. So we set there in the river,
lookin' at each other. I guess we was thinkin' about what was
goin' on 'tween us.

Help me stand up by you. I did. *Walk me out to where it's more
deep.* I did, 'til we was standin' in the river up to our chest. *Hold
on to me, so I won't fall.* I did. I put my arm around him and
pulled him right close to me so's we wouldn't get swept away by
the current. He turned his face to me. *I got one more thing to ask
of you. It's real hard for me to ask it, but I want to, real bad. If'n
you'd let me, I want to feel you, and take you, so I can know the
part of you that's goin' to bring my baby. I want to do that real bad.
I hope you'll let me, kind of to seal the bargain. Can I do it? Is that
all right with you?*

Well, it was a thing I never thought of or heard about. But
somehow, it rung a bell in my heart. I knowed kind of what he
was talkin' about. And I had by now got the drift of his feelin's.
It warn't no never mind to me to let him do it. And I could feel
as best I could his feelin's about it. *Yeah, my buddy, that's all right
with me. You can do it.*

And he went about doin' it, feelin' all over me, like I'd do to
Julia, and then down to me and took me slow and easy. I felt
him standin' against my side but there was nothin' hard there to
be felt. When he made me shoot, he felt me shoot, and he held
me so tight I couldn't hardly breathe. We stood there a minute,
me still holdin' him, and him holdin' me, so's we wouldn't go
down the river with the current.

Then it was over. Nothin' else was said. Truth to tell, there warn't nothin' else to say. It was like we'd shook hands on the deal. We got out of the river and on with our clothes, me helpin' 'im with his drawers and his pants, like I did. I helped him up on his mule. He set there a minute, lookin' down at me.

Then he give me a salute, like we was still in the army. I give him one back, and he rode away.

Him and me never went to the river agin. I went, by myself, when I'd had a hard day workin' in the field and needed coolin' off. But he never asked me to go and I never asked him. It was like that was all over. When I was with him I could tell his leg was hurtin' him bad and Julia said it was. She said the end of the stump was real dark in color and that there was streaks runnin' up to'ard his knee. I figured for sure that was a bad sign. But he never said anymore about goin' to Gainsbora to see a doctor.

Well, after what was 'tween him and me at the river that day, it looked like I had to do some of what some sergeant would call follow through. I studied that, that day and the next, not knowin' how I was goin' to go about it. The question was, what did Julia make of it. Her and me had hardly spoke, outside of this and that, and I hadn't never been with her much by herself. I shore was stuck on her, but there was what did she make of me?

Well sir, it fell to place like this. She brung me dinner in the field. I saw her comin' in her buggy and I stood there waitin' for her. When she reached me, I took her hand and led her over to the edge of the cornfield, where the grass was sweet. I et my dinner, watchin' her all the time.

We talked about this and that but I knowed what was on our mind. I asked about John. She said he was hurtin' real bad. She said he told her to bring my dinner. *Is that all he told you?* She nodded and then shook her head. *Did he tell you what he wants me to do? What he wants you and me to do?* She nodded and started to cry, bringin' her apron to her face. *I got to know what you make of it.*

She wiped her eyes and looked at me. *I'm all mixed up about it. He never liked me to talk to the other boys when we was courtin'.*

So I didn't know what to make of it when he kept talkin' about you and askin' me if'n I liked you. I sed, of course I liked you. Why wouldn't I? She let it be quiet. *That day we got home from the hair cuttin' at the river, he wouldn't let it be. He sed you liked me doin' that a lot.*

She looked down at her apron, with a half way smile. *He didn't have to tell me that. I could see with my own eyes that you liked it.* Then she looked away from her apron and me, over to the woods. *Then he told me what he had in mind for me and you.* She was quiet. *The thing is, one part of me didn't know what to make of it.* She shrugged and looked back to me. *But one part of me knowed what it was all about. It's about he ain't any good with a woman. I figured at first it were me. But it ain't. It's him.*

She pulled up a piece of grass and sucked on it. *It's about him wantin' to give his folks a grand baby and he cain't do it.* She spit out the grass and looked at me. *I told him if'n that was what he wanted me to do, I'd do it. He said last night when we was in the bed that you said you'd do it.* She said that like it was a question.

I nodded. *I told him at the river I would do it. But I warn't thinkin' straight when I said it. Now, I got to know how you feel about me and what he wants us to do.*

She shrugged agin, showin' a frown, like she didn't know what I was talkin' about. *I don't rightly know. I like you well enough and I guess you like me. But I've got to tell you I ain't never done it with a man. I don't know if'n I'll like it or not.*

Well, I guess the only thing to do is to find out. I reached out and took her hand. *There's still one thing I have to say. If we do what John wants us to do, we cain't let him be 'tween us all the time. We have to shut him out. It ain't his fault and it ain't ours. But we cain't have him with us.*

And I moved over to her, still holdin' her hand, and I kissed her mouth. She didn't draw back but she didn't give much. I leaned back on my elbows. Kissin' her had got me started and I figured it was all I needed. It sounds quare to say it to you, but I thought to myself, there ain't much time here, so we better get to it.

She watched me shed my clothes. There warn't no hurry that I could see and I let her look at me, figuring maybe she ain't ever seen a man like this. She laid down on her back and pulled up her skirts and pulled down her drawers. Then she laid there, lookin' up at me, waitin'. Well, it warn't what I'd dreamed of with her, but I went ahead and done it. There warn't no sign from her, one way or other. I laid there on my back, not knowin' what to say.

She was lookin' up at the clouds. *You figure that will make me a baby?*

I got no idea how it works, 'ceptin' what you and me do.

She raised up on her elbows and looked me over. She had a kind of a grin, first one I'd seen since we started this whole thing. *You figure it'll take more'n once?*

Well, I knowed right then it was goin' to be all right. Maybe it wouldn't be sweet milk and teacakes, as my brother Sam would say, but it was goin' to work out. I let out a belly laugh and set up. *Yeah, I figure it'll take more'n once.* I looked at her. *You ready for that?*

She down right giggled. *Maybe.*

I was goin' along with her play actin'. *You seen enough? Can I get back on my britches? And you get gone. I got corn to chop.* She smiled and nodded, and fixed her clothes back. We picked up the leavin's of the dinner. I handed her up to her buggy with a kiss on her mouth.

Then she froze, lookin' over on the other side of the cornfield. There was John, settin' on his mule. She looked like she was startin' to cry and I pulled her back down by me, holdin' her in my arms. *Julia, he's wishin' he could be here, but he cain't. It's you and me that are here. Look at me. It's you and me and it's what he wants. And it's what I want. You hear me?* She nodded, and got back up in the buggy and left.

I chopped corn in the blazin' sun the rest of the day for all I was worth, cussin' at John Tinsley all the time. Damn him! He cain't do it. He wants me to do it. He wants Julia to do it. And now he wants to watch! The more corn I chopped, the madder I got. The weeds was flyin' like they had wings.

After I quit, I was on my way to the river to cool off and I
went past their house. There he was, settin' on the porch, whittlin'.
There was no howdys. *Where's Julia?*
In the back of the house.
I spit out what I had to say, as quiet as I could, for fear she'd
hear me. *John, you cain't do this to us.* He put down his whittlin'
and looked at me. *I seen you today at dinnertime.* He put his
hands out like as to say it warn't so. *You cain't be watchin' us. Julia
ain't easy in her mind about doin' this, to start with. And you're
goin' to have to live with her and make her happy when this is all
said and done.* I stood there, my fists clinched, mad at him, mad
at me for gettin' in this mess. *I catch you doin' it agin, I'm goin' to
thrash you to a pulp.* And I went on to the river. But I never
caught him watchin' us agin and Julia never said any thing more
about it.

I ain't goin' to tell you any more partic'lars. She was slow to
come around but little by lettle she opened up to me. Or maybe
I opened up to her. It don't matter which. It warn't long that she
liked to be nekkid with me. Her nekkid body was all pink and
white and all of what I'd dreamed about and more. The more I
had her, the more I wanted her and it come to be the same for
her. Once she opened up, it seemed like she wanted me all the
time and couldn't get enough of me. When we was together I
felt this power to make her filled up with me and make her cry
out for me. Sometimes the feelin's was so strong I couldn't keep
from bellerin', like a damned bull yearnin' for a cow in season.
Only thing was, I warn't yearnin'. I had it.
We come together when we could. Once I was workin' the
hay at the barn at their house and she come down with a drink of
fresh water for me. I was glad to have the water but what I wanted
was her.
One day it was rainin' and I couldn't work in the fields and I
come to their house on Thunder. I told John I'd come to set a
spell and talk. We talked a while and he asked me to help him up

in the buggy. Said his leg was hurtin' real bad. Said he wanted to go talk to his daddy. So he left us there alone and we went in and laid down in their bed. I guess I should of felt bad about takin' Julia in John's bed, but I didn't. Maybe I felt like I was takin' her partly for me and partly for him. He was gone for a hour or two and I was gone afore he come back.

One thing we couldn't never do was to sleep together of a night. One time Julia said she wanted to do that, and cried a little when she said it. But we knowed we couldn't do it. We couldn't do it when he was there. And it didn't seem right for him to go to my barn to sleep at his daddy's house while all the time I was sleepin' in their bed with her, holdin' her like he'd never do.

Then, it all come to a end. I was workin' in the field down by their house. About the middle of the evening, long afore supper, here come the buggy to the field. Julia was cryin' and come runnin' into my arms. *Luther, I need help bad.*

What's got you so upset?

She strained against me, out of my arms, now near yellin'. *He went to the river this mornin' afore dinner and he ain't come back. Somethin's happened to him. I know it has.*

Hush now. We'll go see. I led her to the buggy and left Thunder grazin' and we went to the place at the river where we went in. We warn't even near gettin' there when I could see his mule there on the river bank, tied to a saplin', like he allus did. When we got there, there was his clothes and his boot and his crutches layin' there on the bank where he allus put 'em. There warn't no sign of him. Now she near fell in my arms agin, cryin' like her heart was gonna break. *When did you say he left the house?*

Middle of the mornin'. I was doin' the washin', hangin' it out. He said his leg was hurtin' real bad. He said the hurtin' hadn't never let up all night. Then he said that he was goin' to the river to cool off. He said maybe that would ease the hurtin'. I said to wait and I'd come too. He said no, no need for me to. I said go get

Luther. He'd be hot and want to cool off. He said no, not 'til evenin'.
She started in cryin' agin. *Then he did somethin' he didn't do much,
when he left the house. He took me in his arms and he kissed me.*
Then she was sobbin' real hard, like she was gonna cry forever.
We stood there in each other's arms 'til she quieted down
some. By that time, I was near to cryin' myself. I figured I knowed
full well what he'd done and that maybe I was a party to it. *Can
you pull yourself together to go in the buggy for his folks? And I'll
stay here to watch. Or do you want me to come too?*
She pulled away from me and more or less stopped cryin'. *I
can do it. You stay here, watch for him.*
I held her still. *You tell them what you told me and how we
come here and what we found.* She nodded. *And don't say anythin'
elsewise about you and me.* She shook her head. I wanted her to
kiss me afore she left but she didn't. I guessed she didn't think it'd
be right. Anyway she headed for the Tinsley house at a fast clip.
I stood there on the river bank where we allus set to talk,
him and me. And I looked hard up and down at the river goin'
by. I started to holler. *John, damn you, where are you? John, what
have you gone and done? We was workin' it out, you and Julia and
me.* I started to cry. *What'd you have to go and do this for? Did
yore leg hurt real bad? Was you afraid of what was happenin' to yore
leg?* I started to sob just like Julia had. *John!* I yelled at the river.
Did you go to yore grave hatin' me? Then I started throwing rocks
in the river, like him and me did when we come here.
I got hold of myself just when Julia and Mr. Tinsley pulled
up in the buggy. He nodded at me and climbed down and come
over to where I was standin' by John's clothes. *Julia said he's been
gone since afore dinner.* I nodded. *Must be three, four hours now.* I
nodded. *He's a good one to swim.* I nodded. *Has been since he was
a boy.*
*Maybe something happened. Maybe he got hit by a log comin'
downstream. Got caught in the current. It's runnin' fast today.*
Maybe. He was real quiet, lookin' at the river, with the current
goin' by fast. He turned to Julia. *You say he's been feelin' bad these
days?*

She nodded. *Past week his leg was hurtin' him bad. He said Luther here said he'd go with him to see the doctor at Gainsbora.* She started cryin' agin. *He said he wouldn't go. He said they'd just take off all his leg.* And she started to sob. *You seen anythin' since you been watchin' here? No sir, I ain't. Ain't likely I guess with this river runnin' so fast.* I saw his eyes start to tear up and he wiped 'em with his fist. *I guess we all know what he did. Life's been hard for him since he come home from the War and I guess he just give up. And give hisself to the Cumberland River that he loved since he was a boy.* He put his arm around Julia, and held her close to him. *We'll have to go tell his mama. Luther, you ride along with us to yore horse and then come back here for his clothes.*

They got in the buggy and I held on the side 'til I got close to where I'd been workin' when Julia came for me. Thunder was waitin' for me. I petted him on the head. *Thunder, old boy, it looks like John has gone and done it in the river. I hate to see him do this but I guess I can see why he did. He was in a lot of torment and I guess he dreaded the end he saw ahead. He admired you a lot and wanted to try to ride you, but I guess he just didn't have the nerve to try. I'm real sorry about that.*

Then I got up on him and we went back to the river bank. Seein' it now, it looked real peaceful. I wondered where John was now. Maybe a long way downstream. Lord, I hoped he wouldn't turn up around Gainsbora. He would of liked it better if'n he'd be in a backwater somewhere. A backwater, I thought, where the varmints could get to him. Joe Dale would say that's the way death is.

Some days after John left us in the river, I went to the big house after my field work was done and afore suppertime. She was settin' on the porch shellin' beans or doin' something like that. *Evenin' Julia.* It was the first time I'd seen her after he went.

Evenin' Luther. I stood there lookin' at her. I wanted to take her in my arms real bad right then. I wanted her to touch me real bad right then. But I just stood there, lookin' at her. *Whyn't you set down here if'n you will. I'd be obliged if'n you would.* She looked up at me and I guess I'd of done anythin' for her right then and there if'n she asked me. *You have a hard day in the field?* I nodded. *It was a hot one, warn't it?* I nodded, not able to speak. She went on shellin' the beans. *John's mother is real upset we cain't have a funeral for him. But I told her there warn't no need. Weun's that loved him are all right here, and we know where he is.*

I was watchin' her hands shellin' the beans. *That's a right good way to put it, I guess.* We was quiet, watchin' her shell the beans. *You stayin' here now?*

She nodded. *John's mama wanted me to. She fixed up the other bedroom right nice for me.* She started to cry. *I didn't know if'n I could go back to the house or not and she said stay here, so I did.*

You gettin' along all right here?

She wiped her eyes with her hands and nodded. *His mama has been real good to me. And his daddy.*

I was still lookin' at her hands in the pan with the beans. She'd stopped shellin' 'em. *I better tell you that I'm about to move on.* She nodded. *I halfway want to stay here.* I stopped talkin'. *But it ain't right that I do. I won't ever forget you all.* I couldn't say just you, 'cause I thought somebody might hear me. I cleared my throat to keep from cryin'. *I won't ever forget you and John and his folks and Tinsley Bottom and the good times we had, him and me at the river. And that day you cut away our hair and all the rest of it. But I need to go on home to Stewart County.*

She nodded, and wiped her eyes agin. *I know that. I feel the same way as you do.* She looked up at me. *You know John loved you a lot. He loved you like the brother he never had.*

I nodded. *I know that and I loved him back, more'n any man I ever knowed.* I was wonderin' if'n that was true. But it seemed like the thing to tell her right now.

She picked through the beans to see if'n there was any she had missed. *John's daddy and mama say it's all right for me to go see my family across the river.* *It seems like a good time to do that. When you plannin' on goin'?* *Soon as his daddy says he can take me. We'll have to go by way of Gainsbora. John used to have a boat but it got washed away while he was at the War. His daddy don't like boats anyhow. John was the only one that made use of the boat.* She looked over at me. *John's daddy is goin' to talk to you about takin' me. He says somebody's got to stay with John's mama. He says he can go and you can stay.* She was quiet, lookin' at me with those beautiful eyes. *Or he says he can stay and you can go.*

My old heart leaped up and sank down at the same time. I leaned over close to her, pickin' at the beans in the pan she was holdin' in her lap. *Does he know about us?* Our hands touched in the pan of beans.

She pulled her hands back out of the pan. *I don't know. I don't think so. I ain't seen any sign he does.*

If he asks me to take you, what do I do?

She moved my hand out of the pan and stood up quick. *I don't know.* And she went into the house.

But it turned out that I didn't have the say so about goin' or stayin'. Mr. Tinsley come in for dinner and said he wanted to take Julia to her family's place. He said he wanted to see her daddy agin, that he hadn't seen 'im since the weddin'. And he said he needed to get some supplies as he come back through Gainsbora. He said he'd be gone for three, four days and he asked me if'n I'd stay here with Miz Tinsley. I said I would. He said they'd leave on the next mornin' and said he'd take the buggy. That settled, we set down to eat dinner.

You can figure out what my feelin's was. I wanted like sin to be with Julia some more. I wanted to hold her, and kiss her, and touch her, and lie down with her, and be in her. If'n he said I would take her, we could of done that on the way there.

But as Aunt Polly used to say, the handwriting was on the wall. I couldn't be with her for any time at all if'n I was goin' to Stewart County. And I was still thinkin' about marryin' up with Nadine. So it looked like I had to end it with Julia as bad as I wanted her right now. If'n I had gone with her to her family's place, I would of done something on the way that was shore to be foolish. On top of what I'd already done foolish, I guess. So, I knowed it was best to end it this way.

Only thing left was to say goodbye. The next mornin' we met face to face on the front porch afore Mr. Tinsley come out to leave. *This looks like a goodbye.*

I guess so. She was smilin' at me but I seen some tears in her eyes. *It's best this way.*

Looks like it. I took her hands and kissed them quick. *You know I'll not never forget you.*

She took her hands back. *I know that. I know that you'll never forget me, me and John.* And she left me standin' there and went and got in the buggy. Mr. Tinsley come out with Miz Tinsley, and he said goodbye and that he'd see us in a few days and they drove away.

We was standin' there on the porch. I didn't know how it was goin' to go with Miz Tinsley with him gone. I bet in all the days and weeks I been there, she hadn't said more than ten words to me. *Well, that's that.*

Yes mam, that's that.

It'll be good for her to be with her people for a while, what with loosin' John.

Yes mam, it will.

I hope she comes back. I didn't look for her to say that, not with what I heard about her not wantin' him to marry up with her and her not givin' Julia hardly the time of day when she was here. I swear, she must of read my mind. *You didn't look for me to say that, didn't you?*

Well, no mam, I didn't. But it ain't none of my business.

No it ain't I guess. But I need to talk to somebody about it and I guess you're the only one I got.

Yes mam.

It ain't time for dinner. If'n you don't mind, let's set down and let me talk a while.

Yes mam. So we set down. There was a rockin' chair on the porch and she set down in it. I set down in a straight chair and leaned it against the wall. My state of mind was that I didn't know if'n I wanted to do much talkin' about John. Or Julia. And I figured that was what I was in for. And I was right about that.

She started to rock and started out to talk. *John was real taken by her from the first. Afore her, he hadn't paid much attention to girls. Next mornin' after he met her at that play party he said he met a girl from across the river. That she was real purty and real nice to him. I asked about her family and said she was a Bibey. I was a girl in Gainsbora when I met John's daddy and I knowed some of the Bibeys. I knowed they was a pore family back then, just gettin' by. I figured they was still just gettin' by. I figured she knowed the Tinsley farm was a good'un and I figured she'd tried to set her cap for him, to get to the Tinsley place.*

She kept rockin', lookin' out at the place. *His daddy and me have allus worked hard to keep it up, and it was then and still is a real purty place.* I nodded. *I figured she knowed that. I didn't say anything to John about that but I asked about what other girls had been to the play party. He named some names. Afterwards Mr. Tinsley and me talked about it and he said best to leave John to make up his own mind.*

Then I found out John was takin' his boat across the river. I figured it was to go see her. One time her daddy and her brothers and her come over to spend the day. She didn't say much but I could see how she looked at him and how he looked at her and I knowed in my heart what was goin' on.

Some weeks went on, him goin' over in his boat to see her. Then he come home one evening and told us he was goin' to marry up with her. I didn't like it but there warn't nothin' I could do to stop it, I guess. So him and her and her brothers went to Gainsbora and got married by a preacher there. They come back here and we set them up in the little house. She stopped rockin'. *I want a drink of water. Will you get me one?*

Yes mam, I will. So I did and brought it back to the porch. She took a long drink and set the cup down and went on.

We set them up in the little house. I been in pore health for several years and I didn't need anybody else in my house. You can see that, cain't you?

Yes mam.

Mr. Tinsley went along with it. He said they needed to be by theirselves. You can see that, cain't you?

Yes mam. That seems like a good thing to do.

Then come the War. They'd not been married more'n a week or so and he come in and said he was goin' to join up. Him and some other young men around these parts. So he went off and left her here. I tried my best to talk him out of it. John was my only child. He warn't ever very strong. He did the farm work with his daddy but ever since he was a boy it seemed like he didn't want to work on the farm. His daddy would get after him and he'd say he'd do better but it was the same thing over agin. She turned to me. *You like it on a farm?*

Yes mam, I do. I allus have.

I could tell that after you first come. I used to watch you from the house, goin' about yore business. Mr Tinsley was real pleased with you about that. He ever tell you that?

Yes mam, he did. Him and me have got along real good.

She kept on rockin'. *She stayed down at the little house. She'd come up here every day or so but allus wanted to go back to the little house. I never pressed her to stay.* She looked out around her. *Maybe I ought to of. I don't know. Some months went by and we never had word from him. Then one day we did.*

She looked like she was about to cry and she wiped her face with her apron. *Here he come home with one leg gone. It near broke my heart. I didn't want him to go in the first place and here he went and got shot and come home a cripple.*

She stopped talkin' and took another drink of water from the cup. *John warn't never a strong boy. I could tell he was different from the other boys all along. He didn't never get in fights or get drunk or do anything like that, that I knowed the other boys his age done. His daddy done his share of that when he was a young man. I had my trouble with him like that but we made it out, him and me. Anyway, I figured maybe goin' to the War would make him different, make a man out of him. But all it did was make it worse. You can see that, cain't you?*

Yes mam, I can.

You and John get along?

Yes mam, we shore did. We didn't know each other very long but we felt like we was brothers.

I'm real glad about that. Maybe you was the brother I never could give him. You think that is the truth?

Yes mam, I do. Him and me said that one time at the river.

She started in rockin' agin. *Yes. The river. He loved that Cumberland River.*

Yes mam, he did.

And it took him away from us. She wiped her eyes with her apron tail. *I guess better said he give hisself to it.*

Yes mam, I reckon so.

We was quiet for a while. *Well, that's that. Cain't take any of it back, can we?*

No mam, we cain't.

She got up, lookin' at me. *Well, I'll go put dinner on the table. You look like a man that likes baked sweet taters.*

Yes mam, I shore do.

I got some good ones. It'll be ready directly. She turned to go. *I got a favor to ask.*

Yes mam?

Will you sleep in the other room while Mr. Tinsley's gone? I'd feel better with a man sleepin' in the house.

Yes mam, I'll do that.

She kind of laughed. *It's a better bed than what you've had in the barn.*

Yes mam, I bet it is.

Well sir, that was the most I ever heard from Miz Tinsley any of the time I was in Tinsley Bottom. I was there for nigh on to another week and there was not a peep out of her aside from small talk. She tended to me the three, four days Mr Tinsley was gone. We'd say good mornin' and talk like that. And where did you work today and was it real hot in the field today.

But nary another word about John and Julia. I didn't bring the subject up. I figured she'd had her say and didn't have anymore to say.

Truth to tell, the hardest part was sleepin' in the bed where Julia had slept afore Mr Tinsley took her away. I swear I could smell her in that bed. It was hot and you didn't need any covers but the piller smelled like her. The first night I wanted her so bad I near cried. But by the third night I couldn't be for certain I smelt her or me or us both. So I just went to sleep huggin' that piller, wishin' it was her, and feelin' real, real sorry we never got to sleep all night together in a bed like a woman and man ought to.

Mr Tinsley drove up one day afore supper time. In a little while, after he'd unloaded the supplies to the house, he brought the buggy down to the barn to unhitch. We said our howdys. *You have a good trip across the river?*

He nodded. *It were a good trip. The Bibeys had heard about John and I guess they was more or less thinkin' Julia would come to see 'em. They was real glad to see her. They made over her right smart and I could tell that was real good for her. When she comes back, Miz Tinsley and me are goin' to have to try to do more of that.*

You figure she'll come back?

He shrugged. *Well now that is a right good question. I shore do hope so. I shore do. I figure we're goin' to need her, now that John's gone.*

Beggin' yore pardon, but did you tell her that?

Yes, I sure thing told her that. We had some long talks while we was on the road. She said maybe she'd come back if'n she was for certain that we wanted her. Mainly she said if 'n Miz Tinsley wanted her.

He picked up a piece of the harness I was workin' on. *We'll leave her that a few weeks and then John's mama and me will go over and see if 'n we can get her to come home with us.* All this time I was tryin' to finish up work and at the same time scared to death he was goin' to say she'd told him about her and me. But if 'n she did, he never let on. He was still holdin' the harness, but lookin' at me. *You figure it's time for you to move on?*

Yessir, I figure it is. You're right near caught up here 'til time to gather corn. I don't want to stay that long, 'til the hard frost.

He nodded. *I figured as much. I've got yore money at the house. Maybe you'll stay on for a few more days?*

Yessir, I'll do that.

Miz Tinsley said you been right good company for her while I was gone. She said she was real glad to have you while I was gone. I'm obliged to you for doin' that. He was quiet. *She talk any about John?*

Yessir she did a little. I was glad to hear about him. You know I was real fond of him. Him and me felt like brothers. He said one time him and me looked alike enough to be brothers.

He nodded. *Me and his mama remarked about that.* He was quiet agin. *She talk about Julia?*

Yessir, she did. A little. I don't hardly know but I figure she'd be real glad to have Julia come back.

I hope so. I'd like to hope that Julia could be the daughter we never had.

Yessir, that'd be real good.

We can give her a better life here than she'd have with her family. I hope she can see that.

Yessir, I figure she might. She thinks a whole lot of you and maybe could of Miz Tinsley. She told me oncet she never knowed much of her own mama. I warn't for certain that was so, but it seemed like a thing to say.

We put things away and started up to the house. *I got some news to tell you.* I waited, wonderin' what he'd say. I didn't figure there'd been time for her to decide she was carryin' John's baby but maybe she would. *While I was comin' back through Gainsbora I met up with a man, a widder man. He'd lost near ever'thin' in a fire and was lookin' for a place to go. He's closer to my age than John and you but he said he was a good worker. And him and me made a deal for him to come and live in the little house and work with me on the farm.*

I stopped in my tracks and took hold of his arm. *Mr. Tinsley, that sounds like the right thing to do. I'm real proud for you. You told Miz Tinsley?*

He nodded. *I did right after I drove up. She was real pleased about it.*

So that's how it went. I stayed on a few more days, sleepin' in the bed where Julia had slept and I had slept. He paid me off, more'n I expected but he pressed it on me. One mornin' I packed up and got Thunder ready for the road. We all said our goodbyes. Me and Mr Tinsley teared up some sayin' them. Miz Tinsley didn't say much. She just give me a parcel of vittles to take on my way and she give me a big hug. That was enough for me. I figured I knowed what they both was feelin'.

I got on Thunder and we rode on our way to Gainsbora, past the Tinsley graveyard, as we left Tinsley Bottom.

B ut I warn't ready to go to Gainsbora just yet. Mr. Tinsley
had said this road the other way went to Celina. That'd be
up the Cumberland. I recollected my army buddy Joe Dale tellin'
me he lived thereabouts Celina and I ought to stop to see him
if 'n ever I was in the territory. Well I was in the territory and I
warn't in no hurry to get to Nashville, that's for sure. Maybe I
wouldn't even go to Nashville if 'n I could help it. Just thinkin'
about gettin' Thunder and me around in Nashville give me a
terrible feelin', like I had when we was about to go into battle.

Anyway, I headed up the valley, goin' to Celina. The road
left the river and went up into a valley and then over a ridge. It
was real purty country with some pasture land and a few cows
grazin' and then some timber. The road was right good, except
for a mud hole here and there. Thunder felt as good as the road
was and the countryside looked, and he let loose.

We got up on the ridge in no time flat, as Billy Jones would
of said, and there was a man on a mule, standin' there by the
road. *Howdy.*

Howdy. That's a right purty horse.

I nodded. *He is that.* I grinned. *He knows it, too.*

He laughed. *I've seen 'em that way. You passin' through?*

I nodded. *I been stayin' down in Tinsley Bottom for some weeks,
hirin' out.*

Old man Tinsley?

Yeah, that where I was.

I heard tell he lost his son to the river. That so?

Yessir, that's so.

Was you there then?

Yessir, I was there then.

He shook his head. *Terrible thing. I didn't know John but the boys did. Afore he went to the War he used to come up Pea Ridge to our place. Looked like he liked to come. He was allus welcome.* He was quiet, thinkin' about it. *He lose a leg in the War?*

Yessir, he lost a leg. Or most of it.

One of my brother's boys ain't come back from the War. We ain't had any word from him. I reckon he was kilt.

I nodded. *Might be.*

You in the War?

Yeah, I was in the War. Now I'm trying' to get back home. Stewart County. Headed now to Celina.

He shook his head. *Never heard of it. But I ain't never got very far from the home place. Maybe I ought to of joined up, and seen somethin' 'sides Pea Ridge.*

I shrugged. *Might of got kilt, too.*

You ever been to Celina?

No sir, I ain't. I had a buddy in the War from there. Said to see him if'n I was ever in the countryside. Name's Joe Dale.

He nodded. *I know some Dales. Maybe a Joe Dale. He a big man?*

I grinned. *A big man. He'd likely make two of me.*

All them Dales is big men. He fell quiet agin. *You gonna stay with them?*

I shrugged. *Don't know. I reckon so, if'n I can find 'em.* I looked at him straight. It warn't a likely question to ask me. *Why'd you ask?*

Well, sometimes it looks like they're still fightin' the War in Celina. It's allus been a rough town but seems like more now after the War.

Some of the men went one way and some the other?

Yeah, that's how it was. This part of the country is nearly Kaintuck. Celina is maybe twenty scant miles from the line. Folks

*was divided about the War. They still is. I got to get on my way. So
long.* And him and his mule headed on over on a side road, I
guess to out on Pea Ridge.

There warn't no trouble goin' down the mountain. One big
switchback made me think of crossin' the big mountains with
the wagon train. And, then, with the Gates wagon. Beulah Gates'
story was a bother to me. If'n you believed her story, I could see
why she shot Elmer. If'n you didn't, it looked like it was shootin'
a husband she wanted to get rid of. But it warn't no matter to
me. I got away from Knoxville soon enough I guess, if'n the law
found him and was askin' questions. Then there was what was
'tween her and me. Good thing I got out of town when I did.

My killin' that outlaw fellar comin' from Knoxville was a
bother to me. I wondered if'n I was right in doin' what I did.
But I guess maybe it was him or me. I tell you, though, I was
right glad I didn't never see his face. When I was fightin' in the
War it was allus hard for me to pull the trigger if'n I looked at
his face. Like I said, it was best if'n you didn't know what he
looked like

Goin' down the ridge, there was a store on the bank of the
river. The storekeeper said the store was called Butler's Landing.
He said it was a good place to ford the river, when it was low. He
said not much river traffic was comin' up this far at this time of
year. I got some more of that cheese and some hard tack there,
and went on my way. I rode on a piece, and come to a good place
to stop. It looked like the river went to a bend. I figured it was
likely the road would leave it. So I found a place to set, under a
sycamore tree, and I turned Thunder out to graze.

I was real glad to set a while. It seemed like I warn't ready to
be with more folks. If'n I could find Joe Dale, there'd be a lot of
talkin' to do. And I didn't want to a lot of talkin'. Not just yet,
anyway.

My old head was goin' around from what went on at Tinsley
Bottom. I couldn't figure out how so much had went on in such

a short time. I wouldn't of believed it, if'n I hadn't been there. In a way, it was like the time with Dulciemay. I wouldn't of believed that neither, if'n I hadn't been there. Thunder was standin' there by me. He'd grazed some and was just standin' there, maybe waitin' to go. *Yeah, I know you're ready to go, but I ain't.* He looked at me. *I used to talk to Ole Mule a lot. But I ain't done that much to you.* I laughed. *Well, here it comes.*

I set there, lookin' out at the river. *Truth to tell, I want to get my head on straight, if'n I can, from all I seen and done, since I've been on the road.* I turned to him. *You got to take my word for it. I've done a lot of things on the road. I've met up with a lot of folks on the road.* I stopped to eat on my piece of cheese. *Some of 'em warn't so good, but mostly they was. The Wood family pro'bly saved my life from the fevers. And I'm beholden to Dulciemay and Granny for helpin' me see better about slavin'.*

I went on eatin'. *It's the women folk that stay with me. The ones the age of Aunt Polly, like Miz Collins, give me a notion about life that I never had afore. But it were the women my age that caused me all the trouble. Lord have mercy, did they ever! It seems like I was allus wantin' 'em. I was wantin' 'em, in the face of knowin' it warn't goin' to lead nowhere, for them or me.* I put the rest of the vittles back in the kit bag and set back, lookin' out at the river. *It were my crotch doin' the talkin'. Jump in the hay, do it, and there ain't no tomorras.*

I owe it to Miz Collins for makin' me see into what love is about. That was when she was talkin' about Mr. Collins and her as a young woman. Aunt Polly and Uncle Gray had it, too. Puttin' it that way, it was Betty Lou that I could of loved that way. But, like I said, she had strings and I didn't want to take 'em. The others was a matter of wantin' 'em, just for the time bein'. Never mind what's comin' down the Pike.

Thunder had got tired of standin' and had walked a piece away. I fell quiet, lookin' at the river and how it moved. The river looked real peaceful from where I was settin', but I knowed it warn't. I knowed about the fast currents and the sand bars that would shift with the current. You could feel 'em move as you stood on 'em.

And I knowed full well and good that the river would take you, if'n you wanted it to. *John ain't out there. He went downstream. But he might as well be, from how it looks. Wonder what in the holy hell that was all about? It looks like from here, he used me and my wantin' a woman like I was a gol danged bull. I loved bein' with Julia. Them times I had with her in the grass was somethin'! But all the time, in the back of my mind, I knowed it were my crotch that John wanted me for. Maybe that was part of what Julia wanted me for. I don't like to think that of her, but it could be.*

I felt real sorry for him. He was a troubled man. I told Miz Tinsley I loved him like a brother. That ain't so. I shore didn't love 'im like I do Sam. I guess I out and out loved Ed. At that time of my life, I was a boy, studyin' to be a man. John and Ed was cut from a diff'ernt piece of cloth. I didn't hold it against 'em that they was. They was good men. I liked 'em and I liked to be with them. I let 'em do with me what they wanted real bad to do. It warn't no never mind to me. For a fact, it warn't no differnt than me usin' my hand. But I guessed it meant more to them than that. That's why I let 'em.

But my piece of cloth is women. I laughed out loud and Thunder looked over at me. *Lord howdy, there ain't no doubt in my mind about that! A feller over at the Mill oncet said in my hearin' that some man he knowed was out tom cattin' around. I guess, Thunder, that's what I've been doin', tom cattin' around.* I stood up. *But we're gettin' close to Stewart County now. I better keep to the straight and narrow. And keep my pants on.* Thunder had come back over to me, standin' there. *All right. I'm done talkin'. I'm ready to go to Celina.*

I rode into Celina the next day, sometime after dinner, hungry. A man at the courthouse square told me where to go for some eats. The woman put some beans and some cornpone and fresh milk on the table. I et my fill and asked her about the Dale place. It was on the Obey River, she said, maybe four, five miles away.

I went the direction she said go, and come to the place afore sundown. The dogs started barking like crazy and out come Joe Dale, big as life, to see what was the matter. He looked at me a minute or two, then he hollered. *Luther! Luther Morris! Is that you?*

It's me all right, Joe Dale. I come all the way from Virginny just to see you! I got down off Thunder, and me and Joe gave the other a bear hug. I was real glad to see him. We stood there, grinnin' at each other. He said I had to stay the night. He said I had to stay a week. I said I'd be pleased to stay a night or two, if'n he had the room for me. I said I could sleep in the barn. But no, he said, he slept in a bed and there was room for me! And we laughed at the joke and at seein' each other again.

It had been more'n two years since I seen him. He was a bigger man than I recollected, taller'n me and heavier by maybe fifty pounds. Last time I seen him, he had brown chin whiskers and curly hair. Now he was clean shaved and his hair was cut short. He looked real good. His old blue eyes still looked right through you, like they did when we was in the War. Maybe it was his eyes lookin' at that lieutenant that time that made him back down, and leave us be. I was real glad to see him again.

At supper, him and me told some things about what we'd done in the War. His mama said she'd not heard him talk so much about that before. His daddy didn't say much. He looked like he was on the verge of bein' real sick. Joe said the next day that his daddy warn't right in his head. He said his daddy had started to fail a year ago and was gettin' more feeble by the day. He was real forgetful. Sometimes he didn't know where he was. He had worsened since Joe got home from the War. Joe told me next day he had two sisters married and livin' over in Kentucky, He said there was a brother. The brother had gone to the War and never come back.

It turned out he was courtin' the school marm at what he called Dale Hollow School. He said it'd been a good sized school afore the war but not hardly anybody now could pay the teacher. He said him and her was in a tough place. She wanted to marry up with him, but if'n she did they might not send their younguns to her school. Men teachers could be married, but people thought a woman teacher ought to be single. She was puttin' him off, hopin' they would change their mind about it. He said he told her he wouldn't wait forever. I laughed to my self when he told me that, 'cause one night I was there, he never come home from her house 'til mornin', and I reckoned he warn't sleepin' nowheres in no barn!

Next day after I got there, he took me to meet her. *Rose, this here is my old army buddy, Luther. Luther Morris*

Howdy Luther. I'm real glad to make your acquaintance.

Howdy, Miss Rose. I'm real glad to see you. She was a tall woman with brown colored hair tied up at the back. Some of it had come loose and hung down almost in her face. She warn't what you'd call a purty woman, no where near as purty as some women I'd knowed. But she had a knack of lookin' at you when her and you was talkin'. She made you feel like she was listenin' hard to what you had to say, like she was wonderin' what was goin' on in yore mind.

I could see right away that she was a school marm. And she didn't talk like all of us did. She didn't slide over words or say if'n or words like that. I loved to hear her talk. I told Joe the next day I could see why he wanted to marry up with her. Kiddin' him, I told him if'n he didn't, I would. He chased me around the barn lot for sayin' that, like we was two boys.

Joe has told me about you.

I nodded. *Him and me was together in the War. I tell you, mam, he is a good man.*

She smiled and looked at him. *I think so.* Her smile turned into a grin. *At least he tells me he is.* Joe turned red in the face and looked at the ground.

I grinned at him, then at her. *He told me he wants you to marry up with him. Is that so?*

Now she was the one lookin' down at her shoe. *That's what he says.*

You gonna do it?

She shook her head. *I guess I am.* She giggled like a girl. *I've not had any better offers.* His face turned red again. *You going to be in Celina long?*

I shrugged. *Maybe. Maybe as long as Joe'll let me stay.* I looked at him, then at her. *Maybe I'll stay for the weddin'. When are you all goin' to do it?*

She shook her head. *I don't rightly know. My daddy and mama are gone, so that's not a problem. But I've got two little sisters that depend on me. Daddy left me a little farm, but I can't teach school and farm too. I hire it out on half share. It doesn't bring in much, but we make do with my teaching school. The trouble is, I'm not making much money teaching school these days. There's not many families out here in Dale Hollow.* She said Hollow, not Holler, like Joe did. *Some of the families out here can't pay me.*

All the time she was sayin' that, she looked at me, then at Joe, then back at me. Now she went over to Joe and took his hand and he looked at her like he thought she had made the moon. *There's folks here that don't think a teacher should be married. No, I said that wrong. I meant to say a woman teacher. It's all right, I guess, if a man teacher is married.* She shook her head. *I can't see the difference, but they can.*

I told her already I'd go get 'em and make 'em change their minds, if'n I have to do!

She laughed and give him a hug. *He'd probably tell them he'd beat the tar out of them if they don't listen to what he says.*

I laughed. *I don't rightly think the Joe Dale I knowed would do that. But he might tell 'em if'n they didn't, he'd pin their ears back!*

She was lookin' at Joe all the while, all smiles and her eyes full of love light. I never had a woman look at me like that. She put his arm around her waist and leaned on him. *We're going to work it out. I love to teach the children and I'd do it almost for free. But Joe and me need the money. If some of the families go along with a married woman teacher, we'll marry and I'll take my sisters and live on his place. The girls and me can help in the house and help take care of his daddy. Have you seen him?* I nodded. *He's right sick and is going to be worse, I expect. Joe says he can farm his place and mine too.* She looked up at Joe. *Do you think he could do that?*

I smiled. *Yeah, I think he could do that. I think he could do that if'n he had you with him in his cold bed at night.* Joe's face turned red again.

She laughed like I had told her a funny. *Luther, how you do talk!* She looked up at him again, with that same love light shinin' in her face. *I really do want to be there, to keep his feet warm. I guess I've loved him since I was a little girl. He used to come to my house with his daddy and I'd hide behind the rocking chair and look out at him.* And she kissed his cheek.

Maybe I better go along with 'im and hold 'em, while he pins their ears back.

She laughed again. *I bet the two of you would scare the living daylights out of them! Well, here I am, doing all this talking, and I've plumb forgot my manners. Let's all go in the house and you meet my sisters and I'll get us a fresh drink of water.* She shook her head. *Water's all I've got these days, things being what they are.*

Her house looked like all the rest of the houses I'd seen. We was standin' in the front room. I could see the kitchen to the back and a room, maybe two, to the side. It was neat as a pin, as Aunt Polly would of said. Joe and me set in the rockin' chairs in front of the fireplace.

She went out back to round up her sisters, she said. They'd been out, doin' chores, I guess. The biggest one looked a lot like her only maybe more purty. She might even be what Bill Jones would call bee-u-ti-ful. The other one looked a mite like rag tag. Her hair was all mussed up and she was follered by a good sized dog. She looked for all the world like another Thelma Wood.

We had our drink of water and talked about this and that. *You look like a girl I knowed oncet in North C'lina. Her name was Thelma. She had a dog, too. Two dogs. It was her and them that found me in a ditch when I had the fevers bad. If'n it hadn't been for them, I guess I'd of died.*

She nodded. *Dogs are real smart. But mine ain't ever found a man in a ditch.*

Maybe you want to show me around the place?
She nodded, and looked to her sister. *You want to come too?*
Her sister said she'd see to things in the kitchen, so her and the
dog took me out back and showed me the garden and the hen
house. We looked out at the cow pasture. She said she'd named
the cows and she pointed out which one had what name. I could
see that she liked doin' that.
Yore dog good at herdin' cows?
She laughed. When she laughed I could tell she had a laugh
like Rose. *He ain't, isn't, much good at that, but he tries real hard.*
He must of knowed she was talkin' about him, since he come to
her, waggin' his tail. She scratched his ears and his head. *He's a
real good watch dog. Rose says he'd bark at anything that passes by.
Rose says that's a real good thing. It scares off anybody comin' to the
house that's not bein' friendly.*
That happen a lot?
She nodded. *Sometimes. Rose says we need a good watch dog,
bein' a house full of women folks.* She looked up at me. *You hear
tell Joe wants to marry up with Rose?*
That's what I hear. You and yore sister feel good about that?
She nodded again. *We're real fond of Joe. He's real good to us.*
She was quiet, studyin' her dog again, like Thelma would do.
*The only thing is, I guess we'd have to leave this place and go live
with the Dales.*
I guess so. Would you mind that?
She shrugged. *Maybe not. Rose says I could take this old dog
with me. They ain't got.* She shook her head and started over.
They don't have a dog over there.
*I bet they could use a good watch dog. They got a cow pasture
and cows over there, for yore dog to herd.*
She laughed. *I guess so.*
Maybe you can ask Joe about that.
I guess so. She giggled. *I don't care much if we took the cows
along, but I'd shore miss the sweet milk.*
Maybe you can tell from what I've said that Rose had a lot of
learnin', like a school marm had to have. The girl looked like she
was tryin' to talk like Rose. She'd start the country way of talkin'

and then change it. I'd heard that way of talkin' from some of the soldiers in the war. But I loved to hear Rose talk, and I tried to pay attention in the short time I was there. Later on, when we was married, Narcissa helped me to talk more like that way. She'd had some schoolin' while I was at the War. I try sometimes, telling you this story, to talk that way, but I guess maybe I talk the country way most of the time. Like, it's hard for me not to say if'n.

I didn't see Rose and her sisters for a few days. Joe's family was real good to me and made me feel at home. His daddy was real shaky. He mostly set on the porch and he had a walkin' stick by his chair for when he got up. At first I couldn't get much of what he said when he talked to me, but by the third day I could make it out. He talked about the farm and the weather. Sometimes he talked like Joe and the other boy was still little boys. Another time, he kept sayin' the same thing, over and over. One time he asked me if'n I'd had any trouble on the road here. I said I had, but I didn't say much else about it. He never asked me about the War. Sometime along then, he said he wisht they had a good dog. He said he had a good dog oncet but he didn't know what went with it.

Joe's mama was real sweet to me. She was more like Aunt Polly than Miz Collins or Miz Tinsley. She said she was right sorry she couldn't set a better table. I told her I was well satisfied and that I could see she was a real good cook. One day I was out with her gatherin' eggs. *I'm real sorry to hear about yore other boy.*

She nodded. *Thankee for yore feelin's. It were a hard blow to take. And we didn't know if'n Joe was alive 'til he showed up one day. The War took a terrible toll on us all.* She stopped and looked at me. *Do you reckon the folks that started it knowed what it would do?*

No mam, I reckon not.

Well, we got to go on. She was quiet. *Joe took you to meet Rose?* It warn't really a question, since she knowed he had.

Yes mam, he did. She seems like a real good woman.
She nodded. *She is that. And she's had a hard life, tryin' to keep her farm up and watchin' over her sisters and doin' the school.* She was quiet, puttin' eggs in her apron, holding the edges with one hand and taking the eggs from the nests with the other. I'd seen Aunt Polly do it that way. *Joe says he wants to marry up with her.*
He told me he did. And she said she was willin'.
She turned to me. *I shorely do hope they do it. Hit'd be good for him. A man his age needs a wife. Hit'd be good for her too. A woman by herself needs a husband.*
It ain't none of my business, but how do you feel about that?
She looked under a settin' hen to see if'n the hen was keepin' the eggs warm. *I guess that's all the eggs for today.* We started back to'ard the house. *It won't be easy. I'm used to keepin' house by myself. And she ain't lived with a older woman since her mama died. We'd have to sort some things out. But the house is big enough to take her and her sisters in.*
She shook her head. *I could shore use some help takin' care of Joe's daddy. He's gonna get worse, time goes by. I cain't hardly leave him by hisself as it is. He wanders of, like a youngun just learnin' how to walk. Joe and her could have the side room. He could make up the attic room for the girls. It'd be real good to have girls in the house again. I don't see much of Joe's sisters in Kentucky. Joe's daddy and me are real partial to Rose. We've knowed her since she was a girl.* We stopped in the kitchen for her to put the eggs in the egg pan. She laughed. *But it don't matter what I think. Joe's real stuck on her. That's all that matters. We'll make do with the rest.*

I went with Joe agin to see Rose on what must of been the next Sunday. Her and the girls was out workin' in the garden. She stopped what she was doin' when she saw us comin'. We said our howdys and went to the porch to set a while. *Miss Rose, I'd like to ask a favor of you. Two favors.*
She nodded. *Ask away.*

First off, I'd like to ask you to write a letter for me to my Uncle Gray.

She grinned. *It's not to a girl back there?*

I shook my head. *No mam. There's a girl back there he'll tell it to. I ain't had a chancet to tell the folks back home that I'm still alive and on the way back to Stewart County. I thought maybe, seein' you are a school marm and know how to do such things, you'd write a letter for me.*

You want to do it now?

Yessum, if'n you got the time

She got up from her chair. *I've got the time all right and it would be a pleasure to do that for you. Let me get my writing materials.* She went in the house and come out with what she called her writing materials, and put 'em in her lap. *What do you want to say in your letter?*

I started out. *It goes to Mr Gray Morris, Bumpus Mill, Stewart County, Tennessee.* I watched her write that down, dipping her quill pen in a bottle.

Go on.

I started out slow. I'd never done this afore and I warn't for certain how. Rose said to talk slow so's she'd have time to do the writin'. *I am sendin' you this letter to tell you I am alive and I am on the way back to Stewart County.* I waited for her to catch up. She nodded, and I started agin. *I was sick with the fevers for a long time in North C'lina.* I stopped agin. *I am now with my friend Joe Dale and his family. They live in Clay County.*

I stopped agin, wonderin' what to say next. *It's might nigh time for the first frost. I hope to get to Stewart County by Christmas.* I stopped agin. *Miz Rose Bean is writin' this for me. Please tell Nadine Cherry I am alive. Luther.*

That's a real good letter. Let me read it back to you, to see if I got it right. She did that, and I said it was all right. She said she could mail it for me. She stopped what she was doin', foldin' the paper. *Can you sign your name?*

Yessum, I can do that. Do you think I ought to?

I think you should. She showed me where to sign and I did. I couldn't get the pen to work at first, but she helped me. It was the first time since I joined up that I had to sign my name. I didn't know if'n I did it right, but she said I did.

Joe was watchin' us do the letter. *I'm proud you and Rose can do the letter. Yore Uncle Gray will be real glad to get it. I never could write a letter home so's they would know I was dead or alive.*

She finished with the letter and took it and her writin' materials in the house. When she come out again, she asked what was the other favor. *Ever since I left Richmond, I've been traveling by what somebody told me. They'd say go this way and I'd go this way. They'd say go that way and I'd go that way. I never have knowed where I was, 'cept that I was tryin' to find the Cumberland River and foller it. I was thinkin' that way since I knowed the Cumberland River went right next to Bumpus Mill. Do you figure in any of yore books there'd be a map of Tennessee that would tell me where I am and where Stewart County is and how I can get there?*

She nodded. *I'm not all that good at looking at maps myself, but I think I can help you. Let me think about it for a day or two, and we'll see what I can do.*

I would thankee with all my heart, if'n you could.

It were the next day, maybe two, that a rider come up Dale Holler. Joe said his name was Ralph Stone and he lived out of Celina on the other side of the river. We said our howdys. Ralph said he was ridin' up the Holler to tell folks that some men up from Merfeesborra was makin' trouble. They'd been in Celina and the sheriff had run 'em out. The sheriff had Ralph and some men ridin' around the county, spreadin' the word. *What'd they want? We ain't got much to take.*

The sheriff says they say they're lookin' for runaway slaves. He says he don't like the looks of 'em. He says he don't know but what slaves ain't all they're lookin' for.

You figure they mean to cause real trouble?

The sheriff said he figured they did.

I better go get Rose and the girls and bring 'em here. I'm much obliged, Ralph, for you warnin' us. Now you go on up the Holler and warn the t'others up there.

Joe, whyn't you let me go get Rose and the girls and you stay here with yore mama and daddy. If they's trouble, they'll need you here. I know how to get to Rose's place. He didn't want to do it but he let me go. I saddled up Thunder and got my rifle and kit bag out of the barn. And I headed to her place as fast as we could go. She was in the front room, mendin' clothes. I told her what was happenin' and that Joe had sent me for her and the girls.

It's probably a fuss about nothing, but I'll do what Joe says. She put her mendin' on the bed. *I'll go call the girls. You think I should bring the dog?*

Sounds like a good idea. I'll go hitch up yore buggy. And I'll load my rifle.

She went out back and I heard her call the girls. I went out to the lot and caught her mule and hitched up the buggy. I was standin' there by Thunder, workin' on the rifle when she come from around the house.

Mackadoo has gone after Mary. She's over by the spring house.

Mackadoo?

She grinned. *Daddy named her Maxine, but she doesn't much like that name. Somehow, I don't remember how, the name Mackadoo stuck. I have to admit, it fits her better than Maxine.* She looked over to'ard the spring house. *I wonder where they've got to. Joe will be worried about us, won't he?* She looked at the rifle. *That come from the War?*

Yessum.

You had to use it a lot?

Yessum, more'n I wanted to. You think maybe you better go call the girls again?

Yes, I guess I better. And she went over to the side of the house and hollered for 'em again. I got to say she had a right good holler. She could be heard from here to kingdom come.

She come back to where I was standin'. *They're on the way. I see them coming down the hill in the cow pasture.* It looked like she was frettin', waitin' for them to come. So was I. *My daddy had a old gun. He used to go squirrel hunting. He taught me to shoot it, but I didn't like it. It carried a powerful punch when you pulled the trigger.* She looked over that way for them agin. *I can't see why they are taking so long to get here.*

No mam. Come to think of it, you know anythin' about a pistol? She laughed, but her eyes was on the lot where the girls would come through. *Not a thing.*

You reckon you could hold it like you did? She looked at me to see if'n I meant what I said.

I guess I could.

So I took my pistol out of the kit bag and looked to be sure it warn't loaded and handed it to her. *Here's how you hold it. If'n you want to show like you're about to shoot, hold it up even with yore eyes, and yore arm stretched out. Let's see you do it. Don't worry, it ain't loaded, but nobody knows that 'cept you and me.* She showed me she could do it. *You got a pocket in yore apron? Put it in there. You right handed?* She nodded. *Put it in the right hand pocket, so's you can get to it, easy like.*

She nodded and put the pistol in the apron pocket. *I haven't ever done any thing like this before. What if I do it wrong? Oh Lordy, finally, here come those girls. Where all have you been? We've been standin' here a hour, waitin' for you! Get in the buggy. Put the dog in too. Joe said there might be trouble at his house. He sent Luther for us, and here you two were out gallivantin' around! I'll explain while we're goin' there. Now hurry up!* So, it looked like Miz Rose could show some spirit when she had to. The girls never said a word, but got in the buggy, the dog, too, and we left, Thunder and me in the lead.

It was maybe two mile to the Dale place. The last mile was in timber and I stopped at the edge of the trees and motioned to Rose to stop alongside. We could see the Dale house but I figured they couldn't see us 'less'n they was lookin' for us there. Joe was out in the front yard, talkin' to three men on horseback. Mr.

Dale was settin' on the porch. Joe's mama was nowhere to be seen.

The dog started to bark. One of the girls tried to get him to stop, but he didn't. Joe and the three men looked over our way, and Joe motioned for us to come ahead. We did, slow like. I had my rifle out, at the ready, so's the men could see it. I told Rose to get out the pistol and hold it so's they could see it, but no need to aim it. She did. I'd of loved to see old Joe's face when she pulled out the pistol. Pro'bly he was thinkin' where'd she get that? But I couldn't look at him for lookin' at the three men.

This here is Luther Morris, a buddy of mine from the War. He didn't say anything about Rose and the girls.

What's goin' on here?

These three fellars are lookin' for runaway slaves.

You fellars mean to cause us some trouble?

One of 'em spoke up. *Naw, we ain't lookin' for trouble from you. We been hired to bring back runaway slaves.*

It ain't legal to have slaves nowadays.

Well, we ain't gonna get into that. The man down in Alabama says when his slaves was set free he told 'em they could leave or they could stay on his place and work like always. But he told 'em if'n they stayed, they have to go back to bein' slaves. They sed they would, but then they'd run off. He hired us to find 'em and bring 'em back.

Well, I ain't never heard anythin' like that, but I figured it was up to Joe to say next what he had to say. So I set there on Thunder, holdin' my rifle, and Rose set there in the buggy, holdin' the pistol in her lap on top of her apron, in plain view, like she'd allus done it that way.

The dog had jumped down off'n the buggy, soon as we got stopped. He was still barkin' and growlin' maybe fifteen foot away from one of the men on horseback. I didn't know why he picked on that one, but he did. While the other man was talkin', this one circled his horse, tryin' to make the dog back up. Out of the corner of my eye, I could see one of the girls start to get down off of the buggy to go get the dog, and I could see Rose motionin' her to stay still. *We ain't got any colored people here.*

Well, folks in town say differnt. They say sometimes negras come up this holler on their way to Ohio. They say some come up this way two days ago.

Mebbe they say that. But I'm a tellin' you we ain't got any colored people on this place. He said it slow like, word by word. I recollected he talked that way that time to that lieutenant in the war. *So you fellars best be movin' on.*

We aim to look around some. You mind if'n we look around some?

Yes, I danged shore do mind. You ain't got any right to look around. You'd best take my word for it, and get to movin' on. Right then, I don't know why, that dog started in barkin' like he was gonna bust if'n he didn't. And he kept on circlin' that one horse, like he was herdin' a sheep. The man on the horse raised his rifle and aimed at the dog.

I quick waved my rifle around and aimed at him. *You best lower that rifle!*

He didn't. *What's it to you? That dog is makin' me nervy and I'm a gonna stop it from barkin'.* And I could see him draw a bead on the dog, still barkin' for all it was worth.

I raised my rifle to draw a bead on him. *You do, and it'll be the last dog you ever shot! Miss Rose, you cover them other men.* I saw her arm raise and point to'ard the other men. It was real quiet, 'ceptin' for that barkin' dog. It crossed my mind if'n he knowed what a lot of trouble he was causin'. The man aimin' the gun at him looked at me, and lowered it, and shot at the dog. He missed, and the dog kept right on barkin'.

Then, out of the corner of my eye, I seen Joe's mama come out of the house, holdin' a old musket. Without missin' a beat, she shot that old gun at the feller still aimin' at the dog. It must of gone over his head. He turned his gun at her and looked like he was goin' to shoot at her. I trained my gun sight on him agin. *So help me God, you shoot one more time, and you are a dead man*

298 HUGHLETT L. MORRIS

for sure. He looked over at me, and in what seemed like a long time, lowered his gun. Then he turned his horse and headed down the road, not waitin' for the other two. They turned their horses and follered him on up the holler. I was still shakin'. I guess all of us was. Joe went over to his mama, and took the gun from her. *I'd plumb forgot you knowed how to shoot that thing!*

She give a kind of laugh and shook her head. *I was shootin' a gun afore you was born. Oncet you know how, it comes back. I'd clean forgot about it when I recollected where it was ahind the door. When I heard all the commotion, I poured in the powder and come out shootin'. I warn't for certain it would shoot. Them old guns didn't allus shoot when you wanted 'em to.* Now she set down by Mr. Dale. *I'm right shaky from doin' it.* She looked up at Joe, with a grin on her face. *You goin' to get on me for doin' it?*

Lord no, I ain't goin' to get on you. You done right. He laughed. *I guess I'm thankful yore aim was so high!* He stood there by her for a little while. We was all quiet. *I guess if'n we was still in the army, we'd call that'un a close call.* The girls got down from the buggy and them and Rose went to Joe's mama. Joe watched 'em and then looked over to me. *You folks aim to go squirrel huntin'? Or can you set a spell?*

Yeah, we can set a spell. I put my rifle back in the rope on my saddle and got down. *I guess, maybe, Miss Rose, you can hand me back yore pistol, unless'n you want to keep it.*

She laughed, that good belly laugh of hers, and handed me the pistol. *You can have it back. I don't have any use for it, unless I need it to make Joe marry me. If'n I do, I'll call on Joe's mama!* We was kiddin' back and forth to hide that we'd had what Joe had called a close call. We could have had a lot of bloodshed, I guess, if'n that fellar had shot the dog. To this day, I don't know if'n I'd of killed a man over a dog. Maybe I would of missed. Charlie allus said I couldn't hit the side of a barn with a gun. If'n I'd of missed, and the fellar shot the dog, then what do you guess Rose would of done? Well, no way to know. Maybe she'd of pulled the trigger, and maybe not.

Then when Joe's mama come out and shot at the feller, that was a differnt story. If'n he'd shot at her, I'd of shot him for sure. Then we'd of had a real mess on our hands, with maybe a dead man to do somethin' with. But after it was over with, we had a lot of kiddin' to do to get over what had near happened, maybe all because of a derned yappin' dog.

Anyway, I took the pistol she handed me. *I don't reckon you'll need it to get 'im to the Preacher.*

Joe shook his head, tryin' to scowl. *Ain't likely she'll need it for that. More likely I'll be the one that'll need it if'n we have to go see if'n a woman what's married can be a school marm.* We kidded around some more, but it looked like everybody was feelin' better. Rose and Joe and his mama and the girls and the dog went for a walk over in the timber. I figured they was talkin' about what happened and what it was all about. I stayed close to his daddy and chopped and took in some stove wood.

Truth to tell, I was wonderin' what it was all about myself. Mostly what I knowed about slaving was what I got from that time with Dulciemay and Granny. Studyin' about it, I could see some how it was.

Bein' free was all what Dulciemay and Granny would want. But when they was free, what was they goin' to do? Do you reckon Granny could make the trip north? It warn't likely. If'n she left the farm or somewheres like it, how was she to get by? Where was the vittles to come from? Tryin' as hard as I could, a white man, to see her side of it, I could see if'n the Massa come back, as she called him, and said she could stay on the farm, she'd do it. Maybe she'd think to herself that just 'cause he said she had to be a slave again didn't mean anything.

Now Dulciemay was a differnt story. She thought she knowed all right and good enough what it would be to be free and she had the wherewithall to go north, and I bet she did. Maybe she didn't go 'til after Granny died or was took care of some way. But she'd go.

Rose and the girls stayed at the Dale house that night. Bed time come and me and the girls went up to the attic to sleep. Nothin' was said about it, but Rose slept downstairs in the side room with Joe. All his mama did was to make sure the girls and me had enough covers up in the attic. I recollect that afore bed time, the girls made over his daddy and brought in the dog for him to pet. It seemed natch'ral and made me wish I had a family like that.

The next mornin' Joe said for him and me to go to Rose's place to do some chores. When we got there and tied up, we was standin' lookin' around at the place. *You gonna tell me what that yestiday was all about?*

I reckon I owe it to you, seein' as how you helped out so. I couldn't do much about 'em, afore you and Rose come with the guns. I was skeered to raise a ruckus, skeered they'd put their questions to my daddy. And I didn't know what he'd say, bein' like he is. I didn't know what Mama would of done, if'n they had done that. I figured maybe she'd of taken to 'em with her butcher knife.

He laughed. *I didn't reckon with her and that old musket!* He shook his head. *She's some woman, my mama is. I'd forgot how nervy she could be.*

Anyway, they's been word around here of them bounty hunters. Maybe bounty hunters ain't the right word for what they do, but you know what I mean. Daddy told me when I come home that sometimes colored folks come through here on their way to Kaintuck, to go on to Ohio. The Kaintuck line is over that about ten miles. He pointed to the north. *He said there warn't but a few. Since I got home, there's been more or less a steady stream of 'em.*

Them riders yestiday had it right, all right enough. He picked up a rock and thowed it at the barn. I set on the fence railin', waitin' to hear him out. *There's a right good size cave on this place. It's in the heavy timber and nobody could find it if'n they didn't know where to look.*

He thowed another rock, this time down to'ard the pond. *I guess when the first slaves come through, some of 'em come to the house and ast if'n they could stay the night somewheres on the farm. Mama give 'em somethin' to eat, and Daddy took 'em to the cave and told 'em they could stay the night but to move on the next mornin'. That was afore he got sick and crippled up. Then the word must of got around to others comin' this way. They don't come much to the house, just go to the cave. At least it looks that way.*

He quit talkin', and stood there, with his arms folded, lookin' out at the pond. I thought he was done but I kept my seat on the fence, waitin' to see what we was gonna do next. *Tell the truth, they warn't too happy with me when I joined up with the South. Lookin' back, I don't rightly know why I did.*

He turned and looked at me. *My brother went to the other side. I don't know why he did and I didn't. Him and me never talked about it much. I didn't know he'd do that. I figured him to be just a kid when I left. He never come back.*

I got home and Daddy told me first off about the cave. Mama didn't say much but I figured he was talkin' for her. He never asked me to go along but the first time some of 'em come through I took over. By that time he was startin' to be feeble. That was more'n a year ago. Like I say, we're out of the way up here.

But Kentucky is right over there. He thowed a rock in that direction. *I do what I can.* He thowed another rock at the barn. *I didn't lie to them fellars. There ain't no colored folks on this place. Not right now, that I know of.*

He turned to me. *Trouble is, ain't ever'body in Celina or Clay County for giving shelter to the colored folks. The folks in this part of the country was split down the middle on the War. My family was like that. Some folks look like they're still fightin' the War. My mama's own sister has called her a nigra lover. I guess that if'n she knowed about our givin' shelter, others do too.* He shrugged. *I'm in a right quare place. Here I am, a soldier for the Rebels, givin' shelter to the colored folks. Life shore is funny. Rose has helped me to see that.*

Now he was done, I thought. I got down off'n the fence and he led the way to the barn and the lot to do chores there was to be done. It didn't take us long. We got done and put things away and was about to leave. *I'm real sorry about yore brother.*

He nodded. *He was a good boy. I wish now I'd paid more mind to 'im. It feels like I never got to know 'im.* He stopped walking and turned to me. *I'm much obliged you stopped here to see me. Like I told the man you and me are good buddies, as good as they ever come. You're welcome to stay as long as you want.* Grinnin'. *Maybe stand up for me at a weddin'. I'm much obliged to you for takin' me in. I feel right at home with yore family. I guess that means Miss Rose and the girls too. I'm aimin' it turns out that way.* And we rode on back to his place.

I was with him and Rose some more times afore I left Dale Holler. Every time I seen 'em together I saw what looked like so much love between 'em. It set me to thinkin' agin about the women that had been in my life up to then.

Like I said, I knowed there hadn't been them kind of feelin's twist me and any of the women. Not Maybelle. Her and me had come together, natch'ral like, to be sure, but there warn't any love in it. I knowed it and she knowed it, and it didn't matter. Same way for what I felt about Josie. I wanted her, all right enough, but we both knowed it was a one time thing to happen. Same as for Dulciemay. Her again. What Dulciemay wanted from me, like I said, was maybe a way to get back at some other white man that had took her when she didn't want him.

Julia fits in the same way. Them times we was together, they was somethin' special for both of us, if'n I can judge such for a woman. It seemed a sure thing I was givin' her what John couldn't. Maybe when she closed her eyes with me, she was seein' John. But in actual fact, I was there doin' what John had asked me to do. I figured she knowed that, and it was all right with her. Lord knows what there was 'tween Beulah Gates and me.

That there might be a baby with any of them women has always been in the back of my mind. I never told nobody about my times with them women, not Narcissa, not Missouri. I guess I might of, but I was always uneasy about how they would feel about it. They both come to know that I loved women a lot, 'specially them. So I guess it wouldn't be a su'prise to them that I loved women afore I got together with them.

But a baby is a differnt matter. Recollectin' my times with them women always set me wonderin' if'n somewhere out there in Tennessee and North C'lina, there was a baby I had helped make. That would be a baby that I'd never know about. It ain't a good feelin', wonderin' about that. I loved all my babies with Narcissa and Missouri more'n I can say, and it pained me to think about any babies I never knowed about.

But there warn't any thing I could do about it. What was done was done. Truth to tell, when I left Celina, I thought about goin' back to Tinsley Bottom to find out if'n Julia was with a baby. One part of me wanted to know. But the stronger feelin' in me was that it was best if'n I didn't. Knowin' if she was or if'n she was not with a baby warn't goin' to change what I wanted to do, go back to Stewart County.

The last time I saw Rose afore I left Dale Hollow, her and me looked at the map she'd drawed on a piece of cloth. *You still of a mind to follow the Cumberland River?* She said follow, and not foller, like I would of. I loved to hear her talk.

I ain't made up my mind yet for sure. What do'y think I ought to do?

Well, look at the Cumberland River I've drawn on the map. It goes south by west here and by Nashville. She said Nashville, not Nashvul, like Joe and me did. She traced the river with her finger on her map. *Then it heads back up north by west, to Clarksville.* She looked at me, smilin'. *Do you and that big horse of yours want to see the sights of Nashville?*

I caught her drift. *That's a big town, ain't it?*

She nodded. *It is that. It's so big the word town doesn't fit. The word city is a better fit.*

I looked at her map. *You figure maybe I couldn't find my way through?*

Oh I think a man's that's traveled like you can always find his way through. You can always ask how to get to Clarksville. I was still lookin' at the map. *It'd cost a lot of money there, won't it?* She nodded. *More than it costs here, that's for sure.* I looked at the map again. *What if'n I go due west from here? I'd foller, I mean follow, the state line with Kentucky all the way across Tennessee.* I traced it on the map with my finger. *That'd lead me right to Stewart County, won't it?* She nodded. *It'd lead you right to Stewart County.* I kept lookin' at her map. *Stewart County ain't on the Mississippi River. That's on further in west Tennessee, ain't it?* She nodded. *I forgot to put in the Mississippi River, but you know where it is.* And she traced it with her finger. *It goes down from Kentucky to Memphis and on down to New Orleens. New Orleens is on what's called the Gulf of Mexico.*

Does the Cumberland River and the Tennessee River empty into the Mississippi River?

She laughed and shook her purty head. *I don't rightly know. There's the Ohio River somewhere over there. I know it empties in the Mississippi. I don't know any more than that. You've tested my map reading skills as far as they go. When I copied this map, I didn't know you'd have all these questions! The next time I look at the book where I copied your map, I'll look for that.* Her face turned all solemn. *But I guess you'll be gone by then.*

Yessum, I guess I will. I looked at the map again. *How far do you reckon it is from here to Stewart County, if'n I go straight across, like we said?*

She measured it off with her thumb and a finger. *Maybe a hundred miles, give or take.* She grinned at me. *Let me be the school marm here. How many miles a day can you and that horse Thunder make in a day?*

Maybe twenty. I grinned. *Give or take.*

She laughed at that. *Joe said you were good at figuring. Twenty miles a day, a hindred miles to go, how many days would it take?* I used my thumb to measure it off. *Five. Maybe more.*

He was right. You're good at figuring.

*So, if'n I rode hard, I could be there in a week. Maybe less'n
that.*

It looks like it. She laughed. *Maybe two weeks, if'n you get
stopped along the way by a pretty girl.* She said it pretty, not purty,
like I did.

Well, it took me longer'n that. But I had a notion about it
all. I left Dale Hollow one mornin' on a summer day, headed
west. Oncet again, I said my good bye to some good folks. We
said we'd see each other again but of course we knowed we warn't
likely to. Miss Rose give me a big hug and said it was good to
have me come by to see 'em. Joe's mama did the same and give
me some vittles to put in my kit bag for the road. I told her to
keep her musket handy. She laughed and said she would. His
daddy and me shook hands. Me and Joe give each other a bear
hug. We didn't say much except take care of yoreself and such as
that. I hated to leave Joe Dale real bad. He was as good a friend as
I ever had.

We knowed that about the other one. We knowed we'd never
see each other again. 'Twarn't no need to say anythin'.

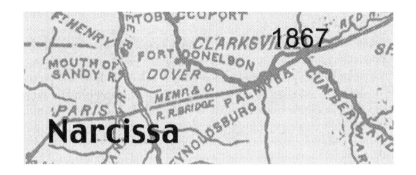

Narcissa

N ow, for certain, I was on my way to Stewart County. I got to tell you right here that the rest of this story ain't near as excitin' as maybe the first part has been. You'll find out that from now on to Stewart County, I didn't meet up with any robbers or bounty hunters or anything like that. And it turned out that I didn't do any more of what I called tom cattin'. I was on the straight and narrow all the way back home. But it ain't that the rest of the story ain't worth listenin' to. At least I hope not. So, let's go on with it.

Anyway, the first stop after I left the Dale place was the courthouse square back in Celina. Miz Dale had give me some vittles but I figured I better see if'n I could find some jerky. Miss Rose didn't know for sure but she said it looked like there warn't many towns the way I was goin', so I better have all the supplies I could carry in my kit bag.

Afore I went in the store on the square, I looked around. It looked like there was three roads leadin' out. One of 'em went out to the Obey River, Joe called it, and to Dale Hollow, the way I just come. I was tryin' to copy Rose when I said Hollow, even to myself. It didn't sound right to me, but that was the way she said it. I knowed another road. It was the one I come in on from Tinsley Bottom. She said it went to Gainesbora, I knowed that, and the Cumberland River, I knowed that too. And to Nashville. I said to my self Nashville, not Nashvul. I knowed that road, and I shore didn't mean to go that way.

The other one looked like it went north, to'ard Kentucky. The man at the store said it got to a crossroad named Moss, first, then it left north to go west to Red Boilin' Springs. He talked like a right smart man. Afore the war, when he was a young man, he'd traveled some. He pulled out a map and showed it to me. It was maybe better'n Miss Rose's but it showed about the same. I ast 'im how long it'd take me to get to west Tennessee. He said a month. It turned out he was more right about that than me and Rose was.

While I was standin' there, talkin' to him, a man older'n me come up. He said he'd heard us talkin' and he was ridin' over to Red Boilin' Springs, if'n I wanted to ride along. I took him up on it. I recollect he was a Stone. He said he knowed the Dales. He didn't have much to say. We just rode along. The countryside up to Moss looked like I was goin' back to Standin' Stone. It was real purty, goin' up out of the Cumberland River valley out of Celina. The hills was heavy in timber, with rock bluffs here and there. It looked like a spring crossed the road ever' half a mile. He said the bluffs was limestone, and there was a lot of springs where you find limestone bluffs. He said the water from the springs was real sweet. I swear that was about all he said the whole way.

We got to Moss afore dinner time. It was a crossroads. Like the store keeper said, one road went north to Kentucky and the other one went west. We stopped to eat a bite and take a piss. I recollect he was ridin' a short legged red mare. It looked like my little red mare but it had some white here and there. We got back on the road. He was in the lead and took off. The mare was fast, all right enough, but Thunder could keep up without hardly raisin' a sweat. We come to a creek and stopped to water the horses. I told him his mare looked like a good runner. And I told him I oncet had a mare like his'n. He grinned, but didn't say much. Like I said, he warn't a big talker.

We got to Red Boilin' Springs afore supper time. He said so long and went his way. I found a boardin' house and told her I'd look around afore time to eat. It was a purty place. It looked a lot like Standin' Stone but it didn't have any real big houses that I could see. But what it had was a place with a hot spring, where you could take a bath in it. The men was on one side and the women was on the other. They'd give you a piece of soap and a fair size rag to dry off with. I set there in the warm water, thinkin' about all the times on the road I'd washed up in a pond and a river. But that time I had to put back on my dirty clothes.

Like I allus did, I ast the woman at the boardin' house about the way west. She said there warn't much, this side of Lafet. I didn't know the right spellin' of it 'til years later, from Narcissa Anyway, the woman said I better plan on sleepin' out. She said there was allus talk of outlaws along that stretch. When she give me back my rifle, she said to keep it close and to keep it loaded. I didn't tell her about the pistol in my kit bag. But I knowed to keep it close too. But I didn't run into any trouble.

For one thing, most of the country along in there was open. I'd figured out from travelin' like I did that it was ridin' through a long stretch of timber that made me uneasy. It was a right good ride. The weather was good. I didn't go through but one rain and it didn't last long. I got good and wet but it warn't cold, so I didn't mind it.

I got to Lafet about dinner time on the day after I started out. If'n you look on a map, you'll see a town along there spelled Lafayette. Narcissa pointed that out to me later on. She was a real smart woman. She'd been schoolin' while I was at war. It was her that learned me how to write my name better. She learned me to read a little and she helped me with my figures. She called 'em numbers. It was the same thing. When we was havin' trouble makin' ends meet with all them babies, she was the one that kept the money and all that. My part of the deal was to do the best farmin' I could. Anyway, nobody there I heard talk said anythin' but Lafet. I don't recollect a thing about the town except that was where I got Buster.

I found a boardin' house and took a room and left my gear and my rifle. Thunder was fed and tied up out back. So I took a walk around the square to stretch my legs. Maybe I'd find a saloon

and have a drink of whiskey. I come up to a store and was about
to go in and look around.

Mister, you want a dog?
Over to the side of the steps was this boy and a little dog. The
boy looked maybe Thelma's age. It looked like his pants was a mite
short, old boots, pro'bly hand me downs, shirt tail hangin' out,
shaggy hair fallin' down in his eyes. A real good lookin' face, what I
could see of it. *What'd you say? You talkin' to me?*
Yessir. I said you want a dog?
I cain't say that I do. But she looks like a good one. I walked
over the few steps and squatted down by 'em and petted the dog.
It was a little bitch dog, maybe weighed out at ten pounds. She
had brown curly fur with two white stockin's and some white on
her nose. She rolled over on her back when I petted her and
looked up at me upside down. *She's a good lookin' dog. Is she right
smart?*
*Yessir, she's real smart. She can chase varmints out of the hen
house and the coons and ever'thin' like that.*
I stood up. The dog got on her feet and stood there lookin'
at me, waggin' a tail as long as her. *She yore dog, I guess?*
*Well, she is and she ain't. She was my granpa's dog and he died
and I'm takin' care of her 'til she finds a home.* He was rubbin' her
behind the ears. She was lookin' at him like she was smilin' at
'im. *She'd make you a real good dog.*
*Well, sir, I cain't take you up on that. I'm ridin' horseback clear
across Tennessee and I ain't got no way to take a dog along.* She
looked like she knowed we was talkin' about her. She got to her
feet and looked back and forth 'tween him and me, waggin' that
tail. *It looks like she's real stuck on you. Whyn't you keep her?*
He looked down at her. *I wanted to, real bad. But we got two
dogs at home and my Pa says that's aplenty. So I got to find her a
home.*
I'm real sorry I cain't take her but I shore cain't. She was lookin'
up at me. *She got a name?*

Yessir. It's Buster.
I busted out laughin'. *Buster? Her name's Buster?*
Yessir. I reckon it funny namin' a bitch dog Buster. But that's what Granpa named her, and she comes to it. It looked like she knowed her name for sure, 'cause when he said it, she got all excited and wagged her tail even harder. *You got a horse?*
Yep, I do. He's tied up while I go in here to the store.
He that big black horse tied up behind the boardin' house?
That's him. He's a big horse all right enough and runs fast when he gets goin'. A little dog like her couldn't nowhere near keep up. I don't 'spect she could keep up with him for more'n a hundred foot afore she'd give out.
I seen him over there. He shore is a purty horse. He shook his head. *She's a good runner but she ain't that good.*
I got to go. I offered him my hand. He took it and we shook, man to man. *It's been real good to talk to you. I hope you find Buster a real good home.* And I went on in the store.
That boy Tom out there tryin' to get you to take that dog?
I nodded. *He shore is. He made a real good pitch.* I laughed and he laughed. *He said it was his granpa's dog?*
Yep. The old man died a month ago. The little dog follered him everywhere. Tom's daddy says they cain't keep her. He says they got too many dogs as it is. What can I get for you?
I named some things I needed and helped myself to some cheese and crackers on the counter, with some pepper sauce on it. He asked if'n I wanted a little drink of whiskey and I said I wouldn't say no. So we stood there, talkin' about this and that while I et and had my whiskey. I paid him and thanked him and went back out on the store porch.
Truth to tell, all the time, I was thinkin' how good it would be to have a dog along. We allus had dogs about on the farm and I'd missed 'em a lot in the War. And it were Dog that found me. And Skunk that stayed with me on Preacher's place. But I knowed that if'n I took 'im he'd be a burden for sure. No, I had that wrong. The little dog was a she, not a he. No matter. I warn't

gonna take her anyway. Her little short legs couldn't of kept up with Thunder, even if'n he was walkin'. And Thunder didn't never hardly walk.

The boy and the dog was still on the store porch. *Mister, is it all right if'n Buster and me come to see the big horse?*

Yep, you can shore come along. So the three of us walked down the road and ahind the boardin' house where I had Thunder tied up. I thought to myself, if'n Buster starts to bark at Thunder, he ain't gonna like it. He could make a hash out of that little dog. *You, boy, better keep yore distance with the dog. My horse may be a little nervy about you. He ain't much used to boys and dogs.* That warn't exactly so, but I figured it would do the trick. Well, 'pon my soul, no sooner'n I'd said that but what Buster run up to Thunder and Thunder didn't do anythin' but put his nose down by that little dog, like they was talkin' to each other.

Mister, do you see that? That big horse likes Buster! He looked at me and I could might nigh read what he was wantin' to say.

Don't he bark a lot? A dog his size gen'lly barks a lot.

He shook his head. It looked like he knowed he was makin' some headway with me about takin' Buster. *Not so much, she don't bark. But Mister, she's a real good watch dog. If'n she sees somethin' she don't know about, she barks her head off.*

I stood there, lookin' at the little dog and the big horse. *I don't rightly know how I can feed her. I travel real light, with only enough vittles for me.*

The boy was now gettin' the drift that I might take her. *Oh Mister, she don't eat much. Just a scrap now and then.* I said to myself, I bet. I bet that dog could out eat me, if'n she had the chance. By now, the dog was runnin' around under Thunder and he was follerin' her with his head, like they was playin' some kind of game. *Mister, why don't you see if'n she'll ride on the big horse, in front of yore saddle? I bet she would.*

I was thinkin' the same thing, but I didn't say it. *Well, I'll try it. If'n it don't work, ain't no way I can take her. Buster, come here!* And she come to me right away, waggin' that tail of hers. I scooped her up, and with one arm full of dog, I swang up on Thunder with the other one. I settled her in 'tween me and the saddle horn. She wiggled around 'til it looked like she had her place to set. I rode Thunder around in some circles and she never moved, even a mite.

The boy was laughin' and jumpin' up and down and clappin' his hands. The woman from the boardin' house come out to see what all the fuss was about, and she stood there, laughin' at what she seen. There was one more thing to see about. I stopped Thunder and told Buster to jump down and she did. She didn't exactly hit the ground runnin', as one of my old sergeants used to say, but she didn't break her neck in the jumpin'. I figured she'd get the hang of it.

The boy could see that the deal was done. He petted Buster and told her to stay with me, and headed home, I guess, at a run. There I was, left settin' on Thunder, Buster lookin' up at me I guess to see what was next. The boardin' house woman was still havin' a good laugh and shakin' her head.

I figured that if'n I stayed on Thunder, Buster would get the idea and foller the boy home and that'd be the end of that. But she didn't. She just stood there, waggin' her tail. Then she set down, like she had all the time in the world for me to say what was next. Leavin' the boardin' house woman still laughin', I rode Thunder back to the store, thinkin' maybe Buster would go home. But no. I got there and there she was right behind me, and when I stopped in front of the store, she stopped and set down again.

By that time, word had spread. The boy was back with his daddy. The store keeper come out. The boardin' house woman foller us over. Two or three other men and women were standin' there watchin'. *Mister, show us how you can carry Buster on yore big horse.*

I looked at the boy and then at Buster lookin' at me and I figured I was licked. I might just as well go along. So I got down and stood there a minute lookin' at Buster. She acted liked she knowed what was up, standin' there might nigh jumpin' up and down with all four feet at oncet. I scooped her up, put her in one arm, and got back on Thunder with the other.

It was a wonder. Thunder held real still while her and me got her settled 'tween the saddle horn and my crotch. We rode some circles for the folks and they cheered like they was seein' a travelin' show. I stopped for her to jump down, and I got down and got up in the saddle again with her. One of the men went in the store and come out with a piece of cheese, he said, for her to have on the road. The woman at the boardin house went and come back with a big piece of cornpone, she said, for the little dog to have on the road.

Finally, I told 'em the show was over and we had to get goin'. Everybody waved and wished us luck. I thought to myself I'm gonna need it, with this here danged dog. So we took off to'ard Portland. The boy and a gaggle of kids follered us out of town.

Truth to tell, that little dog Buster was a big difference in my life at that time. I reckon I was so used to ridin' by myself that I didn't see how bad it could feel, 'til I had her down in front of me, actin' like she'd done it all her life. I talked to Thunder sometimes like I did Ole Mule. But it seemed like Thunder was standoffish by his nature and he didn't care if'n I talked to him or not. I recollected that, when I talked to Ole Mule, he'd turn his head and act like he was listenin'. At least he acted like he was. Maybe he warn't. I don't know.

Anyway, Buster was a right good 'un to be with. Like I said, she rode up front of me like she'd done it all her life. I figured at first she'd shy away from my scoopin' her up to get on Thunder. But she never did. Fact is, when we'd stop for somethin' and it was time to go again, it looked like she knowed it and would wait for me to pick her up. I was worried at first that she'd jump down wrong when we got off Thunder and break somethin'. Then I'd be in a pickle with a dog with a broken leg or worse. One time she ended up end over teakettle, as Aunt Polly would say, but she didn't seem to mind. She never acted fearsome about jumpin' down.

But what I started to say was that I talked to her a lot. When I rode by myself, I'd catch myself talkin' to myself. Now I had Buster to talk to. I'd say somethin' to her and she'd wiggle like she knowed I was talkin' to her. When we was down off the horse and I'd talk to her, she'd look at me, waggin' that tail for all it was worth. It warn't but a day or two and I saw what company she was for me. It made all the difference in the world to me at that time.

The only thing I had to worry about was if'n I didn't have enough for her to eat. When I was on the road, I just didn't eat more'n I had to. I could get by. It was a four day ride to Springfield and warn't much in between.

But right after I run out of vittles for her and me, we was saved. We come to a farm place and I begged. The woman there at first didn't like the idea of me comin' up to the house, and her big dog was raisin' a ruckus at us. But when she saw Buster comin' up to her, waggin' her tail, she took to that little dog right away. She told her dog to come ahead and see this little dog and he did. They smelled each other, like dogs do, and nobody made any trouble. Buster let the woman pet her and make over her.

I told her the story of how I come to have her. She laughed a lot over Buster bein' a bitch dog with a name like that. She asked how we traveled and I showed her how we got in the saddle and down again. She said she never had seen a smarter dog! I figure I could of left Buster with her, if'n I was a mind to, but I warn't of a mind to.

Anyway, we stayed a hour and got fed some fried meat and cornpone and some to take on our way, along with two eggs. I never did figure out how to carry eggs without them getting' broke. Sometimes I put 'em in some moss and leaves, and that helped. It was allus a mess when they got broke in my kit bag or whatever I had 'em in.

The day afore we got to Springfield I was plumb out of vittles again, and worryin' about what I was gonna do. Pro'bly I'd have to beg again, but I had'nt come across a farm place all the day before. It looked like they was few and far between in this part of the country.

But luck was with us again. Mid morning we caught up with a wagon train. The driver of the wagon last in line saw us and pulled to a stop. *Howdy.*

Howdy.

You folks headed to Springfield?

He nodded. *Yep, and beyond. We're headed to Missoury.*

I nodded. *I rode with a wagon train back over the mountains that was headed to Missoury. It looks like a lot of folks are doin' that.*

You ridin' by yore self?

Yessir, I am. Me and my dog here.

He laughed. *That's some dog you got there. I never seen a dog ride a horse that way.*

I laughed with him. *Me neither, til I met up with Buster.*

Tell you what. I got to get goin' or I'll be left behind. Whyn't you ride along with me and the missus. We mean to make camp at dinner time. Two of the boys got lucky and got a big mess of rabbits last night and we mean to cook 'em for our dinner. Maybe we'll stay the night afore movin' on. We'd be pleased to have you and yore dog to take dinner with us.

The Missus was settin' there by him on the springboard. *We'd be pleased to have you.*

That's mighty good of you to offer. I'd be much obliged. I grinned. *This here big dog has et me out of house and home.* Him and her laughed at that, the idea that this little dog could eat anybody out of house and home. *Are you for sure it's all right?*

He nodded. *It's all right.* He started up his team and we follered. It was maybe a hour and the wagon train pulled to a stop at a wide place in the road. I seen there was maybe five or six wagons. There was a lot of bustle when they stopped. It looked like they all knowed what to do.

HUGHLETT L. MORRIS

First thing I knowed there was a big fire built and the rabbits on a put together spit. Like he said, the boys had been lucky. They had maybe ten rabbits cookin' in no time. I said my howdys to everybody. They all made over Buster, more the women and the youngun's than the men. They had a few dogs with 'em. One of 'em was of right good size and right away started in to try to hump Buster. She acted like she didn't know what it was all about and come to me as fast as she could trot. I picked her up and 'til a boy come and got the dog and tied him up to their wagon, I guess. It warn't his fault. He was just doin' what a dog does around a bitch.

After all these years, I still recollect the smell of them rabbits cookin' and the taste of 'em. As Preacher would of said, it was manna from Heaven. When I seen there was goin' to be enough to go around, I gave Buster a bite now and then. She gulped 'em up like she'd been starvin' for a week. They camped there for the night. Supper was leftover rabbit and cornmeal mush and some greens some of the women had picked from around the camp. I kept offerin' to help, but nobody took me up on it 'til one man ast if'n I knowed how to mend harness. I said I did and he set me to work on doin' that. I was proud to be able to help out.

It turned out they was from North C'lina, down south of the Virginny state line. It sounded like they'd crossed the mountains south of where we'd done it and they'd had a easy time of it. The lead man must of knowed about that afore they set out. They was as het up about goin' to Missouri as Henry and his people was.

But as far as I could tell, they didn't know any more about where they was goin' or what they was gettin' into than the others did. It seemed like they was all goin' by what somebody else had said. One of these men said he had a cousin and his family that had gone out last year. He said the land was for the takin' if'n you would farm it. And he said it was good farmin' land. Later on, when I got back to Stewart County, I heard a man say the same thing but the land he was talkin' about was to the north and the west of Missoury.

Anyway, all that talk give me cause to think about goin' west, myself. But I knowed I wanted to farm. And I wanted to farm in Stewart County. The offer made to me by Mr. Cherry was real good. You recollect what he'd said. It was that if 'n I come home, and got Nadine to marry up with me, we could farm that Oakes place. Her and me figured we wanted to do that, and I told him so. But maybe he'd changed his mind since then. If 'n he had, I'd have to figure out somethin' else. Maybe I could farm with Uncle Gray and hire out as best I could. Anyway, Nadine would have a say so about goin' west. Maybe she wouldn't want to. I knowed from hearin' some of the women on the wagon trains talk, that leavin' their families behind was terrible hard for them to do.

So I kind of put the notion of goin' west to the back of my mind. One thing I should say here, talkin' about gettin' a piece of land to farm, I still had them three pieces of gold. I didn't know how far they would get me, but maybe they'd be a start. I'd never told anybody I had 'em, and I didn't know what they'd be worth. It would rest on what land in Stewart County was worth. Maybe any land worth farmin' would be already took.

They was headed to Clarksvul, as they called it, and I stayed with 'em all the way. I struck the same deal with them as I had with the other wagon train. I spelled the drivers and did any fixin' there was to do. I mended harness and worked on two of the wagons when they broke down. There warn't much scoutin' ahead to do, except for a time or two after a heavy rain and there was need to see if 'n the wagons could get through. I did some huntin' with the boys to keep us in fresh meat. I figured I was so close to home that there warn't any need to save the bullets. And I pitched in to buy supplies when we'd come to a store with some of what little money I had left.

Maybe I didn't earn my keep like I could of, but I did the best I could and what they'd let me do. It seemed like Buster earned her keep. She played with all the youngun's and the women made over her. It was a blessin' she didn't come into heat while we was with 'em. If 'n she had, their dogs would of given me a heap of trouble tryin' to keep 'em away from her. I pro'bly couldn't of done it and I'd of had pups on my hands before long.

I don't recollect how long it took us to get to Clarksville. Maybe it was up to two weeks. The weather was mostly good, with one or two stormy days. One day I recollect it rained all the live long day. We stopped and set up a pitiful camp and waited it out. Cold and wet, it made me think of the days like that when I was in the army. Havin' a wagon didn't mean you didn't get wet. Them canvas covers leaked like a milk strainer when they got soaked clean through.

Up 'til we got to Clarksville, the countryside was flat, not much hilly. There was some farms here and there. And we come to some little settlements, with a store and a mill, if'n there was a good size creek to run it. On to'ard Clarksville, it started to be more hilly, comin' down to the valleys of the Cumberland and the Red rivers. It looked more like Stewart County to me. I got in a real hurry to get there. A wagon train moves slow but I stuck with them 'til we got to the edge of town.

We parted company there. The lead driver said they was goin' on to'ard Dover to cross the Cumberland River again and then the Tennessee and then the Mississippi at a place called New Madrid in Missoury. That was what that man's cousin sent word for them to do. I was goin' that way, to'ard Dover, but they wanted to push on and I meant to stop. I wanted to see if'n I could find out anything about Aunt Polly's family and Ed, and the man named Willie Barnett, the man that give me the two gold pieces.

So we said our goodbyes at a store right by the Red River bridge. I waited around while they got their supplies. I gave the lead man a little money to pay for my keep. He didn't want to take it but I pressed him to. Then I went around and shook hands with 'em all, the women too. They'd all been good to me and Buster. The youngun's petted Buster for the last time, and they took off. I was right sorry to see 'em go.

I asked the storekeeper if'n he knowed anything about the Barrow family. That was the family name of Aunt Polly and Ed.

The last I knowed they had a store in Clarksville. He said he did. He said old Miz Barrow had sold her store and took sick last year and died. That'd be Ed's and Aunt Polly's mama. I asked him if'n he knowed the son Ed. He said he'd knowed there was a son but he'd heard the son had left when the War started and gone up north.

I asked him about Willie Barnett. He said everybody knowed Willie, and he told me where to go find his place of business. After lookin' around for it, I found it. It was a store front with his name on it. I went in, Buster follerin'. *Howdy.*

Howdy. What can I do for you?

Nothin', I guess. I come in to say howdy to you.

He looked hard at me. *I don't reckon I know you. Ought I to?*

Maybe. It's been nigh on to five year since you seen me.

He shook his head. *I'd be much obliged if'n you told me yore name and when I seen you last.*

The name's Luther Morris. This here is Buster. You seen me last right here in Clarksville at yore house. I rode with you into Clarksville one time you was drivin' a wagon in from Dover. It was right afore the war started.

He looked at me, his head cocked to one side, like he could see better that way. *Well, I'm damned! You're the young feller that rode with me that time and skeered off them hoodlums when we was on the Dover Pike!*

I laughed. *That's me all right. I didn't know what I was doin' but you and me together skeered 'em off.*

Well, I swan. I'd not never knowed you. Back then you was just a boy and here you a man. And he shook my hand and patted me on the back. *I'm real glad to see you again. Now that you tell me, I can see it's you, only older.* He laughed. *'Course I'm older, too.*

But you look the same as I recollect. I'd of knowed you anyway, even if'n yore name warn't on the store front. You and yore family got through the War all right?

We did that. It was touch and go there for a while. The Yankees took Clarksvul and it was a bad time. I guess not as bad as some towns that were took later on in the War. They come through here early on in the War and warn't in sich a need for supplies and livestock. So they was more easy on us. But some of the battles around here tore up the country here and to the south and 'tween here and Nashvul. The country around Franklin was tore up terrible, I hear tell. We made it through without gettin' hurt too bad. He stopped talkin' and motioned for me to foller him out back.

Out back was maybe four or five big wagons and a stable. I could see in some of the stalls in the stable and could tell they had mules in 'em. I kept an eye on Buster to be shore she didn't cause any trouble with the mules. She went out of the barn and I could see her set down by where Thunder was standin'. He looked around. *Folks in business hire me to do their haulin'. I started out just in Clarksvul, but now I take 'em to Dover and Springfield and all around. Next week I got a load to Kentucky.* He grinned. *Truth to tell, I don't do much of the liftin'. I got some young fellers to do that for me.* He looked at me, still grinnin'. *You lookin' for work?*

Not right now. I ain't even been to Bumpus Mills yet. I'm on my way there now. It sounds like yore business is doin' real good.

He nodded. *You got time to set a spell? There's a story to tell about the last time I seen you.* We went back in the store and set so he could see the door. He looked around to see if'n nobody was in ear shot. *You know what I had in that wagon?*

Maybe. You told me a little about it when we got to yore house. I was wonderin' if'n he recollected that he'd give me them two gold pieces. And I wondered what I'd say if'n he wanted 'em back. I figured I'd lie and say I didn't have 'em any more.

So you know there was gold in that wagon. They was gold pieces. They was the property of my wife's family. They'd put 'em in the bank safe over in Dover where they used to live. Her family lived over on the Cumberland River. I never knowed how they'd come to have the gold. I never ast and nobody told me.

Anyway, when the War broke out, she got nervous about havin' it over there and she begged me to go get it. I was skeered as all get out to do it, but she kept after me 'til I said I would. So she give the key to the lock box in the bank safe and I got it out without any trouble. The main worry I had was if 'n I'd have any trouble on the way back to Clarksvul, would anybody find out about what I was carryin'. That's where you come in handy.

He stopped talkin' and went outside to see if 'n anybody was around. *I ain't ever told anybody this next part of the story. But hit's all right I reckon to tell you on account of what you did to help me get it here.*

Anyway, I got it home and her and me dug a hole under the house and put it there. She said it was gonna come in handy. She's a right smart woman, she is. He fell quiet. *Well, we never told anybody about it. Fort Donelson fell and the Yankees come in. 'Bout that time, here comes her brother. He had a store in Dover. Afore he left Dover when Donelson fell, he went to the bank to get the gold pieces and they was gone. He figured she'd had a hand in it. Him and her had a big fight about it.*

I figured she'd give in. After all, he was her brother and family and all that. But she didn't, and he finally give up. Truth to tell, I felt kind of bad about it, but bein' that he was her brother, not mine, I didn't say anything. We ain't never heard from 'im since. We used the gold, or most of it, to start the haulin' business.

I didn't know what to say. It seemed queer that he was tellin' me, a stranger, all this about what his wife had done. Maybe he figured he needed to tell somebody and I was a safe bet. *It looks like you and her have a good business goin'.*

Yeah, me and her. It turns out she's got a real good head on her shoulders for business. He laughed, kind of. *She does the plannin' and I do the workin'.*

I thought maybe to change what we was talkin' about. *I recollect you had some younguns.*

He nodded. *You was here, we had two boys and a girl. A boy died of the fever in the War. T'other one works with me. The girl goes to school. Her mama wants her to do that. We got the money to pay for it.*

I stood up. *I better get goin'. Looks like you done well. It must of been hard, startin' up.* I thought to myself, maybe not so hard, with all that gold.

He stood up. *It was hard, all right. There was a lot of trouble at first. First off, it was that we was doin' haulin' for the Yankees. They was the ones with the money to pay. Then I had trouble gettin' men to work. All the young ones had gone to the War. So I started in hirin' colored men, payin' 'em like I would if 'n they was white. There's a lot of colored folks in Clarksvul, and the men was glad to be able to work. Well, some of the white folks here, the ones I wanted to hire me, was agin what I was doin'.*

They didn't like it that I was haulin' for the Yankees. And they shore as hell didn't want me to hire the colored men. We lost two wagons in a fire that must of been set. Three of our mules was cut so bad I had to put 'em down. Nobody would own up to doin' it. The law warn't no help. Nothin' bad has happened after that but some of the folks won't do business with me to this day.

He straightened his shoulders. *Now it's picked up and goin' real good. It's a wonder you caught me here. Tomorra I got a load to go up to Oak Grove, up to'ard Kentucky.* He laughed. *If 'n you'd come through here a year ago, I'd of hired you to ride shotgun for me on a load. Like you did afore. I was much obliged to you for doin' that.*

It worked out all right. You guessed, I figure, that I warn't even sixteen when that happened.

That so?

Yessir. I joined up when I was fifteen. That's what I was goin' to Clarksville to do. So if 'n them outlaws had pushed, I don't know if 'n I could of stopped 'em.

Well, I reckon you put up a good front. I can still see you with that old black hat pulled down almost over yore ears. He laughed, recollectin' how I must of looked, a boy actin' like a man.

I figured I better say somethin' about the pieces of gold. *You recollect you paid me well and good for doin' that?*

He nodded. *I recollect. I never told the missus about doin' that. It felt like the thing to do, and I'm not sorry a bit. If 'n you hadn't been along, she wouldn't of got any gold and her husband would be layin' in a ditch, dead.* He laughed again. *I recollect now where we put 'em!*

I nodded. *They stayed in the hem of that old coat for a long time in the War. Soldiers kept tellin' me to swap it in for a better one. But I wouldn't. They didn't know the worth of that old coat! It finally give out.*

You still got 'em?

One of 'em. I lied, not knowin' if'n he meant to try to get 'em back. If'n he did, I meant to put up a real good fight about it.

But he didn't. *That's real good. It'll give you a head start when you get home.* We went on out. Buster was settin' there by Thunder. *Whoee, where'd you get that big dog? Ain't she a fine 'on.* And he leaned over and petted her.

Willie, it's a long story. I got to get goin', so I'll save it for another day. We shook hands, and me and Buster got on Thunder and rode away. I recollect thinkin' as I rode back across the Red off to'ard Dover that was some story he had to tell. And, I guessed, it was some wife he had, fendin' off her brother to keep the gold for herself.

As for Willie, there must have been a lot of talk around town about where their gold had come from. For sure, there'd be that kind of talk when he started in to deal with the Yankees and hirin' the coloreds. Truth to tell, I liked to talk to the man. I figured that if'n I ever got back to Clarksville, I'd stop in on him. It turned out in some years to come I went back to Clarksville and I saw 'im again.

By the time I got away, it was near dinner time. I found a saloon that served vittles, so I et my fill there and give some to Buster and started off again. I figured it was more'n a day's ride to Bumpus Mills and I wanted to get there in good daylight. So I figured since I had a late start it'd mean two nights on the road. It turned out that way. That first night I didn't quite make it to Red Top but near so. When I made my camp, I recollected there was a family in Red Top Uncle Gray knowed, but I couldn't bring up their name.

Next mornin' it was hard for me to believe that after so long a time I was back in Stewart County. I didn't know 'xactly when I crossed over from Montgomery County. But after Red Top I could tell by the lay of the land. There was more timber and scrub. The pastures was green, with some cattle and horses here and there.

The turn off from the Dover Pike to the road down to Big Rock come up on me almost afore I saw it was there. There was a good size house at the crossroads. I asked if 'n I could stay the night there, and the woman said I could. So I had one more night to go at a boardin' house. Near sundown, a bunch of riders pulled up and they stayed the night. There warn't no saloon, so we set on the porch after supper, talkin' about this and that. They did the talkin' and I didn't have to. It was mostly about happenin's at Dover that I didn't know anything about. One of 'em liked old Buster and I had to tell the story of how I come to have her. I turned in early and was on the road just after we had our breakfast.

Now I was in a real fret to get there and I guess I run Thunder ragged. We come down by the crossroads above Big Rock. Then, on past maybe two mile was the road that went down the ridge along the S'lene Creek. I knowed where I was, and me and Thunder and Buster pulled up and stopped at Uncle Gray's house good season afore dinner.

A woman come out. *Howdy.*
Howdy.
What can I do for you?
Name's Luther Morris. Gray Morris is my uncle. Does he still live here?
She wiped her hands in her apron and held them out to me. *Oh my. You're Luther! We was lookin' for you but we didn't know when you'd get here. Where's my manners? Get off 'n yore horse and you and the little dog come on up on the porch. I'll go ring the bell for Gray.* Buster jumped down and I got down off of Thunder and tied him up. *I'm Gray's wife, name of Elizabeth. I guess you didn't know Gray was married again. No, of course you didn't. No way you could of. Don't mind me runnin' on like this. I'm just so taken aback. You set here on the porch and I'll go ring the bell for*

Gray. He will be real pleased to see you after so long. And she went around to the back of the house and I heard the bell ringin'.

I set down and Buster jumped up in my lap and I looked around. The place looked good. It looked like what it did when I left to go to War and all the time between when I tried to recollect it. The barn was over there. The spring house was on the other side. The fence around the lot looked like he'd kept it up good. Maybe the trees was taller. I could hear some pigs squealin'. I didn't have to wait long.

From around the corner here come Uncle Gray and Miz Elizabeth and a boy maybe ten years old. Uncle Gray held out his arms to me. *My God, it's good to see you!* He give me a big bear hug. Then he held me at arm's length. *You look real good.* He grinned. *Maybe a mite hairy!.*

I laughed. *Maybe. It's real good to see you. You look real good.* I grinned. *What's this about a woman?*

He laughed and turned to her. *This here's my wife, Elizabeth and our son Jake.* He turned back to me. *Elizabeth and Jake, this here's Luther Morris. He's my brother's boy. He's been to the War and now he's back.* We all said howdy and shook hands. Miz Elizabeth said she'd go get Sarah from the turnip patch and then they'd put dinner on the table.

She's a real purty woman.

He nodded, smiling. *She is that. And a good one, too. Her husband died of the fevers, about when you left to go to the War. Sam was still home then, but the house felt empty already. I knowed he'd go, soon as he could pass for sixteen. So I started in courtin' Elizabeth. We've been married a little less'n two years. She's real good to me.* He grinned, like he was a boy. *It's real good, holdin' a woman in my arms agin.* He looked at me, still grinnin'. *You now what I mean?*

I laughed at what he'd said. *I know what you mean.* I reached over and punched him on the shoulder like we used to do. *I'm real proud for you.*

Miz Elizabeth called time to come to the table. I told Buster to stay with Thunder. Sarah was tickled at the little dog settin' by the big horse. We went in to dinner. Inside the house looked like it allus did in some ways and then agin not. It looked like the rockin' chairs was the same, in front of the fireplace, but everything else looked differnt. In the same place as before, but differnt. The clock on the mantle piece didn't look like the one I knowed.

On inside, the kitchen looked the same and in the room where we et, the table and chairs looked the same but there was two pie safes, one from afore, one differnt. Miz Elizabeth asked Uncle Gray to say blessing as he allus did before. It sounded like the one Preacher said, up until the end when he said thanks for the soldier man comin' home from the war. I recollect wonderin' if'n all the blessin's was the same, everywhere in the world. It sounds silly I would of wondered that.

The dinner was real good and afterward there was dried apple pies. Miz Elizabeth said she was right sorry for havin' no coffee. She said it was still hard to get and she saved what she had for breakfast. Like I said, Jake was about twelve years old. Sarah looked maybe 16. She favored Josie so much I couldn't hardly keep from lookin' at her.

Settin' at the table, I thought how real good it was to be there with some family. I shore didn't want to go travelin' again. After Uncle Gray and me went about the chores, takin' Buster along. The farm and the livestock looked real good and I told him so. He said he'd been havin' some help from Sam. *Where is Sam? When am I goin' to see him?*

Yeah, you'll see him. He stayed here for a while after he got home from the War. He slept in the barn. Elizabeth didn't feel right about him sleepin' in the room with Sarah. He looked at me. *She'll feel uneasy about you bein' in there, too.*

I nodded. *Sarah is a right purty girl. You want me to sleep in the barn tonight?*

He shook his head. *I asked Elizabeth a while ago. She said no need to. Truth is, Sam and Sarah was kind of stuck on each other. Anybody could see that. Him and me talked about it and I said it best if'n he stayed som'ers else. He could see that. He's over at the Taylors. Billy didn't come home from the War and Miz Taylor needed the help. So he's livin' over there. He comes to see Sarah now and agin, but they ain't courtin'. At least he ain't asked her mama and me if'n he could. You'll want to ride over and see him. Maybe tomorra.*

He looked at me, kind of sideways. *You thinkin' of goin' over to the Cherry place in the mornin'?*

I nodded, wonderin' why he was lookin' at me that way. *I thought I would, yessir. They all right over there?*

Tolerable. Miz Cherry ain't been feelin' so good since the middle of the summer. Nadine and Narcissa been takin' care of her and the house. Nadine's just as purty as ever. You won't know Narcissa. She's growed up to be as purty as her sister.

We were done feedin' and were leanin' on the fence to the lot. *While we're doin' some talkin', you and me, let me tell you what Elizabeth and me have been thinkin' about. I ain't told you yet, but all the folks over at my mother's house is dead. Tobe went first, then Cele and Mama. They died a day apart. It seemed like one couldn't get along without the other. It happened over a year ago. The house is empty. I just left everything in it like it was. I asked Sam when he come home if'n he wanted to live there, and he said no. When the chancet come up to go to the Taylor house, he wanted to do that. So, I figured maybe you'd want to live there when you come home.*

He looked over down to'ard the pond. *'Course, I didn't know if'n you was gonna come home, 'til we got yore letter.* He looked back at me. I could see his eyes shinin' like they was teared up. *So now, you are shore enough back. Maybe you want to live over there? Elizabeth thinks that'd be a good idy, if'n you're willin'.* I could see that me bein' over there would save me from sleepin' in the same room as Sarah and elsewise sleepin' in the barn.

I nodded. *That sounds real good to me. It'd give me a place to stay while I figure out what I'm goin' to do next. Can I move in right now or does it need some work done on it?*

I figure you can move right in. Last time I was there, it looked all right to me. The roof don't leak, as far as I could tell. The cook stove and the fireplace was drawin' all right, last I knowed. One

*thing. The old bed Cele and Tobe was sleepin' in is fallin' down.
The straw tick and the feather bed is still good, I figure, but the
rails and the slats are near all broke through. Mama's bed is still
good.*

*But I got a idy for you to hear. Maybe you don't recollect it, but
when yore mama left for good, she had me and some of the boys put
her bed and a table and a dresser up in the loft of the barn at
mama's place. My mother allus claimed that our daddy was borned
in that bed. I know for a fact that yore daddy and me was. I ain't
looked in the last year, but I 'spect they're still there. Like we feared,
some Yankees come through in the War. Word was that they tore up
some places bad this side of the Cumberland. It was said they was
burnin' houses and barns. We knowed they was comin' this way. I
tried to get my mother to bring Cele and Tobe over here, but she
wouldn't do it. She said if'n she warn't there, they'd burn the place
down. I guess maybe she was right.*

*Anyway, her story was that some Yankee soldiers come and she
told 'em she'd feed 'em and then they have to leave her alone. She
said her and Cele got out their old guns and scared the Yankees
away.* He was laughing and shaking his head. *I don't doubt it for a
minute. Her and Cele with their old guns would scare anybody
away. All I know is that the Yankees was gone by the time I got
there. And they never come to my place.* He turned and looked at
me. *You recollect much about her?*

I shook my head. *Not much. Speakin' of scarin' people off, she
allus scared the pants off'n me!*

He laughed. *You ain't the only one that felt that way. My
mama was a fearsome woman. She was a good mother to me and
yore daddy but she never cottoned much to Polly or yore mother. I
never figured out why. As far as that is, when I got to be a man, I
never figured out what our daddy seen in her. Maybe she was a lot
differnt when they was young.* He shook his head. *It ain't no matter
now. I figured her and Cele and Tobe had as good a life as they
could of in their last years. I'm real glad she had them to live out
her years with. Nobody else could of put up with her. Anyway, her*

place come to me when she died. I hate it to set there empty. I'd be right pleased if'n you'd live there.

You shore it's all right with Sam?

He said he didn't want to live there by hisself. Maybe with you there, he'll change his mind, but I wouldn't count on it, if'n I was you. Maybe you better ask 'im yoreself.

All right. If'n he don't mind, can we figure it's settled?

We can figure it's settled. And we shook hands on it.

If'n it's all right with Miz Elizabeth, I'll stay here the night and then go over there to stay on the morrow.

She'll say that's fine. Afore you go, I need to say to you again that I'm real glad to have to back. He was grinnin'. *Aside from needin' a haircut you look real good. You ain't changed all that much. I'd of knowed you anywhere, 'cept maybe for them chin whiskers.* And like I was a boy again, he reached over and give me a big bear hug. I figured I was home in Stewart County.

He let me go and we started back to the house. *I figure I'll go over to the house after I go to the Cherry place.*

He nodded. *I reckoned you'd want to do that.*

Can I get in the house?

Yep. I've barred the front and the back doors, but I left that side door unlatched. You recollect where it is? It's over on the side where Cele's shack is.

I nodded. *I'll find it.*

Well, that night I slept in the bed with Jake in the side room where Sam and me had allus slept. Sarah went in first, them Jake and me. I kept on my drawers so's not to take the chancet of offendin' Sarah. Next mornin' at breakfast, we had some of Miz Elizabeth's coffee. I bragged on it and told her how much I thought about coffee when I was in the War. And I had two dried apple pies. She was real tickled about that. Then I went to the barn and saddled up Thunder and rode him out to where Uncle Gray was standin'. Buster was standin' there, waggin' her tail, ready to go. Sarah had come out of the house. *Sarah, you want to have a big dog?*

She laughed. *I might as well. We ain't had a dog for a long time, not since Daddy died.* She stooped down. *Buster, go to see Sarah.* Buster looked at me and at Sarah and at me and at Sarah. *Go on, go see Sarah.* And that little dog did. I was real glad to see her do that. I figured I didn't need no dog where I was goin' visitin'.

Uncle Gray was standin' there, watchin' all this. He looked Thunder over. *That shore is a good lookin' horse you got there. Best I've seen in many a day.*

He's a good 'un, for sure. I'll tell you how I got 'im some day. Him, and the little red mare you give me. And a old mule I called Ole Mule, that saved my life. I been real lucky with mules and horses. I'll see you at supper time.

The Cherry place was maybe four miles away. It looked like how I recollected it. It allus was a real purty place with more trees around it than some houses I knowed of. The house was bigger than Uncle Gray's. It was a fact that the Cherrys was good farmers. Uncle Gray said they had been ever since he knowed them. They allus had a big garden and a big tater patch and more cows than they could milk. Mr. Cherry was in the barn lot. *Howdy.*

Howdy. He come up closer to me and I could see him squint his eyes. *Gol dang, Luther Morris, is that you?*

It's me, all right. I got in yestiday, stayed last night at Uncle Gray's.

How is him and his family?

They're in good shape. I was proud to meet Miz Elizabeth.

She's a good woman. He's lucky to get her. Well, get down off of that horse! I did. He come over and rubbed Thunder on the flank. *That's a good lookin' horse you got there. What's his name?*

Name's Thunder. I got him in North C'lina, where I've been. I got real sick with the fevers and like to of died. A family found me and took me in. I stayed with them for a while. That's why I'm so long gettin' back to Stewart County.

Gray told Nadine about yore letter. He shook his head. *We figured we'd never hear from you again. We figured you'd been kilt in the War.*

I can see why anybody would think that. I'd of writ sooner but I didn't have anybody to do it for me.

I figured that, when we got yore letter. Tie up yore horse and come on in the house. Nadine must of heard us talkin' and she come out on the porch afore I got there. *Nadine, honey, look who's here!* He started up on the porch. *I'll leave you be. Luther, I'm real glad to see you. Don't be a stranger around here.* And he went on in the house.

Luther, you've got here!

It's me all right. We stood there, lookin' at each other. It warn't exactly the kind of homecomin' with her I'd looked for, but I figured four years was a long time. *You're just as purty as ever. Can I give you a kiss?*

She nodded, and turned her head for me to kiss her cheek. *We didn't know when to look for you.* And she drawed back.

I grinned. *I was too busy comin'. I'm real glad to see you.*

I'm real glad to see you too. But the way she said it I couldn't tell if'n she meant it. *My hair's a mess.* She smoothed her purty reddish brown hair with her hand. *I been workin' in the kitchen and my apron's all dirty from makin' cornbread.*

I bet you make good cornbread. I wondered why we was talkin' about cornbread.

Daddy says I do. Me and Narcissa do the cookin' since Mama's been porely.

Is she bad sick?

I don't rightly know. She says she ain't hurtin bad anywhere. She says she just feels weak in the knees. She smiled. *I'm feelin' weak in the knees, seein' you.* That's more like it, I thought to myself. *Lordy, where are my manners? Come on in the house. Mama and Narcissa will want to see you. You won't know Narcissa. She's growed up while you was gone.* She took my hand and led me in the house. *Mama, Narcissa, look who's here. This here's Luther, come home from the War to Stewart County.*

Miz Cherry was settin' in the rockin' chair in front of the fire. I could see she was wrapped up in a quilt where she set. There warn't much light to see by, but I could see her well enough to know her. Narcissa was standin' behind her chair, off to the side. Miz Cherry turned in her chair and held out her hand. *Oh my, is that you, Luther? Hit looks like you left a boy and come back a man. It's real good to see you. Here. Set by me in front of the fire.*

It's real good to see you, Miz Cherry, but Nadine says you're feelin' porely

I shore am. I don't know what's the matter with me. It's been a month, maybe more, since I've had any get up and go. My mama used to say, weak as dish water, that's how I am, weak as dish water. I don't know what we'd do if'n we didn't have our girls to help out. And she reached out and took Narcissa's hand. *They're both real good around the house. Narcissa here is takin' hold real good, now that Nadine's leavin' me.*

And she reached out and pulled Nadine closer to her by her skirt tail. What's that all about, I wondered. Does she figure Nadine and me are gonna be married real quick? I shore hoped not. I figured I warn't ready to do that so fast after just comin' home. She turned back to me where I was settin. *Well, you been gone a long time. We figured you'd been kilt in the War like Billy Taylor.*

Yessum. I'm real sorry to hear about Billy.

She went on like she hadn't heard what I'd said. *We didn't know what to think. Then Gray got yore letter. You should of writ sooner. We thought you'd been kilt.*

Yessum. I'm real sorry about that.

Afore I could say anything else, she started in again. *You'll have to tell us where all you've been.*

Mama, let's don't make him do that right now. We have to get dinner ready.

Narcissa spoke up. *I'm goin' to the garden for some greens.* I looked up at her. It was still hard to see, but it looked like she had her hair tied up in a rag like Betty Lou used to, with some sprigs escapin' at the edges. Her voice was strong, like Miz Collins' was. When she left the room, I could see that she was as tall as me, taller'n Nadine.

I'm takin' Luther with me to the springhouse to get the sweet milk and the butter for dinner. You'll be all right 'til Narcissa gets back. Maybe we'll get back first, I don't know. Daddy's out back.

Miz Cherry nodded. *You go ahead. You got a lot to talk about, him bein' gone so long. I'll be all right, settin' here by the fire.* When she said that last part, I wondered if'n she was making a play for sympathy, as Aunt Polly would say.

When we get back, mama, maybe you can show him yore quiltin'. She turned to me. *Mama is real good at quiltin'.* Afore anythin' else could be said, she took my hand and led me out the back way to to'ard the spring house.

It seemed like we didn't know what to say or how to start talkin'. We was quiet on our way out there but kept lookin' at each other sideways as we walked. It was a right cool day and she pulled her shawl closer around her. Then we both started to talk at the same time. *Nadine, I'm real glad to see you. Where are you stayin'?* Talkin' at the same time broke the ice, and we started to laugh.

Let me go first. I'm real glad to see you. I've thought about seein' you for a long time, knowin' you was growin' to be a woman. Now that I'm here I don't rightly know what to say or where to start.

She nodded. *I know what you mean. You look so differnt from what I recollect. I don't know if'n I would of knowed you if'n I'd seen you at the store. Yore face is all brown. You been workin' in the field? And you growed them chin whiskers! You don't hardly look like the feller that went off to the War.*

We set down on the log by the spring house. I recollect thinkin' I was allus settin' on a log by some spring house. *For sure, I reckon I don't look much the same. I was just a boy when I left you that day we said our goodbyes. A lot has happened to me since then. I'll tell you about it, if'n you want to hear about it. I may not be good at the tellin' of it. Some of it I ain't never told nobody. Maybe I've been savin' it up to tell you.*

She smiled at me and I figured I was makin' some headway with her. *You look the same and you don't. When I left, you was a girl and I can tell now you're a woman.* We was lookin' at each other. I took her hand. *Can I kiss you again?*

She nodded that I could. I moved closer to her and took her in my arms, proper like. She held her face up to me and I kissed

334   HUGHLETT L. MORRIS

her on the mouth. First off, it was a short kiss. Then I pulled back and looked at her and give her a long kiss, like we was tryin' to get our mouths as close as we could. I felt myself getting hard in my pants. She pulled away. *I ain't never been kissed like that afore.*

I been savin' it up for you. I was still holdin' her hand. *Can I do it again?*

She shook her head, and got up and went in the spring house and brung out the milk pail and the butter pan. And she set down on the log again, but not so close to me. She set the pail and the pan down in front of her, and she was studyin' them like she'd never seen them afore. *It'd be better if'n you didn't kiss me again.*

What's that mean?

Then she looked up at me. *A lot has happened while you was gone.*

You mean yore mama bein' sick?

That too. But Narcissa is here to help with her. No, the main thing I have to tell you is about LeRoy Campbell.

LeRoy Campbell? Who's he? And the minute I asked that, I knowed there was trouble ahead.

She straightened her dress tail, and looked down at it. *He's the man I aim to marry up with.* And she looked up at me.

I was real set back at that. I expected trouble, but nothin' like that. *You got some man you mean to marry? You didn't wait for me like you said you would?*

No, I guess I didn't. I know I said I would. Her words come tumblin' out. *That was five years ago. I was just a girl and I didn't know what I was sayin'. Afore yore letter, we figured you was kilt in the War and warn't ever comin' back. Mama said I'd best forget about you. She said I'd best be thinkin' about another man. She said I was the marryin' age and I'd best be careful or I'd end up a old maid. I could see the truth in what she said.* She was quiet. *Can you see that?*

My old head was spinnin'. *It don't seem right to me, but I can see why she said it. You all was thinkin' I was kilt and never comin' back.*

She nodded. *That's what she kept tellin' me. I could see the truth in it. So when LeRoy come courtin', I said I'd let 'im. Him and me hit it off right away. We aim to be married in a month.* She looked at me again. *Him and me had got together afore I knowed you was comin' back. I thought you was dead. Can you see that?*

My old head was spinnin'. *I guess I can. Is he a good man?*

She nodded. *He's a good man. Him and me get along real good.* She giggled. *Truth to tell, he ain't as good a kisser as you, but I'm workin' on it.*

I had to laugh at that with her. Nobody ever told me I was a good kisser. But then I hadn't of kissed all that many women. I thought to myself right then that I must not be in too bad a way if'n I can laugh at somethin' like that. But I had to ask one more question. *Ain't there any chance for me?*

She come back right away with her answer. *No, there ain't any chance for you. The weddin' set for a month, over in Dover. Mama and Daddy like him. Narcissa will see to Mama after I'm gone.* She looked down at the milk jug. *One part of me is real sorry. But I like LeRoy a lot. Him and me is good together.*

I stood up. *Well, I guess that's that, ain't it?*

She nodded. *Yes, like you say, that's that.*

I turned and walked back to'ard the lot where Thunder was tied. I could hear her walkin' behind me, but there warn't anythin' else to say. I could hear by her footsteps that she turned off and went around behind the house. Mr. Cherry and Narcissa was standin' in the porch.

We nodded to each other and I stopped in front of them. *I take it by the way you look that Nadine has told you about her and LeRoy Campbell.*

Yessir, she did.

I ask you not to be too hard on her. She figured you was dead and she had to think about what she was goin' to do.

No sir, I don't mean to be too hard on her. It'll take me some time to get used to it. I thought about her a lot all these years, that's for sure. In a War, a man's got to have somethin' to hang on to.

Elsewise, he'll go crazy. I tried to laugh. *But it shore ain't the homecomin' I was lookin' forward to.*

He nodded. *I can see how that'd be.* He stepped down off the porch to stand in front of me. *But look here, we don't want you to be a stranger around this place. Nadine's soon to be gone, but the Missus and me and Narcissa want to see yore ugly face from time to time. While we're talkin', I better tell you that I shore could use some help farmin'. So come around and talk to me when you get settled. Stay for dinner. Narcissa here makes some real good dried apple pies*

I looked up at her, standin' above me on the porch. She smiled, like she knowed somethin' I didn't. *They may not be as good as Nadine's, but Daddy likes 'em just as well.* I guess I muttered somethin' to him and her about not stayin' for dinner, and bein' shore to come back, and got on Thunder and rode away.

After I left the Cherry place, I rode around some. The roads was all the same as ever and I recollected where I was and which way I was headed. Thunder wanted to gallop, so I give him his head, just settin' there, feelin' him run. We'd come to a crossroad and I'd nudge him which way to go and he wouldn't even break stride. We cut over to the creek, down the creek to the Mill, and on into Kentucky, just ridin' and thinkin'.

First off, I figured my heart was near broke, as Aunt Polly would say. I had this picture in my mind when I was at the War, and on my way back, of Nadine and her waitin' for me. Now that picture was dashed to bits, like a dish that fell on the floor.

On the one hand, I couldn't see why she couldn't of waited a little longer for me to come home, to be shore I was dead.

On the other hand, well, she was right. It looked for all the world to her like I was dead and warn't comin' back so she better get on with her life. Gettin' on with her life turned out to be with this here LeRoy Campbell feller. I thought back over it. Truth to tell, I could of writ a letter to her from the Wood place.

Shorely somebody there knowed how to do it, if'n I had asked. But I didn't.

We went some miles into Kentucky and I turned Thunder around. At the rate he was goin', we'd be to the Mississippi River afore I knowed it.

The more I thought about it, the more I settled down. Truth to tell, I didn't even know how I felt about Nadine. I was 15 last I seen her. She was 13. You can't bank on feelin's from back then. All I'd done here was kiss her. I liked it and I figured she did too, but you can't bank on a kiss just like that. Thinkin' about it, I figured I'd made a picture in my head of what her and me would be when I got back to Stewart County.

I guessed now the picture was only in my head. Dulciemay and Maybelle and Josie and Julia and Beulah Gates hadn't been no pictures. They was real and I knowed more about them than I knowed about Nadine. Even if'n she hadn't been promised to LeRoy Campbell, I'd of had to get to know her as we are now, I thought, and not 13 and 15.

By the time I got to the Mill, I was restin' a lot more easy about the whole thing. It hit me that all the time I was on the road after Richmond my aim was to get back to Stewart County. Lookin' at it fair and square, it warn't so much to get back to Nadine. My pride was hurt by her goin' to marry this LeRoy Campbell, but Aunt Polly would of said, pride can take you for a fall.

I rode up to Uncle Gray's house and tended to Thunder, takin' off his saddle, givin' him a good rubdown. Then I took 'im to the pond for a drink and back to the lot, give him some corn, and turned 'im loose. Buster was no where around. She'd taken to Sarah and Miz Elizabeth, and I figured I'd lost my dog for sure. I knocked on the door and went in.

Uncle Gray was settin' in front of the fire mendin' harness. I took up two pieces and started in splicin', not sayin' a word. Miz Elizabeth come in from the kitchen when she heard me. She stood there in the doorway, watchin' us. Uncle Gray looked over at me. *You been to the Cherry place?*

Yessir.

I seen them look at each other. Miz Elizabeth was the first one to talk. *You get to talk to Nadine?*

Yessum, I did. She told me about her and LeRoy Campbell.

I'm real sorry about that. She's a right good young woman.

Yessum, I guess so.

Uncle Gray spoke up. *We all thought you was dead afore we got yore letter.*

Miz Elizabeth took it up again. *It was too late by then. Her and LeRoy already loved each other. When we got yore letter, she come over here to see us and looked at it. That was the first we knowed you was alive.*

I put down the harness I was mendin'. *I can see that. There ain't nobody to lay the blame on. I was on the way back to Stewart County. You all thought I was dead. Nadine had to get on with her life the best she could.* I shrugged my shoulders. *So that's the end of that. I wish her and LeRoy Campbell a good life.*

Well, you set there by Gray. I'm fixin' to put dinner on the table. You want to stay and eat with us.

I put the harness I was mendin' down. *I thankee. I'll not stay, but I'll take some corn pone and fried meat, if'n you can spare it. I'll go on over to the other house.* She went to get it.

You feel all right? You want me to go over to the house with you?

Naw, ain't no need to. I'm all right. I just need to be by myself some. I took the vittles from Miz Elizabeth and thanked her for 'em. *If'n it's all right with you, I'll be back here tonight to sleep with Jake agin. I'm goin' now to the other house to look at it and tomorra I'll go over there to stay.*

You're welcome to do that. Gray here will be pleased to have somebody over there. He's been worried about the place, it bein' empty.

When I got to Grandmama's place I could see that it was kind of run down. The house and the little barn looked good. There wouldn't be much needed there. But the fence around the lot was broke down here and there. Without no cattle around, the weeds was maybe waist high. The door to the hen house was swingin' on one hinge, and I didn't see no sign of any chicken. The only chair on the front porch was halfway come apart. The paths and the wood pile was all growed up with weeds. It'd take some work to get it to look any good again.

The door to the shack where Cele and Tom had lived when I was a boy was hangin' open. Tobe must of died some time ago or maybe he'd gotten old and crippled so's he couldn't fix it.

Standin' there, it seemed like I couldn't recollect much about Tobe. Him and me allus said our howdys but we didn't say much more'n that. He was allus busy around the place. At that time there warn't much farmin' to do. It was mostly in the garden and the tater patch. I couldn't even recollect much about how he looked, 'cept he was real light and had a head of kinky hair. He allus called me Massa, even when I was a little boy.

I tried to recollect Cele, and I could see her face better'n his. She was darker in color than him. I guess her hair was kinky too but I never saw it much. She allus had a rag tied around her head. It seemed like her and Granny at Dulciemay's place favored. It was down right peculiar, I thought then, I never looked much at colored people's face 'til I was with Dulciemay and Granny.

Now, years later, if'n I could draw, I bet I could draw their faces with their dark color of skin, and the brown black eyes, and their teeth showin' against the dark skin when they smiled. Both of the women was snaggle toothed, Granny worse than Dulciemay, since she was older, I guess. But when they smiled at me, I didn't see where the teeth was gone, only the ones that was there. But, back then, and still now, lots of folks are snaggle toothed. I've lost a few myself.

That shack looked awful pitiful to me. I stood there, wonderin' why they didn't have a better place to live. Maybe my grandmama didn't see how bad their shack was, or maybe she didn't pay it no mind. But she must of knowed how much she depended on them to live there, more as her and them got old. If'n she didn't have them, she couldn't of lived there by herself and would of had to move in with Uncle Gray. I knowed she wouldn't of wanted to do that. Uncle Gray wouldn't of wanted it either.

I stood there feelin' the cold and thinkin' it would of been real cold in this shack on a day like this. I didn't go in, just stood there lookin' at it, wonderin'.

Like Uncle Gray said, the side door to the main house warn't barred and I got in wiithout any trouble. It come to me when I went in that I couldn't recollect much about my grandmama's house. Maybe I didn't go there much. Anyway, when I got in, I could see that the layout warn't like the others.

Her house only had three rooms. There was a front room and a kitchen to the back and a side room of not much size. The side room had a bed in it, but looked like a store room. The kitchen looked real good. It was bigger'n Uncle Gray's, with a cook stove, and a meal chest and a pie safe and some shelves somebody had put up. The table was good size and there was four chairs around it. There was a door to the front room and it closed good and tight.

It looked to me like I could live mostly in the kitchen, goin' to the front room just to sleep. That way, I wouldn't have to fool with havin' a fire in the fireplace. No need to. Everything in the kitchen looked passable, but the old table. It was rickety and looked like it would fall with just a dish on it.

Like Uncle Gray said, the bedstead in the front room was fallin' down. Maybe she slept in the side room. The bed in there was still standin' all right. Maybe after Tobe died, Cele slept in the big house. Maybe the two women slept in the same bed. That was a right funny thing to think about. But I'd allus heard that old people slept cold, so why not?

Standin' there, thinkin' about that, I wisht I knowed more about Cele and Tobe. Somebody told me oncet they was slaves give to Grandmama Morris by her mama when she married Granddaddy Morris. That was a long time ago when I was a boy I was told that, and I reckon I didn't know then what that meant.

Fact is, I never thought much about slavin' one way or the other 'til I was in the War. You'd of thought I'd of wondered what them colored people was doin' on this place and how they come to be there. But I didn't. Stewart County, best I say this part of Stewart County, never had any colored people that I knowed about.

Anyway, I'll go on with the story about Grandmama's house and me movin' in. The next day Sam and me moved them pieces of furniture down from the barn loft, where they'd been put when our mama had left to go to Kentucky with Mr. Fritzell.

We took down the old bedstead in the front room and carried it and the old table from the kitchen out back of the hen house. Then we put the other table in the kitchen. It fit in there real good. The bedstead and the dresser from the loft went in the front room. It didn't look like there was any harm done to any of 'em, except one of the spindles on the headboard was gone. I'd have to beg some tickin' for a straw mattress and a feather bed from somewheres. Maybe Miz Elizabeth or Miz Taylor had a spare. We got the movin' and the settin' up done and stood there lookin' at it all. *You recollect where we lived when our daddy died?*

Naw, I don't. I don't recollect the place or any of them pieces of furniture. My earliest recollection is in Uncle Gray's house.

Him and Aunt Polly was real good to us, warn't they?

Yep, they shore was. It was a good thing they was there. Elsewise, I don't know where you and me would of gone. I nodded to'ards the bedstead. *This here furniture is as much yore's as mine. You tell me if'n you want any of it. For that matter, you tell me if'n you want to move in here.*

He nodded. *I'll do that, but right now, I cain't forsee doin' it. I'm likin' it at Miz Taylor's and she says she needs me.*

I looked at him. If'n I looked at him hard, I could see some of the brother I had left when I went off to War. But he'd changed a lot in looks, o' course. I knowed I had too. *We ain't had much time to talk together. I hope we can sometime. Maybe you want to tell me about bein' in the Yankee prison?*

Maybe. I don't like to think about it, much less talk about it. He stood up. *I got to go. Maybe I'll come over in a few days, see how you're settlin' in.*

I hope you'll do that.

He stopped at the door and turned back to me. *Are you all right in yore head about Nadine?*

I guess so. I guess I ain't got much of a choice. I'm obliged for you're askin'.

He nodded. *Maybe that's what a brother is for.* Right then, with him lookin' at me, I could see what I recollected of his face as a boy. And he went out the door.

I spent the night for the first time in that house. And I stayed there for some years, by myself, and after Narcissa and me was married. Fact is, we lived there 'til we moved to the place that was Mr. Cherry's. I come to like Grandmama's house a lot. I can still feel how good the kitchen was, with the cookin' stove keepin' it warm.

The winder looked out the back to some timber and I loved to watch the squirrels play around and the birds come and go. Narcissa said she allus liked the house too. 'Course when the babies started to come, we needed a bigger house. That was when we moved to her daddy's farm he let us live at.

My comin' home and movin' into the little house happened around Christmas time and the first of the new year. The new year was 1867. It was a good year. I worked like a dog. I got the Morris place all cleaned up, fences mended and all that. I even fixed up Cele's shack for a store room. Uncle Gray give me two cows and some chickens and two little pigs. I put in a good garden and a tater patch and a patch of corn.

Spring come early and stayed late, with a lot of good rain. The spring run good and the little pond filled up to the banks. It was a good farmin' year. The pastures all around made good hay. We got two cuttin's easy on all of 'em, and a third cuttin' on two of 'em. I worked with Uncle Gray when he needed me and I hired out for Mr. Cherry and at a place around there and about to make some money.

But what money I made that way warn't much. Times was hard that year, even if'n the crops was good. Nobody had any money much. The Confederate money was long gone. The Federal money was long in comin' and what there was, was hard to get ahold of. If'n you had some calves to sell, nobody had the money to buy 'em. Takin' 'em to Clarksville to sell was real hard to do 'less'n you drove 'em all the way. Most folks had to do swappin' of what you had for what you wanted. That had allus been the case, I guess, for folks livin' in the country.

You took a bushel of corn to the mill to have it ground by the miller and you got back a tow sack of meal less'n his share. He'd then swap his share of yore meal for somethin' him and his family needed. Somebody didn't have hogs swapped some sorg'um 'lasses they'd made for some side meat.

People in this part of the country have been doin' that kind of tradin' for a long time. But the thing was, afore I went to the War, somebody allus had a little money. Now there warn't hardly none to be had. Salt was the hardest to come by. That and coffee. O' course you could get by without coffee, but everybody knows yore body needs the salt.

The store keeper got so he wouldn't hardly trade for salt 'cept when he knowed it was a hardship case. What you had to do was tend the best garden you could and depend on chickens for meat and eggs, and maybe try to kill a hog in the fall when it turned cold. Then the meat had to be smoked good, so's it wouldn't turn rancid. In the War weun's had all the rancid meat we could swallow for a long time.

My money from the road home was near gone. There was only a little left. I wouldn't let Uncle Gray pay me. He was havin' a hard time just like everybody else. And Mr. Cherry, good farmer that he was, didn't have any money to spare. I took supplies from him instead of money for my work. I did the same for the farmers I hired out to.

Well, sir, you recollect that I had the three pieces of gold and that gold ring. Two of them gold pieces come from Charlie Barnett. The other one and the gold ring come from the old man Zeke. My aim was to use that gold to help me buy a farm.

But there warn't any worth much for sale. In the meantime, I had to get by. So round about early spring, I took one of them gold pieces and went to the store at the Mill. *Howdy.*

Howdy, Luther. How you getting' along?

I'm doin' tol'able well, thankee. It's real good to be back in Stewart County. Uncle Gray says I can live at his mama's place and that's workin' out real good.

I hear you're doin' some hirin' out, too.

Yessir, when a body needs me.

You need some supplies?

Yessir, I do. I looked around. There warn't anybody else in the store. *I want to strike a deal with you.*

He nodded. *What kind of a deal you got in mind?*

I took the gold piece out'n the pouch I was carryin' it in, and held it in my hand for him to see. *This is what I got in mind.* I handed it to him. *You want to see if'n it's the real thing?*

He nodded, and held it up to the light comin' in through the winder in the store. After a little while lookin' at it and turnin' it over and lookin' at it again, he handed it back to me. *It's the real thing, all right. Can I ask you, where in the tarnation did you get it, a soldier in the War.* He laughed. *Maybe you don't want to tell me. Maybe you stole it from a Yankee!*

Nope, I didn't get it that way, though some did. But I'll tell you. A feller give it to me one time for helpin' him out of a tight place with some men set on robbin' him. You could say I got it fair and square. I played with the gold piece, holdin' it so's he could see it. I could tell by the way he was lookin' at it that he wanted it, and maybe wanted it bad.

What I've got in mind is to sell it to you to build up some credit in the store with you. You tell me what it's worth to you and that'll be my credit with you for supplies. I'll trade with you 'til I've used up all my credit.

He was quiet, lookin' at the piece of gold and at me and back again. *If'n you don't want to do it, I'll take it to Big Rock, maybe Dover, and see what I can get there.* I didn't want to do that. I knowed that the store at Big Rock warn't as big as his'n, so I wouldn't get as much credit. And Dover was too far away to be handy.

You got any more of 'em?

I shrugged, and put it back in the pouch. *You want to make a deal? If'n you do, name yore price.* I figured I had the upper hand. Likely, pieces of gold didn't come his way much and he could use it to good purpose in tradin' with peddlers that come through with goods. What with the mess about Federal money and Confederate money, gold was the real thing. Anybody would take gold. *You want to see it again?* And I took it out of the pouch again for him to see.

You ain't gonna tell me if'n you got more of 'em?

Maybe I have and maybe I haven't. But that ain't what's on the table here. You want it, name yore price. He named a price. It was way too low. I shook my head and put it back in the pouch. *Naw, Mr Phillips, that's too low, and you know it. I may look to you like a country boy, but I been all over, to North C'lina and Virginny, and I've got a real good notion of what this gold piece is worth.*

He stood there, lookin' at me and the pouch and back again. *I'll tell you what. I want to trade with you real bad. I figure you're a honest man. My family has traded with you since afore the War. I'll take twicet that price and you throw in the supplies I come in today for.*

He grinned. *You strike a hard bargain.*

Yessir, I do. But, like I said, I know how things is when it comes to gold pieces. I held out my hand. *You gonna take it?*

I'll take it. He held out his hand and we shook on it. *You know how to figure?*

Yessir, I do. I learned it in the War. You keep a set of figures and I'll keep one. I grinned. *That way, it'll keep us both honest.*

A while ago, I slipped up in my tellin' you the story and let it be known that it was Narcissa Cherry that I married. Maybe you already knowed that. I got to know Narcissa little by little. Like I said, she was eleven years old when I went to the War. Now she was sixteen and a whole diff'ernt person. I guess you'd say we come together natch'ral like. I'd see her at the Cherry place. Maybe I'd be at the barn and she'd come out to gather eggs. Maybe I'd see her go to the spring house and I'd go see if 'n I could help her carry the milk and butter to the house. I cain't recollect anything we talked about at first.

Not that she was what you'd call quiet. When she got to know you, she'd talk yore head off. She was right smart, too, even as a girl. She'd had some schoolin' while I was at the War. She could read 'most anything. She was good at numbers too. The time come I told her about the deal I'd made with Mr. Phillips at the store. She said that was real smart of me to do, and she helped me watch to see he did it right. After a while, I left it up to her.

So here she was 16 and I was 20. Our families was friendly with each other. I hired out to her daddy. One day I was over there and she was hangin' out the wash. I stood there, watchin' her, recollectin' how I had watched Betty Lou do it. I started out wishin' she was Betty Lou. Then I saw to myself I didn't want her to be Betty Lou or anybody else. So I went over.

Howdy. She stopped what she was doin' and looked at me. I saw that she was a right good lookin' woman. Her hair as a reddish brown and she had it cut shorter than other women like her mama and Miz Elizabeth or even Nadine. She had a rag tied around her head, keepin' her hair out of her eyes. Her eyes looked like they was maybe light brown or maybe dark blue, I couldn't tell which.

Fact is, I never could tell which. She used to tease me about not knowin' what color her eyes was. She was a middle size woman, not tall and not short. I couldn't tell right then about her bosums, but later on I saw they was full and womanly. *Can I help you do that?*

She grinned, and the grin made her eyes crinkle up. *Shore thing, if 'n you want to.* She giggled. *My daddy is always sayin' shore thing. He likes to talk country talk.* I handed her something to hang up. *Do you like to talk country talk?*

I figured I was in over my head. *I don't know if 'n I do or not. I guess I talk how I talk.* She reached for what I was handin' her and our hands touched. And inside I gave a start.

I like to hear you talk.

You do? Even if'n I talk country?

Yep. She grinned again. *Even if'n you talk country.* She was sayin' it as near like me as was possible.

I half way frowned. *You're raggin' me!* She laughed and held out her hand for something else. Our hands touched again and inside I got another start.

Well sir, that was the start of it. I knowed what was happenin' and she did too. When I et at the Cherry place somehow we'd set together. I'd watch for her and go to the spring house with her and go gather eggs with her. If'n I was at the barn, she'd come over and watch me and pass the time of day. We never talked about anything special but it seemed all right with us.

She was real easy to talk to. Sometimes I'd find myself talkin' about the War and what had happened to me there. She'd talk about folks around them parts and the schoolin' she'd had and when she was a little girl. Sometimes she'd bring a sausage biscuit and some fresh water and we'd set somewhere and eat and talk about whatever come to mind.

One day after maybe a month goin' on that way, she come to the barn with my dinner. I was up in the loft, pitchin' hay down for the cows. I stopped when she come over, down from where I was standin' *Howdy. You look mighty purty today.*

Thankee. I got yore dinner. Mine too. Whyn't you come on down. I got a question to ask you. I looked down at her. She warn't smilin' like usual, but she had on a straight face. I shinnied down the ladder and brushed off my hands and pants where the hay dust had stuck. We was standin' there, facin' each other. I could tell by her face that this warn't any kind of small talkin' like we'd been doin'.

She was lookin' at me straight with them purty blue brown eyes. *You don't have to answer me if'n you don't want to. But I want to know, if'n you can tell me.*

Ask away.

Are you sorry Nadine has gone and married LeRoy Campbell?

I knowed what she was askin' me. *My answer to yore question is no.* I reached out and took both her hands in mine. *You want to hear me say it again? My answer to yore question is no.* She halfway smiled at me but didn't say anything. *I guess maybe I better explain how it is with me. Come over here with me and set with me on this log.* She did, smoothin' out her dress tail as she set down, and she looked up at me, watchin' to see what was next.

I stood there in front of her. *I don't know if'n I can tell this story right. You'll be the first one I ever tried to. But let me try. When a man is away at the War, figurin' at any time he'll be kilt, he needs something to keep in his mind to keep from goin' crazy. I was keepin' Nadine in my mind. But it turned out that what I was keepin' in my mind warn't the real thing. Nadine the real thing was thinkin' I was dead and warn't ever comin' back to her. So she got to know LeRoy Campbell.*

I stopped talkin', thinkin' about what to say next. *It's a shore thing, I was set back when she told me.* I stopped again. *But it warn't long, maybe no more'n a few days, for me to come to know that I didn't need to keep her in my mind any more. I had lived through the War and come back to Stewart County and I was my own man.*

I was lookin' down at her and she was lookin' up to me, not movin' or showin' any thing in her face. Then she said what I'd said. *You are your own man.*

I am. I am my own man. The War is over and I don't need to keep her in my mind any more. So, no, I ain't sorry one bit that she has gone and married LeRoy Campbell. I squatted down beside her. *Do you believe me when I say that?*

She nodded. *I guess I do.* She shook her head. *I never thought about it that way.*

I smiled at her, still holdin' her hands. *You figure you are your own woman?*

She let go my hands and stood up and smoothed out her dress tail. She grinned down at me, still squattin' there, the grin spreadin' to her eyes. *Maybe I'm not yet, but I plan to be.* And she started out the barn door.

When I saw her about to leave, I got up and went to her afore she could go. *Wait a minute. I got a question for you.* She stopped and turned to me. In my mind's eye I can still see her after all these years, her purty hair tied back with that rag, standin' in the barn door, lookin' back at me.

Lookin' back, I figure it was right then that I started to love her like I never loved a woman before. But now that I had her stopped, I didn't know what to say or how to say it right. *What I want to know is do you like me? Can we be together some and talk about things?* I held out my hand to her. I didn't know why I did that, but I did.

She reached out and took my hand. She warn't grinnin' and she warn't laughin'. *Yes, Luther, I like you and yes we can be together and talk about things.* And I kissed her hand. Now that sounds funny. Here I was a man been with some women like in the bed and here I was askin' a woman if'n she liked me. But it's the truth, and that's how it started. I stood there, stiff as a board, not movin' a inch, lookin' in them blue brown eyes She took her hand back and went on out.

I stood there, watchin' her go. She didn't walk like Dulciemay had, like she was dancin'. She was walkin' like she was floatin' along, like a leaf in the creek. If'n I couldn't see her feet, I'd figure she didn't have any, but was just ridin' in the air above the ground. She allus walked that way even when she was carryin' a baby and said she felt like a cow. But on that day, I watched her walk away and went back to work.

Like I said, we was together like it was in some kind of plan to be follered. I'd see her at church or at the Mill. I'd see her at the Cherry place. Come spring there was a box supper at the churchhouse and the boys quit biddin' agin me for hers, knowin' that was what her and me wanted. There was play parties and we'd dance together 'til another man would claim her. But I always got her back for the last set. It went that way. We was together a lot and I allus felt good about bein' with her.

I'm gettin' ahead of my story about Narcissa and me. One Sunday in the spring time I had dinner at the Cherry place. After we got done, I set with Miz Cherry on the front porch, talkin' about this and that. Narcissa come out after she'd done the dishes.

I figured it was time to ask her another question. *You want to go for a walk with me? Mama, you think you'll be all right if'n I'm gone with Luther for a while? Daddy said he'd be back directly.* Miz Cherry nodded. *You go ahead, sweet child. I'll just set here 'til yore daddy comes.*

So off we went, holdin' hands, around the back of the house, over to the cow pasture and walked along the fence. She looked for wild flowers and she told me their names. Some of the cows come over to where we was, I guess to see what we was doin'. It was a real purty spring day. The sky was a clear blue with some white clouds here and there. I felt real good, bein' there with her. I knowed it was the right time. *Narcissa, it's real good, bein' with you. I like bein' with you a lot.* She smiled and nodded. *We've been friends now ever since I come home.* She nodded again and bent down to look at a little white flower. *I want to ask you a question.* She laughed. *You want to ask me again if'n I like you?*

Naw, I know you like me as a friend. What I want to ask you is can I come to court you, a man come courtin' a woman.

She stood up straight and turned to look at me with them blue brown eyes, not grinnin' or smilin' at me, just lookin' at me. *I've been wonderin' about that. All we've done to hold hands and dance together and set next to each other. I've been wonderin' if'n that's all you wanted to do.* She frowned. *I got to ask you my question again. Are you still thinkin' about Nadine?*

I could see why she'd want to ask that. Maybe she thought I was still thinkin' about Nadine since all I'd been to her since I come home was to be friendly. I shook my head. *No, you got to believe me. I don't think any more about Nadine. Like I told you that time at the barn, I'm my own man.* I reached over and took both her hands in mine. *What I want most in all the world is to be a man to you, come courtin'.*

She smiled her sweet smile to me. *I'd like you to do that if'n you want to.* She was still smilin' at me as she shook her head. *But you'll have ask Daddy.*

I took it that was a yes from her even if 'n she didn't out and out say it. I nodded. *I'll do that.* I grinned at her. *I'll ask 'im real nice so he'll say I can.*

She laughed. *He'll put up a fuss maybe. That's his way. But Mama and Daddy like you a lot. She'll likely tell him he's to say yes.* She looked at me, with a little frown. *So do I like you a lot.*

And right then, not thinkin' what I was doin', I pulled her to me and kissed her on the mouth. She didn't pull away at first, then she did, and held back, lookin' at me, like she was wonderin' what she'd done. And I leaned to her and kissed her again. We was holdin' on to each other like no holdin' I'd ever done afore. It was a long kiss, and she was kissin' back. And for the first time with her, I felt myself gettin' hard. I knowed I wanted more, more kissin' and more huggin' and bein' close together.

Like there warn't anything else to say, we turned and walked back to the house. We could see Miz Cherry was still settin' on the porch, looked like she was half asleep. *Can I go talk to yore Daddy now? You know where he is?*

She nodded, laughin' at me. *You want to do it this minute?*

I laughed with her. *I shore do, so's I can get started in on this courtin' business!*

Go look in the spring house. Lookin' at her mama, to see if 'n she was watchin' us, Narcissa kissed me again on the mouth. I went.

She was right. He was in the spring house. *Howdy.*

Howdy. You come to help me clean out this spring?

Well, now that I'm here, I can shore help you do that.

Hand me that long handle prong stick over there. It looks like it's stopped up a little further up than I thought. I handed him the stick and he got down and run it up in the spring two or three times, twistin' it this way and that. The spring started to run better, dirty at first, then it run clear. He got up and watched it. *I guess that done the trick.*

I was waitin' for the right time to ask him my question. *The box looks good.*

Yeah. I made a new one last summer. He laughed. *The butter kept washin' downstream. I don't know why this'un stops up. The one that feeds the pond never does it. It must be a better flow to the spring.* He turned to me. *You seen many springs where you went in the War?*

I nodded. *Same as here, mostly. Lots of creeks fed by springs. Me and Thunder crossed a lot of 'em on the way home. Ole Mule and the little red mare was better at crossin' creeks than Thunder. Seems like he hates to get his feet wet.*

He laughed a good belly laugh. *Some horses and some mules is like that. I had a horse oncet when I was a boy that would be damned afore he'd cross a creek he couldn't see the bottom of.* He looked at me again. *That little red mare was the one Gray give you when you went to the War?*

Yessir. I rode her when I was ridin' with the cavalry with General Morgan.

How long did you do that?

I didn't want to talk about ridin' with the cavalry right now. But he did, so I went along. *Maybe a little over a year. Word come one day he was goin' north on a raid in Kentucky, maybe Ohio. I didn't go along. It was a good thing I didn't. Him and some of his men was taken prisoners. He got away and come back to Tennessee. That's where he got shot.*

What happened to the mare?

She got shot by a cannon ball. I was real sorry about that. I cried like a baby when she was kilt. She was some kind of a mare. Losin' her was a real bad thing to happen to me. If'n I didn't have her, I had to quit the cavalry and fight on foot.

That must have been bad fightin'.

Yessir, it was real bad fightin'. It was worse'n ridin' with the cavalry. The cavalry was how I wanted to fight. But after the mare was kilt, I didn't have any horse to ride so I had to do it.

You mind talkin' about it?

I nodded. *It ain't easy to do. It seems like I want to put it all behind me.*

*I can see that. I won't press you. Maybe someday you can tell
me more about it.*

I'll try to do that.

Afore we quit, I got one more question. What was Ole Mule?

*Well, I don't know if'n it's a good story about me. We got to
Richmond and I come down real bad with the fevers. I seen a lot of
soldiers die of the fevers. I kept gettin' worse and I figured I was goin'
to die. Then come the day I made up my mind if'n I was goin' to
die I was goin' to die on the way back to Stewart County. So I stole
Ole Mule and him and me left the War and got as far as North
C'lina afore I couldn't go one more mile. I passed out on 'im and fell
in a ditch. That was when the Wood family found me. I was with
them a year. I left him with one of the girls in the Wood family
when I got Thunder and started up again for Stewart County.*

The Wood family nussed you back to health from the fever?

Yessir, they did. They was real good to me.

*I'm obliged to you for tellin' me all that. Mebbe there's more for
the tellin' some day.* He was quiet. I was thinkin' about what to
say to him about courtin' Narcissa. I looked up to see him lookin'
straight at me, with a kind of smile on his face. *But I bet you
didn't come here to help me with a stopped up spring or to tell me
about Ole Mule, did you?*

*It's real good to talk to you about any thing. But no sir, I didn't
come here to talk to you about that. I come here, Mr. Cherry, to ask
you if'n I could come courtin' to yore daughter Narcissa.*

He was still kind of smilin' at me. *Well, now, I allowed as
how you'd ask that some time. She's a right purty woman, and a
good one at that.*

Yessir, she shore is.

You asked her about if'n she wanted you to come courtin'?

*Yessir, I asked her and she didn't say no. She said I'd have to ask
you about it.*

That sounds like what she'd say. Now he out and out grinned
at me. *If'n she didn't say no, if'n I was you I'd take that for a yes.*

Yessir.

354 HUGHLETT L. MORRIS

Fact is, she's ahead of you. He laughed. *Seems to me most women are ahead of us men. You found that out already?*

Yessir, I guess so. I ain't dealt much with many women.

He laughed again. *I 'spect you're bein' careful what to say. A soldier boy away from home must of met up with a woman here and there. It'd be natch'ral if'n you had.*

Yessir.

Anyway, she told her mama and me all about how she liked bein' with you. Her mama and me talked about it some after she'd gone to bed one night. He picked up a stick and got out his pocket knife and started to whittle. *Her mama ain't feelin' so good. I don't know what it is. She don't talk about hurtin', she just don't feel real good. She leans on Narcissa to help. Now that Nadine's gone.*

Yessir, I can see that. I figured I knowed what was comin' up.

Her mama likes you. She said she recollected you as a good boy, afore you went away to the War. She recollects you around the place when you did some hirin' out with me.

Yessir. She's always been real nice to me.

I figure givin' her some time to get used to Narcissa gettin' married, movin' away, will do the trick. Afterwards, if'n she needs help about the house, I'll find some woman to come in.

Yessir. Are you sayin' I can come courtin', if'n I don't hurry it?

He laughed again, a good belly laugh. *You catch on quick. That's what I'm sayin'. Just don't hurry it along.*

Yessir. I'll do that. I grinned. *It won't be easy. I'm real stuck on Narcissa. She's a purty and a sweet woman.*

He laughed again and kept on whittlin'. *Man to man, I can see how you want her and you don't want to wait too long to have her.*

No sir, I don't. But I want to do what's right.

I'm obliged to hear you say that. He kept on whittlin', lookin' at the stick he was holdin'. *There's something else I better tell you.*

Yessir.

There's a man from over in Trigg County that has had his eye on her. Name's Hershel Duncan. He's got a good farm. Never been married. He took care of his mama 'til she died last fall. He's talked to me about coming to court Narcissa. He stopped whittlin' and looked at me. I was quiet, wonderin' what he was gonna say next. *He's 'tween you and me in age, older'n you, younger'n me. Her mama 'spects he wants a woman that can give him some children.* I was still quiet. He was studyin' the stick he was whittlin' on. *He comes off too strong for her mama. She don't take to him much. She don't want him comin' to court Narcissa but she said she'd go along with what Narcissa wants.* He looked at me. *What'd you think about that?*

I was quiet for a minute or two, lookin' down at the spring that was runnin' good and clean. *I guess I'd say to let us both men come courtin' and let Narcissa say what she wants to do.*

He throwed the stick he'd been whittlin' over to the side. *Speakin' as her daddy, I figure that's the right thing to do. Let Narcissa say what she wants to do.* He looked at me sideways and grinned. *You figure you can hold your own up against him?*

I shrugged and kind of laughed. *I figure I can. Leastwise I'll do my damnedest.*

He laughed again, his belly laugh. *I figured as much. One thing in yore favor, he ain't got no where as purty a horse as yore black 'un.*

I laughed with him *Maybe that'll help my case!* That was all we said about it at that time. We went on our ways.

So that's what we did. When I asked her when I could come over to see her, she said Sati'day evening. I didn't ask why she didn't say Sunday. I reckoned that was when she'd told Hershel Duncan he could come.

At that time, I didn't say any thing to her about him. But I knowed what he looked like. I went to the store at the Mill the next week with Uncle Gray and he was there. Him and me said our howdys and passed the time of day. I couldn't tell at the time if'n Uncle Gray knowed about Hershel and me and Narcissa. Maybe he did. News gets around fast in Bumpus Mill. They allus have. I'd see Hershel Duncan at the store from time to time. It looked like he come to the Mill down from Trigg County to do his tradin'.

Only thing was said about him and me courtin' Narcissa was from Miz Taylor oncet when I was over there. *Luther, I need a word with you. Let's step out to gather the eggs.* Yessum. I follered her out. *Sam tells me you're goin' over to the Cherry place some.* Yessum. *You courtin' Narcissa?* Yessum. She was talkin' to me and puttin' eggs in her apron tail at the same time, like Aunt Polly used to do. *I hope you're doin' this in the right spirit.* She turned to me, lookin' at me with a frown. *I hope you ain't still moonin' over Nadine. That wouldn't do any body any good, least of all Narcissa. She's a real sweet girl and don't need to play second fiddle to no body, least of all her sister! You get what I mean, boy?*

Yessum, I get what you mean. Since you asked, can I tell you how it is with me?

I was hopin' you would. You know I love you and Sam like you was my own boys. She looked off across the pasture. *Now that Billy didn't come home, I ain't got much to live for.* Then she looked back at me. *So, you tell me how it is with you.*

Well, how it is with me is that all in the War I had to have a picture in my mind to keep from goin' crazy. The picture I come up with was Nadine. And it was Nadine when she was somethin' like 16, still a girl. But I had her in my mind. When I got home to Stewart County, I found out she was goin' som'ers else. She figured I had been kilt and she had to go on with her life. So she did it with LeRoy Campbell.

It hit me real hard at first that the picture in my mind warn't the real thing. But I come to know that I didn't need that picture any more. It had done its job in the War. I hadn't gone crazy. But now I was back in Stewart County and I didn't need it any more. I stopped talkin' and looked at her. *Does that make any sense to you?*

She nodded. *It makes sense to me. But better it makes sense to Narcissa. You told her all that?*

I have, the best I could. It ain't easy to talk about.

But you got to try hard. You got to make her believe it's her in your mind now, and not Nadine. She frowned at me again. *You get what I mean?*

Yessum, I do. I'll keep tryin'.

Well, my boy, you better do more than try. She went back to feelin' around in the nests and under the hens for more eggs. *You know about Hershel Duncan?*

Yessum. Her daddy told me about him.

He's knowed to be a good man.

Yessum.

She laughed, a good belly laugh. *Is that all you got to say?*

No mam, that ain't all I got to say. I know him and me is courtin' Narcissa. But I know I'm the better man for her and I aim to get her!

She laughed another belly laugh. *That's what I wanted to hear you say. If 'n it matters, I'm on yore side.*

I laughed with her. *That's good to hear. If 'n you're on my side, I'm bound to win!* She was done gatherin' eggs and we started back to'ard the house. *Do you mind if 'n I ask if 'n the folks around here know about him and me and Narcissa?*

She kind of giggled. *Lawsy yes, they know. You cain't keep anything like this a secret around here. There's allus talk around the quiltin' frame about who's courtin' who.*

Who they bettin' on?

She laughed again. *Well, now, that'd be tellin'. Hershel's a right good man. He took care of his mama like he did. I figure he put off marryin' 'til after she was gone. Women think real good of him for doin' that. But don't you pay any mind to that. You just go in there and get her!*

Yessum, I will.

We got to the house and went in the kitchen and she put the eggs in the basket there on the shelf. *When is it you go see her, if 'n you don't mind my askin'?*

No mam, I don't mind. I go on Sati'day evening, after dinner, maybe stay 'til suppertime.

Well, now, I tell you what. Why'n't you bring her over here next Sati'day night. Have supper and stay the night. She laughed. *You can sleep with Sam. Narcissa can sleep with me.* She laughed again. *I guess I better not let any bundlin' go on in my house.*

She smiled, thinkin' about it. *That's what Mr. Taylor and me used to do when we was courtin'. He'd come for supper and I'd tell my daddy warn't no use in him goin' back home in the dark. My mama would fix my bed for bundlin' and we'd all go to bed when bed time come. Nary a word was said. We just did it. I recollect how good it was to go to sleep with him next to me in the bed, even if'n we both was all bundled up.*

I smiled at her tellin' the story. In my mind's eye I could see her as a young woman that Mr. Taylor must of loved a lot. *If'n you don't mind my askin', did you ever do away with the bundle?*

She smiled a real purty smile of the young woman she used to be, and shook her head. *I ain't tellin'!*

Well, Narcissa and me went to the Taylor house some after that time. I figured her mama might say no to that, but if'n she did, I never heard about it. There warn't no chance of bundlin', since we slept like Miz Taylor said we would.

But bundlin' or no, it was real good to have the time with Narcissa away from her home place. And Miz Taylor seemed glad to have us there. She was a real good woman and I missed her a lot after she was gone. It was mighty good to have Sam there, too. I got to know him from talkin' to him at the Taylor house.

All this time I was pressin' my case with Narcissa. I'd talk to her about farmin' and what I wanted to do about growin' corn and how to tell when to cut and stack hay and the like. She'd tell me about what she was doin' around the house and what kind of garden she liked to put out.

Little by little she'd ask about the War and I'd tell her where I'd been and what I'd seen and how it made me feel. When I got to the parts where there was women I'd just mention them, along with everybody else. She never asked me any questions about the women.

One time soon after that, when I was at the Taylor place, helpin' Sam with some farm work, Miz Taylor pulled me aside. *You recollect I said there was allus talk at quiltin'?*

Yes mam, I do. The bets been placed? I grinned.

Well, it looks like all bets are off. I hear tell Hershel Duncan ain't comin' to the Cherry place nowadays. He's startin' to show up at the Dade place just across in Kentucky. Mr. Dade got kilt cuttin' timber last winter. Looks like Hershel's courtin' his widder. She smiled at me. *I guess you didn't know about that?*

Nome, I didn't. It's news to me. I give a good belly laugh. *But it shore is good news!* She smiled, and went on with what she was doin'.

It was in the early harvest moon one night Narcissa and me was at the Taylor place. The weather had warmed up some. After supper was cleaned up, I asked Narcissa in front of Miz Taylor and Sam if'n she'd go for a walk with me to look at the moon.

Now, you understand that Narcissa and me was doin' this courtin' business proper. Like I said, we'd be together a lot, but not by ourselves 'cept in the day time and around the farm. We'd done a lot of hand holdin' and some kissin', but that was all. This night was the first time we might go out of the house at night. So when I asked her to go look at the moon, she looked at Miz Taylor like she was askin' her if'n she could. Miz Taylor must of knowed what the look was about, and she said that was a good idea and for us to go ahead.

We walked down to the pond and set on a log there, me huggin' her as tight as I could. We talked about the night and the weather and the moon. I told her how I had watched the moon in the War, thinkin' the moon I saw was the same moon that was shinin' in Stewart County. I didn't tell her that in battle a full moon could mean trouble, since the Yankees could see where to attack. Anyway, she named some stars her daddy had learned her about.

Then we fell quiet. *Narcissa, I figure it's time for me to ask you a question.* I could see her purty face in the moon light. She had a shawl over her head but some of her hair had come loose from it and was hangin' down her cheeks. She looked at me, but didn't say anything. I started in again. *Narcissa, the question it's time for is will you marry up with me?*

I could see her smile in the light of the moon. *I figured that was what you was goin' to ask.*

I started in again. *I know Hershel Duncan has been comin' courtin' to you. I don't know much about him, but I hear he's a good man and he's well to do, to top it off. And I figure he wants you to marry him real bad. Any man would. You are a bee-u-ti-ful woman and you're real good around the house, helpin' with yore mama.*

I was huntin' in my head for the right thing to say next. *You've knowed me since you was a girl and I was a boy. You know my mama left me and Sam to live with Uncle Gray and Aunt Polly. I ain't got nothin', to compare to what Hershel Duncan's got. But I know how to work hard and I'll make you a good life if'n you'll let me.* She still was quiet. *Uncle Gray has let me live in Grandmama Morris's house and it's real nice there. You've seen how nice it is. And you could go see yore mama a lot. And yore Daddy says if'n you married up with me and left home and yore mama needed takin' care of, he'd find a woman to do it.*

I could see her turn her head and look at me. *He said that?*

He did.

What else did he say?

I was still huntin' for what to say. *Nothin' much. He told me that when I asked him if'n I could come courtin' to you.*

Did he tell you about Hershel Duncan?

He did. And I said I figured I could beat Hershel Duncan's time with you.

She smiled at me in the light of the moon. *Why'd you figure that?*

I figured that 'cause I love you more than any body else in the whole word loves you, 'ceptin' yore mama and daddy. And I need you real bad. And I want you so much, the wantin' hurts. And I took her in my arms and I kissed her for all I was worth. And I could tell she was kissin' me back and I figured I knowed right then that she'd say yes to marryin' me.

She pulled away from me just a little, but our mouths was still near touchin'. *Can you hold off 'til Christmas?*

Our mouths was still near touchin', but I let loose with a belly laugh. *Does that mean you'll marry up with me if'n I can hold off 'til Christmas?*

That's what it means. And she pulled my head back to her with her hands and kissed me. All along I figured I had a good chance with her but now that she'd said yes, I couldn't find the words to say. So I pushed her away from me a little so it wouldn't be so loud and I yelled the Rebel yell. She laughed. *What in the world was that?*

That's the Rebel yell that us Rebel soldiers did when we was goin' to battle and when we'd won the battle. I ain't got the right words to tell you how I feel right now, so I made our yell. And I drawed her back in my arms and we kissed some more. I got hard, kissin' her, but it seemed like a differnt feelin' than I ever had before with a woman.

So, holdin' hands, that was all that was needed, we went back to the house. Miz Taylor and Sam was still up, settin' by the fire, Miz Taylor doin' some mendin' and Sam whittlin'. Sam looked up when we come in. *What was that yellin' I heard all about? For a minute there I thought it was the Rebel yell.* He was grinnin'. He knowed what that yell meant.

I laughed at what he'd said. *You're right there, my brother. That was me doin' the Rebel yell, 'cause Miss Narcissa says she'll marry up with me!* There was handshakes and hugs all the way around. Miz Taylor wiped away a few tears with her apron tail. They went on to bed. We set up a while by the fire, holdin' hands, not sayin' much. It seemed like there warn't no need to talk.

I ain't talked much about Sam yet. Like I said, he was two years younger than me. When we was little we was together near all the time. I was bigger than him but not by much. It was near even when we got in a rasslin' match.

When our mama left and we went to live with Uncle Gray and Aunt Polly, we stuck together. Maybe I needed him more'n him me. He was too young to know what was happenin' to us. Aunt Polly got to him real fast. He latched on to her real quick. I guess it took me more time. The times our mama come back to see us was hard for him. I guess hard for her. I recollect he ast me oncet after she'd come to see us if'n she was our mama or if'n Aunt Polly was. I don't know what I told him. At the time, I was just a boy myself.

Truth to tell, what do you say when a mama leaves you to live with somebody else? I guess while Sam was latchin' on to Aunt Polly, I warn't latchin' on to nobody. Her and Uncle Gray was good to me and I'm obliged to them for that.

But the hole in my heart that was made when our mama left us warn't ever filled for a long time. Maybe it warn't filled 'til I fell for Narcissa. Even then, she used to say that sometimes I was far away from her and the childern. I didn't mean to be that way, but if'n she said I was, I guess I was. She come to know me like a book, as a school marm would say.

Anyway, to get back to Sam, when I got back to Stewart County I was 20 and him 18. When I left for the War I was 15 and him 13. There's a heap of difference in some people growin' up between 13 and 18. Them five years can change anybody a lot. Now he was more like Joe Dale than me. Maybe not so tall and heavy as Joe Dale, but he was shore bigger'n me. I recollected him to be a towhead. Now his hair was brown, and his chin whiskers, what there was of 'em, was near black.

That first time, he ast where I was stayin'. I told him I was goin' to our Grandmama's house and could he help me with the bed and things. At first I felt uneasy about it. Uncle Gray hadn't said why Sam warn't in that house. Then he said he was settled right good at the Taylor place. He said Miz Taylor told him she was glad to have him since her son Billy hadn't never come home from the War. So I figured that was all right. I told him he was always welcome to come to see me there. He helped move the bed and all.

At first, he'd come around some, but not much. Later on that summer, it looked like he liked to, and he'd come to help me with this and that and stay the night and we'd talk.

At the first we didn't talk much about the War. I guess it was still too close to us and we just didn't want to go there. But little by little, we did. Something would happen that made one of us recollect something that happened to us in the War. We'd tell about it. I told him about where I'd been and what I'd done and bein' sick and the Wood place. I never told him about Dulciemay and Tinsley Bottom and Beulah Gates. I was fearsome he'd let something slip to Narcissa and I didn't know what to tell her if'n she asked.

It turned out that he was in the battles around Spring Hill and Franklin and he'd been took prisoner by the Yankees. He never said much about that and I never pressed him. I figured he didn't want to talk about it. Best it left unsaid.

He stayed on at the Taylor place a year of two. Fact is, he stood up with me when Narcissa and me was married. I was real glad to have him do that. Then Miz Taylor sold her place and moved away and he left to go up north. I never saw him agin for a while. Then he come back and bought a little farm over in Trigg County with his wife he'd married up that way. They never had no children.

There warn't many of us around Bumpus Mills that come back from the War. We knowed that each other had done that, but we never talked about it much. One of 'em said he'd been fightin' at Richmond when Lee surrendered. I told him I'd been there too. We talked a little about how cold and how hungry we'd been, but not much else. It seemed like all of us that had gone to the War and come back wanted to put it ahind us.

One thing that made me real uneasy was when they would talk about where they got parole. You can see why that kind of talk would make me uneasy. I never got parole. A soldier that walks away don't get parole. I guess we better say it the right way.

A soldier that deserts don't get parole. When they talked about that, I made up some story about where I'd got parole and nobody said anything about it.

But I allus felt real bad about that I'd deserted. I hope I've told you enough about how I come to do it that you don't lay too much blame on me. In my life, I've tried to be a upstanding man who done right by his family and neighbors. But that don't wipe the slate for me for bein' a deserter. That will go with me to my grave.

It were Sam that led me to go see our mother. The first time he said anything about it we was movin' the pieces of furniture down from the loft. It warn't much of a job. There was only the three pieces, a bed, a table, and a dresser. Uncle Gray said there was a meal chest and some straight chairs but he needed them for his house, so he took 'em.

We was standin' there, lookin' at 'em. *When yore daddy died and she broke up housekeepin' to go marry Fitzell, she didn't want to take them pieces with her. She said they'd belong to you boys. So we put 'em in a stall in my barn. They stayed there for several years. When Fort Donelson fell we all in Stewart County got nervous about if'n the Yankees would come through and make trouble. Word was they was takin' any vittles they could get ahold of. And takin' livestock. And word was some houses was set fire. Yore mama come about that time. She was worried about them pieces of furniture, and we moved 'em up into the loft here at yore grandmama's house. They've been up there ever since.*

Did the Yankees come through?

He nodded. *They come through and made some trouble. I've told you how my mother and Cele claimed they'd fed 'em and then run 'em off. I don't doubt it. They was gone by the time I got here. I was real thankful they didn't give more trouble in these parts. It'd of been real hard on us. I guess you boys have seen what soldiers can do like that.*

Me and Sam didn't say much. I knowed what trouble soldiers like that could make. We was on the makin' side, when I was ridin' with the cavalry. That was all that was said at the time. But the time come one night Sam and me was settin' by the fire at my house when Sam brought it up again. He was lookin' at the dresser. *I don't recollect much about this here furniture. Do you?*

No, I guess I don't. We was both too little to know much about where we was livin' and what was in the house.

He was quiet, lookin' at the fire. *Do you recollect what our mama looked like?*

Not much. We never saw her much after she moved away.

He was still lookin' at the fire. *You ever wish she'd of taken us with her?*

I shrugged. *I guess so, when I was a boy old enough to figure out what had happened. Aunt Polly said it was the only thing she could do. Her bein' a woman by herself with two little boys, she couldn't make it by herself. And they never had any youngun's and they wanted us. So she give us to them.*

We was quiet for a while, studyin' the fire. *You recollect when she come and give us the ribbons?*

I nodded. *Yes, I do that. It was right afore I left to go to the War. I hadn't thought about them ribbons for some time. You still got yore's?*

Yes, I've still got mine. Havin' it with me helped a lot to get me through the time I was in the Yankee prison. I had it tied around my neck when I was took prisoner. A Yankee soldier guardin' us saw it and started to take it. I told him my mama give it to me and he changed his mind and let me keep it. I would feel of it under my shirt when I got scared I wouldn't make it through. It helped me a lot, more'n I can say right now. It looks raggedety but I still got it. And he opened his shirt and I could see it hangin' around his neck.

I ain't got mine any more. And I 've got no notion when it got lost. I don't recollect when I had it last.

He was lookin' at the fire again. *I've been thinkin' about her. When Miz Taylor gives me leave, I'm gonna go see if'n I can find her.*

I thought about doin' it when we was passin' through Kentucky in the War, but I never got away. You figure you want to do it, after all these years?

Some way I figure I need to do it. He turned and looked at me. *You want to come along?*

Maybe. I set there, lookin' at him and the fire and the dresser. The bed was ahind me and the table was in the kitchen. She left them for us to have. She could of took 'em with her and nobody would of laid any blame on her for doin' it. But she left 'em. And I was sleepin' in the bed her and our daddy had slept in and the bed me and Sam was born in. I'd not have it if'n she hadn't left it. I was beholden to her for that.

On the other hand, the truth is, I didn't know how I felt about seein' her again. I wondered about her and her life but it warn't a very big worry to me. Maybe she'd tell us something about our daddy that we didn't know. I couldn't see that seein' her again could do no harm, 'ceptin' maybe stirrin' up old feelin's. But what turned the trick, I guess, was the trip would give me more time to get to know Sam. *I'll go with you, if'n we can both get away at the same time. I don't guess it'll be hard to do. By next week, crops'll be laid by, and there ain't much heavy farmin' to do again until corn gatherin'.*

I could see his face in the flight of the fire, he was lookin' at me, grinnin'. I guess he was afeared I wouldn't want to do it, and he was down right glad to hear me say I would. *You better do it afore you marry up with Narcissa. After, she may not let you get away!*

I laughed with him. *Maybe she won't. Maybe havin' her in my bed, I won't want to go nowheres!* We was quiet, lookin' at the fire. *Talkin' about that, can I ask you some questions?*

He nodded. *Ask away. I bet I know one of 'em. It's why ain't I courtin' some girl.*

You mind my askin' that?

I don't mind. You're my brother. You can ask me that. Fact is, I've asked myself that. I guess I ain't ready to settle down. Maybe part of why I want to go see if'n we can find our mother is I want to see some of Kentucky! He laughed at what he'd said. *That ain't much of a answer, but it's the best I got.* He laughed agin. *'Sides, I*

*had a woman in mind to court but my danged brother come along
and beat my time!*

You mean that? Or are you just joshin' me?

*I warn't payin no mind to Narcissa 'til you started to. Then I
looked at her with new eyes. She's a right good lookin' woman.
Smart, too. You are a real lucky bastard to get her. What's the other
question?*

*It's about these pieces of furniture. I've got 'em in my house but
they ain't any more mine than they are yours. Any time you want
some of 'em, you tell me.*

He nodded. *I'll do that. Right now, I don't need 'em or want
'em. I ain't got any place to put 'em.* He looked around the room.
'Sides, they look right at home here in her house.

He reached back and took hold of the foot board. *'Sides,
you're gonna need this bed for some lovin' with yore gal Narcissa!
Brings up a question from me, good brother that I am. I been around
here since you been courtin' her, and I ain't seen hide nor hair that
she's been here for the night. What's the matter? You scared of her?*
We both laughed, and he held up his hand. *You don't have to tell
me. It ain't none of my bees wax!* He grinned. *But I am yore brother,
and I get to ask questions like that.*

I shook my head and I laughed. *You are my brother and you
get to ask questions like that. Now, if'n I know the answer. I guess
it goes like this. I guess you can figure I been with a woman afore. I
give you my word I know how to do it. And I want to do it bad
with Narcissa.* I reached back and took hold of the knob on the
foot board. *Lots of nights this here old bed has been cold to me
when I thought of havin' her here with me. So I have to do the best
I can.*

We both laughed. *Truth to tell, I figure Narcissa knows I want
her here in this here old bed. I figure she wants to be here, too, like
me. But we made a deal that we'd wait 'til around Christmas.
And she ain't said anything about comin' here afore then. And I
ain't asked her to come here night time in so many words.* I was
quiet. *Truth to tell, I want to do this woman right. I don't want to*

fall in the bed with her like there was no tomorra. When she comes to my bed, I want it to be right, and for keeps. I figure she sees it that way too. So I'll sleep in my cold bed 'til the time comes.

He smiled that good brother smile at me. *That's a right good story. I figure I want it to be that way with me, when I find the right girl. I thankee for tellin' me.* We set there a while, in the quiet, and went outside to piss. Standin' there, we looked up at the stars that could be seen. Then we come in and went to bed. I lay there, afore I dropped off to sleep, thinkin' about what I'd said. I guessed I'd been thinkin' that way afore I said the words to him, but I never said the words out loud. I was real happy, havin' him to say 'em to. And I felt real good about Narcissa and me. It felt right. Recollectin', I didn't feel much guilt about Maybelle and all the rest of 'em. But I wanted it to be differnt with Narcissa. I've never in my life felt any sorry about that.

In about a week, him and me got it cleared with everybody that we'd get away from farmin' to go look for our mother. Ever' body was for it. Uncle Gray and Miz Elizabeth said it was the right thing to do. Miz Taylor said so too. She said the quiltin' women was real pleased we was goin' to do it. Mr. Cherry said so too.

Narcissa didn't say much at first when I told her, but I could tell she thought it was the right thing to do, too. She give me hugs and kisses and told me to hurry back. She said maybe I wanted to ask our mother to come to our weddin'. I hadn't thought of that, but it seemed like a good idea. She allus had good ideas. When we left, she give Sam a hug and a kiss on the cheek and told him he'd better bring me back or he'd have her to answer to! He got real tickled at that, and said he shorely would do that for fear of her.

She pulled me aside right afore we was leavin' *Can I tell you what's on my mind?*

I kissed her again. *You sweet girl, you know you can allus tell me what's on yore mind.* I said yore, like her daddy did. *From now on in.*

I ain't got any notion about what you'll make of what you find. Of what she'll say to you and Sam, or what you'll make of what she says. She frowned. *But I want you to be easy on her. I'm only a girl and I ain't never been in her shoes when she did what she did, givin' you and Sam up to marry Mr Fritzell.*

But I figure a woman has to see things differnt from a man. Lookin' at it through her eyes, she didn't have many ways to go. She knowed your Uncle Gray and Aunt Polly. She loved them a lot and she knowed they would give you boys a good home. But she had to look after herself, too. She had to do something about herself, too. She hugged me again, and drew back to look at me with them blue brown eyes. *Will you do that?*

My eyes teared up and I wiped 'em with the back of my hand. I tried to smile at her, but it didn't come out right. *I promise to do that. And I thankee from the bottom of my heart for what you said. I'll try as hard as I can to recollect yore very words when I see her.*

She kissed me on the mouth again, a long kiss, and drawed back. *Then go.* And I left her, standin' there, feelin' like I was the luckiest man on earth to have her on my side.

Uncle Gray told us what he knowed about where our mother might be. He said, the best he knowed, the Fritzell place would be this side of Guthrie. He drawed us a map in the dirt about how to get to that part of the country. Him and Miz Elizabeth said good bye and for us to come back when we could, and we left.

We didn't shoot for makin' good time, and was on the road for maybe three days. The weather was good and we slept out in the open. I had some money along, so we stopped here and there to eat well. I hadn't never had such a good time of it, bein' on the road. I'll never forget how good it was.

After that night at my house, when Sam and me had that talk, we was real easy with each other. I recollect thinkin' with sorrow about the brothers who split up on diff'ernt sides in the War. That must of broke your heart to see that happen, to loose yore brother that way. It made me thankful I didn't. Anyway, we didn't talk much about what we was up to, just the weather and the country side. There didn't seem to be any need to do more than that. It seemed like it ought to be that way always 'tween brothers.

It worked out the way Uncle Gray said. We rode into Guthrie and stopped at the first store we come to. Sam asked the storekeeper if'n he knowed the Fritzell place and he told us how to get there. We got there mid mornin'. It was a right purty place, with a good house and some out buildings. It warn't much diff'ernt from any other place, with a lot and a cow pasture and a spring house and a pond. Everythin' looked well tended. A boy about fifteen was sloppin' the hogs in the pig pen. He come over to where we'd stopped the horses. *Howdy.*

Howdy.

Name's Luther Morris. This here is my brother Sam.

Name's John. John Fritzell. Get down off'n yore horses. What can I do for you? You want to talk to my daddy? He'll be here directly.

We got down off the horses. *We'd like to see yore daddy and mama if'n we can.*

He took the reins and put the horses on the hitch. Then he turned to us. *You say yore name is Morris?*

Yessir, it is. I wondered if'n he knowed the name and the story.

Just then, a woman come out of the door. She stood there on the porch lookin' at us. *John, what is it? Do they want to see yore daddy? Did they tell you who they was?*

Yes, mama, they did. It's Sam and Luther, Sam and Luther Morris.

When he said that, she come down the steps to over where we was standin', and looked at us one to the other. Then she give a little cry. *Oh my, it's my boys!* She put her hand to her mouth. *Luther! Sam! Is it really you?* She turned to the boy. *John, it's your brothers! Luther and Sam, this here is yore brother John.* Then like it was all she could take, she started to cry.

Sam made the first move and took her in his arms and rocked her like she was a baby, 'til she got quiet. Then she got free and put herself 'tween us, one on each side of her, and she looked at our faces, back and forth, holdin' on to our arm. *You are such grown men. It's been so long since I seen you. I cain't hardly believe you are really here. I've dreamt of this comin' to pass and now it has. You boys give me a hug and a kiss on the cheek and shake hands with yore brother John.* We did that.

When I give her the hug, I tried to recollect the feel of her body from the last time we hugged each other. I couldn't. This woman in a hug felt like any other woman her age, like Miz Collins or Miz Taylor. I looked at her face, to see if'n it was the face I recollected as a boy when she come to see us.

What I recollected was her voice. That sounded right to me. *I am so glad to see you! I been hopin' for a long time to see you boys again.* She stood there, still lookin' at us, one and the other. *It's been so long since I seen you.* And she started in cryin' again. *Here you are grown men, come to see their mama.* She wiped her eyes with her apron tail. *Mercy, we cain't keep standin' here in the sun. You all come up on the porch and set. I want to hear all about you.*

We went to the porch, all of us, and settled. It worked out that Sam set next to her and he set there holdin' her hand. John was 'tween her and me. I couldn't tell if'n he wanted to be there, but maybe he figured he ought to be. Sam and her was doin' the talkin', about how we come and how we'd been farmin' and talk like that. John and me set there, mainly watchin'.

Now that I saw her some more, I recollected full well what she looked like. She was older, of course, but I seen in her face what I recollected. And like I said, I recollected her voice. I cain't tell you exactly what about her that was differnt from any woman her age. Her hair color was more like Sam's than mine, and pulled back at the back of her neck. I could see her eyes was brown and they crinkled up when she smiled. And she was smilin' all the time, but still wipin' her eyes now and then with her apron tail.

You all will stay for dinner. I ain't got anythin' but taters and beans, but there's a plenty of what there is. Mr. Fritzell will be comin' in for dinner in a little while. Then it was quiet for a little while. It seemed like nobody knowed what to say or how to start. Me and Sam was lookin' at her, tryin' to connect what we was lookin' at now with what we recollected. I guess she knowed that. She smoothed her apron and dress tail and pushed some hair that got loose back where she had it done up. It seemed like her hands wouldn't stay still.

It was John that started the talkin' again. *How long you men been back from the War?* Sam talked first. He said a year or more. He said he was livin' with a family nearby, helpin' a widder with the farmin'. I said I'd been back since Christmas. I told how I'd been sick with the fevers and that was why it took me so long to come home. It looked like that broke the ice. We all started talkin' with more ease.

Tell me about yore Uncle Gray. Is he doin' well?

Yessum, he is, and he sends his wishes to you. He says you folks are welcome to come to see him and Miz Elizabeth any time. You know about Miz Elizabeth?

No. I ain't heard about her.

Her and Uncle Gray've been married two years, maybe three. I don't know for sure how long. She has a daughter and a son. She's been real good to Sam and me.

Are you stayin' with them?

No mam. I'm stayin' at the house where Grandmama Morris had.

I got word from somebody she had passed away.

Yessum. It was quiet. *I've got the pieces of furniture you all put in the loft that time.*

She put her hands to her mouth. It looked like she was goin' to start to cry again. *Oh, I am so proud you have done that. When I come that time Gray was worried that the Yankee soldiers would come through and cause trouble. He thought maybe there'd be a fire and them pieces of furniture would get burned up. I don't know why he thought the loft would be a safer place for 'em, but he did, so we did that. I wanted like everythin' to save them pieces of furniture for you and Sam. That's all I had left of what yore daddy and me ever had. He didn't even have a watch and chain for me to keep for you boys.*

She wiped her face and smoothed down her apron tail. *I want you boys to know he was a good man, struck down in the prime of his life. I loved him a lot.* She looked at John and smiled a real big smile. *Yore daddy is a real good man too. He saved me from havin' a real troubled life.*

Sam reached over and took her hand again. *Mother, do you recollect them ribbons you give us that time?*

Oh, I shorely do, It warn't much to give you, but it was all I had.

He opened his shirt to show her. *I've still got mine. I want you to know it is what saved me from goin' crazy when I was in a Yankee prison camp.*

Up went the apron and her hands to her face again. *Oh, I am so proud to hear that.* It was the first time I'd heard Sam call her mother. It looked like it was the right thing to do for her. I couldn't of called her by that name then and I never could after. She warn't my mother. Aunt Polly was my mother.

She went back to smoothin' her apron tail. *I don't know how to say this. It give me real much pain to let you boys go. It seemed like I had to do it. Sometimes after I felt like the pain was more'n I could stand. I knowed Gray and Polly would treat you like their own. It seemed like it was the best I could do.* She looked at us, one, then the other. *It's real hard for me to ask, but I hope you don't blame me too much for what I did.*

Sam spoke up. *No, we don't blame you. Speakin' for myself, I was too little at the time to know what was happenin'. But I'm a man now and I can tell you I can see that you did the best you could.*

I didn't want to answer her question, less'n I had to. I nodded my head over at John. *It looks like you got a real good son here.*

She smiled and looked at John. *Yes, Luther, he is a real good boy. He's just like his daddy that way. He come to us when we needed him and we treasure him like gold.* John looked down at his hands and didn't say anything. Just then, here come Mr. Fritzell. We all got up. *Look here who's come to see us. This here is my boy Sam and this here is my boy Luther. Boys, this here is John's daddy.* We all shook hands and he motioned for us to set again. *I'm real proud you boys come to see yore mother. She's been wantin' to see you for a long time.* He went on to ask about our family and how we'd found his place and the like. He seemed like he was glad we was there. He was a tall man, brown from the sun like any farmer would be. I thought when I looked at him that he'd be the age our daddy would be if'n he was alive. Funny, I never had looked at Uncle Gray or Mr. Cherry in that light. Maybe it was 'cause this man was my mother's husband.

John, you want to help me put dinner on the table? John nodded and they went in the house.

I'm real glad to meet you boys. You look like fine young men. You been through a lot in the War.

Yessir, we have. Luther here got bad sick to'ard the end and it took him more'n a year for him to get back to Stewart County.

Sam got home afore I did. He had a real bad time of it there for a while in a Yankee prison. But we made it. Lots of soldiers didn't. Both of us has seen many a soldier die on the field of battle. And Sam seen many of 'em die in the prison. But we made it, and we lived to come back home.

Mr. Fritzell nodded. *I can see how you boys had a bad time of it. We all thank the Good Lord that you come out of it alive. Some our neighbor's boys never come back.* He was quiet, lookin' out in the front yard. *I hope you boys will come back to see us, now that you know how to get here. Yore mother would shore like that a lot.* John come out to tell us to come to the table. When we got set, Mr. Fritzell said the blessin'. It was like all the other blessin's I ever heard. But afore he got to the amen, he give thanks that we was there to see our mother. Out of the corner of my eye, I saw her reach over and take his hand when he said it.

We set on the porch a while after dinner. John did some talkin' about his part of the farmin'. He'd been some to a school and he said he knowed how to read some and his numbers. I told him to keep on that, that it'd caused me a lot of trouble that I never knowed how to read and write. I told him about Jake, Miz Elizabeth's boy and how I liked to have him around.

I said maybe sometime he could come see us for a while, if'n his daddy could spare him from the farm. Mr. Fritzell said he thought that was a good idea and they'd see what they could work out. Sam told 'em I was courtin' a young woman. Our mother asked me some questions about Narcissa and said she hoped we could come to see them after the weddin'.

Then John asked about Thunder. I told him a little of that story and asked 'im if'n he was a good rider. He shrugged, but his daddy said he was real good with horses. So I asked him if'n he wanted to ride Thunder. He said he shore would like to, so him and me and his daddy went out to where the horses was tied up. I made his 'quaintance with Thunder, like I allus did with a new rider. He got up and did a few circles and I told him to go for a little ride. I could tell he took to that right away. And Thunder acted like it was all right with him. So away they went.

Mr. Fritzell and me stood there by the hitch, watchin' John and Thunder ride off. Sam and his mother was settin' on the porch, talkin'. Mr. Fritzell turned to me. *Can you boys stay a little longer? I've got some right good cattle I want to show you.* Well I didn't know what that was about, but since he asked that way, I figured I'd better go. So we walked over in the pasture, just out of sight of the house. We looked at the cattle and talked about this and that havin' to do with farmin'.

We fell quiet. He was lookin' out over the pasture, not at me. *I guess you're wonderin' why I brung you over here. It was to say something out of earshot of John and his mother. Maybe it has to do with that you are about to be married.*

First off, I'm much obliged to you boys for comin' to see yore mother. She's carried the burden of leavin' you for what might seem a life time for her. We never had any babies of our own and I thought her heart would break that it turned out that way. Then John come to live with us and that was a help to ease her pain. I'm his daddy by another woman. But that's another story. Anyway, havin' one son didn't never make up for the other two she'd lost.

He fell quiet again. *I need to tell you that if'n there's blame to be placed over her givin' you boys up, it has to be placed on me. It were near twenty years ago. I was a young man lookin' for a wife. I warn't thinkin' of nothin' but havin' a wife. I knowed about you boys. I seen you when I come courtin'. But I figured what was I gonna do with two babies. I never was around youngun's much and I couldn't see how I could feed you and raise you. When I told her that, she cried and said she couldn't leave you all. But she let slip that yore uncle and aunt would take you, and that was all it took for me to take a hard stand. It was me or you.*

He fell quiet again. I figured he was done tellin' his story. I was goin' to have to come up with somethin' to say, but I didn't know what. But he started up again, still not lookin' at me. *It were trouble from the first. Lookin' back I can see the trouble was that she didn't want to marry me and she didn't want the bargain of marryin' me. She cried and cried and I told her to stop and she did, leastwise to my face. She was good in the house and in the garden and warn't ever mean to me, like I've heard some wives can be. But at night, she'd let me have her but she didn't take me, if'n you know what I mean. I figured she was bein' fearsome and I chalked it up to that.*

He turned to me. *I'm talkin' man to man here. But I want you to hear from me how deep her feelin' was about leavin' you boys.* He turned away, back to the pasture again. *This is the first time I ever told any body this. The truth is, I reckon I paid a high a price for her leavin' you boys. Sometimes I figured she'd always hold that agin me. It got better after John come and she knowed the story of him. But she allus grieved for you. But the Good Lord has pulled us through. You and Sam lived through the War and here you come to see her. I thankee for doin' that, from the bottom of my heart.*

I could see by his face that it warn't a easy thing for him to say, about her blamin' him. I was tryin' to think of what to say. *Like Sam said afore you come in, weun's are men now and we know what a lot of trouble life can be. You all did what you did.*

That's all in the past now. We're obliged to you for givin' her a good life and for her havin' John as a son. I don't know why I did, but I held out my hand. He nodded and took it and we shook. Nothin' more was said and we headed back to the house.

Sam and our mother was still settin' on the porch where we'd left 'em. John and Thunder was down at the pond for a coolin' off drink. John had Sam's horse along too. *It looks like you folks have got a real good farm here.*

She smiled and nodded. *John and his daddy are always workin' on it. It seems like they work all the time.*

I was just tellin' Mother we better get on the road.

It seems like we should.

You are welcome to spend the night with us.

John was back by that time. I was teasin' him. *Naw, we better not. We'd hate to kick 'im out'n his bed, make 'im sleep in the barn!* Everybody laughed. *But if'n Thunder ever starts to give me a bad time of it, I'll send for John here to straighten him out!*

Luther, you goin' to marry up with Miss Narcissa any time soon?

Yessum. Christmas time. Her mama ain't all that well, so we put it off 'til then.

You figure maybe you can let us know when the time comes? She looked at Mr. Fritzell. *Maybe we could come. I shore would like to see one of my sons get married.*

He smiled and nodded. *I figure we could do that. You'll let us know ahead of time?*

Yessir, I'd be pleased to do that.

It was time to go. We all walked out to where John had hitched the horses. Sam went over and give our mother a hug and I follered suit. Then we shook hands with John and his daddy. *I hate to see you go. There warn't near enough time to do the visitin' I want to. It's been real good to see you boys. It's been a dream of mine for a long time to see you. I hope you won't stay away so long again.* I figured she might start to cry, but she didn't.

Luther here's gonna be busy with getting' married. But I'll be back to see you folks when I can. I've been thinkin' about comin' up to Kentucky when Miz Taylor sells her farm and won't need me to help her any more.

So that was it. It seemed like Sam had said it all. We got on our horses and waved to them and headed out. The first night on the road, we come to a good place to stop and made a little camp with a fire. We set around the fire, watchin' it get dark and the moon come up. *I feel real good about comin' to see her. You glad you come?*

Yeah, I'm glad I come. I owe it to you. Maybe I wouldn't of, if'n it hadn't been for you. I'm much obliged to you for that.

He was quiet, looking at the little fire. *You still blame her?*

I studied what to say. *I don't rightly know what to say about that. One part of me can see how she come to do what she did. She were in a tight spot, as my friend Billy Jones would of said. I can see that. But the other part of me will allus recollect how you looked as a little boy when you asked me about where our mama was and if'n she was ever comin' back. It was real hard for you. I recollect feelin' real bad for you. You used to cry for her at night when we was in bed.*

That's talkin' about me. What about you?

I cain't say. Maybe I got used to not havin' her faster'n you did. I cain't say. It warn't long afore I lost her for my mama and put Aunt Polly in her place. I was quiet. *Truth to tell, I felt the loosin' of Aunt Polly as my mother more'n I felt the loosin' of her.* I was quiet again. *Today, bein' with her, I looked inside myself to see if'n I still had any love for her. I guess I don't.*

I guessed that was happenin'. If'n you don't mind my sayin' so, you acted cool to her, like she was just some woman you just got 'quainted with. He'd said it out loud. There warn't anything else I could say that seemed right. We laid down in our bed rolls and I could tell he went right to sleep. I laid there awake for a while, thinkin' what I'd said and what he'd said. I felt my eyes tear up.

Many a time in the War and on the way back to Stewart County I'd felt all alone in the world. You try to get used to feelin' that way, but I guess you never do. Then, I thought I warn't goin' to be alone anymore come Christmas. I'd have Narcissa.

I'm at the end of this here story. We got back to Bumpus Mill, and there was a lot of work to be done. The time for corn gatherin' come, after a early hard frost. It'd of been a good year and there was a good crop. I worked for Uncle Gray and Mr. Cherry and some more farmers around. Narcissa and me was together when we could. She'd come to my house of a day when she could get away. The Cherrys was always good to me. I come to feel a real part of their family.

Miz Cherry never got much better, but Mr. Cherry found a woman to help out. But she was able to help Narcissa make her weddin' dress. It was real purty, all white with some ruffles around and some flowers sewed on that the quiltin' women had made. I got the store keeper to mail order me a new shirt and a coat and a hat.

Time come for the weddin', Sam stood up for me. Nadine come for the day and she stood up for Narcissa. My mother and Mr. Fritzell and John come for the day. Uncle Gray and Miz Elizabeth and Sarah and Jake was there. Miz Taylor was there. Thunder and Buster was out in the horse lot. A preacher from over at Pugh Flat come to do the weddin'.

My ring for Narcissa was the gold ring I had from the old man's pouch. I figured he'd be proud about that.

The weddin' was held in the front room of my little house. Narcissa and me stood by the foot board of the bed where I was born and my daddy was born. It felt right.

It was on the Twenty-second of December, in the year 1867.